I0779948
SEATTLE
SEA

Uniquely In Love

COUSINS COFFEE CLUB

JENNIFER CHIPMAN

Family Tree

THE BEST FRIENDS BOOK CLUB & COUSINS COFFEE
CLUB UNIVERSE

Noelle & Matthew Harper (Academically Yours)
- Owen Harper, 24 (Uniquely in Love)
- Penelope Harper, 22

Angelina & Benjamin Sullivan (Disrespectfully Yours)
- Zachary Sullivan, 23
- Wesley Sullivan, 23
- Lucy Sullivan, 16

Gabbi & Hunter Sullivan (Fearlessly Yours)
- Quinlan Sullivan, 23

Charlotte & Daniel Bradford (Gracefully Yours)
- Abigail Bradford, 25
- Beau Bradford, 23
- Ellie Bradford, 21 (Uniquely in Love)

Tessa & Oliver Graham (Famously Mine)
- Avery Harper-Graham, 20
- Amelia Harper-Graham, 17

Seattle Seals Team Roster

Forwards
- Jonah Campbell, #14
- Finn Evans, #81
- Maverick Hendrix, #11
- Stefan Kovac, #26 (C)
- Rhodes Larsen, #42 (A)
- Carter Meyer, #73

Defenseman
- Owen Harper, #8
- Brooks Hendrix, #79
- Andrei Morozov, #65
- Mikhail Sorensen, #38 (A)
- Lucas Tremblay, #20

Goalies
- Reid MacKenzie, #33
- Matthias Farkas, #92

Coaching Staff

- Coach: Tristan Donovan
- Assistant Coach: Victoria Monroe

Please note that while an NHL hockey team can consist of up to 23 players, the above are players who appear in Uniquely In Love as on-page characters.

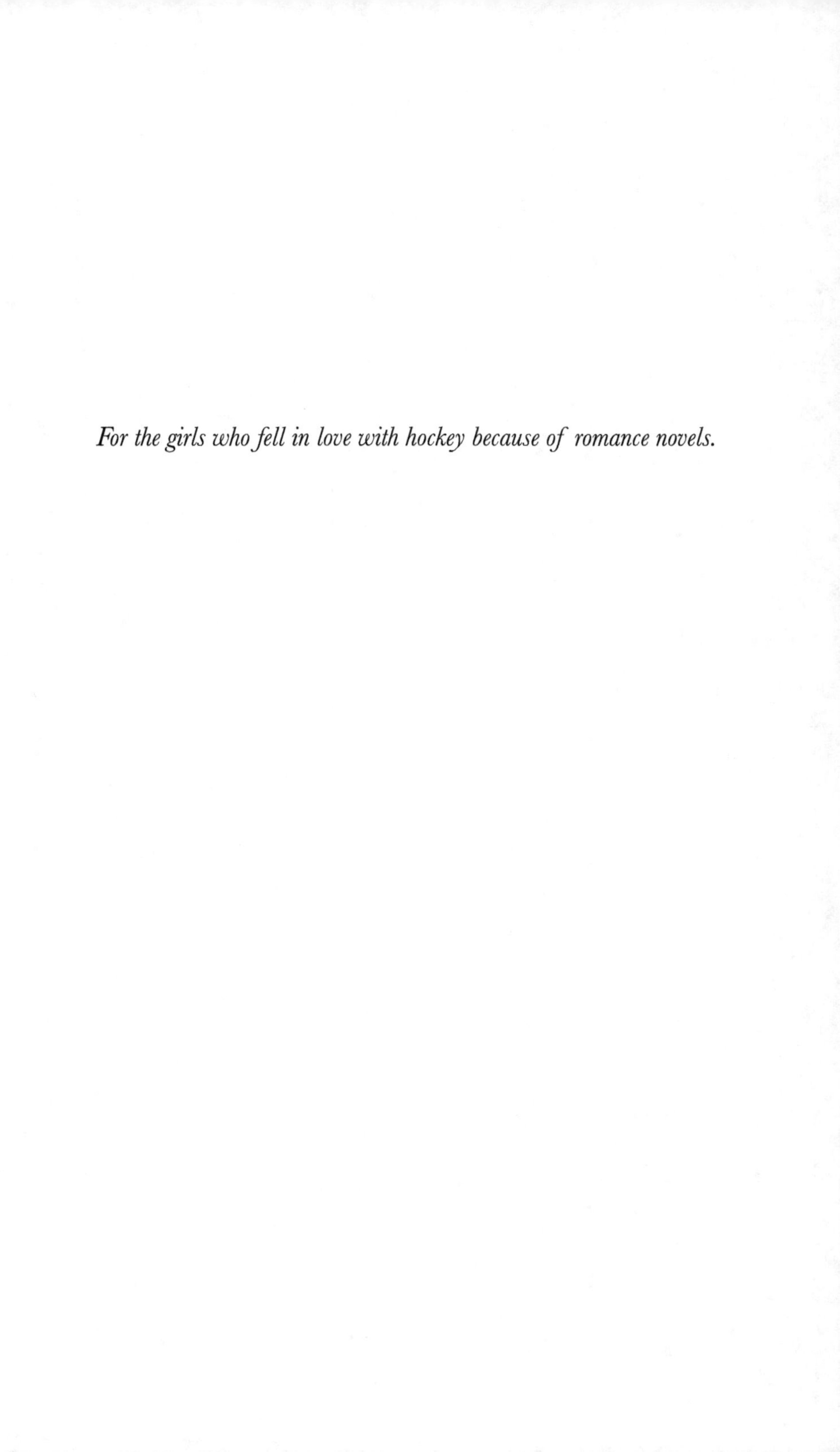

For the girls who fell in love with hockey because of romance novels.

Playlist

- Imagination - Shawn Mendes
- I'm Only Me When I'm With You - Taylor Swift
- 18 - One Direction
- 21 - Gracie Abrams
- Hold On - Chord Overstreet
- Last Kiss - Taylor Swift
- Before You Go - Lewis Capaldi
- Someday - Michael Bublé, Meghan Trainor
- the 1 - Taylor Swift
- Love Of My Life - Harry Styles
- loml - Taylor Swift
- Bags - Claire
- We Don't Talk Anymore - Charlie Puth, Taylor Swift
- right where you left me - Taylor Swift
- see you later (ten years) - Jenna Raine
- Remember That Night? - Sara Kays
- happier - Olivia Rodrigo
- A Little Too Not Over You - David Archuleta
- Suburban Legends - Taylor Swift
- Forget Me - Lewis Capaldi

- That's When - Taylor Swift, Keith Urban
- Back To You - Selena Gomez
- As It Was - Harry Styles
- Never Get to Hold You - Carly Rae Jepsen
- Never Really Over - Katy Perry
- Stay - Rhianna, Mikey Ekko
- The Alcott - The National, Taylor Swift
- Comeback - Jonas Brothers
- Stay Stay Stay - Taylor Swift
- Love Somebody - Alex G, Jon D
- Dandelions - Ruth B.
- Crazier - Taylor Swift
- Can I Have This Dance? - Vanessa Hudgens, Zac Efron
- Two Is Better Than One - BOYS LIKE GIRLS, Taylor Swift
- Hits Different - Taylor Swift
- Until I Found You - Stephen Sanchez
- You Are In Love - Taylor Swift
- Thinking Out Loud - Ed Sheeran

Contents

Prologue

ELLIE

The first time I'd fallen in love with the ice, it had been watching him play hockey. My five-year-old self had been dragged along to a game, and I hadn't been able to take my eyes off of the way the players glided across the ice.

Especially not off of him.

But I'd turned to my mom—tugged on the edge of her big, cozy sweater, and then I'd asked a question that would change the trajectory of my life forever. "Mommy, can I learn how to skate?" My eyes grew wide.

I was already in dance class—my mom taught lessons, so I'd basically grown up in the studio—but I couldn't explain the rush it gave me to watch the blond-haired boy float on his skates.

And two weeks later, when I was laced up in my first pair of ice skates and holding my mom's hand at the mall ice rink, I didn't give up. Not once.

No matter how many times I fell, I kept getting up.

Maybe my mom saw the determination there. Whatever the reason, she let me keep going.

THE SECOND TIME I'd fallen in love with the ice, I'd been twelve years old, training as a competitive figure skater after I'd taken lessons for the last seven years. It was my dream. One day, I hoped to make it to the olympics. I'd already competed in competitions at the state level, but I craved *more*.

Staring out across the rink at our local practice facility, I waited for my ice time to begin. My coach was somewhere around, and I'd already warmed up, but the hockey team was still practicing.

His hockey team. My best friend's brother. Though in a lot of ways, he felt like my best friend, too.

I swung my legs back and forth as I watched Owen hit a slap shot. He was *good*. At least, I was pretty sure he was. He was fourteen, growing like a weed, and the most beautiful boy I'd ever seen, with that soft, dirty blond hair, and a pair of warm, chocolate brown eyes. I felt gooey inside whenever he looked at me. He had no clue that I had a giant crush on him.

Owen skid to a stop, creating a spray of snow behind him, before resting his arms on the ledge. "Hey, Skater Girl."

"Hi, Hockey Boy." I smiled shyly at him as he heaved his leg over the wall, hopping over it in a way I could never even hope to.

And he hadn't even finished growing yet. He was already almost five foot ten, and his fifteenth birthday was still a few months away. Owen sat down next to me on the bench, bumping my shoulder with his before undoing his helmet and running his fingers through his hair.

"You waiting to start practice?"

"Yeah." I nodded, just watching him as he grabbed a bottle, squirting the water into his mouth.

God, it should have been wrong how much of a crush I had on him. He was practically family. Our mothers were best friends, and we lived on the same street. I saw him as much as I saw my brother, who was a year older than me, and as into football as Owen was into hockey.

Part of me loved that this was our special thing. Owen and I's.

Even if he had no idea that I liked him like that. I was just his little sister's best friend. His cousin. That was all he saw me as.

It was okay. I was alright with that.

"How's your solo coming?" Owen asked, and I watched as the rest of the guys headed off the ice and into the locker rooms.

"Good." My cheeks warmed. Had he been watching me? "It's fun. Mom's making me a new costume for it, too."

His eyes brightened. "What color? Yellow?"

That was my favorite. I cleared my throat. "No. It's um… It's blue."

"That'll be pretty," he muttered, looking away.

"I should go," I said, stumbling to my feet. "Get on the ice before my coach gets here and sees me talking."

"Okay," Owen said, standing up from the bench himself. "Bye, Skater Girl. Catch you later." He winked, and I skated out onto the ice, trying to ignore the butterflies in my chest. How much I *liked* having his attention on me.

What he didn't know was that I'd picked the fabric of my new skating dress because it was his favorite color. Light blue.

And god, I loved this building, because here, I didn't have to share him with anyone else. Here, I could pretend he was all mine.

THE THIRD TIME I fell in love with the ice, I'd been fifteen, wearing his last name on my back and his hockey sweater on my body. It was a big game for him, and I knew there were scouts in the stands watching him.

He was amazing out there.

And he was *mine*.

The way he commanded the ice was beautiful. Even under his pads and hockey gear, his body was finely sculpted and honed to perfection. There was no doubt in my mind that he was going somewhere, and I couldn't wait to watch him climb.

I balled up my fists in the sleeves, holding them against my nose. If I inhaled deep enough, I could still smell him on the jersey that was several sizes too big for me. Even though it had been washed, it still had the faintest scent of ice and cologne. I blushed, thinking about what it was like to have his body weight on top of me. We hadn't gone all the way yet, but we'd had some hot and heavy make-out sessions.

Sometimes, it still felt surreal that he'd asked me out last year. That we were dating. I was trying hard to forget about the fact that in a few months, he'd be graduating, and we'd have to do long distance. He'd decided not to enter the NHL draft right out of high school, deciding to go to college and get his degree, so when he was done with his hockey career, he'd have something to fall back on. It was something I knew his dad, a finance professor, had encouraged him to do.

It wouldn't be easy, but this was *us*, after all—Hockey Boy and Skater Girl.

My first kiss. My first boyfriend. My first love.

I loved him the way I loved being on the ice. When I was skating, the world went quiet. It was just me and my blades as I lost myself in my routine. The world, normally chaotic and frantic, was calm when I was with him, too.

I was sitting on the edge of my seat the entire game, watching him any time he was on the ice for a shift. It felt like I wasn't breathing when he had control of the puck, passing it to a forward. Like I was so finely attuned to him, to his body, that I couldn't help but track him unconsciously. I didn't even have to try.

As the final minutes of the third period ticked down, I watched as the opposing team tried to make another shot on goal, but the Wolves' goalie blocked it successfully, and Owen hit the rebound down to the opposing team's ice as the buzzer sounded, the game coming to an end. And with that, the Willamette Wolves won the game.

I couldn't wait to tell him how proud of him I was.

Just like he did every time he watched me at one of my skating competitions. We supported each other, and everything was so good.

Later, when Owen came out of the locker room, hair damp from his shower, his face lit up as he saw me.

"Hey, Daisy."

I blushed. He'd started calling me that after we'd started dating—my middle name. It was a nickname only he called me, and it felt special.

"Hi, Owen."

He stepped in close to me, wrapping his arms around my upper back before tugging me into a hug.

"I'm so proud of you," I murmured in his ear. "You played amazing tonight."

Owen nuzzled his face into my hair. "Thank you for coming. I love being able to look up and see you in the stands."

"You know I'll always be here," I promised. I meant it, too. I'd sit in the stands for him at all of his games.

He drew back, pressing a small kiss to my lips, before interlacing our fingers as we walked out to where his family was waiting.

IT ONLY TOOK a moment to fall out of love with the ice. Good things didn't last. I knew that now. Twelve years after I stepped on it for the first time, and it felt like everything I'd worked for crashed down around me with one decision. One mistake.

One goodbye that hurt more than anything ever had before.

That was the day I left the ice behind.

The day I knew I'd regret for the rest of my life.

Ellie

NOW

They say you never forget your first love.

If only that wasn't true. Especially considering we'd grown up on the same street. I couldn't tell you when I fell in love with Owen Harper. It wasn't one moment, one instant. It had been a slow, gradual thing, until I looked up one day and realized I loved him. He was my first everything—first love, first kiss, first… Well, you know. I never thought there would be any *lasts*. That I'd call him anything but mine. But that was the thing about first loves. They weren't supposed to be forever.

Today was supposed to be happy. A monumental, joyous occasion. The *end of an era*. Putting my college years behind me.

That was why we were all here, celebrating. The ceremony was tomorrow afternoon, and then we'd go back to my house for a big grad party. My family took up two tables in the coffee shop, and for the first time in a long time, everyone was here.

Okay, *almost* everyone. There was one person missing, someone whose absence I felt deeply. I stared at the text I sent. The one that hadn't received a response. Maybe it was wishful thinking that he'd reply. But he should have been here.

ELLIE

Are you coming?

Sighing, I locked my phone and looked around at everyone.

The eight of us had grown up in this coffee shop. It was my Aunt Noelle's—though we weren't related by blood—and somewhere I'd visited at least once a week for years. All the people surrounding me were my cousins—some of them by blood or marriage, and some by choice, since our moms had been best friends since college. When we were little, our moms used to bring us here, and we'd play on the floor while they'd talk about books.

I tried not to explain my family tree in too much detail to people, since their eyes glazed over when I did. Aunt Angelina —my dad's sister—was married to my Uncle Benjamin, and his brother was Hunter, who was married to Gabbi. That entire clan shared the last name of Sullivan. Then there were the Harpers, Matthew and Noelle, who might not have been related to me by blood, but I loved just the same. My parents, Charlotte and Daniel Bradford, rounded out the group. Between the four couples, there were nine of us kids, and they were some of my best friends and closest confidants.

"I can't believe you two graduate tomorrow," my older sister, Abigail, muttered. She ran her fingers through her dark, curled hair, separating the individual strands before smoothing down her pink tailored dress, one I knew she had designed. Abigail was twenty-five and thriving, running a successful fashion line. I'd always looked up to my older sister, probably because she'd always had everything together.

My cousin Zachary Sullivan, sitting by her side, snorted. "I'm just glad we have a few years until we have to go to another ceremony after this." He'd graduated two years ago with his degree in history, and now he was in grad school, with his goal to be a history professor. His twin, Wesley, was sitting on the opposite side of the table. They were identical, and I couldn't count the number of pranks they'd pulled on us over the years. Wes was the quieter twin, though he had a mischievous side too.

Penny was walking tomorrow too, which meant there would only be one of us left—Angelina and Benjamin's youngest, Lucy. She was fourteen and desperately wanted to be one of the big kids.

Between all of us, there had been college graduations the last four years in a row.

Lucy rolled her eyes, taking a sip of her iced pink drink as she thumbed through a young adult book from the bookstore portion of the shop. Aunt Noelle was a bestselling author, and when she'd been younger, she'd always dreamed of opening up a bookstore and coffee shop.

I wondered if she knew she'd be creating the future home of the Cousins Coffee Club. That we'd hang out here during college breaks and summer vacations even after we'd grown up. Though after today, who knew how often that would happen? Everyone had jobs and was getting busier. Beau, my older brother, had moved to California to play professional football in Los Angeles.

I nudged Penny at my side. "You ready for this? Getting our diplomas?"

We'd been roommates through all four years of college, driving home together some weekends when we missed our family—not that it was very far away. Growing up on the same street and only being ten months apart, our friendship had always been assumed, but from the time we'd been walking, we were tied at the hip—practically inseparable from birth.

Penelope was graduating with her degree in English and a minor in art, while I'd studied Elementary Education. While I'd been student teaching all of last year, I hadn't found a placement at any of the Portland-area schools yet, so I was going to have to move back in with my parents after our current lease ended. Her dad was a professor at the University of Portland, the same school we were both graduating from.

While she'd found her love in art and writing, my love had always been figure skating.

Until it wasn't.

And then there was my massive crush on her older brother. Owen Harper.

A crush, until it… wasn't.

But I'd lost both at the same time.

"So ready. I'm so glad to be done with classes." My best friend nodded, her red hair catching the light with the movement. She was the spitting image of her mom, all curves and freckles, but with her dad's blue eyes.

Not that I could talk, since I was practically my mother's twin, with her blonde hair and a set of blue-gray eyes. I could never quite describe the color, though my dad always said they reminded him of storm clouds on a typical Portland day. I was a few inches taller than my mother, though I'd also inherited her slender build. A body I'd worked hard to keep strong when I skated, loving the sensation of the air flowing past me as I soared across the rink. But I hadn't laced up my skates in four years. Not since the accident.

"Is Owen going to make it back?" Beau addressed Penny. He was home for a few weeks from California, since the football season was over and he didn't have to report back until later in the summer for training camp. Though he spent a lot of his time in the gym, keeping in shape.

"I don't think so," she frowned. "At least not for the ceremony. He's driving down from Seattle."

My heart leapt at the mention of my ex. I never asked about him, and somehow, I'd avoided him over the last four years since I'd ended things. It was easier said than done, considering his childhood home was on the same street as mine and our mothers being best friends. But there were perks to him being a NHL hotshot. Namely, that his visits were few, and I was pretty sure he had no desire to see me.

"Ellie?" My name was called, like it had been repeated a few times.

"Huh?" I turned, and Quinlan had an amused expression on her face.

"Whatcha thinking about there?" She sipped on her dirty chai latte while giving me a knowing look.

Looking down at my coffee on the table, I shoved the straw of my iced coffee in my mouth, drinking deeply. "Nothing."

Chuckling, she readjusted her long braid. Quin worked as a zoologist at our local zoo, and I was pretty sure she had the coolest job out of all of us.

Of course, I still didn't have an actual job, so that was probably the reason for the apprehension in my gut. That, and the unread text message on my phone.

Hopefully, a teaching position would open up over the summer, otherwise I'd just be substitute teaching until I could find something. It was a strange limbo to be almost twenty-two, a college graduate without a job lined up, and planning on moving back in with my parents. I was grown up, but it didn't feel that way.

And I knew my mom—she would love on me and dote on me, treating me the same as she always had. I was her baby. But she also had treated me differently ever since the skating accident where I had hurt my knee. Like I was *fragile*. Like she knew my dream of being an Olympic figure-skater had shattered with one wrong move. A lot of my plans had fallen apart that year.

"Okay, maybe not nothing. I need to find a job," I said, letting out a deep sigh.

"You can always come work here with me," Penny said, gesturing to her mom's coffee shop. She'd also lined up a job teaching ESL—English as a second language—classes online, but I knew she felt the same way that I did. We'd talked about it a lot, with all our siblings and cousins being so successful. How we were both worried we wouldn't live up to them. How we hadn't really made it. It felt like everyone around us was doing great—professionally, at least.

In the love department, we were all a little lacking.

At least Penelope was writing her first novel, though. She wanted to follow in her mom's footsteps as an author. I'd already told her I'd be the first one in line to buy it when she published. Pen also had her art studio, and I loved to sit and just watch her paint.

"Don't worry, El," Beau said, leaning over and messing with my hair. "You're going to find the perfect placement. I just know it. Look at you. Who could say no to that face?"

"You're just saying that because you're my brother," I said, rolling my eyes as I leaned away from him, feeling like he was about to pinch my cheeks like I was still a toddler.

"Maybe," Abigail shrugged. "But it doesn't mean it's not true."

"Thanks, Abs." That meant a lot coming from her. She'd always had this air about her, confident and put together. My sister had been a dancer for years, and I'd been mesmerized watching her on stage, so graceful with her long legs and slender frame. I'd danced too—it was really helpful with figure skating, and I loved seeing my mom at the studio, but there was something different watching her.

"Alright," Wesley said, sitting down at the table with a fresh cup of coffee. "What'd I miss?"

Zachary rolled his eyes at his twin brother. My cousins were spitting images of Angelina and Benjamin, but the Bradford genes were strong, and when they were with Beau, people often mistook the three of them for triplets.

Everyone burst out laughing, and then we all continued our various conversations.

Penny looked over, squeezing my hand.

No matter what else, I had my family. The people crowded around me as we shared laughter and love while we drank coffee in the place we grew up.

The people I loved more than anything else.

Even if there *was* one person missing.

MY GRADUATION GOWN WAS UNZIPPED, and I was clutching my diploma case and my decorated cap as I searched through the crowd, looking for my family. I was desperate to take my heels off, but we'd still have a bunch of photos to take, so I hadn't yet.

When I caught sight of them, I practically beamed. "Hi!"

"There she is," Mom announced. "I need to take pictures. Oh my gosh. Our little girl, all grown up." She pulled out her phone, snapping pictures of all of us before asking someone nearby to take one of our family.

"Proud of you, sis," Beau said, handing me a bouquet of white roses.

I smiled, looking at the beautiful flowers. "Thank you."

My older sister pulled me into a hug, whispering in my ear, "You're going to do amazing things, Ellie."

"Congratulations, El." My dad wrapped his arms around me once Abigail had pulled away, holding me tight. "I'm so proud of all you've accomplished." I'd always felt safe and loved in his arms. He'd always been the best dad—driving me wherever I needed to go, sitting on the benches during my time at the rink, and always making sure I felt loved and supported.

"Thanks, Dad." I hugged him back, he squeezed me tighter.

One more minute, I thought. I just wanted to be their little girl for one more minute.

It was just my mom who was left, standing there with her arms open for me.

"Mom," I breathed as I stepped into her hug.

"Hi, sweetie pie. Look at you. My little graduate." She kissed the side of my forehead. "Happy graduation day, my sweet girl."

"Thanks, Mom. I love you guys so much."

As the youngest Bradford sibling, I never could have asked for a better family. Beau was a year and a half older than me, and all throughout school had been fiercely protective of his little sister. And while Abs and I had barely attended the same school, my big sister had been there for every school dance, every skating competition, and every big moment in my life.

The decision to stay in my hometown for college hadn't been an easy one. But after the skating accident that had left me with a bad knee, dashing my dreams for the olympics, I hadn't known what I wanted anymore. Except I didn't want to be alone in a new city for the first time in my life, and instead, I'd followed in my parents' footsteps, attending the same university that they'd both attended. I was proud to wear the purple, and happy that there was no ice rink to remind me of what I was missing.

Who I was missing.

"Ellie!" My head perked up, and I saw one of my friends waving at me. "Let's take a picture!"

I turned to my family. "Be right back?"

They smiled, and I ran over to hug my friends and take pictures with them. It was strange to think that we'd never all be in one place like this again. That after four years of college, I might not see some of my classmates ever again. We all said our goodbyes, promising to keep in touch.

I made my way back to my family, my heart full and my camera roll full of even more photos.

"The rest of the family's back at the house, waiting for the party," Beau said, slinging an arm around my shoulder. I hadn't been able to get as many tickets for today as I had people who loved me. All of my aunts, uncles, and cousins had been watching the live stream, but as soon as we got home, we'd be throwing a huge joint graduation party.

"Speaking of, has anyone seen Penny?" I looked around, scanning the crowd for a curly head of ginger hair. "I wanted to get one last picture."

As if summoned, my best friend's curls bobbed as she ran over to me, throwing her arms around me even as her cap dislodged from her head.

"We did it!" Penelope laughed as we jumped up and down in each other's arms.

"You ready for the party tonight?" I asked, the smile practically splitting my face.

But her face grew solemn. "Yeah, but…"

I winced. "Oh. He's… not coming?" I knew she'd hoped that her brother would make it to watch her walk, but he wasn't here.

Penny shrugged. "No, he said he's on his way, I just…" She bit her lip. "I love him, but it's been hard, you know. I barely get to see him anymore."

"Yeah. Beau's only been gone a year, but even in college, I didn't see him as much."

Still, getting drafted to the NFL last year had been incredible for him. Our family was so proud of him, even if he lived down in California now. My Aunt Lavender, my mom's sister, lived down there too, so we had plenty of excuses to go visit. Plus, we'd practically grown up going to Disneyland down in Southern California and Disney World in Florida, so going down to Los Angeles wasn't anything new.

I hugged her tight to my side as her parents caught up with us.

My dad looked at all of us before wrapping his arm around my mom's waist. "Everyone ready for the party?"

I nodded. "Let's go."

TWO

Owen

———

NOW

What the fuck did I think I was doing? My grip tightened on the steering wheel as I stared at the Bradford house. A house I'd spent almost as much time in growing up as my own.

But I couldn't seem to get *out* of the car. Maybe it was because I knew that when I did, everything would change. I hadn't seen her in almost five years. Since she'd walked out on us, walked away from our relationship, leaving my heart shattered in pieces on my dorm room floor.

Her text was still unread on my phone.

ELLIE DAISY

Are you coming?

I hadn't even had the balls to open it.

Today, she graduated from college, but I'd been too much of a coward to go to the ceremony. Even if my little sister Penelope had also graduated today, and I'd promised I'd be here. My team didn't make the playoffs, which meant our season was over. I didn't have an excuse to hide anymore. To avoid seeing *her*.

"You're twenty-four," I muttered to myself. "You can do

16

this." I was over it. It was fine. Really. I could see my ex again. The word was sour on my tongue, but that was what she was.

Stepping out of the car, I shoved my hands in my pockets as I looked up at the house that Daniel had built Charlotte. Unlike the rest of my family, I never called them aunt or uncle. Beau was one of my best friends, and my sister Penny was best friends with Ellie, but it had never felt *right*.

Maybe because she'd always felt like *mine*.

I leaned against the car. There were two packages on my front seat—a gift for my sister, and a bouquet of daisies for her.

As if summoned by my thoughts, the door opened, and my mouth went dry. There she was. Dressed in a light blue sundress, her honey blonde hair tumbling around her shoulders in light curls.

Ellie Bradford.

Beautiful as ever. Maybe even more beautiful, if that was possible. Only now, she wasn't mine.

"Hey, Skater Girl." I don't know who moved first. Only that I was catching her as she launched herself at me, wrapping her arms around my neck and burying her face in my neck.

"Hi, Hockey Boy," she murmured against my skin.

Four years I'd been avoiding this. But I was home.

I set her back down on her feet. "Happy graduation."

"You're here," she whispered.

"Promised I would be, didn't I?" I'd made that promise a long time ago, though, before things changed.

She looked at her bare feet. "I didn't know…" Ellie's voice trailed off.

"Yeah. I know." I hadn't known either. Not until today. "Ellie…"

She shook her head. "Can we just… go inside? I can't do this now."

"Yeah." My voice was hoarse. "Let me just grab something," I said, turning back to my car. I scooped the gifts out, watching as her eyes widened as she caught sight of the flowers.

"Are those…"

"Daisies. Yeah." I nodded, handing her the bouquet. "For you."

"Thank you." She buried her nose, inhaling the scent.

I followed her inside, the entire room of my family bursting to life as soon as I walked through the door.

"Hey, everyone." I waved, grinning as all the guys stood up to hug me and slap my back.

There was a wide spread of food on the kitchen counter, something I was sure my mom and Ellie's had spent multiple hours baking and prepping for. They'd always loved throwing parties ever since we were little, though I suspected it was mostly just an excuse for our four moms to sit around and gossip or talk about the romance novels they'd read.

"Owen!" A redhead dressed in a yellow sundress came rushing towards me, a grin on her freckled face.

"Hi, Pen," I said, grinning at my younger sister. All of us kids were tight, especially since we were all close in age, but she and I had always been thick as thieves. We fought, but she was also the one who would cheer me up when I was feeling down. I'd do the same for her, of course. I was her fiercest protector, always making sure no guys at school were going to mess with my sister. "Sorry I'm late."

She punched me in the arm. "It's about time."

Wrapping her up in a big hug, I held her tight against my chest. "I know. I promise I'll make it up to you."

"How long are you staying in town for?"

I looked over at Ellie, sandwiched in the middle of her two siblings. God, I was supposed to be getting over her, and yet one look at her, and all I wanted was to orbit her like the sun.

"A few days, maybe?" Though that depended on a lot of things.

Penelope pouted. "Don't you get the summer off from hockey? You should stay for a few weeks. It would be good for you. You've barely spent any time in Portland the last few years."

"I know," I sighed. "I'm sorry, sis." She was right. Ever since I'd gotten drafted to the NHL and made my debut on the Seattle Seals, I'd barely come home. More often than not, my family had come up to spend the few days I got off for Christmas with me. Grabbing the wrapped package I'd set on the island, I handed it to her. "This is for you. I'm so proud of you, Penelope."

Her eyes were watery. "Owen…"

"Just open it." I tapped on the wrapping paper.

She did, finding a leather-bound notebook inside with her name embossed on the cover. *Penelope Elaine Harper.* "It's beautiful," she gasped.

"For you to write your story ideas down in," I said. I'd had it custom made, and I really hoped she liked it. "And there's something else inside."

I'd found a beautiful necklace of a little book that opened and a message could be inscribed inside. She let out a small gasp as she pulled out the gold chain, opening the little hinge to see what was written in it. *More than words.* My parents always said it to each other, a little phrase that meant *I love you,* and I'd had that engraved because I knew how much it would mean to her..

"Thank you. I love it." She wiped away a tear, opening up the clasp before putting it on. "Guess I forgive you for not seeing my ceremony earlier."

I laughed. "I'll make it up to you, I promise."

"Good." She nodded. "I have to show mom!" Squealing, she headed for the kitchen, and I joined her, shoving my hands in my pants pockets.

A lot of my friends throughout college and my teammates in the NHL didn't understand how I was so close with my family, but my parents were some of the best people I'd ever met. They were both so supportive of Penelope and me with all our dreams, even when she'd told them she'd wanted to follow in mom's footsteps as a writer and with me playing professional hockey.

I grinned as my mom opened her arms for a hug. "Hi, Mom."

"Hey, baby." My mom squeezed me tight before pulling back. "How's Seattle?"

"Good," I said, wrapping my arms around her. She always smelled like baked goods, and the scent made me feel like a kid again. It took me right back to all the afternoons spent studying in her bookstore & coffee shop, surrounded by all the cousins and siblings who currently filled the living room. "Not that much different from Portland, really." Especially considering how much I traveled throughout the year.

"Hey, Dad." I grinned.

My dad was the best man I knew, and I'd learned everything from him. He was a college athlete, too, playing basketball, but he hadn't gone pro afterwards. And I knew that even though he'd wanted me to graduate from college with my degree, he'd understood why I couldn't turn down my chance to join the NHL and play for the Seals.

"It's good to have you home, son."

I nodded. "I've missed you guys. You're going to come up for some games this year, right?"

They'd come up a few times each year, and they were some of my favorite games. I loved knowing they were in the stands cheering for me.

My parents nodded, but it was dad who responded. "Yeah. Of course we will. I know we were planning on coming up for Thanksgiving. We're still trying to figure out Christmas, too."

"Yeah. Maybe I could come down this year?" I offered. "Schedule pending, but I could drive down after the last game."

My mom was practically beaming. "I'd love that."

Dad pushed a strand of mom's hair back behind her ear. "Of course you would, sunshine."

"Sorry if I just want to have all my babies in one place," she muttered, patting his stomach. "Even your sister is planning on spending it in Portland this year."

My dad's sister, Tessa Harper-Graham, was married to my mom's cousin, Oliver. She was an actress, and they spent part of their time each year in California, and part here with the family. They had two daughters: Avery and Fiona. I couldn't remember the last time we'd all been in town for the holidays.

"That sounds nice, Mom."

She nodded, and after giving me another hug, I headed into the living room where everyone else my age was gathered.

Ellie was sitting on the couch next to her older sister as they chatted about Abigail's fashion line and the designs she was working on.

For the first time in my life, I felt like an outsider looking in on my family, on the people I'd grown up with. It was my fault. The distance I'd put between me and everyone here felt necessary back then, partially because my heart ached just being in the same room as her after everything that had happened between us.

Beau handed me a beer, and I eagerly chugged it down, not wanting to be sober as I had to stare at the girl who got away sitting across from me, her smile bright.

Because despite everything, all I wanted to do was to sit by Ellie's side. To hear about every minute from the last four years.

The daisies I'd given her were in a vase on the counter, alongside a vase of white roses. Suddenly, my flowers felt dumb. I should have known her family would have given her flowers. And yet, a gift like Penelope's was too intimate for my ex-girlfriend. We weren't together.

I needed to get over her. That was what this trip was

about. *Closure.* I finished the rest of the beer, guzzling it down before going and grabbing another one.

"Where are you staying tonight?" That was Pen, plopping next to Ellie. I tried my hardest not to look over at the two of them, pretending I was listening to the conversation Beau and Zach were having about football.

"Thought I'd spent one last night in the apartment and get a head start on packing up tomorrow. That way, I can be out before the lease ends."

My sister nodded. "Yeah. That makes sense. I'm figuring I'll stick around here tonight. Especially with Owen at home. Maybe I can bribe mom to make cinnamon rolls."

Out of the corner of my eye, I could see Ellie fidgeting with the edge of her sweater. It was her tell that she was nervous, and I wondered if the thought of *me* being back was making her uncomfortable.

We needed to get over this. We couldn't keep avoiding being in the same room for the rest of our lives. Not when our families did everything together.

"What do you think, O?" Zachary asked, elbowing me.

"Huh?" I focused on the guys. "Sorry, what was that?"

"We were just talking about going out tomorrow. Celebrate all being in town at the same time." Beau raised an eyebrow.

"Oh. Right." I shrugged. "Sounds fun." A few drinks and some good company would definitely help me get my mind off the girl who had run into my arms like she'd never left, right? I hoped so. Something had to help this empty ache in my chest.

She doesn't want to be with you. Not like I wanted, anyway. It was the reminder I needed to steel my spine. To lock my feelings away behind a brick wall. To forgive and forget.

I could be the fun-loving, cheerful guy I'd always been.

Ellie Bradford might have broken my heart four years ago,

but starting tonight, I was getting closure, and then I'd move on.

It was time to stop dwelling on the past.

THREE

Owen

THEN

Junior Year

*H*ey, Skater Girl," I said, grinning as I leaned up against a locker at our high school.

Ellie gave me a small smile. "Hi, Owen."

"First day, huh?" It was a question, but I already knew the answer. She'd turned fourteen this summer, and it was both her and Penelope's first day of freshman year. My sister, of course, had missed the cut-off with an October birthday, so she was almost a year older than the blonde in front of me. "It'll be great, I promise."

She nodded, still quiet.

"Where's your first class?" I asked, cocking my head as I watched her. I'd never seen her like this before. Fidgety and almost… *nervous?* The Ellie I knew was a ball of sunshine, plus she was always so poised and elegant on the ice. "Maybe we're heading in the same direction, and I can walk you there."

"Oh." She lifted her head, her blue-gray eyes meeting mine. "That would be great."

She handed me her schedule, and I grinned after looking

over it. "Look at that. I have history in the room right next to your English class."

"Really?" A little warmth trickled back into her voice, and I tightened the grip on the backpack I had slung over one shoulder.

"Really. Come on. Let's head there."

I knew from looking over my sister's schedule that she and Ellie didn't have the same classes, and I wondered if part of that was the reason she was feeling out of place.

"You know, between me and all your other cousins at the school, there's always someone you can go to for help."

Ellie scrunched her nose, looking up at me. "*We're* not cousins though, Owen." Her cheeks were a little pink.

God, she was tiny. I'd never really noticed how much taller I was than her before. Even at the ice rink, I didn't normally stand next to her for very long, and mostly, we were coming and going in passing, or chatting with each other on the bench. This felt different.

I chuckled. "No, we're not." That felt important. I didn't know why, but it was. Even if we'd grown up together, we weren't related. Even if I didn't remember life without her.

She fidgeted with the strap of her backpack. It was a bright, sunshiny yellow color. One I knew was her favorite. "I'm glad you're here," she finally whispered.

"Yeah?" My chest puffed up, and I didn't know why that thought made me feel warm inside, but it did.

Ellie nodded. "Beau would act like an over-protective brother if he was walking me around."

And her older sister, Abigail, was a senior. It was strange to think that once she started college, I would be the oldest of the pack. The one who could drive to school, since I'd gotten my license this summer. My dad had given me his old blue truck, and I felt so much pride that he trusted me enough to drive it around.

Sure, the twins, Zachary and Wesley, were both in the

same year as me, but I was six months older, and I felt that responsibility immensely.

But standing here with Ellie, I didn't feel like her older brother. I wanted to protect her for a whole different reason.

I wasn't sure I'd ever noticed how adorable she was before. She was wearing a white t-shirt under a denim overall dress that was embroidered with flowers with a pair of white sneakers, and it was so *her*. Her hair was pulled back in a braid, with little wispy tendrils falling out the front, and she had the barest amount of makeup on: a little shimmer over her eyelid, a swipe of mascara, a touch of blush and this hint of lip gloss that sparkled on her lips.

Lips I *shouldn't* be looking at. I had no business looking at Ellie like that. Especially as that blush returned to her cheeks, and she looked away quickly. What was that? I'd never thought about kissing Beau's little sister before. She was Penny's best friend, on top of it. But she was also my friend.

Honestly, I'd never thought about kissing *anyone* before. I'd always been too busy with hockey and classes to even spare a second glance around girls. But maybe it was that in the last year, my voice had deepened, and I'd gained more inches in height. Plus, all my time on the ice was already bulking me up. My dad was six-three and a big guy, so it wasn't much of a surprise.

Still, girls noticed me now. I was uncomfortable with all the attention, brushing it off the best I could. Because the only one I wanted to notice me was walking by my side.

It was a thought I pondered long after I dropped her off at the door to her classroom. After wishing her good luck on her first day and telling her to text me if she needed anything.

She'd blushed again before ducking into class, and I knew that no matter how hard I tried, I'd never quite be able to get Eleanor Bradford out of my head.

THE SUN WAS SHINING as I walked across the street to the Bradford house, shoving my hands in my jeans pockets as I let out a breath. It was an unusually nice day for fall, and that felt like a good sign. All week, all I could think about was her.

We'd grown up together, but it felt like in the last year, I'd blinked, and she'd grown up. Ellie Bradford had gone from the adorable little girl whose pigtails I used to tug on to a graceful young woman. And our relationship had changed, too. This year, it felt like we'd gone from friends to… *more*. I'd catch her glancing my way when we walked through the halls at school, her cheeks pink, and my heart raced.

I liked her. So much more than I could have ever imagined.

Which is why I needed to get this right.

Raising my hand, I knocked on the door. It was the first time in a long time that I'd needed to. I'd been coming to this house my whole life. Namely, on account of the fact that my mom and Ellie's mom were best friends. Some of my earliest memories were with the Bradford-Sullivan clan, spending almost every holiday at one of their houses.

Daniel Bradford—Beau and Ellie's dad—opened it, grinning at me. Thanks to the height I'd inherited from my dad, we were almost eye to eye. That should have made this less intimidating, but it didn't. My palms were sweaty, and I was more nervous than I'd ever been.

"Hey, son." Her dad clasped a hand on my shoulder. "I don't think Beau's here right now, but I can find him for you—"

"I'm actually here to see you," I said, swallowing down my apprehension as I followed him inside, wiping my palms on my jeans.

"Oh?" He raised an eyebrow. "Is everything okay, son? I know your dad would—"

"Everything's great." I nodded. "Can we sit?"

"Sure." Daniel gestured to the couch, running his hands through his now-salt-and-pepper hair.

We sat down, and I took a deep breath. "I wanted to get your permission to date your daughter."

"Ellie?" He raised an eyebrow.

"Yes." They had to know how much time we spent together. How we'd sit out on the back porch for hours late into the night, looking up at the stars. How every time she came into the rink and I spotted her on the bench, waiting for her skating practice, my heart leapt into my throat. "I care about her. I really like her."

That was an understatement.

"What happens when you go off to college?" As if I needed the reminder that I'd be leaving. It was why I wanted to take advantage of every moment we had now. He crossed his arms over his chest. "She's a freshman."

"I know." Daniel said that like I wasn't hyper aware of the age difference between us. How the two and a half years felt so big now. But my mom was five years younger than my dad, and when we were older, it wouldn't even matter. "That would be up to her, sir. We can always do long distance. It's not like I won't come home all the time." And when she started college, then things would change. We hadn't really talked abut the future yet. Because I wanted to do this right. "I was going to ask her to be my date to prom."

He rubbed his fingers over his jaw, like he was contemplating what I was saying. "I don't want to see any funny business, Owen. Don't forget I know where you live. You both have bright futures, and I don't want to see you ruining that."

My cheeks went pink at the insinuation. "No, sir. I'll bring her home straight after the dance."

He nodded. "Okay. I can't see any reason to object to that. But it's Ellie's decision, of course."

"What is?" Charlotte, Ellie's mom, asked, entering the room and draping her arms around Daniel from the back of the couch.

"Owen's going to ask Ellie to prom." He said to his wife, eyes beaming as he looked up at her. It was clear, even now, just how much he loved her. The two of them had been best friends since college. Maybe that would be El and me someday. *If she said yes*, I reminded myself. If she liked me the way I liked her.

"Oh!" Her face lit up with delight. "I'll have to make her a dress, and—"

"Assuming she says yes," I cleared my throat. Even though I doubted she'd say no. We were friends, and though I hadn't taken her out on an official date yet, I planned to remedy that soon.

Her mom giggled. "Oh, she'll say yes. She is *smitten* with you."

It was my turn to run my hands through my hair. Somehow, everything felt so much more real now.

"Mom, Dad, I'm home!" Ellie's voice carried through the house as she opened the front door. Her skating bag was over her shoulder, and her skates in her hands. She did a double take, seeing me sitting on the couch. "Owen?"

"Hi." I stood up, going to stand by her side. "Can we talk?"

She nodded, her eyes wide. "Okay. Upstairs, or…"

"Treehouse," I offered. Up there, we'd have some privacy. Though I didn't expect Charlotte and Daniel to eavesdrop, the thought of someone listening in was a lot.

Ellie's expression morphed into a warm smile. "Yeah. Treehouse sounds good." She set her stuff at the base of the stairs before turning to me. "Let's go?"

Our parents had built it when we were all much smaller,

and it had been our preferred hangout spot. Sometimes when we were young, the guys and I had all taken sleeping bags up there and slept outside. All of those were amazing memories, but somehow I suspected this would be even better.

We headed outside, Ellie climbing up the ladder before I followed behind her.

"Smaller than I remember it," I murmured as I stood up in the space, ducking so my head didn't hit the ceiling. Sitting on the ground, I had my backpack with me, and I set it to my side, fidgeting with the strap.

Ellie sat across from me, draping her legs all ladylike and putting her hands in her lap. "What did you want to talk about?" She had that sparkly lip-gloss on again, and I wondered what it tasted like. Knowing her, it would be birthday cake flavored, but I tried not to pay too much attention when she swiped it on her lips.

Focusing on her lips was not a good idea.

"So, prom is coming up," I started.

"Right." She laughed awkwardly, then made a face. "Well... I don't get to go, since I'm a freshman."

"Unless..." I reached in my backpack, pulling out the flowers I'd hoped would be safe in there. A small bouquet of daisies. "If you wanted to go with me?" I swallowed, hoping she couldn't tell how nervous I was.

She blinked. "*Me*?"

I nodded, handing her the daisies. "Do you see anyone else in this treehouse, Skater Girl?"

"This is just... are you sure? I'm sure there are a lot of other girls in your classes that you—"

"I don't want to date any of them, Ellie."

Her teeth dug into her lower lip, and her words came out in hardly more than a breath. "Then... who do you want to date?"

Flashing her a smile, I sat up on my knees. "You."

"Oh." She blushed, looking down at the flowers. "Are you sure?"

I chuckled. "Yeah, I'm sure. I like you a lot, Eleanor Bradford."

She gave me a shy smile. "I like you too, Owen Harper." Her eyelids fluttered as she looked down at the flowers. "I just… *Wow*. I didn't expect this today."

There was no way the grin could be wiped off my face. "Yeah? What did you expect?"

She blushed, tucking a strand of hair behind her ear. "I don't know, honestly. What will everyone think?"

"Well, I already asked your parents, so they're cool with us dating."

"Oh." A giggle slipped free from her. "You asked my parents?"

"Your dad, mostly." I shrugged, like it was nothing. As if I hadn't been nervous beforehand.

"You're something else, you know that?"

I nodded. "I am when I know what I want, Ellie."

You.

She rolled her eyes, but she didn't stop smiling. Not as she told me how her practice had gone today, how she felt more comfortable with her routine with each passing day and how excited she was to perform it. Scooting closer to me until our thighs were touching, it felt like there was no one else in the world, just the two of us in that tiny tree house together. We shared our hopes and dreams for the future. How she wanted to go to the Olympics. My dreams of the National Hockey League.

After all, in here, anything was possible.

And today… Today was the beginning of us.

FOUR

Ellie

NOW

*H*ours after my graduation party had ended, I sat outside in the old treehouse with a pile of snacks I'd smuggled up. My parents had built it when I was a kid, and I still loved it.

I'd told Penelope that I was going to go back to our apartment tonight, and I meant it, but right now, I was enjoying my last night where I didn't have to think about being an adult or getting a job. About the fact that soon, I'd be living with my parents again. At least I wouldn't have to pay rent.

It felt like I had blinked, and my time in college was over. Looking back, it felt like it was last fall that I'd been moving into my dorm for the first time.

"Damn," I muttered, looking down at my pile. "Maybe I should have brought some wine." I'd had more than a few glasses throughout of the evening, a lot of them to distract from the fact that I'd practically *flung* myself into Owen's arms when he'd shown up outside my house. And then we'd spent the entire night less than five feet apart, and I could almost convince myself I'd hallucinated it. But no.

He was here.

I leaned my back against the wall, looking at the structure

fondly. I had so many amazing memories here. It was where Owen had asked me to prom. Where we'd shared our feelings over summer breaks. How many kisses had we shared in this very spot?

Over the years, as I'd gotten older, I'd stopped spending as much time up here, but it was no less special. Still, being up here made me a little heartsick.

"Ellie?" a deep voice called. The voice I would know anywhere. Was it even deeper now? Maybe. Even after all this time, it was a balm to my heart.

I poked my head out, looking down to find him standing in the middle of the yard, looking just as handsome as he had earlier. Maybe even more so, with his hair mussed like he'd been running his hands through it over and over, and an extra button undone on his shirt. Though maybe that was the alcohol talking.

Owen. *My Owen.* Only he wasn't mine anymore, and he hadn't been in a long time. He went out with models now. I'd seen photos of him up in Seattle, with different women on his arm for hockey events. It had hurt like hell every time, but I'd tried to ignore it. It shouldn't bother me. I was the one who'd ended it.

"Owen." My breath caught. "What are you doing here?"

He shoved his hands in his pockets. "Thought maybe we should talk."

"What is there to talk about?" I bit my lip.

"What isn't there, Ellie?" He shook his head. "It's been four years." *Almost five.* Did he think I didn't know that? I didn't respond, and he moved to the ladder, climbing up quickly.

Drawing my legs up to my chest, I stared at him as he settled onto the floor across from me, not saying anything.

This space seemed even smaller with him in it. Maybe it was all the years of professional hockey, but he was much bigger now. All six-foot-three of him, with those broad shoulders and thighs that didn't quit. If I let myself, it would be so easy to salivate over this man. His eyes were the same warm brown, and his hair the shade of dirty blond that it had been since I was little. I'd expected it to get darker, but it hadn't.

"Four years," he repeated, running his hands through his hair. "We went from being each other's everything to *this*, and you're asking me what we have to talk about?"

I shrugged, feeling hopeless. "I don't know what you want from me, Owen. We never would have worked in the long run. You were always destined for greater things. And look at you now. You're living your dream. Playing in the NHL. You got everything you've always wanted."

"But did you?" He looked… *wrecked*. But that couldn't be right.

Did I? I looked down at my bare feet to my freshly painted nails. I'd kicked off the fancy sandals I'd changed into for my party before climbing up here, though I was still wearing my light blue dress. I didn't know how to answer that, so I didn't.

"So, elementary education, huh?" He asked, changing the subject.

Tucking a strand of hair behind my ear, I nodded. "I always liked kids, you know? And after everything, I just…" I closed my eyes. I didn't enjoy thinking about the time after my accident. When everything had fallen apart around me and I'd had to rearrange my entire life my senior year of high school. "It made sense. And I love it."

"You didn't tell me." Now, there was an edge of hurt to his voice. Owen sounded… *defeated*.

I blinked. "What?"

"You got hurt. The accident." He gritted his teeth. "You— you didn't tell me you were hurt. I had to find out about it from my mom. Do you know what that did to me, El? Knowing you were hurt and I couldn't even comfort you? Knowing that I was away at college and couldn't come and make sure you were okay?" He shut his eyes.

"We were broken up," I whispered. "I ended it. I didn't think—"

"Of course you didn't think." His thumb reached out, swiping over my cheekbone before tracing that same line down my ear. "Because you didn't ask."

"Owen, I—"

He shook his head. "Why do you think I stayed away all these years, Ellie?"

"Because you hated me," I murmured, avoiding his eyes. "Because I broke your heart."

His voice was soft when he cupped my chin, tilting up my head till my gaze met his, and said, "Ellie baby, I never hated you."

My eyes fluttered shut. How was I going to survive this? Survive *him*? It had taken me so long to move on. To stop feeling like my heart was missing from my chest. To find happiness again in the little things.

"You should have," I said, miserably. He should have hated me for the things I did. For the way I left.

"It would have been easier if I did," Owen agreed.

Now it was my turn to shake my head. "It doesn't matter now." The whispered words were all I could offer him. "It's in the past. We're in the past."

It was what I'd had to tell myself to keep going all these years. That the moments we'd shared—no matter how good—were in the past now. Though this didn't feel like anything had passed. Not when he was holding my face so reverently, his mouth only inches from mine.

And the worst was knowing what those lips felt like against mine. It had been so long since I'd been kissed by him, and all I could think about now was I wanted him to.

His eyes dipped down to my lips, and I wondered if he was thinking the same thing. How easy it would be to fall back into what we'd been before. How much we both wanted it.

I reached up a hand and ran my fingers through his hair.

It was longer than it had been when we were together, though that shouldn't have been surprising.

"What if—" I started, at the same time he opened his mouth.

"We should—"

Pulling back, I motioned for him to go first.

"We shouldn't."

I frowned, starting to pull away. The rejection stung. "Oh. But…"

"We shouldn't, but *damn* if I don't want you." Owen's hand wrapped around the back of my neck, dragging us closer together. If I moved even a hair, my lips would be on his.

"I know," I murmured, trying to resist the pull. The urge. There was a magnetism between us, pulling us together. That was how it had been our whole lives. The only reason we'd been able to stay apart for this long was avoiding each other. It was a cruel fate to have each other, to want each other, but not be able to keep each other.

"What if we just have tonight? One night," I promised. "You're going back to Seattle, anyway." And then he'd be gone, back to his life of hockey and models, and I'd be here.

"One night," he agreed.

And then his lips were on mine.

Everything else melted away.

Because Owen Harper kissing me was better than anything else.

The kiss was soft at first, a gentle press of his lips against mine, like he was re-acquainting himself with my mouth. His palm was warm against the back of my neck, and I slipped mine around his as I shifted my position, climbing onto his lap. The first stroke of his tongue against my lips, encouraging me to open for him, and I melted, kissing him back with just as much fervor. I needed more. Rocking my hips against his, I moaned when my core pressed against his length through his jeans.

It brought back memories I tried not to think about unless I was alone in the dark. He was big back then, too, and right now, I wanted to feel him everywhere.

"*Fuck*," he groaned, as I rubbed myself against his erection. "Baby, you have to stop."

I whimpered. "Why?" It wouldn't take much for me to come. Not like this.

"Because I'm not fucking you in this treehouse, Ellie. Not when anyone could come outside and hear us."

Oh. I supposed that made sense. "Right." I ran my tongue over my lower lip. "Then where…"

"You said you were spending tonight at your apartment, right? *Alone*?" Owen quirked an eyebrow.

"Yes," I said in a rush. There would be no chance of interruption. Penelope was spending tonight at with her parents. That was where I'd expected Owen to stay, too. But I liked the idea of him staying with me.

Closure. It was all that we could offer each other, but I would take it.

"Let's go, Hockey Boy."

His eyes were dark, full of heat. He pressed his lips against mine once more before standing up, taking me with him.

"Wait," I murmured, before he could angle us towards the stairs. "The snacks."

Owen laughed, and the sound was a balm to my aching heart.

AN HOUR LATER, Owen's car was parked in front of the apartment I'd rented with Penny near campus. After a quick stop at the store, there was a bag in the back, and it had been hard just to keep our hands off of each other long enough to make the drive here.

"Are you sure?" he asked, resting his forehead against mine. Neither one of us had moved to get out of the car, and I knew the second we did, everything would change.

But I wanted his mouth on mine. Wanted his weight over my body, surrounded by his warmth. Wanted to feel him inside of me one last time. If this was all of him I got, I wanted to savor it. Part of me knew I'd remember this for a long time.

"Yes, Owen. I want you."

Would anyone else compare to the man by my side? Whose smiles lit up my world in a way I'd never been able to explain? I couldn't even remember when my crush on him had begun. Only that when I'd started high school, our relationship had changed. He'd become as much of my best friend as Penny was. And then we were dating, and everything had been… perfect. Until it wasn't.

He pressed his lips to my forehead and then climbed out of his car without preamble. Part of me missed his old truck, though the blue sports car he drove now clearly showed how well the Seattle Seals were paying him to play on the team.

Owen came around to my side, opening my door and unbuckling my seatbelt for me when I made no move to do it myself. He held out a hand, and I slid mine into it, letting him pull me out of the car. The door shut, and I rested my back against the cool exterior as he traced a finger around my jawline.

"You're so beautiful," he murmured, his free hand resting on the roof of his car. "I can hardly stand it."

Dipping his head down, he kissed me until I was panting underneath him. Needy and hopelessly wet, and all I wanted was *him*.

"Upstairs," I begged.

Owen opened the backseat, grabbed the bag of condoms,

and then interlaced our fingers as I guided him into my apartment.

I'd promised him one night only, but somehow I knew that with every step, there was no going back from this. That I could say whatever I wanted, but I knew the truth.

One last night would never be enough. Not with him. And not for us.

FIVE

Owen

NOW

*H*er apartment door slammed shut behind us, and I pinned her against it, relishing in the taste of her mouth after so long. How had I gone so long without kissing her? Without feeling her skin under mine? She was warm, despite the slight chill to the night air and her bare shoulders. I moved my lips down, pushing the spaghetti straps of her light blue dress off and kissing the crook of her neck.

She let her head fall back against the door as I brushed my lips over her skin while trailing my fingers up the skin of her thigh, dangerously close to her panties.

"Owen," she begged. "Please. Touch me."

I groaned, dropping my head to her shoulder as I pushed aside the material and ran my fingers over her slit.

"So wet," I murmured, spreading her wetness around before pressing my thumb against her clit. She let out a small gasp, and I pushed a finger inside of her. "So tight." Her moan as I thrust my finger in and out spurred me on even more. "Do you need to come, my Daisy?"

"*Yes*," she cried as I added another finger. "So bad. It's been *so long*."

She was mine. The idea that in all this time, she hadn't been with anyone else made my cock harden further, pressing uncomfortably against the zipper of my jeans. I didn't even know if it was true. My mom hadn't told me about her dating anyone else, but that didn't mean she'd been waiting around for me. Especially when I'd spent the better part of five years staying away from her.

I hadn't memorized her body like I'd wanted to the last time, and that was a mistake. This time, I planned to take my time with her. Luckily, I'd picked up some new tricks over the last few years. Listening to my teammates talk about women had been eye-opening, to say the least.

Continuing to fuck her with my fingers until she fell apart in my arms, I felt a smug satisfaction at the feeling of her cunt clenching around me and how fast she'd come. Pulling my fingers out, she slumped against me. As I held her against my body, I pulled us both away from the door.

Grabbing the bag I'd dropped as soon as we'd entered the apartment, I opened the box and stuffed a few foil packets into my back pocket.

"Bedroom?" I murmured in her ear once that was done.

"The one on the left," she responded, wrapping her arms around my neck before lifting her body off the ground to hug her legs around my waist.

Carrying her like a koala, I kicked in her door, dropping her on the bed. Her honey blonde hair spread out around her, and that icy blue dress that complimented her skin so well rode up, exposing her white lacy panties to me. Leaving her dress on and pushing it up her hips further, I tugged the lace fabric down, exposing her pretty pink pussy to me. God, I wanted to have my mouth on her.

"So pretty," I murmured, kneeling at the edge of the bed and tugging her down so her entrance lined up with my face. "I need to taste you, baby."

Ellie whimpered in response as I dragged my tongue over

her slit, tasting her like I'd been dying to do since I kissed her earlier today.

Taking my time, I thrust my tongue inside her, lapping up all of her juices before circling her clit with my tongue. I could tell she was still sensitive from coming on my fingers, and I worked her up, feeling her tighten around me.

Before she could come again, I stood up, kissing her deeply, letting her taste herself on my mouth.

"I need you," she said against my mouth. Her hands reached lower, unzipping my jeans before her hand slid unceremoniously into my boxer briefs, her fingers running up the length of my dick.

I shuddered, eyes shutting as her soft hand wrapped around me.

She used her other hand to push my jeans down, only getting them halfway down my hips before she let out a growl in frustration.

I chuckled. "Someone's eager."

"Fuck me," she groaned, and *damn*. I'd never heard her say things like that before, but it did something to me.

"Does my girl have a filthy mouth now?" I muttered, shimmying my pants off and letting my cock spring free.

Her eyes widened as she licked her lips, taking in my erection, standing at attention for her. Only for her.

"Maybe I'm not the same innocent, blushing girl I was."

"No," I said, holding back a groan as she slid backwards on the bed, spreading her thighs for me. "No, you're not."

She fluttered her eyelashes. "Then what are you waiting for?"

I climbed on the bed on top of her, positioning an arm on either side of her to keep from crushing her body. My cock rested between us, thick and heavy, and I couldn't help but rub it against her clit.

"Ellie," I groaned. "Tell me to stop." I needed her to tell me to stop, because otherwise I was going to be on my knees, begging to have her just like this for the rest of my life.

"I don't want you to stop," she murmured, pressing her lips to my neck and kissing my skin. "Please."

I shook my head as she continued kissing my exposed skin. She didn't understand how badly I wanted her. I was shaking with effort as I tried to control myself, to keep from thrusting into her like a beast. "I don't think I can hold back—I won't be gentle."

She gave me a soft smile, brushing the dirty blonde hair off my forehead. "I don't need gentle, Owen. I just need you. However I can get you."

I wrapped my arms around her back, tugging her tight against my chest. "You have no idea how badly I need you, Ellie baby." It had been too long since I'd been inside of her.

Grabbing a condom out of my back pocket, I rolled it on before positioning myself at her entrance.

She reached up, her hands clutching on my shoulders as I pushed inside of her, holding myself still as I watched her face. Ellie let out a ragged breath as I spread her open. Only my tip was inside, and *fuck*, she was tight. With her underneath me, I was reminded of how much smaller than me she was. Even at five-seven, she'd always had a dancer's body, that lithe frame that came from being on the ice all the time. Except, with a pang, I remembered her injury. *When was the last time she skated?* I hated that I wasn't there when she'd hurt herself. To help her back on the ice and reassure her she was strong enough to make it through this.

I hadn't been there at all. But that had been her decision, not mine.

That was something I couldn't dwell on right now. Not when I was inside of her, her warmth surrounding my length as her fingers dug into my shoulders.

"Fuck, you feel so good," I groaned, thrusting to the hilt. "So tight."

Ellie wrapped her legs around my waist, forcing me in deeper as I began thrusting in earnest. I knew nothing would ever compare to this, to the feeling of being buried tight in her, in the way her cunt felt nestled around my cock.

"God, I missed this. Missed you. Only having you once wasn't enough, Ellie baby."

Leaning my forehead against hers, I took her mouth, thrusting my tongue against hers the same way I rammed inside of her. I wouldn't last much longer. Not when her nails dug into my shoulders, and her heels pressed into my back, every rock of my hips driving us higher and higher.

"Need you to come," I grunted. "Want to feel you come on my cock."

She let out a moan when I reached down between us, pressing my thumb against her clit and giving her the pressure I knew she craved as I gave her a few more punishing thrusts. She came with a cry, and I couldn't hold back as her pussy fluttered around me, milking me for everything I was worth.

"*Fuuuuck*," I grunted, spilling inside of her.

I kissed her again before pulling out, heading to the bathroom to take care of the condom. When I came back, she was on her side, looking flushed, thoroughly fucked, and… beautiful. Though she was always that.

"That was…" I said, shaking my head as I slid back into the bed after pulling my boxers back on.

"I know," she murmured, brushing a strand of hair off of her sweaty forehead. "So good, right?"

I laughed. "One time is definitely not enough." *One night would never be enough.* It had been like this between us before. Teasing each other, a playful banter that I'd missed so much. We'd both been so young that I hadn't appreciated how easy it was with her until she was gone.

Ellie didn't respond. She got up, unzipping her dress as she walked towards the bathroom, letting it drop to the floor before she closed the door, winking at me. Giving me a glimpse of that perfect ass, the perfect handful of soft skin that I wanted to sink my teeth into.

Groaning, I rolled onto my back, draping an arm over my face as I heard the water run in the bathroom.

God, she had no idea what she did to me. It was better that way, though.

If she knew how much of my heart she held in her hands, even after all this time, I'd never survive it.

I LOOKED at her sleeping form, wearing the giant t-shirt she'd pulled on when she'd come back out from the bathroom earlier. Despite both being exhausted, we hadn't been able to keep our hands off each other and it hadn't taken long before wandering hands had turned into another round, and then we'd finally collapsed, falling asleep.

Her chest rose and fell as she slept, her body totally sated after wringing me out. I hadn't come that hard in years. Damn, but I wished I could stay forever.

I wanted to hear her crying out my name when I made her come. To sleep beside her every night. To grow old together, knowing that the love of my life was in my arms.

But that wasn't in the cards, not in the hand that we'd been dealt. I had a life in Seattle, and she had one here. Ellie would find a job, and she'd be her bubbly, outgoing self. Her students wouldn't understand how lucky they were.

Finding my pants, I pulled them on, zipping them up as Ellie rolled over, hugging her pillow tighter. Thankfully, she didn't wake up. I hunted around her desk until I found a piece of scrap paper.

Writing a note, I left it on her bedside table.

And even though every instinct of mine was screaming to

stay, to keep her, I knew what this was. *Closure.* It was a goodbye. One last night.

I pressed a kiss to her forehead, brushing her hair off her cheek, before standing and walking out the door. Leaving her behind.

"Goodbye, Ellie," I whispered as I closed the door behind me.

I wished things were different.

But that didn't change the fact that soon I'd be gone.

Nothing had changed.

Not for us.

No matter how much I wanted it to.

But as I slid into my car, the first rays of sunlight breaking the sky as I drove away, I knew it was time to finally move on.

SIX

Ellie

THEN

Freshman Year

O wen?" I opened the door to find him standing on my front porch, a bouquet of yellow daisies in his arms. "What are you doing here?"

I surveyed his attire. Blue button-up shirt and slacks. Was he trying to impress someone? I looked back at the flowers, and then I realized—oh. *Me.* He was trying to impress me.

"These are for you," he said, offering me the bundle.

I giggled, taking them and burying my nose in the bouquet. "You didn't have to get me flowers, Owen." *Again.* He'd given me a bundle of daisies on the night he'd asked me to prom in the treehouse.

"I did. I do." He cleared his throat. "I want to do this right, Ellie."

A blush covered my cheeks, and I fiddled with the ends of the flowers in my arms. "Do you want to come inside?"

"Actually, I, uh—do you want to get dinner tonight?"

I bit my lip to hold back a smile. "Are you asking me on a date, Hockey Boy?"

"Depends, Skater Girl."

"On?" I fluttered my eyelashes, enjoying the way he was looking at me. Like I was the only girl in the world.

"Whether you're saying yes." He winked.

I looked down at my outfit. I was still wearing the jeans I'd worn to school and my favorite scoop-neck long-sleeved body-suit. "Can I have a few minutes to change?"

Owen laughed. "Of course, El."

Rushing upstairs, I rifled through my closet. What did you wear on a first date, anyway? And it was my first ever. I'd never had a boyfriend before, let alone gone out with anyone. I didn't have time to be flirting, not when I was constantly at the rink skating. But this was different.

Twenty minutes later, I was back downstairs, dressed in a white sundress—with a chunky cardigan in my arms in case I got cold—and a pair of flats.

"Ready." I smiled at Owen—he was standing right inside the doorway, running his fingers through his dirty blond hair like he was nervous.

My mom came out, still dressed in her dance clothes, like she'd just come from the studio. "You two have fun." She pulled her hair out of the tight bun she'd had it in, her blonde hair falling down to her shoulders.

He cleared his throat. "Thanks, Mrs. B. We won't be home too late."

"I know." She focused on him, giving him a look that I'd been on the other end of too many times to count. "I trust you, Owen. Don't give me a reason not to."

He nodded, placing a hand on my back to guide me out the door and towards his truck. "She's terrifying."

I couldn't hold in my laugh. "My mom?" She was five four and built like a dancer, and no one had ever described her as intimidating before. Especially not a six-foot something hockey player who spent his days slamming into people on the ice. *"Really?"*

"Uh-huh. Did you not see the look she was giving me back there?" He shuddered. "Pretty sure if anything happened to you, she'd never let me forget it."

I wrapped my arm around his, leaning on him as we walked to his truck. "Good thing you won't let anything happen to me then, huh?"

"Never," he promised.

It was a statement I felt down to my bones. Because I knew he meant it. That he'd be there for me. He always had been.

OWEN DROVE us to the edge of Forest Park, pulling into a parking lot where one trail-head started.

I frowned, looking down at my shoes as he put the truck into park. "I didn't really dress for hiking…"

"Don't worry," he chuckled, looking over at me. "We're not going hiking."

Raising an eyebrow, I sat up straighter. "Then what are we doing in the woods?"

"Come on. You trust me, right?"

"Of course."

He winked, swinging the door open and hopping out. "Stay here. I'll be back in a second."

After scooping a mysterious bundle and large blanket out of the backseat, he closed the door. I heard him rustling around in the truck bed, but I didn't turn my head to look at what he was doing. Whatever his surprise was, it felt special.

A few minutes later, my door opened, and Owen offered me a hand. Taking it, he guided me out and around to the back of the truck, where he'd lowered the tailgate down. The entire bed was full of blankets and pillows, plus a picnic basket and a bottle of sparkling apple cider in the corner.

"What's all this?" I turned to him, shocked, and he looked bashful.

"Wanted to do something special for our first date." He looked around at the calm woods. There weren't any other cars out here, and it was surprisingly peaceful.

Wrapping my arms around his middle, I hugged him. "Thank you."

He wrapped his hands around my waist, lifting me up into the truck before hopping up after me. I sprawled back against the pillows, looking up towards the tops of the trees.

"It's beautiful here," I murmured.

"You know it's where my parents got engaged?" he asked, sitting next to me, his long legs stretching out across the bed.

I shook my head. I hadn't. Though I'd heard the story of my parents and how they'd gotten together, and I knew that his parents had met while she was a grad student at the University he taught at, I'd never heard how he'd proposed.

Owen continued his story. "He set up a scavenger hunt for her, sending her all over Portland to places that were memorable to them. It ended here, where Snowball was holding the final envelope and when Mom looked up, Dad was down on one knee."

Snowball—a fluffy white Samoyed—was Matthew's dog from before he met Noelle. Though she'd passed years ago from old age and I didn't remember her much, I knew how much the dog meant to the Harpers.

"That's so cute," I said, looking over at him.

He had a faint blush on his cheekbones, and he looked away. "Yeah. They used to come up here and take the dogs on walks and runs. And then Pen and I when we were small, too. I guess it's why I've always loved it. The smell of the pines, the fresh air, looking up at the trees and realizing how small you are… It's grounding. Once I got my license, I drove up here and just sat for a while. Now, whenever I get stressed, this is where I go."

"Wow," I said, suppressing a little shiver. My lips tiltled up when I realized that he'd brought me to his special place.

Owen grabbed a blanket and reached across, draping it over my lap before scooting closer. "You cold?"

"Oh." I played with the plush fabric. "Guess I left my cardigan in the cab." I didn't want to explain that the reason I had shivered had nothing to do with the temperature outside but everything to do with the conviction in his voice.

He hummed, changing the subject by asking, "Are you excited for prom?"

I nodded, watching as Owen grabbed the bottle of sparkling cider, unwrapping the top before popping it open. "I didn't expect to go this year, that's for sure. All my friends are jealous."

"It wouldn't be the same without you," he murmured, handing me a glass.

I took a sip, hoping I could hide my blush. "Mom's making my dress. We picked out fabric last weekend." Knowing my mom, it would be done with plenty of time to spare. She loved sewing, even making her own wedding dress. One day, I hoped she'd make mine, too.

"What color is it?" He asked, perking up like an adorable puppy.

I bit my lip, trying so hard to play it cool. "Why? Are you going to match me?"

"Of course." Owen winked, drinking from his flute of apple cider. "What sort of date would I be if I didn't?"

That made my heart flutter in my chest. "It's this really pretty shimmery light blue."

He closed his eyes like he was picturing it, and I took that moment to appreciate *him*. That firm chest, the bulk of him. I'd never really considered a boy like that before, but suddenly, I was hyper-aware of the fact that this was a date.

At how close we were together. I finished my glass and set

it down next to me. He wasn't a boy anymore. No, he was all man.

"This is nice," I whispered.

"Yeah?" He reached over, brushing a strand of hair off my face.

I nodded. "What's in the basket?"

Owen laughed. "Nothing too fancy. Sandwiches, fruit, and mom made some pastries."

"Yum. Sounds perfect."

He grinned, and we both looked at each other. I wasn't sure I was breathing. Not when his eyes were tracing my face, darting down to my lips and then back up.

Was he going to—?

"Ellie." Owen murmured, tracing my jaw with his finger.

"Hm?"

"Can I..." He swallowed. "Can I kiss you?"

"Yes," I whispered.

I'd never been kissed before. But I *wanted* him to kiss me. Even if this didn't last, him being my first kiss felt special. Owen and I were friends. And now we were *more*.

He held my face with his hand, leaning in and pressing his lips to mine. Soft and warm and... *perfect*. It wasn't more than a soft kiss. No tongue—though I wasn't sure I was ready for that, anyway.

We pulled apart, and I blushed, holding my cheeks in my hand.

"Are you hungry?" He asked, his voice sounding deeper than before.

I nodded, and we ate as the sun set, enjoying the view as I snuggled into his side, feeling like there was nowhere else in the world I'd rather be.

And no one else I'd rather be there with.

SEVEN

Ellie

NOW

*I*n between my legs was deliciously sore, and as I turned over, reaching for the man who had fallen asleep at my side.

But the bed was empty. *Cold.* The sheets were pulled back up, and it shouldn't have been a surprise that he hadn't stayed. I knew what we'd promised each other. One last night. But the disappointment coursing through me… that was a surprise. Because no matter how hard I tried to deny it, I'd never really moved on from him. We were like two magnets who couldn't stay away from each other. The gravitational pull I felt towards him was immense. Unavoidable, yet devastating.

Because he wasn't mine. This was all we'd ever have.

A piece of paper on my nightstand caught my eye, and I sat up, grabbing it.

I wish things were different. - O

Maybe that was what broke me. The note in his sloppy handwriting and him disappearing without even a goodbye.

I probably deserved it. I'd done the same thing to him

years ago, after all. Except I'd ended things completely. With one note, I'd destroyed everything we had.

"Ellie?" Penelope's voice came through the apartment.

"In here," I croaked, crumpling up the note in my hand.

A few seconds later, my best friend opened the door, catching sight of me sitting in bed. I probably looked like a wreck, especially after all the sex last night. Meanwhile, she was wearing a pair of running shorts with a workout shirt, her curly red hair pulled up into a ponytail, like she'd just been out for a run.

Meanwhile, I was wearing a giant t-shirt and a pair of panties I'd pulled on before we'd fallen asleep together, post another round of *amazing* sex.

"Oh, El." Her voice was soft. "Are you okay?"

I shook my head. "N-no."

Kicking off her shoes, she climbed onto my bed, pulling me into her arms. I cried onto her shoulder, not caring about how pathetic I was right now. "I made a mistake."

There was probably snot on her shirt, but she didn't seem to care. Penelope rubbed a hand down my back. "By sleeping with him?" she prompted. So she had known where her older brother had spent the night. I would have been embarrassed if I hadn't been crying. We talked about a lot of things, but never sex with her brother. It's not like we'd had much to talk about, anyway.

"No." I sniffled. "Letting him go." I opened my fist, his note still in my hand. "It's over." He was probably back in Seattle by now. "For good now, I guess." It had *been* over. So why was I so upset? Why did this feel like my entire foundation had crumbled underneath me?

"Oh, babe." She hugged me tighter. "It's going to be okay."

I was blubbering, and I could barely even get the words out. "I know what I told him. It was just supposed to be one night. It was my idea. But—"

"But you want more."

I nodded. "Maybe that's always been the problem. I've always wanted more than I could have. But he's not mine, Penelope." And he hadn't been in a long time.

"What happened?" She was quiet as I rested my head on her shoulder, cuddling against her. "You never told me, you know. Why you broke up with my brother?"

I shook my head. "I can't—" I wasn't ready to talk about it. *Would I ever be?* I didn't know.

"I'm calling in backup," Penny said, squeezing my hand.

Letting out a breath, I wrapped my arms around my middle. "I don't want to see anyone. I feel pathetic. How weak am I?" One kiss, and I was a puddle at his feet. One night, and I wanted everything I'd given up all those years ago.

"Loving someone doesn't make you weak, Ellie. It makes you strong."

I shook my head. It didn't feel like that. She left the room, and I forced myself to stop crying.

Sniffling, I got up, dragging myself to the shower. Part of me mourned losing his scent that still clung to my skin, but the other part of me knew I couldn't move on while I could still smell him. He'd always smelled clean and fresh, with an undercurrent of pine and snow, like the mountains. And then there was something uniquely him, that delicious musk of man that couldn't be replicated no matter how hard they tried with candles or cologne.

My giant t-shirt came off, and I let the water run over my body, washing the places where he'd embraced me with his mouth. Hating that it meant I lost that last connection with him.

The last time we'd been together, it had been nothing like that. Our first time had been awkward and fumbling and yet, I wouldn't have traded it for anything. Because I'd loved him, and we'd shared that moment together.

But now... a sour taste filled my mouth, thinking about

how many women he'd probably been with. How many girls would have thrown themselves at him simply because he was a hockey player in the NHL? That he could have taken a girl up to his hotel room in every city across the country.

You gave him up, I reminded myself. I took a deep breath and then washed my hair, rubbing at my scalp. Like I could wash all of it away.

When I finally dried off thirty minutes later, pulling on a pair of cozy sweats and walking out of my bedroom, I found my mom standing in my living room; her eyes a little too perceptive. Like she knew how long I'd been nursing this broken heart. Like she knew, somehow, that I was broken all over again.

"Mom," I started, falling into her open arms.

"What's wrong, sweet girl?" She ran her hand over the back of my wet hair.

I closed my eyes, inhaling her scent, trying to steady myself. "He's *gone.*"

My mom and I had always been close. Maybe that was why I felt so comfortable falling apart in her arms. She rubbed my back, and even though it felt like I had no tears left to cry, I just let her embrace warm me from the inside out. Penelope had disappeared into her room, probably sensing I needed a moment alone with my mother.

When I finally pulled away, she ran her thumbs across my cheekbone. "Feel better?"

"No," I mumbled, wishing something as simple as a hug could make all my problems go away. "Did I ruin everything, Mom?"

She sighed, guiding me to the couch and then sitting down next to me. "Only you can decide that, honey. What do you want?" That was the problem. I didn't know what I wanted. Except… maybe I did, and that was the problem. Maybe I'd just stuffed it away for so long. And what could I do? "You're miserable."

"I mean, I wouldn't say miserable…" I mumbled, looking down at my bare feet. Before graduation, I'd painted my toenails a bright, sunshine yellow color.

"You've always been the sweetest, brightest, bubbliest of my kids, Eleanor Daisy. Growing up, you were always smiling. And you smiled with him more than anyone else."

"Mom." I shook my head. "I can't—"

She guided my chin up till my eyes met hers. "Ellie. You can do whatever you put your mind to. You've always been able to. It was the same with skating, you know. You were so determined, and nothing could keep you down. Until you came back and the accident—"

Part of me couldn't think too deeply about how closely those incidents were related. How losing Owen had felt like I was losing my love for the ice. And after I'd fallen, after my injury, I'd never been able to get back on the ice again.

I bit my lip. "I don't know, Mom. How can I? It's been five years. And I… I broke his heart."

For whatever reason, she'd never pressed me to find out what had happened. Why we'd broken up. He hadn't cheated on me or hurt me, despite what everyone seemed to think. No, the problem was how he'd always put me first, even when it hurt himself. His career prospects. His relationship with his teammates.

"He was pretty clear about the fact that it was just one night," I whispered. "Especially when I woke up alone. Even if I wanted more, he doesn't."

"You still love him?" she asked, though I suspected she'd known the answer to that for a long time.

"How could I not?" It was a whispered omission. It was the problem with everything. That I'd never stopped. That I loved him was why I'd had to leave.

She cupped my face, her gray eyes—so much like mine— boring into my own. "Then, my sweet girl, what are you still doing here?"

I frowned. "What do you mean, Mom? I can't exactly chase after him. He went back to Seattle. I'm working on getting a job here, and finding a place to live, and—" There weren't very many openings in the area for elementary teachers, and the ones that had been were snatched up quickly. Still, I'd been reaching out to schools. I'd graduated with my degree and my teaching credential in four years, which should have made it easier to find a position.

"Is that what you want?" She repeated her question from earlier.

"What do you mean?"

"Portland isn't the only place where you can teach elementary school, hun."

I blinked. "Huh? Mom, I can't just…" *Leave Portland.* My family, my home? Sure, both of my siblings had already done it, but I'd never even considered moving away from home. *Except when I'd been planning on going to college with Owen.* A nagging voice in my head reminded me of the fact that I'd changed my entire life plan once before. I could do it again.

"If I'd never left California and moved to Portland for college, I never would have met your dad *or* my best friends. And if I had to do it all over again, I would. Because it brought me the most important people in the world. You, Abigail and Beau were the best things I could have ever asked for."

"But that was different, Mom," I insisted.

"How so?" She crossed her arms over her chest.

Because she hadn't moved to Portland for a boy. She'd moved there for herself. "I can't believe you're seriously telling me to move to Seattle and chase after a boy."

"Ah, but he's not just any boy, is he?"

I shook my head. No. No, he wasn't.

"Dad was your best friend, right?" I laid down, stretching out my legs across the couch and dropping my head on my mom's lap like I had when I was little.

She chuckled. "He was. We did everything together. The girls weren't even surprised when I announced we were getting married." My mom shrugged. "I loved him more than anything, but I was terrified that being together like that would ruin everything."

"But it didn't."

"No." There was a smile on her face. "I know you'll have that too some day, Ellie."

"How can you possibly know that?" I whispered.

"Because I watched you grow up. I know how you two looked at each other. But even if you and Owen aren't meant to be, it's time to go live your life. Don't let your fear and worries hold you back. You can always find an excuse to keep yourself from the things you really want, but you'll always wonder what if. What if I took the chance? What if I took the job? What if I moved to a new city? What if I fell in love?" It was really hard to argue with her, so I didn't.

I wasn't sure I was ready for that, but I couldn't deny that a part of me longed for everything that she was saying. That she knew me in a way I hardly knew myself.

"And if all I want is to bury my head in the sand or hide under a pile of blankets?" I whispered. Maybe I could live under a rock. Keep my TV turned off during hockey season.

"You can lick those wounds as long as you need, sweetie." She squeezed my shoulder. "I'll still be here when you decide it is time to come out of hiding."

Hadn't five years of punishing myself been enough? Maybe it was time to take my life back. To reach for the life I wanted. "Okay," I murmured, closing my eyes. Tomorrow. I'd start tomorrow.

Today, I just wanted to pretend I could still smell Owen on my skin, could still feel his phantom touch across my body. Could still feel his lips press against mine. Like if I pretended hard enough, he'd still be next to me, telling me how beautiful I was. How much he'd missed me.

One night would never be enough. Not for us.

Not when one touch from him set my soul on fire. When one kiss made me crave him like nothing had before. The way one glance made me feel like I was finally on solid ground again.

I would have followed him anywhere.

Tomorrow… I'd figure out how to win him back.

EIGHT

Four months later...

There was something calming about being in the rink, the cool bite to the air and the smell of the ice invading my senses. The feeling of my skates gliding across the freshly frozen ice only heightened the experience. It had always been one of my favorite places. Even now, at the tail end of my fourth training camp in professional hockey, it still was.

Here, everything else faded away. I barely even took a breath as I kept my eye on the puck. Every muscle was finely honed for this. Coach Donovan had us playing a scrimmage game, and even though this wasn't my first year with the team, I still felt the pressure to perform. As a defenseman, my primary role was to keep the puck away from the opposing team and prevent them from scoring on us. I'd garnered more assists during my career than I had goals, but that was perfectly fine with me.

Skating up the ice towards the other team's goal, one of my teammates passed it in my direction, and seeing the opening, I didn't even have to think. I just moved. My stick collided with the puck, and I sent it sailing.

"That's our boy!" Brooks Hendrix, the other half of my defensive pair, cheered as the puck hit the back of the net. "Look at that beautiful one-timer."

I pumped my fist in the air as the other guys on the ice came around me, surrounding me in a group huddle.

Our team captain, Stefan Kovac, a left winger, slapped my back. "Way to go Harps!"

"Fuck yeah." I grinned. "It's gonna be a damn good year."

"Hell yeah it is." Maverick Hendrix—right winger and older brother of Brooks—exclaimed as we all skated back to the bench. Him and Brooks weren't twins, even though they looked so similar, with their light brown hair and light eyes, though Brooks had a good two inches in height on his older brother.

Rhodes Larsen, who played center, was the only one who wasn't smiling, though we were all used to his broody behavior by now. He was the tallest guy on our team at six foot seven, and he was an absolute beast on the ice. Despite his size, he often snuck in and scored when the other team didn't even see him coming.

Mav, Stefan, and Rhodes all made up the first line of the team, and watching them together was like *magic*. Though the lines were constantly getting moved around, especially during camp, I knew they'd be a top-scoring line in the league this season. We'd all been training hard, preparing for the season, and the pre-season would start soon. I was looking forward to getting back to it. Last year, we'd made it to the playoffs, but had lost in the first round. This year, we were ready to fight our way to the top.

All of our assistant coaches were also on the ice, working with their respective groups, including Victoria Monroe, who was in charge of the forwards. She was our newest assistant coach and had a pretty spectacular career in the PWHL before she came to us. We were damn lucky to have her. Our goaltending coach was over at the net, working with Reid MacKenzie, our goalie, and Matthias Farkas, our alternate goalie, as well as the other goalie recruits.

Brooks fist-bumped me as we sat on the bench, catching our breath. He took his helmet off, smoothing down his brunette hair, before pulling it back on. "You're playing even better this season, man."

I scratched the back of my neck before guzzling down water. "I don't know about that."

He hummed. "Sure, you do. Something's different. What changed?"

Her. I shut my eyes, trying not to think about Ellie or how I'd snuck out of there while she'd been sleeping. How even though I still missed her like fucking crazy, I felt almost *lighter* now. Like there wasn't this heavy weight resting on my shoulders, dragging me down.

"You've been more relaxed. I don't think I've ever seen you so calm on the ice before."

"He probably finally got laid," Maverick joked from my other side. He was a hopeless flirt, and I knew how much he loved women. That wasn't like me, though.

Rhodes, sitting next to him, slapped his helmet.

"Grumpy old man," Mav muttered, staring down at his skates.

The worst part was he wasn't wrong.

Shrugging, I turned back to the ice, watching as the scrimmage match continued. We didn't have long before we had to go back out there and do it all over again. "I guess I had a nice summer. There's nothing else to it." I definitely would not admit that I had, in fact, slept with someone.

Brooks's lips tilted up in a knowing smile. Of all the guys on the team, I'd spent the most time with the two brothers, and a few of us had a group chat. "You saw your girl, didn't you?"

"She's not my girl," I muttered, rubbing the spot in between my eyebrows under my helmet. She hadn't been mine for a long time. I thought about what it had been like seeing her in the stands at my games. Knowing that the last name on her back was mine. Thinking that one day, it would be hers too. We'd never talked seriously about marriage, but from the very first date, I'd been able to see a life for us.

And when it was all over, it had felt like nothing was left.

"My sister graduated college," I said instead. "I went home for her graduation party."

"*Sure*. Still, tell me about it. What was it like, seeing your *first love* again?"

I was saved from having to answer him as we were signaled back onto the ice. Hopping over the ledge, we quickly immersed ourselves back in play.

What was it like? It was *everything*. And damn if I didn't want a repeat of that night. I'd gladly do it all over again. But I had to remind myself that wasn't happening. She'd been perfectly clear on what she wanted from me. It had given me some strange sense of closure. Maybe all I'd needed to move on *was* to get her out of my system. The next time a pretty girl flirted with me at a bar, I'd flirt back. And I wouldn't be thinking about who I'd rather be with. Hopefully.

By the time we were finished with training camp for the day, I was dripping with sweat. Coach Donovan called us all over to circle up, giving us a run-down for the end of the week with our first scheduled pre-season game. The team was split in half, all the new guys trying to prove their worth, so we wouldn't all play every game, but I was looking forward to getting things underway.

Our first game of the pre-season was at home against Vancouver—our closest team and biggest rivals. Games always ended up heated, with gloves dropping easily and players often chirping at each other while on the bench. We would play each nearby team twice during the pre-season—

once on home ice, and once away, which meant we'd be heading up to Calgary and Edmonton as well.

After Donovan dismissed us, we all headed back to the locker room. Fifty something guys made the room feel even more crowded than normal, but we all knew that by the time the season started, most of the prospects would be gone.

Brooks and Maverick joined me in our corner after we'd all showered, and from the glimmer in their eyes, I knew that the conversation from earlier wasn't over.

"Are you going to see her again?" Mav asked, pulling on his t-shirt as we all dressed.

Well, I certainly hoped she wouldn't avoid me for the next five years, but—"It's in the past." I shrugged.

Brooks raised an eyebrow. "And you're good with that?"

"What is this, a double Hendrix team-up?" They had those on the ice every once in a while, and yeah, they were deadly. "Yeah, guys. I'm good with it. Really, it's a good thing. We talked. Now I can move on." Neither one of them looked convinced, but that didn't matter. "Look, you know I've been hung up on her for years. But she's in Portland, and I'm here. And she made it clear exactly what she wanted."

"Most people would be a grumpy asshole after their girl dumped them," Maverick muttered to his brother. "I mean, just look at Larsen over there. Instead, this guy's like a ray of damn sunshine."

Rhodes Larsen was one of the older guys on the team—he'd spent his entire career with the Seals. He flipped Mav off before pulling a baseball cap on backwards over his dark hair. Secretly, I knew Rhodes didn't mind the guy, but it was part of the rapport they'd built. I grinned. God, it was good to be back with my boys. I loved this place, and I wouldn't have it any other way.

"It was a mutual thing," I finally said. "No dumping happened." Not this time, at least. "It's good. I'm good." I nodded to myself. *It doesn't matter now. It's in the past. We're in the past.*

Running my fingers through my damp dark blond strands, I pulled on a sweatshirt over my t-shirt. It was already getting cold outside. Sometimes, I was damn jealous of the teams in Florida that had warm weather almost year round. Meanwhile, it was late September, and I'd already almost forgotten what the sun looked like. Seattle and Portland weren't all that different, really. They both were drizzly and overcast more months out of the year than I could count, though I'd grown used to living here. When I'd first moved here, I'd spent my entire first year wishing I was back home in Portland. Missing my family. Missing *her*.

I'd entered the NHL draft the summer after I turned 18, getting picked in the second round by the Seals, and then I'd started college here a few months later at the University of Washington, playing for the Huskies D1 Hockey Team. Six years later, here I was.

"What are you up to for the rest of the day, Harps?" Brooks asked as he shoved his stuff in his bag.

I shrugged. It was only mid-afternoon, and I had planned to go on a new hike I'd found and then catch up with one of my new books. I always did my best thinking in the wilderness, surrounded by the blue skies and pine trees. "Not much. Found a new trail. Probably some laundry."

Things I wouldn't have as much time for once the season started.

"I'm heading out," I announced to the guys. Reid, our goalie, nodded at me as he swiped a towel over his mess of red hair. "See y'all tomorrow."

Then I escaped before one more person could ask me about my summer or the girl I'd left behind.

LEAVING THE ICEPLEX, I headed back to my apartment in the city. I'd moved into this unit after signing my contract extension last year, and while it was way more space than any single person needed, I was also getting paid way more than I knew what to do with. It wasn't like I was out drinking every night or wasting it. Most of the money I earned from playing professional hockey went into my savings account.

But I'd stepped into this apartment and it just felt… right. Like I could picture a life here.

Someone curled up on the couch, waiting for me to get home from games. A puppy curled up next to them. Laughter. Love.

One day, I wanted all of that. A family. Though I had plenty of years left until I needed to think about settling down. For now, I was at the top of my game in the NHL, and I wouldn't let anything jeopardize my focus.

Though I'd been wanting to get a dog for the last few years, a companion for the quiet nights in my apartment or to take hiking with me. We'd always had one growing up, and I missed having an animal to snuggle with. Call me soft-hearted, but I'd grown up in a house where we'd never had to hide our feelings. And I wasn't ashamed to admit that I was lonely.

Unfortunately, with my travel schedule, getting a dog felt selfish when I wasn't home for days at a time for road trips and away games.

Sighing, I threw my bag on the floor of the laundry room so I could start it later tonight. All of my gear was handled by the team, but I still liked to wash my under layers myself at home. I wasn't the most superstitious of hockey players, though there were plenty on my team, but I still had my routines that I followed every game day. Putting on my gear in the same order, just like I'd done since I was a kid. Taping my stick the same way each night. Wearing my sleeves tighter and pushed up past my wrists because I liked the way the cool air felt against my skin.

Nothing crazy.

Collapsing on the couch, I debated going for that hike, but decided I'd save it for my next day off, and picked up my most recent fantasy novel recommendation I'd gotten from my mom. The plot was amazing—full of political intrigue, and, yes, romance. My mom wrote romance novels, so I was no stranger to them. Though I hadn't read hers, because reading a sex scene your mother wrote felt wrong.

When I glanced back up a few hours later, it was to the sun setting over the city skyline. One of the best parts about this apartment was the view I had and the large glass windows.

Longing and desire filled my heart.

Longing to have someone by my side. Desire for the only woman I couldn't have. The woman who was practically inked over my heart like the tattoo on my skin.

I pretended I was fine, because really—what did I have to complain about? My life was amazing. I'd always been the happy-go-lucky guy on the team. The one who was happy to talk to the media and always had a smile on my face.

But I'd lied before, when I'd told the guys it was over.

Because as much as I tried to move on, Ellie Bradford would never stay in the past. She haunted me, invading my dreams as much as she did my thoughts each day.

Then and now… She was it for me.

Too bad I couldn't have her.

NINE

Owen

———

THEN

Senior Year

*I*t was the end of the third period, and we were up by two. My entire family sat in the stands, watching what was probably one of the most important games of my junior hockey career. I knew that there were talent scouts here tonight watching me. Despite that, my focus was on the blonde sitting three rows up from the bench, who I knew was wearing my name on her back. *My* jersey.

My girlfriend.

Ellie and I had officially been dating for a year, and things were going great. Nothing had really changed, except now we were free to hold hands in front of our families. And as a bonus, I got to sneak her off alone and take her on dates. Thank fuck our parents trusted us to have time alone.

Not that I was going to do anything to jeopardize that trust. We were taking things slow. While the rest of my teammates might have been bragging about sleeping with their girlfriends, I was perfectly content with the fact that we'd only

69

kissed. Whenever we were both ready, I wanted to make it special for both of us. Though there was no pressure, no rush.

I liked the fact that her smiles were for me. That I could call her *mine*.

Taking another shift on the ice, I tried to put all of that out of my head as I just focused on my role, keeping the puck away from our goal and defending against the opposing team. With less than a minute left in regulation time, we worked the puck down the ice towards the opposing team's net. Seeing an opening, I passed it to my teammate, and he hit a snapshot, burying it in the net.

The buzzer sounded, and—"GOALLLL!"

"Hell yeah!" I screamed, skating over to my buddy to wrap him up in a hug. God, I felt on top of the world. Like nothing could bring me down.

Turning my head, my gaze caught on Ellie, who was out of her seat and screaming. For me.

The five of us on the ice skated over to the bench, high-fiving our team members.

We'd have one last face off, and then we just had to run the timer out and we'd officially have won the game.

Settling back onto the bench, I couldn't keep the grin off my face. The buzzer sounded, and we won the game.

For once, I wasn't worried about anything else. Not when my team had won the game, my girl was in the stands, and my future was bright.

AFTER A SHOWER and a post-game meeting with the team, I headed out of the locker room to find my family waiting for me, including the blonde girl beaming in the front standing next to my sister. Everyone had Wolves apparel on, which felt meaningful, especially considering my dad's favorite animal was a wolf. Even Penelope, my younger sister, was beaming in a dark gray sweatshirt with purple accents, even though she was always dressed in bright colors, often with paint covering her hands since it was her favorite hobby besides reading and writing.

"Hey, guys," I said, smiling.

"Great game, son," my dad said, slapping me on the shoulder before pulling me into a hug.

We basically stood at the same height now, thanks to my last growth spurt. Just another sign that I was growing up. "Thanks, Dad."

I threw an arm around my girl after hugging the rest of my family, dropping a kiss on the side of her head.

"Hi," I said, brushing my lips against her ear.

"Hey." She gave me a beaming smile as she nuzzled in close to my side.

She was sunshine. My Ellie. The girl who loved daisies and yellow and who radiated happiness whenever she was on the ice.

Heading out to the parking lot, my parents started heading for their car, and I interlaced my fingers with Ellie's.

"Ride home with me?" I asked, my voice low.

She nodded. We hadn't spent any alone time today, and as much as I loved my family, they'd get me back at home. Ellie had a figure skating competition this weekend, so I wouldn't even get to see her then. It sucked when we had overlapping events, because as much as I loved her coming to my games, I loved going to see her skate even more.

"We're going to head home," Dad said, nodding at me.

Penelope smiled, tucking her book under her arm. I resisted chuckling—I hadn't even noticed she'd had it on her earlier. Of course, my sister would read at my game. Everyone in our family was a voracious reader, though, so it wasn't anything new.

"Be safe," my mom said, looking between Ellie and I.

My cheeks warmed, and I shook my head. "*Mom,*" I muttered, rubbing my free hand over my face and through my damp strands. It wasn't like that.

Ellie buried her face in her hands, and when my family was gone, I peeled them back away from her eyes.

"You okay?" I asked, chuckling.

She nodded. "I just… don't want them to think we're doing anything bad, you know?" Ellie scrunched up her nose. "It's not like we're having sex." She let out a little groan.

We walked to my blue truck, and I held her hand again, interlacing our fingers before squeezing it reassuringly. "Our families love us. So yeah, they're going to tease us. Besides, they, uh… know we're not actually doing it, El."

"Oh." She grimaced. "It's always going to be like this, isn't it?"

"Probably." I laughed, opening up the door for her and helping her inside. When she was buckled in, I leaned over, bracing one hand on the frame of the truck. "Our moms are best friends. Of course, they talk. But we're best friends too, Daisy." My voice was low. "And it doesn't matter what they think."

My girl blinked, her hand bunched in the hem of the gray and purple jersey. "Doesn't it?"

"No." I shook my head. "It only matters what *we* think."

"And what do you think?" Ellie whispered.

"That I want to spend time with my girlfriend." I pressed my lips to her forehead- before closing the door and walking around to the other side.

She turned her head, watching as I slid into my seat, resting my hand on the gearshift as I prepared to turn on the car. Instead, I moved it to her thigh, letting my palm engulf most of her leg. There was something in her eyes—a spark of desire. Heat. "Owen…" Her voice was breathless.

I pushed my seat back, patting my lap. "Ellie," I murmured. "Come here."

She bit her lip before climbing over the truck console, sitting in my lap.

"Hi," she whispered, looping her arms around my neck.

"Hi." I brushed a piece of hair off her forehead. "You looked so beautiful tonight."

Her cheeks were pink. "Thank you."

There was just something about seeing her in the stands, wearing my jersey. "I love having you at my games."

Ellie smiled. "I love coming to them. Watching you on the ice… God, Owen. You're going to do incredible things. I can't wait to see it."

Did she have any idea how much her faith in me meant to me?

"I couldn't do it without you," I answered, the admission coming out without me meaning for it to. "You're the only person I want to celebrate with when I get a goal. When we win the game."

Her hand ran up my chest, settling on my pecs. While I wasn't the biggest guy on my team, nor did I have a six-pack, I was in great shape from the time I spent on the ice, and working out to keep up while playing hockey.

"We're not having sex until we're both ready," I said, one of my hands resting on her lower back as I cupped the back of her neck with the other. "But I really want to kiss you right now."

She looped her arms around the back of my neck, brushing her lips over mine. "Then what are you waiting for, Hockey Boy? Kiss me."

I leaned forward, pressing our lips together, slowly at first. Just light presses. And then, I swept my tongue over her lips, and Ellie opened her lips for me, giving me entrance into her mouth. With fingers combing through the back of her hair, I got my first taste of her. Sweet, like the taste of the candy she'd been eating during the game.

It had never been like this before with us. We'd always

shared such innocent kisses, but tonight... something inside me needed more. Maybe it was the way she was positioned on my lap, maybe it was the way she kissed me back with as much enthusiasm, the fervor running through us demanding it.

I'd never kissed anyone like this. And maybe neither one of us knew what we were doing, but it felt right. I squeezed her hip, pressing her core against my front.

"Owen," she murmured as I trailed my lips down her neck.

"I know, baby," I groaned. The endearment just slipped out. I'd never called her it before—my nickname for her had always been Skater Girl or Daisy. Because she was *my* Daisy. "I know."

I shifted her off of my lap and into the passenger seat so I could start the truck before either of us would do something we would regret.

But damn, I liked the way she looked, lips pink and a little swollen, cheeks flushed and eyes unfocused as she stared out the window. I turned my attention to the road behind us as I backed up, one arm reaching back to grip her headrest.

Ellie bit her lip, and if I flexed my arm muscles a little, well, who could blame me?

I chuckled, and she blinked, looking over at me. Once I'd straightened out the truck and gotten us onto the road, I rested one of my hands on Ellie's thigh. She interlaced our fingers, letting our adjoined hands rest on her leg.

"I like this," she murmured, her lips tugging up into a small smile.

And damn, she had no idea how much I'd liked it.

"Me too, Skater Girl."

Damn, did I enjoy kissing her. Being with her. Holding her hand. Knowing she was my girl.

I couldn't imagine a life without her. Not now... Not ever.

TEN

Ellie

NOW

My car was loaded, and I was overly aware of the fact that I'd packed my entire life into the back of my little SUV, getting ready to drive to a new city where I knew absolutely no one.

Well, except the one person who didn't even know I was moving.

"Are you sure you're going to be okay?" Abigail asked, wrapping her arms around me and hugging me tight.

I nodded into her hold. "I'll be fine, Abs. I need to do this."

In a turn of events that felt almost too good to be true, one of my mom's dance friends had told her about an opening at an elementary school in Bellevue, and a month later, I was getting ready to move.

Turns out my mom was right. What I really needed, more than anything else, was a kick in the pants. Not to wallow in self pity on the couch. I'd done enough hiding over the last five years.

No more.

Seventeen-year-old me might have walked away from

what Owen and I had, but twenty-two-year-old me sure as hell wouldn't.

Now, I had a job. I had an apartment. And, as a flutter in my abdomen reminded me, I had a reason to see him again. Even if he didn't know it yet.

"Text me if you need anything," she made me promise. "You know I'll be on my way to you faster than you can blink." That was my big sister for you—fiercely protective and one of the most loyal people I knew. Though I supposed that also came with the eldest sister territory,

"I love you," I murmured, not wanting to let go of her yet.

"You better hurry before Mom comes out here and starts crying all over again," Abigail said, squeezing me tight before pulling away. "You know how she gets."

"Yeah." I sniffled. I really did. Mom was a huge crier. She couldn't help it, but if I went back inside, I'd probably end up staying for another hour. "I'll see you soon," I promised. I was already planning on coming back down for Christmas. It was only a three-hour drive without stopping, which wasn't so bad.

"Drive safe." She stepped back onto the porch, watching as I opened the door and climbed into my car.

I was surprised my dad hadn't insisted on driving me up himself to help me move in. I'd found a furnished apartment to rent, so thankfully I didn't have to buy furniture for now.

All that was left was to *drive*.

ONE WEEK LATER...

I'd never been to the Seals Arena before, though there was a first time for everything. I hadn't seen Owen since the night of my graduation party, and I wasn't sure how I was going to feel seeing him on the ice.

Was coming here tonight a mistake? I hadn't even been

planning on coming until I got an advertisement for the game, and less than twenty minutes later, I'd purchased a ticket. Luckily, since it was pre-season, it hadn't cost me an arm and a leg.

I was content just to see him from afar.

Was he even playing tonight? I had no idea how all of that worked.

Now, standing in the one hundred level, I suddenly couldn't believe I was here. Part of me wanted to scurry back to my seat. I tugged on the sleeve of my turtleneck. Years ago, there was nowhere I felt more at home than at the rink. The smell of the ice, the slight chill to the air—all of it was second nature.

A wave of panic wove through me. Was I making the right decision? What was I even doing here? I turned to head back up the stairs, but something stopped me. *Movement.*

The guys were coming out onto the ice, the guy at the front knocking down several dozen pucks across the ice as they each stepped off, peeling out into a circular lap.

Warm-ups had always been my favorite part of hockey games. Maybe it was the figure skater in me, but I loved seeing the guys gliding across the ice, skating backwards and showing off their fancy footwork.

And don't even get me started on watching them stretch.

I didn't have to see the number on his sleeve or the name on his back to recognize Owen. My body was so finely tuned to his, and I'd watched so many games of his over the years that I knew the way his body moved.

The worst part was knowing how his body moved over mine. Maybe if we hadn't had that night together, it would be easier. Because now, all I could think about was his face as he'd driven inside of me. The way he'd sounded when he came. How tenderly he'd held me. The way he'd called me *Ellie baby.*

That was new. I was trying not to look too deeply into it, because I liked it too much.

A little whimper slipped free from my lips, and the woman next to me against the boards looked over at me with concern. "You okay, dear?"

I nodded. "Yeah." Swallowing, I turned my attention back to the ice. Owen was on the other side, and I was pretty sure he hadn't seen me yet, which was fine. I was happy just watching him.

A kid next to us banged on the glass as some players passed, and then—*oh*. He was skating over here, skidding to a stop right before the boards.

The rest of the noise from all the surrounding fans faded away, and it was just the boy I'd loved, staring back at me with those wide, deep brown eyes.

"Ellie?" I could see his lips move, but thanks to the warm-up playlist, I couldn't hear him.

"Hi," I said back, reaching my hand out and placing it against the glass.

Owen blinked at me. Like he couldn't believe I was here. If it wasn't for the thick slab of plexiglass between us, we'd be only a few inches apart. "You're here," he mouthed, his face lighting up in a beautiful smile.

I nodded. What else was there to say?

He looked around, and then shook his head, holding up a gloved hand. Like he was telling me to wait.

I frowned. The entire interaction was brief, but when he spun, heading back down the ice, I found the people surrounding me gaping at me. Even the nice older woman who'd checked on me.

"You *know* him?" The boy asked, looking shocked. I assumed he was around twelve, and he was wearing a blue home Seals jersey with a C on the chest.

I smiled at him, brushing my sweaty palms down my jeans as I watched Owen from the corner of my eye. He skated back to the bench, talking to one of the staff and pointing towards me. "Yeah, I do."

"*Wooow*," he said, clearly impressed. His eyes were wide. "That's so cool. Do you think you can get me a puck?"

I laughed. "I can try, bud. What's your name?" I resisted reaching out and messing with his hair. He wasn't my student, even if it was so easy for me to slip into that role.

"Brady." He turned around, waving to who I assumed were his parents behind him. "We're sitting there," he offered, pointing at the seats only a few rows behind us.

I wasn't even sitting in this section, so I gave him a smile. "Very nice. Do you come to games often?"

He nodded. "We're *huge* fans. I play, too."

"This is my first game," I admitted, tucking a strand of hair behind my ear.

"Miss?" I turned around, putting my back to the ice at the sound of the voice. One of the staff members wearing a polo from the arena was standing there, looking directly at me. "Are you Ellie Bradford?"

"Y-yeah," I said, clearing my throat. "That's me."

"Can you come with me?" The man asked. "I've been informed your seat has been upgraded."

My mouth dropped open. What did Owen do? "It was?"

He nodded, and I turned to Brady, who was more enthralled watching this than warm-ups. Which was probably fair, considering how many of the players tonight were likely rookies or players who wouldn't make the actual team. "Have fun tonight, Brady."

I followed the staff member up the stairs, feeling like a child being taken to the principal's office. Looking back down at the ice, I quickly caught sight of Owen doing maneuvers with a puck. He looked up and smiled at me. Somehow, for a moment, everything felt like it was going to be okay. Even if I knew it wouldn't stay that way.

The man escorting me ushered me down a different

entrance, and each step down the stairs took me closer towards the ice. I should have guessed that Owen would pull strings like this.

"Your seat, miss. Mr. Harper has arranged for everything." He waved his hand, like he wasn't pointing at a seat directly behind the player's bench. Like this wasn't a rink-side seat that must have cost a ton of money, even if this was the pre-season.

"I can't possibly—"

He shook his head, giving me a nervous smile. "It's already been done. Enjoy the game." And then he scurried back up the stairs, like he was afraid I was going to say no.

"Damn him," I muttered, standing in front of my chair so I could watch the last few minutes before the guys went back to the locker room. Every time Owen skated by the bench—or bounced a puck off his stick—his eyes met mine. I knew he was showing off for me.

My head was spinning. I'd come here tonight expecting to sit up in the three hundred level, but I hadn't been able to resist watching the warm-ups near the ice. I hadn't expected this, though. It was a struggle to remember he wasn't *mine* when he did things like this.

He looked so… excited to see me. And I couldn't wrap my head around it. Because he'd *left*. Though part of me knew that if we'd woken up, wrapped around each other in my bed, neither one of us would have been able to leave. We wouldn't have been able to keep it to one night.

Here I was, months later, doing something I'd never thought possible. I would have done anything for him. And maybe that was the problem. Before, he'd been willing to do anything for me. Watching him on the ice, I couldn't help but wonder if I would be a distraction for him, even now. His career was the most important thing. I knew how happy he was on the ice.

And god, the way he looked out there should have been illegal. His wrists were exposed between his gloves and the bottom of his sleeves, and something about that was even hotter than it should have been. My panties were damp, and I definitely should not have been turned on at my *ex-boyfriend's* hockey game, but here we were.

Maybe I hadn't thought out moving here fully, but it felt right. So far, I loved my new school. I had my own classroom, teaching fourth grade, and had already made a friend. Maggie, whose classroom was next to mine, was only a few years older than me and was also single. We hit it off immediately, though I didn't tell her about Owen or what had prompted me to move from Portland to Seattle.

That felt too personal. So was tonight, which was why I hadn't invited her along. I needed to do this alone.

Seeing Owen again, well… maybe after the game, we could talk. I could tell him how I felt. That I wanted to try again. That this distance between us was killing me.

That I never should have walked away from him five years ago, but I'd *had* to. It had almost killed me, but I'd survived.

I reminded myself that I would survive again, even if he'd said no.

Even if I had to accept that he would never be mine again, I'd find a way to move on. To pick up the little pieces of myself again.

I had to, for both of our sakes.

Cousins Coffee Club

ZACHARY

So no one was going to tell me Ellie up and moved to Seattle?

ABIGAIL

No, because you don't pay attention whenever anyone tells you anything.

ZACHARY

Hey. Not fair.

WESLEY

She's got a point, Z.

Sometimes I feel like I'm talking to a brick wall.

ZACHARY

I've just got a lot going on. And this girl in grad school is making my life a living hell.

PENNY

Oooh, someone's got a crush.

ZACHARY

Do not. She's the worst.

ABIGAIL

What's her name?

ZACHARY

I'm not telling you.

QUIN

Definitely a crush.

ABIGAIL

Oh, for sure. And I don't even have to be the daughter of a romance author to call that one.

ZACHARY

Whatever, nothing's going to happen. Ever.

PENNY

Quin, how's the zoo?

QUIN

Good. We just had a new baby rhino born. So cute.

BEAU

Thank you for blowing up my phone during practice. I love coming back to a hundred notifications every time I leave my phone in the locker room.

ZACHARY

What can I say? We're a fun group.

How else would you stay in the loop?

BEAU

… Maybe I don't need to keep up with all the gossip.

Besides the fact that I already knew Ellie moved. She called me before she ever took the job.

LUCY

Speaking of Ellie, she's been mysteriously quiet.

ZACHARY

Ah, the baby sister has arrived.

LUCY

Shut up.

ELLIE

You guys are the worst.

WESLEY

Miss you too, cuz.

PENNY

The coffee shop isn't the same without you.

LUCY

Maybe one of these days, I can actually study
in peace…

ZACHARY

Hey, we're fun to be around. And I study
there too.

LUCY

Do you? Last time, you were too busy flirting
with Aunt Noelle's newest barista.

ZACHARY

Hey, she was pretty cute.

PENNY

Ew. She's my co-worker, dude.

ELLIE

… I'm putting my phone on silent now. I'm
kinda busy at the moment.

ABIGAIL

Hot date?

ELLIE

No.

I'm at Owen's game.

QUIN

So it is a hot date.

PENNY

If he wasn't my brother, I'd high-five you. But he is, so despite me loving the idea of you two getting back together… ew. Gross.

ELLIE

Thanks, guys. Love and miss all of you.

Even Zach.

ZACHARY

Why's everyone always picking on me?

ABIGAIL

You make it so easy.

ZACHARY

You can't see me, but I'm rolling my eyes now.

ABIGAIL

If I wasn't the oldest, I'd be sticking my tongue out at you.

LUCY

Quiet, children. I can't focus with all of these texts.

ELEVEN

Owen

NOW

*T*ying the laces of my right skate—then my left—I stood and observed the scene of the locker room. It felt right, all of us back here. Even if the entire team wasn't playing tonight for the exhibition game, seeing all the guys in their Seals blue felt like coming home.

"Hey, Harps. Have any plans tonight after the game?" Brooks nudged me.

I shrugged. "Not really."

"A group of us were talking about going out tonight for drinks. Let loose a little before the regular season starts." My friend gave me a warm smile. He was quieter and more subdued than his brother, which was probably why I spent more time around him than Maverick. Still, they were my best friends.

"Sounds good," I nodded. It had been a while since I'd gone out with the team, and maybe I needed this. To blow off some steam and let go. To feel like I was a part of the group.

Mav stared at me, mystified. "Sorry, did he just agree to go out tonight?"

"I think he did." Brooks shook his head.

"Fuck off," I muttered. "I go out plenty. Unlike Rhodes over there."

He flipped me off, going back to his pre-game ritual while getting ready.

Grumpy asshole that he was, I couldn't fault him for being an incredible hockey player. He had a record for the most assists in history with our team over his last decade that he'd played, and so I tried not to give him too hard of a time. Even if I rarely saw the guy smile.

One day, someone was going to come into his life and completely knock him off his feet, and he'd have no idea what to do with himself. I chuckled to myself, pulling my jersey over top my shoulder and elbow pads.

Hopefully, I'd be around to see it. After all, some guys on the team had been here for their entire career. I hoped I would be the same. I loved the Pacific Northwest, and I didn't want to leave it. Though I missed Portland, they didn't have an NHL team there, so at least I was close to home.

Imagining leaving this place... even now, it felt wrong. I couldn't imagine how rough it would be to hear I was being traded. Hopefully, the day would never come.

That was why I had to keep my head in the game and stay serious. It was my fourth season in the NHL, and while I didn't feel like I was at risk of being sent down to the AHL anymore—proving my worth over the last two seasons—anything could happen.

I needed to stay focused. Sharp.

IT WASN'T long until we stepped out onto the ice, a giant stack of pucks being knocked onto the ice by Finn Evans, who entered before me. We all took turns shooting at the net, our man Farkas in goal, doing his best to block our shots.

Since he didn't play most of the games during the season, these would give him the extra practice he needed as our alternate goalie.

After a few turns around the ice, I skated over to the boards, coming to a stop next to Brooks. He was almost the same height as me, only an inch shorter. Sometimes, it felt like we could read each other on the ice so well that we didn't even need to communicate. That was one reason it felt like we worked so well together. We were both damn good at blocking the other team's shots and had a record number of hits between the two of us.

He tipped his head, looking across the ice. "Hey, she's pretty cute."

"Huh?" I asked, looking back at him.

He motioned with his stick. "Over there. Blonde. Standing next to the kid in the corner."

I perked up. There was no way. It couldn't be. She wasn't *here* at my game.

We hadn't talked to each other since I'd left that morning. The group chat I never took part in didn't count, though it seemed like she'd been doing okay.

I wasn't even aware I was moving, skating across the ice, until I was right there. The only thing that separated us was the half inch thick piece of plexiglass.

"Ellie?" My eyes were wide.

But it was her. She was here.

Her lips moved, and a hesitant smile covered her face. "Hi," she mouthed, and I wished I could hear her voice.

She moved her hand, placing it against the glass and splaying her fingers wide.

Fuck, I couldn't believe she was standing in front of me. I blinked a few times, trying to decide if it was really my imagination. Had I just hallucinated her?

But no.

"You're here," I said, unable to keep the smile off my face.

God, she was beautiful in Seals blue, wearing one of our jerseys. It wasn't mine, but *she* wasn't mine anymore, either.

Ellie nodded.

Where was she sitting? I wanted her closer to me. So that I could watch her during the game. Something told me she would disappear all too quickly after it ended.

Did she drive up just for the night? While my family came to my games fairly often, since Seattle wasn't too far from Portland, Ellie never had. I puffed up my chest, knowing I shouldn't feel this way but unable to rein myself in. I'd enjoy knowing she was watching me for tonight, and after that, I'd go back to moving on. Letting go of our shared past.

Maybe we could be friends again. We'd been best friends before I'd ever asked her out, and I missed her as my friend as much as I missed her as my girlfriend. She'd always been the one who would sit on the bench in the rink with me growing up as we talked about anything and everything.

That was where it had all began. It felt fitting that we were here once again—me on the ice, and her in the stands. Like this was fate. Like it was meant to be.

Looking around, I shook my head before holding up a hand. Unfortunately, she couldn't hear me through the plexiglass, so I just had to hope she understood the universal sign for *wait.* Especially with my gloves on.

Skating back to the bench, I caught the attention of Coach Monroe, and she walked over to the edge. She was wearing her dark hair back in a tight bun and a powder blue suit for tonight's game. "What's up, Harper?"

"I need a favor."

She raised an eyebrow, but nodded at me to continue.

"There's a girl," I said, looking backwards over my shoulder at where Ellie still stood. "At the glass over in section 110. Can you upgrade her seat? Maybe somewhere behind the bench?"

"I can try, but…"

"Please." I wasn't above begging. Not for this. Not when it came to her. "She's my—" What was she to me? *Ex-girlfriend* felt wrong. *Childhood best friend* didn't quite communicate the depth of feelings for her. She was a lot of things to me. "We've known each other since birth," I said instead. "Our parents are best friends. I'll pay for it. I just need—" *her close by*. To see her. Knowing she was really here was almost enough to have me jumping out of my skin. I shook my head.

"Oh, if she's family, you should have led with that. I'll see what I can do. Keep skating, and I'll have someone go get her. What's her name?"

"Ellie. Ellie Bradford."

She nodded, pulling out her phone and beginning to type furiously on the keyboard. A few moments later, she looked back up at me. "I've got it taken care of."

"Thank you." I turned around, heading back out to the middle of the ice to continue warm-ups, hitting a few slap-shots towards the goal and practicing a few maneuvers with the puck.

It was everything I could do to keep my eye off of the girl who once held my heart.

Especially when a staff member came down the stairs, and she hesitantly followed behind him before they disappeared at the top of the stairwell. I knew I couldn't focus on the spot for too long—even pretending to stretch wouldn't give me enough time to wait for her to reappear—but finally, she did.

Standing rink side, right behind the player's box. During the game, she'd be right there. I couldn't afford to get distracted—there might not be points awarded at the end of the game tonight, but Coach Donovan would be making decisions for the season based on how we played in these pre-season games.

Nevertheless, knowing she was close enough that I could see her filled me with a sense of ease. She wasn't mine, but tonight, I could pretend she was.

For just one more night.

AFTER THE FIRST PERIOD, we headed back to the locker room. I pulled off my gloves once I got into the tunnel, putting them in their spot so they'd dry out during intermission. After dragging my jersey over my head, I pulled my phone out, sitting on the bench as I opened my text message app and found Ellie's contact.

God, I still couldn't believe she was here. It was a struggle to stay focused on the ice, knowing how close she was to me. I was desperate to talk to her face to face.

Would the guys mind if I invited her out tonight? Probably not. Some of them would be too busy entertaining whatever girl they picked up on at the bar. While I hated the term puck bunny, there were plenty of girls who were interested in being with a professional hockey player. Hopefully, they'd be too wrapped up in themselves to even notice me bringing Ellie along.

Because even though I knew it was a terrible idea, I needed to talk to her. Needed to hear her voice. Needed to know why she was at my game, when she'd never come to one before.

Not in *years*.

I missed her being in the stands for me. My junior years felt like a distant memory now.

For a long time, I'd been jealous of the guys on the team whose wives would come for the games and watch warm-ups or hang out in the wives room until they were done and ready to go home. I wanted that. To know someone was there for me. That at the end of the night, we'd be going home together. That I wouldn't be sleeping alone in a cold, empty bed.

Unable to help myself, I typed in a message.

OWEN

Hi.

Short, sweet, and to the point. I held my breath as I waited for her to respond, the dots finally appearing on my screen.

ELLIE DAISY

Who's this?

OWEN

Ellie.

Just kidding.

Hi.

It's just been a long time since you've texted me.

I know.

You never changed your number.

I know.

You never changed yours, either.

I can't believe you're here.

Do you want to come out with me after? Some of the guys and I are going to get drinks. We can talk.

Sure.

You didn't have to upgrade my seat, by the way. This is way too much.

Nah, it's not. Besides, I like it. It was fun being able to turn around and see you there. It's been too long since you were at one of my games.

Yeah. It has.

Alright. I gotta go. I'll see you after.

Good luck tonight, Hockey Boy. You got this.

Thanks, Skater Girl.

I shut my eyes, trying to center myself. To focus on the game, and not the excitement I felt at seeing Ellie afterwards. I was supposed to have moved on, so why did I care so much that she was here?

Because no matter how hard I tried, she was always going to be ingrained under my skin.

But I couldn't risk having her and then losing her again.

She might have been here tonight, but that didn't mean anything. So I needed to be strong. I couldn't be weak and sleep with her again. Even if every cell in my body screamed for it.

What I needed was for us to be friends.

I was tired of being on the outside of her life. When we'd been teenagers, we'd told each other everything. Now, I heard about her through my mom. It was the worst. Like hearing about her skating accident second-hand, months after the fact.

All I'd wanted to do was to drive down to Portland, wrap my arms around her, and tell her everything was going to be okay.

But I hadn't been able to. Because she wasn't mine anymore.

That was the slap to reality I needed.

So from now on, I couldn't touch her. Not until I stopped being so weak.

AFTER THE GAME, I texted Ellie to meet us at our favorite bar, a hockey themed one aptly named The Penalty Box. We loved hanging out here, because people didn't normally bother us, even though it was close by the arena and most of the other patrons were Seattle Hockey fans.

Brooks and Maverick were right behind me, still horsing around with each other after the game. They were two of the closest brothers I knew—well, besides the twins, Zach and Wes. I'd grown up with them, so I was used to their ribbing. Still, the Hendrix brothers always had some good-natured teasing going, and that extended to the other players on the team as well. After so many years together, it really felt like we were all brothers, and this team was my extended family. When you ate, slept, and breathed hockey, it just happened naturally.

Heading inside, I looked around the bar for the head of blonde hair I would recognize anywhere.

Not seeing her, I moved to the bar, ordering my usual porter. It was a label by a local Seattle brewery. I loved supporting the local beer scene. Considering how large the micro-brew scene in the Pacific Northwest was, it was fairly easy. Waiting for Ellie to arrive, I stayed in my spot with a view of the door.

"Who are you waiting for, Harps?" Mav asked.

"Probably that girl he was staring at the entire game," Brooks said with a snort. "Did you give her your number or something? Ask her out?"

Some of the other guys were right behind us, joining us here after the game, and we normally ended up with one of the larger booths crammed full of hockey players. Which was a feat, considering most guys on the team were over six feet tall. Even our shortest on the team, Carter Meyer, was still 5'10. Though no one was as tall as Rhodes.

I shook my head. "I wasn't staring at her the entire game."

"She's cute. Who is she?"

They had no idea, I realized. Probably because I'd never shown them a picture of the girl who broke my heart when I was nineteen years old.

"She's..." How did I even answer that? I tried, but nothing came out.

And then... there she was. She'd taken the jersey off, wearing a coral sweater with her straight blonde hair hanging loose around her shoulders. Ellie had always been beautiful, but now she was *stunning*. I'd noticed it at her graduation party, when I'd barely been able to look away from her all night.

Was it any wonder that I'd followed her up into that treehouse and kissed her? That I'd driven her back to her apartment and spent the night with her? No.

Her eyes lit up as she saw me, and she walked towards me with a bounce in her step.

"Hi, El," I said, trying to look normal. *Casual.* And also trying to ignore the fact that my two best friends were right behind me, clearly also trying to scope out my girl.

Nope. *Not mine anymore.* I needed to remind myself.

"Should we go somewhere we can talk?" Ellie asked, tucking her hair behind her ear.

I nodded. "Want to get a drink first? We can grab a booth at the back." Away from the nosy, prying eyes.

"Okay." She turned to the bartender, ordering a whiskey sour. We were quiet as we waited for her drink to be made. Once she had it in her hand, I grabbed my beer, the two of us walking back to one of the empty booths.

I resisted placing my hand on her back to guide her there, because that wasn't something you did with your friend. And that's what we were to each other now. Or at least, that was all we could be.

Taking a long pull of my beer, I set it down on the table and looked at her. "Why are you here?"

Ellie bit her lip, running her thumb over the rim of the glass. "What do you mean?" I couldn't help but notice how she tugged at the hem of her sweater. Okay—she was just as nervous as I was.

"At my game," I answered. "It's a long drive from Portland. Are you staying the night, or—"

"I moved here last week," she answered quickly. "You're looking at the newest fourth grade teacher at Pine Creek Elementary."

My eyes widened. "You... *what?* Ellie, that's..." I wasn't sure I had words. But I was so proud of her. She gave me a hesitant smile. "Amazing. Congratulations."

"Thank you. I wasn't going to come tonight, but I saw an ad for the game, and I guess I just wanted to see if it felt like old times. Watching you play." Her eyes connected with mine, and I held her gaze.

"And did it?"

She nodded. "Better now, I think. God, you're amazing, Owen."

It was my turn to thank her, but the words tasted strange on my tongue. Maybe because we'd never exchanged pleasantries like this before. We'd never had to. I dipped my head. "Thanks. The regular season will probably be more exciting, but—"

"No, I thought it was fun. A lot of the guys who played tonight are trying to get a spot on the team, right?"

I gave her a nod of acknowledgement. "We lost to the Warriors in the playoffs last year, so that also had something to do with the game tonight."

The guys had been feisty, ready to drop their gloves and chirping at the opposition. And while I tried to keep my time in the penalty box to a minimum, I was always ready to defend my teammates. It was practically an unwritten rule when you saw someone on the opposing team messing with one of your guys.

"You really didn't have to get me a better seat," she said, looking down at her drink. She'd barely touched it, and I was almost done with my beer.

I shrugged. "I know." Maybe I shouldn't have done it, but it had made me feel better. After all, who knew what sort of guy she could have sat next to? Especially being new in the city. She would have been an easy target. "Where are you living?"

She winced. "Oh, well, I'm teaching in Bellevue. I wanted to be closer to the school, but I had to find something I could afford on my salary, so I'm a little farther out. It's okay though. I rented a small apartment, and it'll be fine. It's just for this year, anyway."

It certainly didn't sound fine. And what was *a little* farther out? I wasn't her dad, or her brother, though. Being this over-protective wouldn't serve me well. And what did she mean by it was just for this year? Would she be going back to Portland after that?

A frown covered my face, and she bit her lip. "What?"

"You said one night." My voice was low. I didn't know how else to bring it up. Were we ever going to talk about it? I'd left because I had to. Because she'd left me once before, and the idea of her kicking me out had felt like a punch in the gut. "But you're here."

Ellie nodded. "I know."

Right, then. I took a deep breath, forcing the words out. "I think we should try to be friends again. Like we were before."

She frowned. "Before?"

"Yes. Before we dated."

"Oh." Her face fell.

Fuck, I was an asshole.

Of course, she wouldn't want to be friends. I'd fucked her and then left in the middle of the night. What was I thinking? Sure, we'd always be connected by our families, but maybe that was all we'd ever have anymore.

Maybe that was all I deserved.

No matter how much I wanted Ellie Bradford again, I couldn't have her.

Not anymore.

TWELVE

Ellie

THEN

Sophomore Year

 never imagined how it would feel watching Owen's high school graduation ceremony, knowing that in a few months, everything would change.

That he'd be leaving.

It felt so unfair that we were together, but we'd be forced apart so soon. Long distance wouldn't be easy, but he was only going to Washington for college, so at least he wouldn't be on the east coast. Seattle had added a D1 college team recently, and they'd recruited him to play. Plus, the NHL draft was at the end of this month, and this was his first time being eligible. I knew someone would snatch him up. After all, I'd spent countless hours watching him at the rink. I knew he could do this. I wouldn't have encouraged him to pursue his dreams so hard if I didn't think he could make it. We all did.

Every step towards a future for him just felt like he was leaving me in the past. I hated being two grades behind him. The age difference suddenly felt so *big*.

This fall, I'd be in my junior year of high school and he'd

be a freshman in college. I wouldn't be able to ride in with him to school anymore, or hold his hand as we walked through the hallways. We certainly wouldn't be able to sneak kisses at the ice rink in between practices when we thought no one was looking.

Everything was about to change, and I was trying to remind myself that it was okay. In two years, I'd start college too, and I'd already planned on attending the same school as him. And after he graduated, if he was in the NHL, we'd make it work. We had to. We were *Ellie & Owen*, after all—inseparable since birth. He was my friend before he'd ever been my boyfriend. Probably my best friend besides Penny.

Owen walked across the stage in his graduation gown, accepting his diploma from the Principal before heading back to his seat. He looked over at where we were sitting—me, next to Penelope and his parents and gave me a big, dopey grin before blowing me a kiss. I blushed, too embarrassed to blow him one back with all of our family sitting near me.

On the other side of me was Aunt Angelina, Uncle Benjamin, and their daughter Lucy, who was still in elementary school. Their twins, Zachary and Wesley, were also graduating today. We were having one massive graduation party later today at the Sullivan house, complete with a barbecue and a pool party.

I'd never complain about a chance to relax in their pool while we all hung out. I loved my cousins, even if things got a little crazy with all nine of us. Plus our parents, extended family, and friends.

Owen's cousins Avery and Amelia were also coming to the party later today, though they were both younger than me, so I wasn't as close with them. His aunt Tessa was a big Hollywood star, and their family would often live part of the year down in LA when she was filming something and the rest at home in Portland.

Aunt Angelina and Uncle Benjamin's boss, Nicolas, would

be here with his wife, Zofia, and their two kids, Alexander and Bianca. Alex was the same age as Abigail, while Bee was a few months older than me. We didn't go to the same school, but I still saw her often. She was a singer and a dancer, and I hadn't been surprised at all when she'd announced her intentions of attending Julliard once she graduated high school. If anyone could do it, she could. Plus, the Larsens were two of the most supportive parents I'd ever met—besides my own.

The ceremony dragged to a close. I hadn't been paying much attention, too busy thinking about the party and seeing everyone to focus on what anyone was saying. And then we were heading outside, waiting under the shade of the trees for our graduates to find us.

I'd notice Owen anywhere. With his six-foot-three frame and that dirty blond hair I loved, he was impossible not to recognize in any crowd. He was built like a hockey player, and he had the muscles to prove it, too. My heart sped up any time he was near, like it knew something I didn't. Every kiss, every touch, every smile… They were all mine.

"Hey, Daisy Girl." Owen tugged one of my blonde curls. I'd spent almost two hours getting ready for today. Not that I wanted to impress him, or that I wanted to look pretty for him, but… I liked when he looked at me like *that*. Like I was beautiful. He smiled at me, and my heart swelled.

"Hi." I threw my arms around him, and he picked me up, twirling me around. "Happy graduation."

"Thank you for coming."

"I wouldn't miss it," I said. There was nothing that could keep me from being here today.

His grin was bright enough to rival the sun. "I know. We'll be there for all the big moments, won't we, El?"

I nodded. "Of course we will."

"It's a promise." He leaned his forehead against mine. "I'll always be there for you, El."

I smiled against his mouth. "I'm so proud of you. First,

high school graduation. Next, the NHL draft, and then…
college."

"I might not get drafted, you know." His words were low.
"I might have to walk on to a team after I graduate." From
everything he'd told me about the NHL, that seemed like a
much harder way to make it, but it was doable. Still, I had
faith in him.

"It'll be okay, either way," I promised, curling my fingers
through the long hair at the nape of his neck.

"Yeah?" He held my gaze, those beautiful brown eyes I
loved staring back at me.

"Uh-huh," I nodded. "Because we'll do it together."

"Damn right we will." He placed a soft kiss against my
mouth.

A throat cleared, and we both laughed as he set me back
down on my feet. His parents had let us have our moment—
our bubble that had felt impenetrable—and now it was their
turn to tell their precious baby boy how much they loved him.
How proud of him they were.

It shouldn't have been possible to have been so happy and
yet… devastated at the same time. Because every step forward
he took felt like one further away from me. *We'll do it together.* I
had to believe him, because that was the only way I was going
to survive.

So, I smiled, and I held his hand. I laughed with him, with
our family, with the dozens of friends that gathered in the
backyard of my aunt and uncle's house, and I tried not to
think about the few months we had left before he would be
gone to Seattle.

And I'd still be right here.

Right where he left me.

THIRTEEN

Ellie

NOW

I think we should try to be friends again. Like we were before.

Before we'd dated. Like he somehow expected me to erase all the moments we'd spent together. We'd been together for almost four years, even if we'd spent the last five with radio silence between the two of us.

God, I was so dumb. I'd moved here for him, and he wanted to be *friends*. But I couldn't exactly run back to Portland with my tail between my legs now, crying about how my professional hockey playing ex-boyfriend wouldn't take me back just because I'd moved to his city and gotten a job here.

This was about more than just him now, anyway. This was about finding myself and my identity outside my family. Sure, I'd still talk to my mom every day, and I didn't foresee the group chat of my cousins getting any less active—or annoying —but I'd turned twenty-two this summer. It was time to figure out who I was. Seattle was as good of a place to do that as any. I'd make some friends, and Owen could be one of those. Maybe we'd find our way back to each other. I had to have faith that everything was going to work out the way it was supposed to.

"I can't just pretend like we were never together," I whispered. I'd spent so many hours with him when we were younger, we'd almost melded into one person. Everyone knew us as Ellie and Owen, like we were one unit. My friends were his friends, and his friends were my friends, and everything was great. I never had to sacrifice family time to spend time with my boyfriend, either, because our moms being best friends and all of us growing up on the same street meant we got to see each other all the time.

He grunted. "That's not what I'm asking you to do, Ellie." Owen seemed tormented, and I wasn't sure I'd ever seen him like this before. He'd always been so easy-going. The guy with a huge grin on his face who was always cracking jokes and making me smile. The one who would hang around the rink after his practice to watch me skate, and then drive me home.

"Then what are you asking, Owen?" I picked up my drink, taking a long sip of the strong alcohol. I wasn't a huge drinker, but my dad had gotten me started on drinking whiskey sours, and it felt like a tiny part of him was with me now.

His elbows rested on the table, and he placed his head in his hands. "We used to tell each other everything."

"Yeah." I remembered.

"Don't you miss that?"

I blinked. "Of course I do. But we can't just close our eyes and magically be back where we were half a decade ago. We barely even know each other anymore."

Except I knew him *intimately*. Because a few months ago, I'd had him on top of me. And underneath me. And it was unfortunate that we hadn't made it to the shower, because I was pretty sure that would have been even better. My cheeks heated at the thought of him pinning me against a tile wall, thrusting roughly into me as his lips captured a nipple.

I sucked in a breath. That was definitely not friend-like. And if Owen wanted to be friends, well...

"Okay. Let's be friends, then."

Owen flashed me a grin. One that felt like his normal,

signature smile, but it lacked some of the usual warmth. He stuck his hand out across the table, like he wanted me to shake his. "Friends," he said.

"Friends."

With a little dip of his head, he drained the rest of the beer in his glass. I followed suit with mine, trying to ignore the awkward tension between us. It had never been weird between us before, and I *hated* it.

There were so many things I wanted to ask, but I couldn't make my mouth work. They were all too intimate, too personal. Things a friend wouldn't ask. He was my first love, but now we were basically strangers.

"So, do you guys come here often?" I watched out of the corner of my eye as players I recognized from the game flirted with some girls at the bar.

He nodded. "It might seem strange, but people don't really bother us here. They know we come here often after the games, so usually we just get to hang out. It's refreshing. Like I can pretend I'm not some famous athlete with a handful of endorsements and a contract worth more money than I will ever know what to do with."

"That doesn't seem strange at all. It's like your safe space." We had those, too, when we were younger.

Owen looked down at his empty glass. "Yeah. Exactly."

Two giant brunette hockey players—I assumed, because they both had to be over six feet fall and had that *look*—stood over us. I blinked, almost seeing double. I was pretty sure they were the Hendrix brothers, but I didn't pay attention to most of the guys on Owen's team like I did to him.

"Um, hi?" I asked, sucking more of my drink up my straw.

"Hey." One of the two grinned at me, showing off a set of pearly white teeth. He didn't appear to be missing any, which surprised me, considering the track record of most hockey players. "We had to come over and check out Owen's girl."

"Oh." I blushed. "I'm not—"

The two of them slid in next to us. So much for our moment alone.

"This is Ellie," Owen said. "We grew up together. Our moms are best friends."

"So you got to see this one in his peewee days, eh?" The guy sitting next to Owen elbowed him. "Where are my manners? I'm Brooks. Harps here is my D-man partner."

"Maverick," his brother added, grinning like a fool. "Also known as the better looking Hendrix brother."

I squinted. They had similar facial shapes and coloring, though I didn't particularly find either of them more attractive. Probably because the man I found most attractive was sitting across from me.

"You're on the first line, aren't you?" I asked the man sitting next to me.

"Sure am." Maverick puffed out his chest. "Did you see the goal I scored tonight?"

I nodded. "Yeah. I did." I'd mostly been watching Owen, who had gotten the assist for the goal. He'd kissed his forearm after his teammate had scored, and I wondered when that tradition had started. He'd never done that when we were younger.

"So tell us about little Owen," Brooks encouraged me. "We want to hear more about this guy when he was younger."

"We used to spend a lot of time at the rink together," Owen said, his gaze holding mine. Did he not want them to know we'd dated? Was he… embarrassed by me? "Ellie was a figure skater."

"Oh, you skate too, blondie? We'll have to get you on the ice sometime with us."

I dipped my head. "Well, I did. I haven't stepped foot on the ice in a long time."

Owen frowned. "You don't…" Did he not realize that I stopped skating after my accident?

"No."

We both stared at each other, and I looked away. Both of the Hendrix brothers were looking between us, and I didn't know what else to say.

I cleared my throat. "Well, he was always an incredible player. There's a reason he made it this far, right?"

Owen shrugged. "I was alright."

"Alright? God, Owen, you were..." I closed my eyes, picturing him back in high school. It was a different league with different rules, but he'd been captivating on the ice, even back then. "Incredible."

"I like her," Maverick said to my ex.

Brooks was eyeing me, and I fidgeted with my empty glass. "Anyway. We had good times."

Owen gave me a hesitant smile. "We did."

Maverick turned to me. "So, are you sticking around here for a while, Ellie? Think you'll come to the home opener?"

I shrugged. "Maybe? I don't know. Since I just moved here, I don't know my schedule yet. It sounds fun, though. As long as I don't have school the next day."

"School?" Brooks asked.

"She's an elementary school teacher," Owen said, his voice filled with what I could only assume was pride. "El just graduated college this summer."

"Oh, so it was your graduation too, eh?" Brooks cocked his head to the side, a bit of a Canadian accent coming out. "Owen told us he went home for a graduation party."

"My sister and Ellie graduated from the same university," he said. "Of course, I was there." Was it just me, or did he sound a little defensive? Which didn't make sense, unless he'd told them about me. But then again, he hadn't told them we'd dated, either.

"You *were* late, though," I teased him. That seemed safe.

Owen's ears and cheeks turned pink, and he looked down at his empty cup. "I need another drink if everyone's going to team up on me," he muttered.

I giggled as Brooks and Maverick stood up.

"On me, man," Maverick said. "Ellie, could we get you another drink?"

"Oh, no," I said, shaking my head. "I have to drive home soon, anyway."

"You're not gonna stay and hang out?"

It was a Friday night, but I still had so much to catch up with settling into a new school, and I planned to use the weekend to work ahead. Still, it was good to see Owen. And I enjoyed seeing him in this space, a whole different side of the man I used to love. His teammates teased him in a way that felt so similar to the way my cousins and I teased each other.

"Maybe one more. It's a whiskey sour."

Maverick winked at me, and then the two disappeared back to the bar.

Owen ran his fingers through his hair.

"They seem great." I watched them mess with each other, standing on either side of a barstool of who I assumed was another member of the team. Even sitting down, I could tell the guy was tall. A little older, with a short beard and darker brown hair. He was frowning and definitely looked grumpy as the Hendrix brothers bothered him. "It must be fun for them to be on the same NHL team."

"Yeah, I imagine it is." Owen looked over at them, a wistful look on his face. "When Maverick got traded to the team two years ago, Brooks had been overjoyed."

"This is weird, isn't it?" I scrunched up my nose.

He chuckled. "A little. But we just need to re-learn each other, that's all." Maybe he was right. "Speaking of… Have you really not skated since your accident?" Owen asked, completely changing the subject. It was like the question had been pinging around in his mind ever since he'd brought it up.

I shook my head, swallowing roughly. "I—no."

"Fuck, El." He rubbed his forehead. "Why?"

I raised one shoulder and then dropped it. I wasn't ready to talk about why. Not when it had everything to do with him. And that wasn't fair of me. It wasn't *his* fault I'd messed up my routine during a competition and landed wrong during one of my jumps. Nor was it his fault that I'd given it all up afterwards. My heart just wasn't in it anymore. It wasn't about failing or getting hurt. Even after I'd healed, the ice symbolized everything I'd given up. I couldn't tell him about the anxiety attacks when I tried to skate, either. And by the end, I'd already been second guessing my dream of competing in the Olympics.

"I meant what I said earlier, Ellie. I want us to be friends again. I want to know about everything I've missed."

What did I even say to that? I bit my lip. "Me too, Owen." He used to be my everything. I'd confided everything in him, and I missed having that. Moving here to chase after him might have been a crazy choice, but I wouldn't give up on this opportunity. Even if it was just being friends, at least he'd be in my life.

That was more than I could say before.

I gave him a hesitant smile. "So, you're still number eight, huh?"

He'd worn the number eight on his jersey for as long as I could remember, and I was glad it hadn't changed in all these years.

Owen laughed. "Out of everything you could ask, that's what you go with?"

"Why not? I'm curious." He'd never told me why he picked the number originally.

He smirked. "Is your favorite color still yellow?"

It was my turn to smile. "No."

His brows furrowed. "It's not?"

"Guess people change," I said, looking down at my lap. We both had, though the physical chemistry between us hadn't disappeared. It was explosive when we'd come together in May. But that didn't mean we could just pick up where we left off after all this time.

The Hendrix brothers came back to the table, finally leaving the stoic guy at the bar alone as they carried back another round of drinks for all of us.

Maybe it was strange to hang out with a bunch of pro hockey players, but being in a new city where the only person I knew was Owen—and my new teacher friend Maggie, plus the fourth graders I'd just started teaching—it felt good. Like things were going right, for once.

Just friends.

I could do that, right?

FOURTEEN

Owen

___

NOW

*N*ot your girl, huh?" Brooks said during our practice the next morning, a devilish smirk on his face.

"Fuck off," I said, adjusting my gloves during a break. Coach Donovan was really throwing everything at us this week, and I knew he was just trying to weed out the best of the best. Some guys would end up getting sent down to our AHL team, and the rest would be cut. It was hard to know that guys we'd spent the last month with would be gone soon, but I tried not to get too attached to anyone.

That rule applied to my personal life, too.

"She's the one, isn't she?" Brooks asked, shifting his weight back and forth between his skates. "The one who broke your heart."

I grimaced. "I never should have told you that."

"Ah, but you did. And you're not denying it, which means it's true."

Fuck. I walked right into that one. "Yeah. Ellie's my ex."

"So, what's she doing up here? I thought you said she lived in Portland."

"You heard her. She got a job up here as a teacher. I don't know." I shrugged. After all, if I let myself think too hard about why she had moved to Seattle, the hope in my chest would swell, and I couldn't afford that. *No attachments.* It was why I'd told her that maybe we should just be friends again.

That, and I was dying to be close to her, even if I couldn't be with her. All I'd wanted to do last night was to growl anytime someone got near her. Which was absolutely ridiculous, given our relationship was over. Though it hadn't felt that way when we'd slept together a few months back. No, in that moment, it felt like we had never ended. That we'd simply been waiting for each other all this time.

But that couldn't have been further from the truth. We hadn't been waiting for each other. She'd left me behind and never looked back.

"Maybe it's the universe giving you two a second chance, eh?" His Canadian accent really came out whenever he added an *eh* on the end of one of his statements, and it always made me chuckle. Brooks and Maverick were both from a small city outside of Winnipeg in Manitoba, and it was easy to forget they weren't American until they pulled out one of those. Or when they talked about how much better the healthcare was up north, despite us having an amazing plan being on the team.

"Nah." I shook my head. "It's too late for us. I don't know why she moved up here, but she made it pretty clear from the beginning what she wanted." And that wasn't me.

"You sure about that?"

I wasn't sure about anything anymore.

"We're just friends now, man," I insisted.

Luckily, I was saved by Coach Donovan calling us over, discussing some line pairings he wanted to try today, as well as other defenseman pairings. Our first game had gone well, and we'd won, but we wanted to keep that momentum for the next one tomorrow as well. Especially while we were still on home ice. Since I played the first game, I was off for the next, giving the new guys who were trying to prove themself a chance.

I worked with a few of the prospects for the rest of the day, and while none of us had the chemistry and innate understanding of the way the other worked on the ice like I did with Brooks, they were good. Still, we made some good defensive saves. Hopefully, we'd see some of them during the regular season if they got called up from the Otters, our AHL team.

I remembered my first year here, when I'd been fresh out of training camp and trying to give it my all during those pre-season games. I'd been terrified that after being drafted and making it this far, I wouldn't actually make it on the team. But then, I'd been the rookie on the Seattle Seals, officially a part of the team, and besides a few scratches or minor injuries, I'd been here every day, working hard for the team.

One of these guys would be like that, too. Young and with a lot of talent, ready to prove himself in the NHL. It was exciting to watch, but even more exciting to be a part of.

When I headed back to the locker room, I wasn't surprised to find a small group of my teammates standing around my stall, like they were waiting for me. They were in various states of undress, and I pulled off my practice jersey, throwing it into the bin before finally turning to them.

"Alright, lay it on me," I said with a sigh.

"Come on, Harper. Tell us about your lass." Reid MacKenzie, our resident redhead, spoke up. He'd already removed his goalie pads and was just in his compression shirt and a pair of workout pants. *Your lass.* I resisted a chuckle at his choice of words. He was from Scotland, and his thick accent was definitely popular with the girls.

He was wrong about one thing. I crossed my arms over my chest. "There's nothing to tell. And she's not my lass."

Maverick raised an eyebrow. "*That's* the story you're going with? We saw you at the bar. There was some serious tension between you."

A sigh escaped me. Might as well get it all off of my chest, since Brooks already knew. "We were best friends, okay? And we dated in high school. She was supposed to follow me to college. I thought she was my forever. And then…" And then it was all over.

"But she moved here?" Reid frowned. He was about the same height as me, giving me a look as I stripped off all my layers.

"She got a teaching job." I shook my head. There was no way she'd moved here for me. Not when I'd left her four months ago, naked and asleep in her bed. "It doesn't matter anymore. We agreed to be friends."

"That's what you want?" Brooks asked. I knew he was thinking about what I'd told him earlier. This little intervention probably had something to do with that, too.

I nodded. "Yeah." It was all I could want. "Look, I love you guys. You're like my brothers. But Ellie and I… Nothing's going to happen there, okay?"

"So I can ask her out?" Mav asked, flashing me a smile.

There was no way I could hold back my growl. "Over my dead fucking body."

"Yeah." Reid patted me on the shoulder. "*Nothing's* going to happen." He snorted. "And I'm Irish."

"Was I that obvious?" I asked Brooks, as everyone else walked away.

He chuckled. "Yeah. Even Rhodes noticed the way you couldn't stop looking at her during the game. *Rhodes*. And last night… I've never seen you like that, man. Like in a room full of people, your eyes couldn't help but find her."

"Fuck." I massaged my forehead.

"Good luck." He smacked me on the shoulder. "You're going to need it."

A WEEK HAD PASSED since I'd seen Ellie, and the home opener of the season was just around the corner. We'd texted a little here and there—enough for me to know she was settling into her new school and her role as a teacher. I couldn't wait to see her in action, though I had no idea how I was going to sneak into the school to see her.

OWEN

Hi.

ELLIE DAISY

Hey. How's it going?

Good. Just got home from morning skate.

What are you up to tonight?

Probably will just grab food after I finish class for the day and then watch some TV.

Guess we haven't changed that much after all.

Maybe not.

Do you want to do something tomorrow, maybe? I have the day off.

And it was Saturday, which meant that Ellie wouldn't have classes, either. Saturdays off with the team were rare, so I wanted to take advantage of it.

What the guys had said kept running through my mind. The idea of them asking her out gave me hives. It was one reason I had spent little time at home all those years. The idea of seeing her with another guy, her bringing someone else home for family dinners and having to look out my window and seeing her with someone else killed me.

I needed to get over that, though. Still, my teammates were not getting anywhere near her.

What do you have in mind?

I could show you the city. You haven't really had a chance to explore yet, have you?

No, I haven't.

That settles it. Send me your address. I'll pick you up tomorrow morning.

Hmmm… Are you asking or telling me, Hockey Boy?

Skater Girl?

Yeah?

Would you please come on an adventure with me? For old-time, friends sake.

Of course. See you in the morning.

I grinned to myself before looking around my apartment, trying to see it from her point of view. What would she think when she came over? Would she feel comfortable here?

Was it wrong of me I hoped she would?

THE NEXT DAY, I left my place at 8 AM sharp, heading to pick Ellie up from her apartment.

"Where are we going?" Ellie asked a few minutes later as we drove towards our destination. She crossed her legs, resting her hands in her lap.

It wasn't in the nicest area of town, which I didn't love, but I understood her need to do this herself. We both came from families with no shortage of money, but I'd never felt right taking my parents', either. I'd wanted to make it for myself, and I had. Between my yearly salary, endorsements, and investments, the amount in my bank account was enough to make anyone do a double take. But it was mine.

"Somewhere you'll like," I promised. Today felt like one of our old adventures from our early days of dating, back when we were in high school. Ellie had always come along back then, for everything from hiking to sharing picnics under the stars while laying in the truck bed. Sometimes, I wished I still had the old truck, but a smaller car made sense for living in the city.

This morning, I'd pulled on a dark gray sweatshirt and a pair of jeans, plus my most comfortable pair of tennis shoes. We weren't going hiking, but I wanted to take her some place I'd loved since I first moved here. It was a little off the beaten path, but ever since I'd discovered it, I'd tried to come here once a week and just breathe.

It helped to remind me who I was and where I came from.

Looking over at her, I took in her appearance. She'd pulled her hair back in two double French braids, and was wearing a pair of daisy earrings with a light blue sweater and jeans, as well as a pair of sneakers on her feet. I'd told her to dress casually for where we were going, though I hadn't told her my plans.

I was trying hard not to think about the last time she'd been in my car, which was proving hard with her scent surrounding me, taking me back to that night. Florals and citrus, and fuck, she smelled good. She looked good, too. Better than good.

She was always the most beautiful woman I'd ever seen.

"You know, I can get you tickets for the home opener if you want to come," I said, watching as she bit her lip.

"I couldn't ask you to do that."

I shook my head, not sure how to communicate the sincerity of my actions. "You're not asking. I'm offering. Besides, I get free tickets." And I wanted her there.

"Your family should use those, Owen."

You are my family, I wanted to say.

But I couldn't. That wasn't something friends said, right? And I was trying to keep this strictly platonic. Even if she was the only woman I'd ever loved, and all I wanted was to hold her in my arms and know she was mine.

"I already got tickets for the games they're coming up for," I said instead. "So it's fine. Please come? I want you there. "

Her eyes connected with mine. "Okay."

Ellie being there was important to me. It was like my graduation ceremony and having her at my junior hockey games— something about knowing she was in the crowd for me made me warm inside. After all this time, that hadn't changed.

Having her at the game last week had been one of my best games in a long time. Brooks and Mav had made fun of me for playing better after I got back from Portland this summer, but maybe it *was* just her. Her light in my life.

"Great. Since that's settled, are you ready?" I pulled off the road, heading down the one that would take us towards the park.

"Oh." Her breath caught as part of it came into view. "Owen. It's beautiful here."

"Wait until you see the lake." I said, turning my eyes away from her and back to the road. "It's even prettier in the spring, too, when all the flowers are blooming."

"I don't think I could ever leave the Pacific Northwest," she said with a sigh of wonder. "I love how green everything is. Sure, it's gray and rainy eight months out of the year, but it's nature's wonderland."

We'd always loved places like this. Maybe that was why I'd fallen in love with it when I'd first come here.

Parking the car, I got out first, rounding the car to open Ellie's door and hold out my hand for her. She took it, sliding her palm in mine, and *fuck*, I shouldn't have touched her. I'd been resisting the entire time she was sitting next to me, my hand itching to rest on her thigh. But I'd been good. I was being her friend, just like I'd promised.

Our skin touching felt like a shockwave to my system. And I felt the absence when she let go, walking over to the trail-head with excitement in her eyes. This place wasn't the most beautiful park in the Seattle area—not by a long shot—but it was peaceful, since it wasn't one of the busy touristy destinations. I liked the calm.

"It reminds me of Forest Park," I whispered, shoving my hands in my pockets as we walked down towards the water. "The trees and the quiet."

"It's perfect." She did a little twirl, like she was taking in a full view of the place. "I can see why you like it."

I nodded. "Come on, there's a bench up ahead. You'll love the view."

Ellie followed behind me, and with every step, it felt like we were taking another one away from our past—and towards our future. Whatever that looked like.

FIFTEEN

Owen

———

THEN

Summary

Summer

O wen," Ellie's adorable voice groaned behind me. "How much further?"

I grinned, looking at the trailhead. At the arrow that pointed towards the waterfall we'd been hiking to. "We're almost there."

Pulling her water bottle out of my bag—a yellow one covered in white daisies—I handed it to her as we reached a bench.

She plopped down, guzzling her water. "How is it I'm on the ice every day and I'm struggling, but you have barely broken a sweat?" She wore a racerback tank and athletic capri leggings, and they hugged every curve of her lithe body. Something I was trying hard *not* to notice, especially since I was definitely a horny teenager who was currently alone with his girlfriend.

Wrapping my arm around her blonde ponytail, I tugged it lightly, bringing her eyes up to meet mine. "Because I practically grew up hiking, Skater Girl."

She muttered something under her breath about how she was just as fit as I was, but I had to give it to her. My stride was a lot longer than hers, and I hadn't exactly taken it easy on the way up here.

"We'll go slower on the way down, I promise."

Ellie huffed out a breath, blowing strands of blonde hair off her forehead. Standing up, she handed me her water bottle back, and I stowed it in my backpack before waving my hand towards the trail. "Ready?"

"Yeah." She gave me one of those smiles that melted my heart. God, there was nothing like spending time with her.

This summer, I wanted to make every moment count. After all, I was leaving for college in less than a month. Oregon had so many beautiful trails and places to see, it felt like you could live here your entire life and still not see all of them. The Bradfords had spent a week in Central Oregon this summer, renting a house, and let me come along with them. I'd stayed in Beau's room, of course, and Ellie had roomed with her older sister Abigail, but that didn't stop us from sneaking out onto the deck to make out.

"It's going to be weird when you're gone," Ellie murmured as she laced her fingers through mine, the two of us taking a slower pace than we had before.

I sighed. "I know. I can't imagine not seeing you every day." Leaning over, I pressed a kiss to her forehead. "I'm going to miss you so much, El."

"Me too." She squeezed my hand. "But at least we can call and text each other. And when you're on the ice, just know I'm cheering for you, even if I can't be at your games anymore."

Our destination came into view: a crystal clear waterfall with a shallow pool that was a perfect swimming spot—if you took the long trek up here. Because of that, it wasn't super crowded.

"Oh, Owen. This is beautiful." Her hand rested over her heart as she took in the view.

"Yeah, it is," I said, unable to pull my eyes away from her. The sun had caught on her blonde hair, illuminating it like a halo. Her blue-gray eyes looked even bluer in this light, sparkling the same way the water did. And the expression on her face? She had no idea how gorgeous she was. How attractive I found her.

I knew some of my friends thought it was cliché, going into college while still dating my high school girlfriend. But she was more than that. She was my future, my everything. All my life, I'd noticed Ellie. Even when I was little, I'd always given her a hand when she fell, or bandaged her knee when she scraped it. I enjoyed being her protector. I liked being *hers* even more.

So yeah, maybe I was a fool to think we would last. But I couldn't imagine wanting anyone else.

"Do you want to go for a swim?" I asked, giving her a mischievous grin as I set my backpack on the rocks, far enough away from the water that it wouldn't get wet.

Ellie frowned. "But we didn't bring swimsuits."

I shrugged, pulling off my top. In the summer heat, the cool water was going to feel freaking amazing. "We can just wear our underwear."

"Owen." Her cheeks flushed. "Are you sure?"

"Daisy." I pulled her tight against my body, and Ellie's fingers traced up my hard chest as I pressed a kiss under her jaw. My voice was low, barely above a rasp. "I've seen you in a swimsuit before." We'd gone on family vacations every summer since I was little. More than once, our parents had taken all eight—and then nine—of us to Florida to go to Disney World. We spent most of those trips going to the pool at least once. "It's nothing new."

"Okay." She bit her lip. "I guess you're right."

"Only if you're comfortable," I reassured her. There was

no way I would do anything she wasn't comfortable with. That wasn't what this was about. This was supposed to be something fun for both of us, an experience we'd both remember.

My girl gave me a small smile, stepping up on her tiptoes to place a soft kiss on my lips. "I'm always comfortable with you, Owen."

God, those words.

I kicked off my shoes and socks before pushing off my shorts. I'd worn a loose pair of athletic shorts with a pair of boxer briefs underneath, knowing it was too hot for material that didn't breathe.

"Your turn."

Ellie stripped out of her tank top, shoes and leggings quickly, folding and resting them on top of her shoes by my backpack before turning towards me. She was wearing a teal sports bra and hipster undies and gave me a shy look.

"Come on," I said, holding out my hand for her.

She took it, letting me interlace our fingers, and then we both took off at a run, heading straight for the water. There wasn't an abrupt drop into the pool, so we couldn't jump in, but each step brought us in deeper. I laughed as Ellie shrieked from the cold, but tugged her in further with me.

There wasn't a single part of the pool that I couldn't touch the bottom of, but we paddled around for a few minutes, enjoying the cool water and the warm sun. It was perfect. You could hear the rushing of the waterfall and the sounds of the forest.

"This is perfect," Ellie mumbled, floating on her back as she looked up at the sky. "The perfect day."

"I thought you'd like it. I'll make an outdoorsman out of you yet, Ellie Bradford."

She laughed, moving back up to her tiptoes and weaving her arms around my neck. "I'm not sure that's a bet you can win, Owen Harper."

I winked at her before leaning my head down to kiss her softly. An exploratory kiss.

My girl responded with fervor, kissing me back harder, and I groaned at her sweet taste. She was always so sweet. God, I couldn't get enough.

"I want to show you something," I murmured.

"Oh?" Ellie pulled back, running her fingers through my hair as she wrapped her legs around my waist.

"Uh-huh." I nipped at her bottom lip. "Hold on."

Carrying her through the water, I approached the waterfall. Behind it was a small cave, only a little bigger than both of us.

"Close your eyes," I whispered against her ear, and when she complied, I covered her body with mine before walking through the waterfall. On the other side, I waded up to the edge of the cave. "Open."

Her eyes fluttered open, and she brushed back the wet strands from her face before looking around us. "Wow. How'd you know this was here?"

I smirked. "I have my ways." Helping her up onto the rock, I pulled my body up beside her, both of us sitting on it and staring at the backside of the waterfall.

It was loud in here, and it felt like I could barely hear myself think. But maybe that was what I liked about places like this. That here, I could block the rest out. I didn't have to worry about who I was or my future. I didn't have to worry about the NHL or what would become of my life now that I'd been drafted to the Seals. All I had to think about was the girl by my side, and how much I loved her.

Love. It was a big word. Huge. And even though we'd been dating for two years, I hadn't said it yet. I didn't know why. Maybe it was because we were so young. Maybe it was because I'd *always* loved her. As a friend. Like my family. But things were different now.

"I'm so glad I have you in my life, El," I said, almost having to shout over the sound of the water.

"Me too," she responded, cupping my jaw. "It still feels like a dream, you know. That you like me. That out of everyone, you picked me. Your little sister's best friend."

"You're a lot more than that, and you damn well know it," I almost growled. "You're my best friend too, Ellie. I don't know what I'd do without you. Seeing you is the highlight of my day, every day." She beamed, opening her mouth to say something, but I shook my head and continued. "When I finish practice and I see you there, on the bench, lacing up your skates, it's like I see my future waiting for me."

I rested my forehead against hers. "You are my future, Ellie Bradford. I know that it's going to be hard the next two years till you're in college. And I know the long distance is going to suck. But I'm in this for the long haul. I never want to live without you. I love you."

"Owen…" She stroked my cheek, her eyes filling with unshed tears. "You've always been, and always will be, the best thing that ever happened to me." She gave me a watery smile. "Do you know why I asked my mom to sign me up for ice skating lessons when I was little?" I shook my head. She'd never told me this before. "I still remember going to one of your peewee hockey games. It's one of my earliest memories. But you looked so cool out there on the ice. And I knew, immediately, that I wanted to do that too."

I blinked. "You started figure skating because of *me*?"

She nodded, looking shy. "Yeah. And then I fell in love with it too. I love you, Owen. Always have."

"Come here," I murmured.

Ellie climbed into my lap, and I wrapped my arms around her, holding her tight against my chest.

I didn't know what the future held in store for us, but right now, I knew I held my entire world in my arms.

And I didn't want to let her go. Not now… Not ever.

SIXTEEN

Ellie

NOW

God, my life was falling apart.

And I meant that quite literally.

I'd come home from school to find a pipe had burst in the wall, and there was a few inches of standing water in my apartment.

"Fuck," I groaned. I'd already called the landlord, but that still didn't change the fact that this apartment was now unlivable.

It had been the only place I could find that was within my budget, and now it was ruined.

Where was I going to go?

This felt like a bad omen. Maybe it was a sign that moving here had been a rash decision, one I should have thought through more.

But I couldn't regret it when Owen and I had become friends again over the last two weeks. We texted every day since the day he'd shown me his favorite park. Last week, he'd taken me on a tour of downtown Seattle, showing me all the touristy stuff that I was sure he completely hated. He'd gotten recognized a lot, but anytime someone stopped him, he'd been so nice, signing hats and shirts and posing for photos whenever anyone asked.

He'd always been the sweetest, and I loved seeing that he hadn't changed with his newfound fame. That deep down, he was still the same Owen. We might not have each other memorized now the way we did before, but I still knew that he was a good person. I felt it in every action of his. So I would never regret him coming back into my life, no matter what way it happened.

And right now, all I wanted was for him to pull me into his arms, surround me with that woodsy scent, and tell me that everything was going to be okay.

Because everything was *ruined*.

I'd already cried—and screamed—but the tears started falling again. What was I going to do? I needed to call my parents and tell them, but it felt like I'd failed. And I didn't want to admit that I had.

My phone was still in my hand, but I hadn't moved. Not since I'd done my first sweep of the place after hearing running water and wading through my own personal swamp to check on my belongings.

I was in a trance. Which might have explained why I didn't hear the knock on my apartment door the first time. Or possibly the second.

"Ellie?" a deep voice called out, finally jarring me from my current state. Another knock, and I rushed to the door.

I would recognize that voice anywhere.

"Owen?" I asked as I opened it, blinking in surprise.

"Ellie, what's—" His eyes widened as he took in the sight behind me. "—wrong." He finished, and I knew he'd answered his own question.

"Why are you here?" I murmured, wiping the tears from my eyes.

Today was overwhelming, and all I wanted to do was cry.

Or call my mom.

Maybe both.

But I was an adult, and I could handle this. Right? *What a lie.* I was twenty-two, and I didn't have the first idea about how to fix this.

He hadn't moved from the doorway, just watching me. "I thought I'd come over. Last day off before the home opener, and I just wanted to see how things were going. I just…" I was pretty sure I knew what he was going to say, though he didn't need to. "God, Ellie. This place is terrible."

I laughed. "Yeah. It wasn't great before the water. Now it's just…" I looked around us. *Ruined.* I couldn't come up with another word for it. I shrugged my shoulders.

"What do you need?"

I looked down at the floor, trying to hold back a sob. "Can you just… hold me? I just really need a hug right now."

"Of course." His legs sloshed through the standing water as he moved towards me, gathering me up in his arms. I pressed my face into his chest, holding on tight. "Always," I was pretty sure he murmured against my scalp.

It felt like my graduation party all over again, seeing him again in the flesh for the first time in almost five years. Running into his arms. That night, we didn't talk about why it all went wrong. We just *were.* He kissed me, and it felt so right being with him again. It should have been strange… but this was us.

I had my arms around Owen's back, hard and muscular, as I clung onto him like he was my life preserver and I was drowning. Maybe because it felt that way.

"Ready for me to let go?" He chuckled, rubbing his hand over my back.

"No," I mumbled, taking one last hit of his scent before finally pulling away. "I want this nightmare to be over."

"Did you call the landlord?"

I nodded. "He got the water turned off, and then he's going to come back and get it all pumped out of here. But I have no idea how long it will be till this place is livable again. What am I going to do, Owen?"

"Have you called your parents yet?"

I shook my head. "No. Because I know they're going to be so supportive and offer to rent me a place, and I just…" My shoulders drooped with defeat. "I love them. They're the best parents ever. But I wanted to do this myself."

Owen rubbed his jawline, and I took a moment to appreciate all six-foot-three of him standing in the middle of my water-logged apartment. He made the space feel smaller, if that was even possible. Somehow, he was just larger than life.

"What if…" He trailed off. "Hear me out before you say no."

Nodding, I ignored the churn of nerves in my stomach at whatever he was going to say.

"You can move in with me."

There it was. "*What?*" I shook my head. "I can't possibly…"

"Sure you can. Move in with me. At least until this place is fixed. I have a giant apartment, and there's way more space than I need for myself. Plus, I'm not even there half the time with my travel schedule during the season. I have an empty guest bedroom. It's yours."

I bit my lip. "Owen. I can't move in with you."

"Why not?"

"There's all this history between us. We didn't work." *I broke your heart.* "Besides, what would our families think?" That we were getting back together. I saw the hope in Penelope's eyes when Owen and I walked in together at the party. But we weren't.

"We're friends now, right? We can make it work. Be…" He cleared his throat. "Platonic. Whatever you need."

First, I needed to get my stuff out of here. I needed to not be standing in nasty water. And then I needed food before I made a decision about living with my ex-boyfriend.

"I need to get my stuff out of here. Do you think you can help?"

He didn't even hesitate. "Of course. I'm always here for you, El."

LESS THAN TWO HOURS LATER, I'd gotten all of my stuff out of the one-bedroom apartment. I'd only had to toss a few things that were ruined from the water, and with his help, it had been easy to load everything into plastic bins and carry it out. My landlord started pumping out the standing water when we were halfway done, and I cringed to think of what would have happened if I wasn't in a first floor unit. Especially when I had no idea when the damn pipe had burst today, and that water had probably been sitting for hours.

Either way, I wouldn't miss the apartment. He told me he'd let me know when it was repaired and I could move back in, but that it would probably take a few months as the city was short on contractors. I wasn't holding my breath.

"What now?" Owen stood, leaning against his car. We'd loaded up both, and he had all of my bedding and everything that needed to be washed ASAP.

Maybe a few nights at his place wouldn't hurt.

"Okay," I said, nodding to myself.

"Okay, what?"

"Okay, I'll move in with you."

The tightness in his body dissipated quickly. "Thank fuck. I don't like you living here." His voice was almost a growl.

"It'll just be for a few nights," I reassured him. "And then I'll find a place and get out of your hair."

"Sure. If that's what you want."

"*But* we need to have rules." We would have to follow them to make this work. He nodded. I held up a finger. "No sleeping together. We're friends. That means we can't complicate things with sex."

Owen's eyes heated, and I wondered if he was thinking the same thing I was. How good it had been. But that would complicate things. Especially if we were going to be roommates.

"Should we go home then?" He asked, nodding at the two cars. "And then I can feed you dinner."

That sounded perfect. "Yeah. Okay. I should probably get all the wet stuff in the laundry, too."

Calling his home *mine* was strange. It was his private sanctuary, and I was the one intruding. Which presented a whole different problem. We weren't going to sleep together... but that didn't mean he wouldn't want to bring other women over. The thought soured my stomach.

Nodding my head, I turned back to my car. "Meet you there?"

He grinned, not having a clue about what had ruined my appetite. "See you there, Daisy."

IT WAS EVEN LATER when we finally got everything out of the cars and up to Owen's penthouse freaking apartment. It had views of the Seattle skyline, and it was breathtaking. Compared to this, I'd been living in a dump. Luckily, my commute to school wouldn't be too crazy each day, though the traffic would probably be worse now. Still, I'd make it work.

I'd already started my laundry, not wanting anything to mold if it sat too long.

"Pizza?" Owen asked, leaning against the doorframe as I

folded another shirt, tucking it into the guest room dresser. It was a simple room with a pretty floral light blue comforter, and I was pretty sure his mom had picked it out. There were little touches of his family all over the apartment, from the white wolf statue in the living room to the family photos hung on the wall, and the collection of books on his shelves. Growing up spending so much time in the Harper house, it felt familiar.

I nodded. "Pizza sounds great."

"Do you still like pepperoni and olive?" He ran his hands through his hair, his phone clutches in his hand.

"Of course. And some of those garlic parmesan bites?"

He chuckled. "I'll see what I can do."

I blew him a kiss before grabbing another shirt. "You're the best."

Emerging from the guest room thirty minutes later, Owen smiled at me as I slid onto a barstool, watching as he washed a glass in the sink.

"You settling in okay?"

"Yeah." I'd changed into a pair of cozy leggings, slipper socks, and an over-sized t-shirt of my favorite singer. "Thank you again for letting me stay with you." I tucked a strand of hair behind my ear. "Honestly, I don't know what I would have done."

He shook his head. "It's really no problem."

"This place is nice," I said. "It's really you." Looking around the kitchen, I couldn't help but appreciate it. The size, how everything was sparkling clean, with stainless steel appliances and a quartz countertop that matched the overall vibe of the place. It was bright and open and *beautiful*.

Owen's face lit up. "You think? I mean, I've tried to make it feel like home, but—"

"You did a great job."

He grinned. "Thanks. I'll tell my mom you think so."

I rested my head on my hands as I watched him effortlessly move through the kitchen, grabbing a bottle of wine and popping it open. We'd never drank together before the other night at the bar. It was strange to think we'd both missed each other's twenty-first birthdays when once, we'd promised to be there for every important milestone together. It was just one more reminder of how much had changed.

"Wine?" He asked me, holding up the bottle after he uncorked it.

Was it a good idea to have a drink with my ex? No.

Did I need it after the hellish day I'd had? Yes.

Because after wrangling fourth graders for over eight hours a day, and then coming home to find my apartment under water, I needed a lot more than just one glass. But I'd limit myself, because I wasn't sure what I'd do around Owen if I got too tipsy. I wasn't sure I wanted to find out.

Nodding, he filled a glass for me before sliding it over the countertop. I mumbled a quick "thank you" before the door-bell rang.

"That should be the pizza. Wait here. I'll go get it."

I nodded, sipping my wine as I stared at the screen of my phone. Soon, I needed to call my mom and fill her in on what happened. Better yet, I needed to update the rest of my family, because they were all over-protective and a little overbearing. But I guess that's what happens when you're the youngest cousin for the first eight years of your life.

He came back carrying all the boxes, and my eyes widened. There was definitely more food there than either of us could eat. "Hungry?"

He gave a sheepish smile. "I don't normally eat junk during the season. But this felt like a good time to splurge."

"Oh, so I'm just an excuse for you to gorge your face with pizza like you used to?" I teased. The smell wafting through the kitchen was enough to make me moan, but I held myself back.

Owen winked as he opened the first box. "Maybe." It

was an all meat pizza—that had always been Owen's favorite. He grabbed plates, pulling out a slice for him before opening the other box for me. He put two pieces on a plate before sliding over the box of garlic twists and a cup of marinara sauce.

"You remembered."

"Of course I did." Owen's cheeks turned the slightest shade of pink. Cute. He was a massive six foot three specimen of hockey player, with muscles everywhere that definitely didn't exist when we were in high school, and yet he still blushed over stuff like this. This was the boy I'd loved.

Though he definitely wasn't a boy anymore. No, he was all man. Six foot three, muscled to perfection, *man.*

We both grew quiet as we ate, devouring our pizza. I hadn't eaten since lunch, and my meager meal barely even counted as that. I had been trying to save money wherever I could. Meanwhile, my entire apartment could have fit into Owen's living room. It was not lost on me.

"You're still going to come to the home opener, right?" Owen said a few minutes later, polishing off another slice of pizza.

I nodded. "Of course. I wouldn't miss it."

He grinned, and it filled me up with so much warmth seeing that look on his face again. "Good. I'm glad. I'll have a parking pass for you and the ticket, so you should be all set."

"Please tell me you didn't buy me another rink-side seat. I promise I don't need that."

Owen winced. "Not quite. I thought maybe you'd want to hang out with some of the players' wives and girlfriends? Some guys got together to rent a box."

My eyes widened. "A *box?* You want me to sit in the box with the *WAGs?*" I wasn't his wife or girlfriend, and being with all of them felt intimidating.

"I didn't think it would be that big of a deal. They're really sweet." He frowned, rubbing the back of his neck. "I know you just moved here, and I didn't want you to feel alone."

"Oh." I couldn't argue with that. Because it was sweet. And I *did* desperately want friends that weren't fourth graders or co-workers. "Okay." I folded my hands over the counter as I pushed my plate back, done eating. "That sounds really nice, then. Thank you for thinking of me."

He nodded. "Then it's settled."

"Well… What do they think we are? I mean, if they're all wives or girlfriends, are they going to think we're dating?" I didn't want them to think I was just another girl fawning over Owen for his stardom or trying to get into his pants. Even though I had, in fact, gotten into his pants. They didn't need to know that.

"Does it matter what they think?" He cocked his head to the side, in a move that reminded me so much of a dog.

"It does to me." I didn't want to lie if anyone asked me if we'd dated.

He sighed. "I told the guys that we grew up together and you're my friend." That was true, even if it stung that he didn't want people to know about our history. But maybe I'd just hurt him that much.

"Speaking of women," I said, bringing up a subject that made me uncomfortable, but I had to say it. This was his space. I was the one intruding. I fidgeted with the hem of my t-shirt instead of looking at him. "If you want to… uh… have women over, just let me know, and I can make myself scarce."

When I finally looked up, Owen raised an eyebrow. "What do you mean?"

I shrugged. "You're a man. You have needs. I know you're a famous NHL player and you probably have tons of girls throwing themselves at you, but—"

He scowled. "I'm not having any fucking women over, Ellie baby. Not while you're living with me. Okay?"

"Okay," I whispered.

There was that pesky *Ellie baby* again, making my stomach erupt into butterflies. I liked it way too much. More than I should. And it was becoming a problem.

Especially when he was my ex-boyfriend-turned-one-night-stand-turned-roommate.

I couldn't mess this up. Not again.

Cousins Coffee Club

TEXTS

ELLIE

So, I might have had a little mishap today.

PENNY

Oh no! What happened, babe?

ELLIE

A pipe in my apartment burst and the whole thing flooded. It's going to take awhile for them to repair it.

BEAU

The fuck?? That's not good, Ellie Belly.

ABIGAIL

OMG, what? Did you tell Mom & Dad?

ELLIE

Yeah, they know. I called them after dinner.

PENNY

Where are you staying in the meantime?? Did your landlord put you up in a hotel?

ABIGAIL

He better have.

ELLIE

Ah… I'm staying with Owen in the meantime. Just for a few days, while I figure out my living situation.

PENNY

WAIT. You're in my brother's apartment, right now??

PENNY

And I didn't know sooner?

OWEN

We're just friends, Pen. Of course I told her she could stay here.

ZACHARY

Look at that. Guess we DO have the right number.

WESLEY

How many times can we say "Ah, the prodigal son returns" before it stops being funny?

BEAU

At least one more.

OWEN

You three are just as bad as my teammates.

ZACHARY

Yeah, well you love us, so…

ELLIE

Anyway, yes. Owen and I are living together for the time being.

We're roommates, that's all.

BEAU

I'm watching you, Harper. That's my little sister, you know.

OWEN

Bradford, I'd like to see you take me.

BEAU

Did you forget that I'm a professional football player?

OWEN

I'm a professional hockey player.

ABIGAIL

Quiet, boys. We're here to talk about Ellie's problem, not the two of you in some sort of weird alpha male dominant battle.

ZACHARY

And you all wonder why I didn't go into sports after high school…

WESLEY

No, we don't. You're a nerd.

ZACHARY

Hey. That's not fair.

BEAU

Says the guy getting a PHD in History. Nerd.

QUINLAN

You're all insane, do you know that?

Ellie, text me if you need anything. I'm happy to drive up on my days off if you do.

ELLIE

Thanks, Quin. Love you.

Owen

NOW

Having Ellie here in my space was a terrible idea.

For one, because we were trying this *friends* thing, and it was so hard not to touch her. Ever since I'd walked into her apartment to find her crying, that shitty apartment flooded, I'd been fighting my need to go tell the landlord what was up. Especially considering how long it took him to get the standing water out of there.

A lot of her stuff had been soaked, but I thought we could save most of it—at least, the stuff that wasn't on the floor. Some of it had gotten tossed immediately. After I'd gotten everything carried up to my apartment, we'd started the first load of laundry, trying to get any clothes that were wet in so she'd have stuff to wear tomorrow. It was mostly her bottom drawers of the dresser and what was at the bottom of the closet, but still.

If I'd have known she was moving here, I never would have let her rent an apartment there. It already wasn't in a great area of town, and to make matters worse, it hadn't been kept up very well. There was probably a reason the rent had been cheap enough that she could afford it.

But the icing on the cake for all of it was Ellie telling me I could have women over and she'd go elsewhere. Didn't she know there was no one else? That I didn't want anyone else? That had always been the problem. I scoffed at myself, trying to remember when I'd told myself I'd moved on. *Moved on my ass.* The guys were right. And I hated it.

Would there ever be a day when I didn't want her? *Probably not.*

Ellie yawned, stretching her arms over her head as she stood from the kitchen island. "I should probably get to sleep. Today was a lot."

Wasn't that the understatement of the century?

I nodded. "Are you sure you're okay?"

Her lips titled up into a sad smile. "I will be. I can't thank you enough for letting me stay here."

"Least I could do," I reassured her. For her? I'd do anything. That was how it had always been. "I can throw your laundry in the dryer for you, if you want."

"Oh." She blushed. "You don't have to do that."

I raised an eyebrow. "It's no problem, really, El. I know it's been a long day. Let me help."

What, did she think I was going to freak out about seeing her underwear? As if I hadn't been there when she loaded all of her belongings up. Sure, maybe she'd snuck some of those boxes into her car without me seeing, but… It was nothing I hadn't seen before.

"You've already helped so much," Ellie whispered. "I just feel like there's no way I could ever repay you for this."

"Well, that's the good thing about being friends, isn't it? You don't have to."

"Owen…"

"Night, Skater Girl. Get some rest. The home opener tomorrow is going to be fun, I promise."

She nodded. "Night, Hockey Boy."

Then she quickly disappeared into my guest bedroom, leaving me confused, with my emotions all over the place. No one else had slept in that room besides my parents or my sister when they came into town, but I had to admit… I'd enjoyed having Ellie here tonight.

Even if it was the dumbest decision I'd made in a while, because I couldn't have her.

How long would I be able to keep being her friend before I broke? I had no idea. But I had to try.

THE ENERGY in the arena was *incredible*, and we hadn't even stepped foot on the ice yet. You could feel it, even in the locker room. We were all pumped.

Now that training camp was over and all the guys had been sent back to our AHL affiliate team or dismissed, we were back to having our normal number of guys on the team. There were some fresh faces, thanks to trades and free agents we'd picked up, but we had a strong line-up this year—maybe we'd stand a chance to win the cup.

And damn, there was just something that felt different about this season. Maybe part of it had to do with the fact that Ellie was here. When I'd come back from morning skate, I'd found her sitting on the couch, cross-legged with a pile of books in front of her. What was she doing? Working on lesson plans.

It was a-*fucking*-dorable. She chewed on the end of an eraser and I watched her for a few minutes until she noticed me. Then her cheeks turned my favorite hue of pink. God damn, but I shouldn't find her so cute.

Not when her being in my apartment was going to drive me insane. *You can look, but you can't touch,* I reminded myself. We'd dated for a long time in high school without ever having sex. My hand would have to suffice.

God knows it had for the last five years.

My teammates had no idea that I'd only ever slept with one woman. Most of them probably thought the same thing as the media: that I was *with* the women who went with me to events, the ones hired to stand by my side and smile for the cameras. None of them had been anything more than a one-off here or there. I wasn't interested in dating. Honestly, I hadn't felt a connection with any of the women I'd met. Not since—well, I wouldn't let myself go there. It was in the past.

Coach Donovan came into the room, dressed in his suit, and looked across at all of us. Almost everyone was fully dressed and ready to go. A few of the guys just needed to pull their jerseys on over their pads, but liked to wait until the last minute. Athletes were too damn superstitious for their own goods. Thought I'd learned that a long time ago.

"Alright, who's ready for the starting line-up? Kovac's going to start us off for the season. Let's hear it!"

We all clapped and cheered, Brooks giving a few extra hoots as our captain stood up, half-dressed with just his pads on. I loved this little tradition of announcing the line-up in the locker room before each game, and it was even more fun when a special guest was brought out to share the starters.

"In net, number thirty-three... our legendary scot, defender of the goal... Reid MacKenzie!" Stefan fist-bumped our goalie, the two sharing a half hug, before he jogged back to the center of the room.

"Forwards, we've got number fourteen, Jonah Campbell!" He repeated the same motion with each of the forwards he called out. "And number seventy-three... Carter Meyer!" The team clapped three times, cheering for each of our starting players. "Can't forget number thirty-one, Finn Evans!" Another fist bump. Jonah was a new addition to the team this year, while the other two had been rookies last year. They were some of the younger guys on the team, but they had grit and tenacity, which was needed on the ice.

"And on defense, we've got our killer duo... number

seventy-nine, Brooks Hendrix, and number eight, Owen Harper!"

After Brooks, Stefan got to me, slapping our hands together. "Proud of you, Harps. Can't wait to see you kill it this season."

"Thanks, Cap," I said, feeling so incredibly blessed to be here.

It was an incredible honor to be on the starting line-up for the first game of the year. There was something about standing out on the ice during the national anthem next to our Junior Seal—the youth hockey player who got to be a part of the opening ceremony of the game—that was so incredibly energizing.

Tonight would be extra special. And not just because of who was out there for me.

"Are we ready to do this fucking thing?" Coach shouted, and we all cheered. "Go out there, and kick some ass, and remember what we've practiced. You've got this. Keep those pucks out of our zone and get them in the Warrior's net."

"Hell yeah!" Campbell shouted. He was a left winger on our second line, and an all-around great guy. He was a few years younger than me, and last year had been his rookie year after graduating from University of Michigan. "Let's go kick some Warrior ass!"

I chuckled as I stood up, pulling my jersey on. Winning tonight would be a great start for the season, and it would feel great to do it in front of all of our fans.

Plus, I wanted to win for Ellie. Maybe it was me wanting to show off, but I wanted to impress her.

"Someone's happy tonight," Mav muttered. "Is it because your girl is here?"

"Again," I said, repeating my sentiment from the other night. "She's not my girl."

"No?" He smirked, crossing his arms over the Seals logo on his chest. "Then why do you look so goddamn happy?"

"I always look like this," I said, rolling my eyes.

Brooks punched his brother in the arm. "Leave Harps alone. You know how he feels."

I rubbed at the back of my neck. "About that…"

"What did you do?" Maverick asked. At the same time, Brooks said, "See, I knew that *just friends* thing wouldn't last." If there was one thing about the Hendrix brothers, it was that they loved to give me shit. But I knew it was just the way they showed their love.

Shaking my head, I looked down at the floor. "It's not like that. I meant to text yesterday. It's just that with everything that happened, I didn't really have a chance."

"What's going on, Owen?" There was actual concern in Brooks's voice now, and I let out a breath.

"Ellie's apartment flooded."

"Oh, fuck. Does she need somewhere else to live?" Mav frowned.

A low growl came from me before I could think better of it. Because, of course, I was still possessive about this girl. Nothing had really changed, had it? "No, she doesn't need somewhere else to live, Hendrix, because she's living with *me.*" I crossed my arms over my chest. "And everyone's going to keep their hands to their damn selves."

He chuckled. "You're kidding. So you've got your ex living under your roof now?"

I nodded. "Yeah. And you fuckers better not give her a hard time over that." There were a lot of things I would put up with, but not Ellie upset. And the way she'd looked when I came into her apartment, tears staining her cheeks and devastation in her eyes, had almost broken me.

Of course, I'd offered to let her move in. There was no way I was leaving her there. But it was more than that. I wanted her to feel safe here. To feel welcomed.

Five years ago, she'd made the choice to walk away from me. When Ellie had chosen not to come to college in Seattle, not to be with me, she'd done more than broken my heart. She'd stomped on all of our plans, tearing my heart into little pieces. But this was different.

Everything was different now. I didn't want her to go back to Portland. Not when her living here meant I got to take her hiking like we had when we were younger and have her at my games.

"We would never." Brooks grinned. "Now, *you*, on the other hand…"

Rolling my eyes, I picked up my gloves and helmet, shoving the latter onto my head and getting ready to head out onto the ice for warm-ups.

"Let's just go play some damn hockey," I said, starting to understand why Rhodes Larsen was one grumpy son of a bitch after playing on this team for so long. He was probably so tired of them needling him that he'd stopped smiling. Especially considering he was still single and one of the guys who never had a wife or girlfriend at the games for him.

Though, Maverick and Brooks were also single, which might have explained why they felt the need to intrude into my dating life. Or lack thereof. I snorted as I headed out to the tunnel, stick in hand—freshly wrapped, just the way I liked it—and ready to go.

Nothing else mattered.

Not my new roommate, and not how much I wanted to kiss her at any given moment.

Definitely not.

EIGHTEEN

Ellie

NOW

I wasn't sure what I expected when Owen had told me I'd be sitting in a box with a bunch of the wives and girlfriends of the team, but it hadn't been *this*. The box was absolutely insane—there was an enormous spread of food and drinks on the counter, and everything looked like it was brand new. A few high top tables sat in the middle of the room, and there were stairs leading down to the seats that overlooked the 100 level and the ice. It was an amazing view —from here, I'd actually be able to see the plays versus the last game where I couldn't see much. I'd ended up looking up at the jumbotron a lot, but this time, I wouldn't have to.

"This is just… wow," I mumbled to myself.

Someone had escorted me up here, and now that I was actually in the suite—one full of wives and girlfriends of players—I couldn't help but feel intimidated. Because they were all supposed to be here, and I was just crashing the party. I noticed that none of them were wearing their man's jersey, though most of them had some sort of Seals branded gear on. Really, they looked like they were going to the bar versus a hockey game.

It made me feel a little self-conscious in my attire. Last

game, I'd bought a jersey from the Seals shop on my way in, but this game, I was just wearing a pair of jeans, my favorite sneakers, and a turtleneck underneath a Seals Crewneck that Owen had lent me. It still kind of smelled like him, though, so at least there was that.

"You must be Ellie." A redhead smiled at me. She was wearing an oversized Seals jacket with the number twenty-six on the sleeve, and had an adorable baby bump showing. "I'm Lauren Kovac." The name clicked, and I realized she must have been Stefan Kovac's wife. He was the Seals captain, and had been playing with the team for the last decade, drafted right out of high school.

"Oh." I didn't think anyone recognize me. "Hi. I guess I didn't realize anyone would know who I am."

She nodded. "Stefan told me you'd be joining us. Owen wanted to make sure you didn't feel left out."

God, did he have to keep being so sweet? It made me want to do things I shouldn't. Like run into his arms and kiss him senseless. Which was definitely *not* a friend like thing to do.

"This is all kinda overwhelming," I admitted. "Like, I can't believe I'm actually *here*."

She ran a hand over her belly. "Our boys take care of us. We don't rent out a suite every game. Most nights, we just hang out in the wives' room, but this is a special occasion."

"I'm getting spoiled, honestly," I laughed. "Last time, he got me a seat right behind the player's box."

"He's a great guy, your Owen."

"We're not—" My cheeks warmed, but I didn't deny that he was mine. Even though he wasn't. I just nodded. "I don't know what he told you, but we grew up together."

"Not much, honestly. He's pretty closed off about his past. But he's such a warm, easy-going guy, always laughing and cracking jokes with the team."

A grin split my face. That sounded like him. "He's a great friend."

She hummed. "Yeah. I'm sure he is."

Movement on the ice distracted me as the guys came out for warm-ups, circling the ice in their bright blue jerseys. My eyes instantly tracked the ice, looking for the man whose body I knew like the back of my hand.

Just like last game, it was hard to pay attention to anyone but him. He had this contagious grin on his face as he skated around the back of the net with a puck. I imagined what it would feel like to be down there, with the ice under my blades and the cool air in my face as I raced down the ice, but it was gone in a flash. I hadn't skated in a long time. No matter how much I loved seeing Owen in his element, that didn't mean I was going to lace up a pair of skates and join him.

"Warm-ups are always my favorite," Lauren commented, watching me stare at the players. "I love watching them stretch."

I followed her line of sight to her husband, who was currently stretching out his legs in front of the player's bench. Everyone in the arena was probably enjoying the view of all these large, beefy men showing off. I knew I was.

A dark-haired girl laughed from my side. "That's because you always skip out the rest of the game, Lauren."

She furrowed her brow at the newcomer. "Just because I don't stay in the stands doesn't mean I don't watch the rest." She turned back to me, explaining. "I watch most of the games from the wives' room. There's a tv in there, and it's a little more comfortable."

"Is this your first?" I asked. The idea of having kids was still a long way off for me—after all, I was only twenty-two—but I knew I wanted to be a mom one day.

Lauren smiled, a contented sigh sipping from her lips. "Yes. We got married a few years back, but Stef and I were waiting until I finished my degree to have a baby. And, well, I graduated this summer with my master's in Psychology."

"Oh, wow. That's amazing. I'm an elementary school

teacher, so I definitely understand that. Post graduate education can be a *lot*."

"Did you have to do an extra year?" The new girl asked me. She didn't look too much older than me, and I noticed she didn't have a wedding ring on. Which was good—at least I wasn't the only one here who wasn't someone's wife. "My sister is a teacher, and I know she had to."

I shook my head. "No. Thankfully, the university I attended had a program where you could graduate with your teaching certificate as well. It made it a lot easier to get a job after I graduated." Though mostly, that had come down to chance."

"Oh. I'm the worst. Should have introduced myself sooner. I'm Harlow. Jonah Campbell's my boyfriend." Her words had the slightest southern twang to them, something you didn't hear as often up here in the PNW. But then I remembered her boyfriend had been traded to the Seals this season from Nashville, and it made more sense.

"Nice to meet you. I'm Ellie."

"Oh! And this, right here, is our girl Bailey," Lauren said as a third girl joined us at the railing, all of us paying half of our attention to our guys still warming up on the ice, looking more carefree and relaxed than I knew they would during the game. "Her and Mikhail Sorensen got engaged this past summer."

Bailey's hair was light brown, and she gave me a soft smile.

I was treated to a glance of the shiny new ring. "Wow. That's beautiful."

Warm-ups finished, and the guys headed back to the locker room and everyone was chatting up in the top section, grabbing food, or had left to use the restroom before the game started. I'd officially met everyone in the suite, even though I knew there was no way I'd remember everyone's names.

It was a young team, though there were a few older

players who had been around for a long time and were in their late twenties and early thirties.

Everyone was in different stages of their life, and somehow I felt like I fit in here. I didn't feel like I didn't belong because I wasn't Owen's girlfriend or wife. My worries just seemed to melt away.

Leaning on the railing, I pulled out my phone, typing out a quick text. I had no idea if he'd see it, but I still sent it all the same.

ELLIE

Good luck tonight, Hockey Boy.

Butterflies fluttered in my stomach, thinking of our situation. I still couldn't believe that I was living with him. That this morning I'd woken up to an iced coffee on the counter with a note on it.

Gone for morning skate. Will be back later. Have a good morning and try not to work so hard. - O

I had grinned the entire time I drank it, because of course, he knew I was going to work even on the weekends. It was a new school and my first job, and I wanted to prove I was a good fit. So far, I thought I was doing a good job. *Hopefully*.

Everything felt like it was looking up, and I grinned to myself. A year ago, if someone had told me I'd be living with Owen and at his NHL game, I wasn't sure I would have believed them. But here I was. Strangely, it felt like I was exactly where I was supposed to be.

"Hi." A petite blonde, a few shades lighter than mine, and came and stood next to me. Like most of the women in the box, she wasn't wearing team gear, instead wearing a dark green dress with tights. She had heeled boots on, giving her a few inches of height over me, but I suspected we were around the same height without them.

"Hey." I smiled at her, wondering who she was. She definitely hadn't been here for warm-ups, because I didn't recognize her, but she looked around my age—maybe a year or two older, I wasn't sure—and considering the total amount of friends I had in Seattle amounted to my ex and a teacher from my school, I was desperate to make more.

"Haven't seen you around here before," she said, curling her hands around the rail and then leaning backwards playfully. "I'm Sophia. But my friends call me Soph or Sophie."

"I'm Ellie." I slid my necklace pendant across its chain. "This is technically only my second game." Even if I'd seen Owen play hundreds of times when we were younger.

"Ahhh. I see. We've got a newbie." She smiled. "Whose are you?"

I blinked. "What?"

"Which one of them is yours?" She gestured down to the ice, where the first line was currently playing.

A blush warmed my cheek. "I'm not—"

"Oh, give it a rest, will you, Soph?" Lauren came over, sitting down in a chair behind us. She'd grabbed a plate of food and a bottle of water, balancing the former on her belly. "She's Owen's family friend."

"Thanks," I mouthed to her.

Sophia laughed, her cheeks turning a light shade of pink in embarrassment. "Sorry. I tend to forget not everyone here is a girlfriend. My dad is the Coach."

"Oh." I nodded. That made more sense.

"Come on," Lauren said behind us. "Sit down. It's almost time."

I followed Sophia to the black leather chairs and sunk into the seat.

"What's happening?" I whispered to Lauren as the lights dimmed. There was a large archway set up at the tunnel where the Zamboni normally came out, and it was lit up blue and gray.

She smiled. "It's the opening ceremony for the season. This is the best part."

I looked around the arena as the music started playing and lights bounced over the ice as a video started playing on the jumbotron. It was a packed crowd tonight, and it felt like almost every seat in the house was full. The energy was like nothing else I'd ever experienced before, with almost twenty thousand people here for the home opener, and you could tell how much this community loved their team.

Slippers—the team mascot, based on the native Harbor seals—skated out onto the ice. He was mostly white, dappled with gray, with big black eyes and a blue Seals jersey on as well as an adorable pair of flippers for hands. He skated around the ice, along with skaters waving flags, everyone clapping to the beat.

"HELP US WELCOME TO THE ICE YOUR SEATTLE SEALS TEAM!" the announcer came over the loudspeaker. The team's forwards came out first—in numerical order, all being announced individually as they skated to the center circle of the ice, the crowd screaming and cheering for the guys. Even all of us in the suite were joining in, welcoming our men out onto the ice.

Finally, my pulse raced as I realized who was next.

Lauren reached over, squeezing my hand as I spotted Owen's frame underneath the illuminated arch.

"DEFENSEMAN, NUMBER EIGHT, OWEN HARPER!"

He raised his stick as he skated towards the rest of his team, waving to the crowd with a giant smile on his face. God, he was happy. Watching him, I knew I'd made the right decision all those years ago to let him go. To push him towards his destiny. If we'd stayed together, how much would he have sacrificed for me? Would he have even ended up here, playing for the Seals?

We'd never know. But there was not a doubt in my mind that he was supposed to be here.

The rest of the defenseman skated out, followed by our goalies, and then the two assistant captains—Rhodes Larsen, a forward, and Mikhail Sorensen, a defenseman—were next. Finally, our captain, Stefan Kovac, skated out, waving a Seals flag instead of holding his stick. He circled the group before taking his place in the ring, and then the announcer called out, "YOUR SEATTLE SEALS!"

All the men on the ice raised their hockey sticks towards the center of the rink, and then they took off into a lap around the ice, circling their goal.

"Wow." When I finally dragged my eyes away from our team—the guys were settling onto the bench as the starting line-up was announced. "That was so cool."

Sophia nodded. "They always try to find ways to top it every year."

I couldn't even imagine. "I'm already obsessed," I said, laughing.

The starting line-up got called, and there was Owen, standing on the line with his teammates and their goalie. I recognized Brooks at his side. He and Maverick looked similar —especially in jerseys and full hockey gear—but I knew Brooks was paired up with Owen as defensemen. That made it easier to distinguish between him and his brother, who was a forward.

After the national anthem, we all settled back into our cushy seats and it was finally time for puck drop and the game to begin.

"So, how much do you know about hockey?" Sophia asked me.

I turned my attention away from Slippers the Seal who was running around the section in front of us, creating havoc.

I had to admit, he was adorable. And damn, he had some stamina.

"Oh, you know. Enough." Probably more than enough, but I didn't want them to get the wrong idea.

Especially when Owen was my *ex*.

Something that was getting harder to remember. Especially when all I wanted was him. Was this enough? Being his friend and his roommate? Knowing he was only a few doors down from me last night was excruciating. But I'd kept my distance because I didn't want to ruin what we had now. Because I was the one who insisted we needed rules.

Friends or not, he was the only man I'd ever loved.

And sitting up here, surrounded by the wives and girl-friends, I was realizing that I wasn't sure if I could survive without more. I wanted all of it. I wanted his name on my back. To know that I was the only person he'd be coming home to.

The problem was… was it too late? Could I win his heart back, after all this time?

NINETEEN

Ellie

THEN

Summer

ancing Queen by ABBA was playing over the speakers at my seventeenth birthday party, and I was dressed in a blue eyelet lace sundress with a Birthday Girl sash on. It was a warm summer evening, but that wasn't uncommon for July in Portland. My entire backyard was filled with cousins, family friends, and loved ones. It felt like everyone important to me was here.

And I was thankful, for once, that I had a summer birthday. It sucked during the school year, when everyone else got to have cupcakes or cookies on their birthday, and I never did. But this year, I was grateful for summer vacation.

Because it meant my boyfriend was home, and he could be here.

We'd survived our first year of long distance, and it wasn't easy. Not with his hockey schedule and living three hours away. But luckily, he'd come home whenever he could. And this year, I finally had a driver's license. Which meant I could go visit him on long weekends if my parents said yes. I was pretty sure they would—they knew we weren't having sex, and we somehow got away with way more than my brother and sister ever had.

This year, for the first time, I'd missed Owen's birthday, since he'd been back at college in Washington and had a hockey game on the same day. But having him home made up for that.

I never thought I'd be that girl who was sitting around, waiting for her boyfriend to come home, but this year had felt like it was barely creeping by.

Finally, we were in the same place for more than just a long weekend and I intended to take full advantage of that.

Even if I had no idea where he was at the moment. Since the rest of my guy cousins were suspiciously absent from my party, I assumed they were all together in my parent's basement, most likely playing video games.

"Happy Birthday, El!" Another girl I trained with at the rink came up to me, wearing a short purple sundress with her dark hair pulled back in a braid.

"Hi, Brigitte," I said, hugging her. "Thanks for coming."

"How's your summer been?" she asked, running her fingers through her dark hair. At the rink, she often had it in a slicked back bun.

"It's been great," I offered. "Working on college applications and stuff. You know, the usual."

She nodded. "Oh, I remember that well. I'm so glad that's behind me." She was going to UC Berkeley this fall, a school that was well known for their figure skating program. "What are you going to do about your boyfriend if you go to a different school?"

I frowned, because I hadn't really thought about that. Of course, I'd applied to go to the same school as him. I'd applied to the University of Portland, too, my parent's alma mater, which was also where Penny had applied. She was lucky enough to get free tuition, though, since her dad was a professor there.

I couldn't imagine going somewhere where Owen wasn't. Namely, because the distance was feeling so big.

"We'll make it," I promised, though my voice came out shakier than I meant for it too.

"Gosh, it's been weird not seeing him at the rink this year. You two were always glued at the hip."

It *was* weird, but that was because I was so used to our routine. Us sitting on the bench together. Owen tying my skates for me. Now, I normally sat on the bench before my ice time with a pair of earphones in, listening to my favorite playlist before getting on the ice.

I bit my lip. "Yeah. I know. But he's having a great time up in Seattle." And it didn't hurt that he was going to college in the same city where he'd been drafted to play in the NHL. Though looking around here, I couldn't imagine my life away from home. Yes, I'd applied there, but was that what I wanted?

Yes, I scolded myself. *That's what you want. Owen is what you want.*

Quinlan, Penelope, Bianca and Avery were all gathered around the dessert table, and after thanking Brigitte again for coming to my party, I sauntered off towards them.

"Anyone seen Owen?" I asked, grabbing one of my Aunt Noelle's brownies—she'd made them for me by request—and taking a bite.

"Right here," his voice called out, deep and soothing against my ear. It was strange to think that it had gotten deeper in our year apart, but I was pretty sure it had. Even with endless calls and FaceTime sessions, nothing beat this, having him in person.

He took the rest of the brownie from my hand and ate it.

I laughed. "That was mine."

Owen licked his lips. "It was good."

"Your mom has always made the best ones."

He chuckled. "One of the things I missed the most this school year."

"Oh yeah?" I asked. "What was the other one?"

Leaning in close, his breath warmed my face, and I could smell him—like forests and ice and all *man.* "You."

Stepping up on my tiptoes, I pressed my lips against his cheek. "I missed you too, Hockey Boy."

"And that's our cue," Quinlan muttered to the rest of my cousins.

I giggled as Owen wrapped his arms around my waist.

"They don't want to see us make out, Birthday Girl," he whispered against my ear.

"Mmm." I hummed. "Maybe we should find somewhere more private." I trailed my fingers up his chest. He was wearing a t-shirt and a pair of shorts.

He wiggled his eyebrows. "Treehouse?"

A laugh burst out of me. Sure, we'd made out in the treehouse more than a few times, but *now*? "Everyone's in the backyard, Owen." My cheeks felt warm as I dipped my head down, trying to hide my face from his view.

His lips pressed against my bare shoulder. "Not everyone…"

I groaned. "You're killing me."

Spinning around, I leaned against Owen's shoulder. He wrapped his arms around me, swaying the two of us slowly. It was getting late, and the sun was finally setting, the sky painted in cotton candy streaks. It was beautiful.

"Are you excited about college, Daisy?" he asked, holding me tight.

My heart leapt. "Yes. Just have to get through my senior year, and then I'm all yours." Even if I was nervous about uprooting my entire life, I would never be nervous about him. We were solid. I loved him more every day.

He hummed. "I like the sound of that. You and me, just

the two of us…" His lips brushed over my ear. "Just the way I want you."

"*Owen.*" My voice came out breathy, even to the sound of my own ears. It was crazy how just being around him made me want to straddle him. But we had no privacy here, and I knew it. So, as much as I wanted to lose my virginity to him, as ready as I was, we were waiting. Luckily, making out and dry-humping weren't off the table, assuming we were alone. Which, like I'd pointed out, we were not.

"I know," he murmured, squeezing my hip.

But God, I wanted that. To live with him. To fall asleep in his arms and wake up next to him. The future was so far away, even if it felt like it was right there. Within reach, yet out of my grasp.

For now. I turned, wrapping my arms around his waist. He kissed me softly, leaning our foreheads together.

"One day, Ellie Bradford, you're going to be all mine. You can count on that."

But that was the thing—I already was.

If only I had known that in a few months, everything would change. That being his—really, truly his—would come at a cost.

One I knew I couldn't let him pay.

TWENTY

Owen

______

NOW

We won the game in overtime, 3-2, bagging our first official two points of the season against the Vancouver Warriors. I'd gotten my first assist of the season tonight, too, a pass to Maverick that he'd sunk in the net, and I was riding a high. Sure, I was exhausted—physically, at least—but I could never seem to fall asleep right away after a game.

"That was insane," Ellie said, cheeks pink with excitement as I unlocked the door to the apartment hours later. "I can't believe how crazy of a game that was. I was on the edge of my seat practically the entire time."

"I'm glad you were there," I said, stretching my arms out as I followed in behind her.

Had I played better tonight? Who knew. Though there was something *contagious* about her presence that had me all amped up. I'd already showered at the arena before heading out and finding Ellie, but I knew exactly where I was going to end up the moment we said goodnight. Which was *wrong*. I definitely shouldn't fist my cock while thinking about my ex-girlfriend and current roommate.

But when I'd seen her there tonight, wearing that smile just for me?

Fuck. I was all twisted up inside. I knew exactly what the guys would say. My phone would blow up with texts any time now. The next time we all went out for beers at the Penalty Box, I was sure I wouldn't hear the end of how I'd dropped everything and moved Ellie into my house. But how could I not?

I could use the excuse that she was like family. That our mothers had been best friends since college, and I still remembered peeking over the baby stroller at a tiny, sleeping Ellie and feeling like I needed to protect her. It was different than the way I'd protected my own sister, Penny, though I'd kept plenty of assholes from dating her when she was in school too. I just hadn't understood my feelings until I was much older. Until one day I'd blinked, and I'd realized she'd grown up. We both had.

Still, somehow, I didn't think that reasoning would fly with my teammates. Not when that was too close to the truth.

She yawned. "I should probably get to bed. I'm just glad tomorrow is Sunday and I have a day to sleep in before I have to teach a bunch of rowdy elementary schoolers again."

"Probably." I rubbed at my forehead. "I should turn in myself. Lord knows my sleep schedule is going to change drastically once our road trips start."

Normally, I looked forward to them each year. Sometimes it felt like we were spending every night in a different city, flying to our next stop after each night's game. It took everything in me to crawl into bed those trips before I passed out. When we played back-to-backs, especially multiple in a row, it was grueling.

Now, it would be grueling for a whole different reason.

"Oh." Ellie blinked. "I guess I forgot that you'd be gone."

Though I *hated* the sound of that. Her all alone in this big place? I knew how lonely it was. It was why I'd considered getting a dog all this time, though I hadn't wanted to leave it alone multiple times during the season. Now, though… It was perfect. A way to make sure she wasn't alone, even when I was on the road.

Filing it away for later, I focused on the woman in front of me, forcing out a laugh. "Yep. You'll have the apartment all to yourself when I'm gone, Ellie baby." The endearment slipped out before I could think better of it. *Doing a great job of with being friends, Owen.* I scolded myself. *She set rules. Follow them.*

"Yeah." She gave me a small smile. "Don't worry though, I won't bring anyone home."

A growl formed in my throat and I stepped closer to her.

"Owen." Her voice was breathy. "I'm not going to—"

Another step, and her back pressed up against the wall.

"No. You're not. Because there won't be anyone else. Not for either one of us."

Ellie shook her head.

"Tell me." I dipped my head, brushing my lips over her ear. "Tell me you're not going to go out with anyone else while I'm gone."

She bit her lip, her words coming out as a whisper. "I'm not going to go out with anyone else."

"Good." I nodded, and our eyes held for a moment. My gaze darted down to her mouth, and I watched as she ran her tongue across those soft, pink lips. It was impossible not to notice how she did the same.

I cleared my throat. "I should go to bed."

"Right." She let out a breath. "Me too." Ellie slipped out, dashing towards her room.

Fuck. I rubbed my hand over my face as I headed into my bedroom.

What was I thinking? I had no right to control what she did. She wasn't my girlfriend. We were just friends. But the idea of someone else taking her on a date made my blood boil. It made me want to fight, and I'd never considered myself to be an aggressive person.

But Ellie was mine. She always had been.

I flipped on the light, surveying my room. It was pretty basic, but it was enough for me. No one else had ever shared my bed, slept on my sheets. All this time, there had only ever been one girl for me.

The one who was sleeping a few doors down from me. The one who broke my heart.

The one I couldn't have.

I wasn't sure how much longer I could ignore the pull I felt to her. Especially when she looked at me like she wanted me to kiss her.

And damn, did I want to stop pretending that I didn't want that too.

WE PLAYED Calgary three nights later, and I came home to find Ellie asleep on the couch, the TV channel still turned on to the one that broadcast the game.

I liked her watching me, even when she wasn't in the arena. Part of me wanted to insist that she come to every game, that she was always in the stands cheering for me, but I knew that was a lot to ask of her. Especially when she had to leave early each morning to teach.

Normally, on game days, I'd wake up right before morning skate and head there, but now, I got up early just to have breakfast with her. Otherwise, I'd hardly see her all day. She would come home from school, eat dinner, and then hole herself up in her room each night. I hated it, because there was this wall between us that hadn't been there before.

Grabbing the remote off the coffee table, I turned the television off before scooping Ellie up into my arms, blanket and all, and carrying her into her room. She nuzzled her head against my chest, and damn, having her here was everything. Pulling back the comforter, I tucked her into bed, stepping back to watch her sleep. Was it creepy? Maybe.

Her eyes fluttered, and then they were blinking up at me. "Owen?"

"Hey, Skater Girl. You fell asleep on the couch."

She looked like she was fighting to stay awake. "Oh."

"Good night." I leaned forward, pressing a kiss to her forehead.

"Night," she mumbled, curling up and letting her eyes drift shut again.

God, she was adorable.

Tomorrow, I'd have to get on a plane. At least this time, it was only one game, and then I'd be home. That wouldn't last, though. Our first road trip of the season was looming in front of me, and I already didn't know how I was going to be apart from her for almost a week at a time. No part of me wanted to leave, but this was the life I'd chosen. We had three games to play against the California teams, and unfortunately, our first back-to-back game of the season.

Curling a finger around a blonde strand of hair, I tucked it behind her ear. I didn't know what was happening between us, but I knew I didn't want things to go backwards. I wanted to do so many things with her. To take her skating again. To take her out to dinner the way she deserved. To care for her the way she deserved.

Things I fully planned to do… as soon as I was back.

"GOOD MORNING." Ellie yawned as she reached for the coffee cup, standing up on her tiptoes. A tiny strip of bare skin showed between her tank and her pajama shorts, and I tried not to focus on it.

An impossible feat, but hey, I was trying.

"Morning," I said, voice rough as I sipped on my cup of coffee.

"What time do you have to leave?" Her tone was casual as she poured coffee into a cup, grabbing a bottle of creamer from the fridge and adding it till her drink turned a light brown shade.

I looked at the clock. "Soon." There was still time before I needed to head out, but not much. Not that it would stop me from getting in a few more moments with her. "I'll be back tomorrow night, so you'll only be alone tonight."

She nodded. "It'll be fine. I lived alone before, remember?"

I grumbled under my breath, not liking to think about her last apartment. "Have they given you any updates about that place?"

Ellie bit her lip. "No, but it sounds like it'll be a few months before it's ready, anyway. Besides, I was going to look for somewhere else to live. I can't keep mooching off of you forever."

"Sure you can. I don't mind you living here. It's nice that it's not so quiet anymore."

"Owen…"

"Stay, Ellie. Please."

She sighed. "Okay. Just until it's done."

I grinned. "Good. Now that's settled, I'm going to go shower and get ready."

"You have to wear a suit, right?" Her eyes brightened.

"Yes," I laughed. "Just like I have to for every home game."

Humming, she took a sip of her coffee, walking back towards her room. "Say bye before you go."

"You just want to see me in my suit, don't you?" I raised an eyebrow.

"Maybe." Ellie smirked, walking backwards. "It's been a long time since I've seen that ass in tweed. Who knows, it might look completely different now?"

"Ellie," I warned, my voice low. *What were we doing right now?* "Careful, or I'll think you're flirting with me."

"And if I am?" She winked. "See ya later, Hockey Boy." Ellie blew me a kiss. "You're gonna kill it in Toronto, I just know it." I liked her faith in the team. In me.

Chuckling, I headed back to my room, hopping in the shower and getting ready for the day. My overnight bag was already packed—though I didn't need much, since it was a quick trip.

When I came out, Ellie was dressed in a pair of slacks, a brightly colored cardigan, and a white blouse. She had pulled her hair back into a low bun, and was humming to herself as she rummaged through the cabinets while eating a cup of blueberry yogurt. I knew it was her favorite, so I'd stocked up when I ordered groceries earlier this week.

I ran my hands through my hair as I watched her dance around the kitchen, clearly unaware I was watching her. She had a pair of earphones in, and was quietly singing along to her music as she packed a lunch.

This was why I didn't want her to move out. In these moments, it felt like I could see the rest of our lives. The life we would have had together if she hadn't walked out on us five years ago. If we hadn't broken up then, would we have made it? Would our lives be completely different now? Sure, we were still so young, but I'd known back then that I wanted to marry her one day.

She was my friend again—though she'd always been that. My best friend, my first girlfriend, the only woman I'd ever loved. But she was also my roommate. My ex-girlfriend. The woman who'd broken my heart.

It had taken a long time for me to put the pieces back together. And considering how hard it had been to move on, how it had taken promises of one last night together for me to realize I needed to get over her, I'd never be able to repair my heart if it got broken again.

So, as much as I could see our life together, a part of me knew it wasn't meant to be.

Not anymore.

Not if there was a chance she'd leave again.

Not when she could shatter my heart in a million pieces and leave me all over again.

TWENTY-ONE

Ellie

NOW

So, how's it been?" My teacher friend, Maggie, asked me. She was sitting on the edge of my desk during our lunch period, munching on an apple as I picked at my lunch.

"How's *what* been?"

"You know. Living with your super hot, childhood ex-boyfriend turned NHL hockey superstar."

I grimaced. "Oh, that." I'd confessed to her about my living situation earlier in the week, something I was trying not to regret now. "It's…" Living with Owen was a lot of things. Confusing, mostly.

Because some nights, like when he tenderly picked me up and carried me into bed, it was so easy to pretend that nothing had changed. And this morning, flirting in the kitchen over coffee felt so… *normal* and domestic that it made my heart ache.

Because I wanted that. And even though there were a few moments where it felt like Owen wanted that too, I knew the truth. He'd moved on. We were just friends.

Reasons I should try to find a new place and planning to

move out. But how could I, when he'd begged me to stay with those big, brown puppy dog eyes of his? He'd always known exactly what to say to get me to cave. It was how he'd dragged me on so many hikes when we were younger.

I sighed. "It's great. I don't know." I traced circles on my desk, not making eye contact with her. "It's his first away game of the season tonight." My first night alone in his apartment.

"And how are you feeling about that?"

Biting my lip, I tried to assess my feelings. "Fine." I think. "It's not like I'm so used to his presence after barely a week that I can't function alone anymore. Besides, after I work on lesson plans and class stuff each night, it's all I can do to crawl into bed and pass out." Tomorrow was Friday, so I still had one more day of school before the weekend.

She hummed, her dark ringlets bobbing as she popped another piece of apple into her mouth. "Whatever you say, homegirl."

I laughed. But as much as I *was* fine by myself, it was also true that I missed Owen. Already. He'd been gone for a few hours—hours that I didn't normally see him—and I already wanted to text him.

Undoubtedly, I knew what I'd be doing tomorrow night. I had a date with Owen's giant flatscreen TV. Again.

The other night, I'd fallen asleep on the couch after watching the post-game interviews, hoping that Owen would appear, but he hadn't. Which he must have noticed, considering he'd picked me up and carried me to bed when he got home. But he hadn't mentioned my TV activities, and I hadn't mentioned how warm and cozy I'd felt in his arms. At first, I'd thought I was dreaming when I'd nuzzled against his hard chest, but nope.

Owen Harper had tucked me into bed, and I had barely been awake enough to appreciate it.

Sometimes, it all felt like a dream. Maybe I'd hit my head

on something when my apartment flooded, and I was going to wake up and find out I'd hallucinated all of this.

"Ellie."

"Huh?" I looked up from my desk at my friend. She looked amused, and I frowned. "What?"

"You've got a bit of drool…" Maggie pointed at my face. "Right there."

My cheeks warmed, and I batted her hand away. "I do not."

She giggled. "You really like him, don't you? Like, I know you said you two dated when you were younger, but…"

"Yeah." I looked over at her. "It's different now, but he's still the same Owen that I fell in love with, you know? But it doesn't matter."

"Doesn't it?"

I furrowed my eyebrows. Nothing was going to change. No matter how much I wanted it to. No matter how much I enjoyed seeing him in a suit. Sexy as sin, even when I was watching him leave. God, I hadn't been able to pry my eyes away from him this morning after he'd said goodbye.

I didn't want to go another five years without talking again. We'd avoided talking about our one night together after my graduation. About the note he'd left. *I wish things were different.* That was all it had said.

Now, I was the one who wished things were different.

"No." I shook my head. "We're friends now. And roommates." And that was enough.

"Alright. Well, I'm here for you when you need to talk." She scrunched her nose. "Or if you need to complain about living with a man. I lived with my brother for long enough that I totally understand."

A laugh burst out of me. "Thanks, Mags. I'm glad I have you as a friend."

She gave me a warm smile. "Me too, Ellie. I'm glad you got the job."

I was too.

No matter what else happened, I was thrilled I ended up here.

SATURDAY MORNING, I woke up to Owen in the kitchen, making pancakes and looking surprisingly chipper. Which shouldn't have been that much of a surprise considering the Seals won their game last night—they were now 3-0 for the season, which was good—but I had no idea why he was awake this early.

Or why he was making breakfast.

"Morning?" I questioned, sliding in next to him to get a cup of coffee. He always made a pot, and even though I absolutely detested black coffee, adding in copious amounts of creamer and flavorings, it was at least tolerable. I preferred ice coffee from his mom's shop, but I wasn't in Portland anymore.

"Morning. Thought I'd make breakfast." Owen flipped a pancake in the pan as I stirred my coffee with a spoon.

"Yeah, I see that."

He was wearing a t-shirt and flannel pajama bottoms, and even with hair mussed from sleep, I couldn't help but notice how handsome he was. The white cotton fabric of his shirt clung to his muscles, and I really needed to stop checking him out.

"Do you have any plans today?"

This felt like a trap, but I *didn't,* so I couldn't lie to him. "No." I trailed off, taking a drink of my coffee as I slid onto one of the barstools at the island.

"Great." He grinned. "Then we're going out."

"*Out?*" I repeated, furrowing my brow. The question in my word was obvious, but he ignored it.

"Uh-huh. Wear something warm."

It wasn't even that cold outside yet, though I'd definitely started wearing tights under my dresses when I wore them to school, and I didn't leave the house without a sweater or one of my favorite cardigans on. Perks of teaching elementary school was I could dress cute *and* functional. I hardly ever wore slacks, preferring dresses and skirts.

Still, I couldn't think of a single reason I'd need to dress warmly right now.

"What do you have up your sleeve, Owen Harper?" I asked, narrowing my eyes.

His only response was to slide a plate of pancakes my way. He'd topped them with blueberries, and god, why did he have to remember all the things I'd loved when we were kids? The blueberry yogurt in the fridge was bad enough, but this?

"You'll see." He picked up his own plate, scarfing down bites of pancakes.

When we were both finished, he put our dishes into the sink.

"I guess I'll go shower," I said, feeling full of pancakes but also slightly sticky. Though, honestly, my days were always a little sticky. Maybe that just came with working with kids, though.

Owen nodded, heading towards his bedroom. "Alright. I'll do the same, and we can head out when we're both ready."

"You're really not going to tell me where we're going?"

He grinned as he reached his door. "Nope. Today is all about you, Ellie baby."

And then he disappeared into his bedroom, leaving me standing in the hallway, staring after him, my heart going pitter patter in my chest.

That was that, I guess. Wherever he was taking me, I was in for a surprise.

I just wasn't sure if I liked that a little too much.

"WHAT ARE WE DOING HERE?" I asked an hour later, blinking in confusion as I stared at the complex where the Seals practiced. The parking lot was empty, and neither one of us had gotten out of the car. I was just staring at the building.

"Skating."

He'd told me to dress warm, so I'd pulled on a comfy pair of leggings and an oversized light blue sweater. This wasn't a *date*, and I wasn't dressing up to impress him. Luckily, he hadn't dressed up either, wearing a pair of jeans and a navy hoodie. Now I knew why.

I frowned. "*Owen.*" Panic filled my chest as I imagined stepping out onto the ice. About everything I'd left behind five years ago. "I can't."

He reached over, grabbing my hand and squeezing it. "You can."

I shook my head. "You don't understand."

"Then help me understand." His voice was rough. "Please. Don't shut me out, Ellie."

Instead of answering him, I opened the door, sliding out of the car before taking a few steps. Wordlessly, Owen joined me, guiding me inside. He'd grabbed a bag out of the car, draping it over his shoulder.

We didn't speak. Maybe he could sense there was something I was holding back, but he didn't pressure me. He just walked beside me until we were standing in front of the rink.

Wrapping my arms around my chest, I held myself tight. "I haven't skated in—"

"I know." His voice was soft. "But don't worry. I'll be there every step of the way."

Could I do this? Because it felt like a lot more than just stepping onto the ice again.

"I don't even have skates," I whispered. My old pair were probably somewhere in my parents' house, though I hadn't used them in years.

Owen winked. "Don't worry. I've got you."

He guided me onto the bench, kneeling in front of me as he unlaced my sneakers.

And then he pulled out a box that he must have stashed in his bag, and my heart stopped.

They were beautiful, brand new, and top of the line. I recognized the brand from my figure skating days. These were way too nice.

"Owen." My voice caught. "When did you…"

"When you told me you'd stopped skating." He rubbed the back of his neck. "I probably shouldn't have, but—"

"No." I reached down, pulling one of the white skates out and holding it in my hands. I'd have to break them in, but God, I loved them already. And it would be a shame if these skates didn't get worn. They deserved to be on the ice. "I love them." I shut my eyes, tears welling. But I wouldn't cry. Not over ice skates, and not over him buying me them.

Owen's warm hand cupped my chin, and I opened my eyes to find his. "Why'd you stop, Ellie baby?" He asked, his voice soothing. Like he was trying not to spook a scared animal.

"You know why," I whispered.

He shook his head. "Not because of me." There was hurt on his face.

What could I say? There was so much we hadn't talked about. But once we got it all out in the open… would he even want me around anymore?

He took the skate out of my hand, guiding my foot into it. How many times had he laced up my skates when we were younger? Owen knew just the way I liked it. And clearly, he hadn't forgotten, either. Maybe it was like muscle memory. As easy as riding a bike.

"We can't keep avoiding talking about it, El," he said. And god, how tender he was being was making it worse. Because all I wanted to do was to bury my face against his chest. To inhale his scent that felt like home.

I closed my eyes as he placed a soft kiss to my knee after finishing lacing up my second skate. "I know."

Owen sat next to me, pulling on his skates as we sat in silence. I couldn't spill everything now. It was too raw. If I did, I'd be revealing everything to him. And I wasn't ready for that.

So when he stood up, holding out his hand for mine, I took it.

"I've got you," he told me again as I hesitated at the wall.

I bit my lip. "How do you get back on the ice after an injury? Knowing it could happen again? Knowing that it was one of the most terrifying things that ever happened to you?"

He shrugged. "Same way you do everything, I guess. Put one foot in front of the other. Remind yourself that the world isn't over. Pick yourself up and dust yourself off. Try again."

Was it really that easy? To just… start over? Maybe it was. I thought about moving here. How much courage it had taken to do that. His eyes held mine, warm and brown and full of understanding.

I'd gone to therapy after my accident, back when my anxiety felt crippling. It had helped some—enough to go back to my life—but I'd never skated again.

Owen stepped onto the ice, skating backwards as I stood, a death grip against the wall.

"One step at a time, Daisy. You can do this." He held out a hand, and I swallowed roughly. "Five minutes. Just give me five minutes."

I took a step, and the blade underneath me made contact with the ice. Everything else faded away as I pushed off, skating towards Owen. There was only him and me, and suddenly, the years didn't matter. I just focused on him.

Maybe it would have been easier to turn around and flee

if I was as uncoordinated as a baby deer on the ice, but it felt like I'd built it up in my head to be this big thing and it just… wasn't. I was fine. The world wasn't ending. I was still standing on my own two feet. I could still breathe.

"That's it," he murmured as I took his hand. "That's my girl. I knew you could do it."

My cheeks warmed, but he pulled me in close enough that I could see every color swirling in his eyes and feel the press of his body against mine. And god, I missed him. In a way I *shouldn't*. His hands. His mouth.

And I was all too aware of how close together we were on the ice. If anyone came in, they'd get the wrong idea. I pulled away—not letting go of his hand—and tested out my skates. It was a long way to go to where I'd been, at the top of my game and hoping to compete nationally, but at least I was here. On the ice. Skating. Mostly.

In all this time, we'd mainly been staring at each other.

Then Owen grinned, a mischievous look on his face that I remembered from when we were kids.

"Race ya! Fastest one wins!" He dropped my hand, speeding off down the ice towards the other end.

"That's not fair!" I protested. "You're a professional hockey player."

He winked at me as he came to a stop over the blue line. "Guess you'll just have to try to keep up, huh, Skater Girl?"

I scowled, finally skating towards him, catching up to him quickly.

"Come on." He extended out his hand again, interlacing our fingers before we skated together, making a lap around the rink.

We went slowly, like he knew I wasn't ready to race over the ice yet. But his taunt had worked. And I wasn't worrying about falling or getting hurt like I had been the last time I'd tried to get on the ice. After my accident, I'd had a panic attack the first time I tried to go back to the rink. The next time I'd tried to go back, I couldn't even start the car. So I'd quit.

Just like I'd quit on him.

"I'm sorry," I offered.

It wasn't enough. But it was a start.

Owen

NOW

Something about the look in Ellie's eyes as she stepped onto the ice didn't sit right with me. I knew I had missed a lot. But it was clear, looking at her now, that I had no idea just how much. So I did the only thing I could think of to get her mind off of it—taunted her. Challenged her. When we were younger, we'd raced across the ice countless times.

So, I held her hand and watched her as we took a lap around the ice.

I'm sorry. Fuck, she had no idea what she did to me.

"You don't have to apologize to me, Ellie. I… I wasn't there. I should have been there."

She shook her head. "No. I do. I didn't let you be there for me, Owen. And that's on me."

But I could have fought for her. I should have fought for her. I'd let her go, and I was the one who hadn't been around. Avoiding being home clearly hadn't done me any favors. But she was here now.

She'd come to find me.

And it was my turn to be there for her. As her friend, I was going to help her through whatever she was struggling with.

I squeezed her hand. "It's in the past now, though. Now you have me. Okay? I'm here."

Her eyes met mine, and it would have been impossible to miss the moisture in them.

Tugging her hand, I spun her into my arms, wrapping her up in a hug.

Damn, I was glad I'd rented out the iceplex for the day. The fact that no one was going to walk in on our moment, to interrupt this, was worth how much money I'd donated.

"Okay." She let go of my hand, skating away from me, and I was transfixed. I'd always been whenever she was on the ice. She was still graceful as she skated—there was no amount of time that could take that from her—but she was hesitant. Reserved now, in a way she'd never been before.

Still, she'd done the hard part. She'd gotten out here. I was damn proud of her. She was so brave. Moving to Seattle, alone? She said it was for the job, but I suspected that was only part of it. But if I thought too much about that, I'd start wanting things I couldn't have.

But how could I hold myself back? It was so hard to keep denying the truth: I wanted her. So much. One last night hadn't been enough to temper my desire for her. It would never be enough with her.

I wanted *more*.

Leaning against the wall, I watched as she took another lap around the ice all by herself. *That's my girl.*

Her cheeks were pink, but her lips had curled up into the smallest of smiles as she closed her eyes, like she was feeling the breeze flowing past her, the ice underneath her blades. *Beautiful.* She was always stunning, but I couldn't keep my eyes off of her now.

When she finally came to a stop in front of me, I couldn't stop grinning.

Ellie smiled. "Thank you. I… I needed that."

"Anything," I promised. "Anything you need, El. I'm always here."

I meant it.

HOURS LATER, we were riding the elevator back up to my apartment. After leaving the rink, we grabbed burgers and fries from my favorite spot in Seattle. I was grateful that we didn't have a game tonight, and that I'd been able to spend the day with her.

It felt like old times, except... *better*, somehow. Maybe it was because we were older. Or maybe it was just because I knew what life was like without her.

"Today was honestly the most fun I've had in a long time," Ellie said, stretching her hands over her head.

Her earlier apprehension and anxiety seemed to be gone, which I was grateful for. "I'm glad." I grinned. "We should do this again."

She snorted. "Sure. With your schedule, you'll have *plenty* of time." Ellie rolled her eyes, and I stepped in closer, cupping her cheek with my hand.

"For you? Of course I will. I'll always make time for you." Our faces were a few inches apart, and it would be so easy to kiss her. God, I wanted to. Those soft, lush pink lips were calling my name.

Her tongue darted out, moistening her lips. Did she want this the way I did?

She gave a sharp exhale of breath as her eyes darted from mine down to my mouth, and I leaned in, a breath apart, when—*ding*.

The elevator doors opened.

Goddamn.

Ellie's cheeks were pink as she slid out from between me

and the wall, and she said nothing as she unlocked the apartment.

"Ellie—" I started, wanting to talk about what just happened. That we'd almost kissed. The fact that I still wanted to kiss her.

She rushed towards her bedroom. Strange that in less than two weeks, it already felt like hers. "I'm gonna catch up on some work. I'll… Thank you again for today." Her door clicked shut, and I groaned.

"Fuck," I groaned as I headed back to my room. Alone, like always. Frustrated and aching because the one thing I wanted was the one thing I shouldn't.

It was getting harder to hold myself back around her, especially when the only company I'd had for the last few months was my own hand. Hell, the last few years.

Why was I holding back and resisting this, when I knew damn well she was the only woman I'd ever wanted? The only one I'd ever loved.

Was it really so simple as just… telling her what I wanted? Thinking about her small smiles today, the way she'd been so hesitant until she finally got comfortable on the ice, I let my thoughts wander. What if we tried again?

But I knew how dangerous hope was.

How devastated I'd been when she left the last time.

Why did it always feel like one step forward and two steps back with us? When all I wanted was *her?*

I should have kissed her. I'd known it as soon as the moment passed. When we were younger, I would have done it without thinking. But then again, years ago, everything had felt so easy between us. Nothing felt easy now. Not since she'd walked out on me.

Even though I was a fucking asshole who had done the same thing to her. I hadn't been around to see the hurt on her face when she'd woken up alone. No, I'd left a note like a coward. And then I'd hightailed it out of town, even though I had time off of hockey and didn't need to be back in Seattle for weeks. I should have stayed with my family.

But I'd known that seeing that look on her face would kill me.

And today, I knew nothing had changed. That I still wanted her just as fiercely as I had months ago, and now with her in my space, everything was worse.

Maybe I needed these road trips for some space. To remind myself why I couldn't have her. She didn't want this life. She'd made that clear when she'd ended it.

Seals Singles

OWEN

I have a problem.

REID

Ah, there it is.

MAV

I've been waiting for this. Lay it on us.

OWEN

I want more.

BROOKS

I'm not hearing the problem, my dude.

OWEN

The problem is, we agreed to be friends.
Sleeping together would complicate things.
And you know our schedule.

REID

Plenty of guys are in relationships and play in the NHL, Harps. Nothing is stopping you.

RHODES

Why the fuck am I here?

RHODES LEFT THE CHAT.

MAV ADDED RHODES TO THE CHAT.

MAV

Solidarity, man. We're helping Harper through his problems.

OWEN

I can't wait till the day comes when you have a woman in your life and you have to eat your words.

MAV

Nope. Never going to happen.

BROOKS

So, why don't you just ask her out, dumbass?

OWEN

Are we all just ignoring the fact that we're leaving for a road trip soon? Not exactly an ideal time here.

When would it ever be? That question bounced around my head. And fuck, but it sucked that it was true. How could I possibly give her the life she deserved when my entire life was hockey? I was damn good at it, and I loved it, but was that enough?

At one time, I knew what my answer would have been. *No.* It wasn't enough. Not without her.

OWEN

Besides, she doesn't want me like that.

REID

How do you know? Did you ask the lass?

Dropping my phone on the bed, I rubbed at my temples. Did I ask Ellie? I let out a snort. *No.* I didn't need to. She was the one who insisted that we couldn't sleep together.

Though, that was before.

Before I'd seen her walk around my apartment in those tiny sleep shorts. Before I'd woken up each morning to find her in my kitchen, eating breakfast in her adorable teacher outfits. Before I'd started getting up even earlier so I could make her fresh coffee so I could have just a few minutes more with her each day. Before I'd bought her new ice skates and taken her to the rink because she told me she hadn't skated since her accident.

And fuck if I didn't know what to do with all of that.

Deciding I wouldn't make any good decisions this evening, I shed my clothes on my bedroom floor, heading towards my large shower. I turned on the water, letting the cold spray wash over me. It was the shock to my system I needed to clear my head.

Except thoughts of Ellie crept in, and there was no denying myself. Not when I'd been half-hard all day, and just the thought of her smile had my cock weeping. Yes, I wanted that. Wanted her. I imagined what it would be like if she was in the shower with me now, her lips wrapped around my length as she sucked me down. Wrapping my hand around my shaft, I braced my other hand against the wall.

"Fuuuck." The vision was too good to hold back. Especially when she ran her fingers over her clit, touching herself as I slid in and out of her warm, wet mouth. I couldn't help but think about the way she'd felt wrapped around me, the little noises she'd made when I made her come.

"Ellie," I groaned, shutting my eyes as I fucked my fist harder. Goddamn, I was only seconds from exploding. I needed release, and badly. This was wrong—thinking about my ex, my roommate, my *friend*—like this, but I couldn't stop myself. Not when it felt so damn good. She was everywhere, invading my senses. When I came home from practice, she was on my couch. Her scent lingered everywhere, flowery and intoxicating, and I wanted to bury my face in it.

So close, and—

"*Oh*." A squeak came from outside the shower, and my head whipped up, my hand still fisting my cock. My eyes connected with a pair of blue-gray ones.

Ellie. Fuck. *Shit.* I let out a grunt as I squeezed my dick.

"I'm *so* sorry," she said, her eyes wide. "I just came to ask a question, and the door was open, and—" Her cheeks were bright red as she stayed in the same spot, watching me.

She watched me with rapt attention, her tongue darting out over her lips as I fought to keep my cock under control. Her eyes flared with heat, and—

"*Ellie*." I let out another grunt, turning to face the wall so she couldn't see the entire length of my body. "Please." I didn't know what I was asking for. Her to get out, or to come in?

Her face flamed even further. "Ohmygod. Right. Sorry. I'll just—" She turned and hightailed it out of there, and I slammed my fist against the shower wall, pumping faster.

Something about her watching me, the way she looked so turned on herself, drove me to orgasm quickly.

And the only thought flashing through my mind was, *I am so fucked.*

TWENTY-THREE

Ellie

NOW

*W*hat had I been thinking?

I hadn't. That was the only explanation why I'd stared at him like some sort of peeping tom, watching him moan my name as he jerked off in the shower.

Knowing that he was probably in there right now, finishing himself off, made my face flare with heat.

God, I hadn't taken the time to admire his naked body before. Not properly, at least. But he was *magnificent.* Half of his body was turned to the wall, but I could see his fist pumping his cock, and I remembered what it felt like to have him thrusting inside of me. Watching him, knowing it was *my* name on his lips, *me* he was thinking of…

All I wanted was to slide in there beside him. To run my hands up his muscles, feel his skin underneath my palms, his—

"Ellie." Owen came out into the living room wearing a pair of gray sweatpants and a clean white t-shirt. The hint of a tattoo peeked out under his shirt as he moved, and I tried to remember if I'd seen it before.

My cheeks were still warm. "H-hi."

He ran his hands through his still damp hair. "We should talk."

I nodded, covering my cheeks with my hands. "I'm sorry."

Earlier, he'd almost kissed me. I ran my fingers over my lips. That was what I wanted, right? So why was I avoiding him? Because I was a scaredy-cat. And maybe I had been for the last five years. That was why it had taken me so long to get back on the ice. I'd let my fear and anxiety rule my life, and it had held me back.

Well, no longer.

"You said you had a question?" He crossed his arms over his chest like he was waiting for my answer, and the motion made his muscles flex.

"I—" My mouth was dry. I blinked at him. "What?" I wasn't sure my brain was working properly. Backing up till my legs hit the couch, I sat down, studying his face. He looked frustrated. Maybe we both were.

Owen padded over to where I sat, placing one hand on the cushion on either side of me. "A question," He repeated.

"Right. I…" I bit my lip. "Earlier, in the elevator. Were you going to kiss me?"

He groaned. "Did you want me to kiss you, Ellie baby?"

I did. And I was tired of denying it. To myself, to him. "Yes," I whispered.

His frame was still positioned over mine, caging me in.

"Do you still want me to kiss you?"

I ran my tongue over my bottom lip. Was this insane? *Yes.* Did I care?

"Yes."

Owen cupped my cheeks, his eyes reading mine like he was looking for an answer in them.

"Fuck it." His lips met mine, coaxing me open, and I savored the feeling of his mouth on mine. It had been so long since I'd really been kissed by him, and tonight, I didn't want to rush things. Then he was lifting me up, pulling me into his lap before settling onto the couch.

It wasn't a slow, hesitant kiss. This was filled with need.

Needing to be closer to him, needing to feel his hard body under mine. I placed my hands on his chest, squeezing his pecs lightly as his tongue swept over mine, caressing every inch of my mouth.

A small moan slipped from my lips as he kissed the side of my lips and then down my neck, and I rocked against him, needing more friction. I could feel his length underneath me, already half hard, and it wouldn't take much for me to come like this.

I whined, thrusting my hands into his dirty blond locks, guiding his mouth back to mine. Nipping at his bottom lip, I ground down, letting my head tip back and shutting my eyes.

"Ellie," Owen groaned, his hands finding my hips as he thrust up against me.

"Oh," I gasped. Just a little more—

A phone beeped, and it was like a bucket of ice cold water splashed on us. The realization of what we'd been doing, that I'd been so close to coming on his lap, and how easily this could ruin everything made worry pool in my stomach.

"We shouldn't do this." He pulled back.

My heart sunk as I crawled off of him. "Fuck, Owen. I'm sorry. I shouldn't have—" I covered my face with my hands, not wanting to look at him.

Not after he'd stopped us. Not when he was basically rejecting me. Of course, he didn't want this. Of course he—

"No." His hands gently rested over mine, and he pried them away from my face. Those brown eyes I loved were full of worry and concern as he shook his head. "I'm sorry. You're my roommate and my friend. I'm trying to do right by you."

I bit my lip. It was me who'd said no sex, that it would complicate things. But God, it was so hard to resist. We both wanted each other so badly.

"You *are* doing right by me, Owen," I said, resting my hand over his heart. "You always have. Maybe that's always been our problem."

He furrowed his brow. "How so?"

I sighed. "Can you look me in the eye right now and tell me you wouldn't have given up hockey—given up *everything*—for me?"

Owen's furrow turned into a frown. "What do you mean?"

"I mean, if I'd have asked you to pick. Me or hockey. Me or this life. What would you have picked?"

"Ellie, that isn't fair." No, it wasn't. Because life wasn't that simple. But that was the problem, wasn't it? Life was complex. It wasn't black and white, easy decisions to make. And making the one to end our relationship had broken my heart, too.

"I know it's not." I shook my head. "That's why I never wanted you to. Because this life, Owen… This life was *meant* for you. You're so smart, but you're so talented at hockey. And you love it."

He reached out, like he was going to touch me again, and then realized what he was doing, dropping his arm.

"You were always destined for this. I couldn't hold you back."

Owen shut his eyes. "You never would have. You were supposed to come *with* me. We were going to do it together. All of this."

I gave him a sad smile. "And if you'd gotten traded before I graduated? What would I have done?"

"We would have figured it out."

"Owen…" my voice was quiet.

He shook his head. "*That's* why you ended it? Why you…" His voice cracked. I'd never seen him like this once before. Like he was devastated. "Then why are you *here*, Ellie? Why did you come to Seattle?"

I swallowed roughly. Where did I even start? I wasn't ready to confess all my truths. Not yet.

"Why now?" He continued. "What changed?"

"I-I just…" I looked to the floor. "I *can't*." The confession was hardly more than a whisper.

He sighed, standing up from the couch, dragging his hand up over his face. "Never mind, then. But Ellie, I can't…" He grimaced, like this was causing him physical agony. Maybe it was. My heart ached more than it had in years, and all I wanted was to confess the truth. Every bit.

But what if he didn't want to see me anymore? What if he asked me to leave? After everything we'd been through, I thought that would be unlikely, but the idea still haunted me.

"I can't do this—*us*—until you're ready to talk to me. But I'll be here, waiting." He cupped my face, running his thumb across my cheek. "I always have been, Ellie. I've always been waiting for you to come home to me."

Tears pooled in my eyes. "I'm sorry," I said. It was all I could offer. He didn't deserve this. He deserved someone better than me.

He sighed. "You know where to find me when you're ready." Wiping under my eyes, he dropped his hand, wordlessly walking back to his bedroom.

Doing the same, I curled up on my bed, trying not to cry. I'd done this to us. I'd ruined our chance of happiness years ago, and that was my fault. Why did it hurt so much? Why couldn't I just tell him how I felt?

It shouldn't have been this hard.

I'll be here, waiting.

I always have been, Ellie.

I've always been waiting for you to come home to me.

Home. He was my home. He always had been. Maybe that was why moving here hadn't felt like a crazy decision or a big life change. Because it meant I was closer to him.

The boy who'd stolen my heart in the ninth grade and never given it back. Even if it took me much longer than that to tell him I loved him, I always had. And I always would.

That was something that would never change.

A FEW DAYS LATER, I was dismissing my class for the day when my phone buzzed with a Washington number I didn't recognize. Pocketing the device, I finished saying goodbye to all the kids as they each headed out of the classroom.

Owen had left for his road trip this morning, and it had been strange watching him walk out of the apartment, knowing he wouldn't be home for several days. His face flashed in my mind—that goofy grin and blond hair that he let grow longer during the hockey season. As soon as my classroom was empty, I pulled out my phone, sitting in my chair as I opened the text thread.

UNKNOWN NUMBER

Hi. It's Sophia—from the game last week!

I smiled. Even if I'd felt like an outsider at the beginning, I had really enjoyed being in the box with all the WAGs—and Sophia Donovan, the coach's daughter. She was twenty-four —close to my age—and it felt like she needed a friend as badly as I did.

ELLIE

Hey! How's it going?

SOPHIA

Good. I got my dad to ask Owen for your number. I wanted to invite you to hang out tonight.

Oh. Really?

Yeah! I had a lot of fun. It's refreshing having someone my age who isn't in a relationship with one of my dad's players to talk to.

I snorted as I typed out another message.

Yeah, I bet. I remember what it was like being surrounded by hockey boys growing up.

See, I knew I liked you for a reason!

Anyway, I'm having a little get-together tonight with some of the other girls at my place. Since the guys are out of town, I thought we'd do something fun. Would you want to come?

My fingers paused over the keys for a second, but then I wondered why I was hesitating. Did I want to go back to Owen's empty apartment *alone?* Not really.

I'd love to. Just send me the address, and I'll be there!

YAY. Amazing. Can't wait to see you!

With that, I shoved my stuff into my purse, hurrying home so I could change into something a little cuter. There was a skip in my step that I didn't have before, and I just felt... *lighter.*

A grin filled my face, and even though it was overcast and rainy when I stepped outside to my car, it felt like the sun was shining down on me.

"ELLIE!" Sophia raised her hands up, looking excited to see me. And a little tipsy. "You made it!" She slung an arm around my shoulder, and I smiled at her. Her light blonde hair was curled and loose around her shoulders, and she was wearing a pretty teal blouse with a pair of jeans.

"Hi. Thanks for inviting me."

Looking around her apartment—though that was probably an understatement, even compared to Owen's—I noticed quite a few of the women I'd met the other night were here, wine glasses in hand as they chatted on the couch. The hockey game was on in the background, but no one seemed to watch it. It reminded me a lot of home, back when I'd find myself at one of four different houses on any given night, hanging out with my cousins and best friends.

"Of course!" She guided us into the kitchen, grabbing another wine glass out of the cabinet and filling it with a white. "Normally, Lauren plans these things, but since she's pregnant, I'm giving her a break." Sophia glanced over to the Captain's wife, sitting in the living room with one hand resting on her belly as she chatted with the other wives and girl-friends. She was due in December, during the season, which I was sure was hard for her.

"This is such a nice place," I said, appreciating the giant kitchen as she handed me a wine glass.

Sophia gave me a little shrug. "When I told my dad I wanted to move out two years ago, after I graduated college, he refused to let me get an apartment unless he approved it first. Whatever that meant." She rolled her eyes, adding quotation marks in the air around the word approved.

"And this was the place he chose?" My eyes were wide. It was huge. I didn't even want to know what it cost, much like where I was currently living. Thank God Owen hadn't asked me to pay anything, because I definitely couldn't afford it.

I got the idea that Coach Donovan was pretty protective of his daughter. My dad was the same—I was pretty sure he was going to kill me when he found out about the apartment I'd rented originally. I'd avoided telling my parents the worst of it, though they knew I was staying with Owen after it flooded. There was no way to get out of telling them that, especially when I talked to my mom basically every day.

She snorted. "Yup. He's also paying more than half the rent, since my salary doesn't cover all of this." Waving her hand, she gestured to the apartment. "I definitely didn't need something *this* big, but he insisted." Sophia sighed.

"Wow."

"Such is the life of a coach's *only* daughter. I'm his baby. I'm surprised he even let me get a job outside of the team. When I went to school for exercise science and told him I wanted to be a personal trainer, he about fell over himself, saying I could be one of the team's trainers." Sophia took a long drink of wine. "Now, enough about me. Tell me about you and Owen."

"There's not much to tell. Our moms are best friends, and we grew up together. And we dated in high school, but that was a long time ago." I blushed, thinking about how he'd kissed me three nights ago. A kiss I couldn't get out of my mind.

"I knew it."

"What?" I frowned.

"I knew there was something more between you than just being *family friends*." She smirked. "No wonder he asked if you could be in the box with us."

I opened my mouth to say something, but two of the other girls—Harlow and Bailey, from the box—popped into the kitchen, interrupting us.

"Soph, you're totally monopolizing Ellie over here!" The brunette, Bailey, looped her arm through mine. "And we're supposed to be watching the game."

Sophia did her best to look sheepish, but I could tell that she absolutely did not feel bad about it. Not that I blamed her.

Looking over at the TV, I saw the score was 2-1 Los Angeles. I was too far away to track who was on the ice, but I hoped the guys could bounce back. I knew how much they hated to lose, even though it was just part of the game. No one was out here with a twenty game win streak, but they'd won their first four, so I knew they were hoping to keep up the momentum.

"Ellie was just about to tell me all about her and Owen and how they used to date," Sophia said, and the two girls turned to me.

"I—" My heart leapt as I saw number eight skate off the bench and onto the ice for a shift. *Owen.* The LA players were surrounding our net, taking shots on goal, and Owen hit the puck out of the Seals' end, sending it down towards their red line for an icing call.

I let out a breath when he hopped back onto the bench less than a minute later, and the camera panned over our guys. Brooks Hendrix was sitting next to Owen as they reviewed the game footage. The player next to him—number 20, according to his jersey—was chewing on his mouth guard, and I wrinkled my nose at the sight.

"Earth to Ellie." I was poked in the arm.

"Huh?" I looked back at the girls, realizing I'd zoned out. "Oh. Sorry. I just—"

"We've all been there," Lauren said. "You get used to it."

Biting my lip, I looked away from the screen. They had no idea how many games I'd watched of Owen's, or how many times I'd watched him go down from a hard hit. He'd always gotten back up, and thankfully, he'd never gotten seriously injured, but that fear was always there. "I used to go to all his games," I admitted. "We used to practice at the same rink, too."

"Shut up, you skate?" Sophia brightened. "I practically grew up on ice skates. I think my dad was secretly bummed I wasn't a boy, so I could follow in his footsteps and play hockey, but I learned really young. Tried hockey for a few years, too, but it wasn't my style."

"Yeah." I nodded. I hadn't talked about figure skating in a long time. For the first time, it felt like it didn't hurt as much to talk about my past. "I actually used to be a competitive figure skater."

"Wow. Did you ever think about going to the Olympics?" Harlow asked, tucking her hand under her chin.

"Yeah. But it wasn't in the cards for me." I gave her a weak smile. Even if it didn't hurt, I still didn't want to talk about my injury with all of them yet. "I stopped skating my senior year of high school."

Bailey placed her hand on my upper arm and squeezed lightly. "You're a teacher, right? I remember Lauren mentioning that."

I felt a rush of relief at the change of topic. "I am. This is my first year of teaching, since I graduated this spring. I'm teaching fourth grade over in Bellevue."

"Oh, that's a great district to teach in," Harlow piped in. "They're some of the best schools in the state."

"Are you living near there?" Sophia asked, looking at me with interest.

I grimaced, explaining the story of how my apartment flooded. "Luckily, Owen said I could stay with him. So, we're roommates. *Strictly platonic roommates.*" Roommates who kissed, apparently. It hadn't even been two weeks yet since I'd moved my stuff in, and we were already doing terrible at this friends thing. Not that I could complain.

Sophia giggled, waggling her eyebrows. "And they were roommates."

Bailey rolled her eyes, grabbing Sophia's now empty glass of wine. "I'm cutting you off, sister. What would your dad think if we let you get drunk?"

"I'm twenty-four. I'm a big girl," she pouted. "Besides, I can take care of myself. It's not like he can watch over me every hour of every day. Especially when he's gone half the season on away games."

We all ended up moving over to the couch during the middle of the second period, halfway through regulation. Everyone chatted about their upcoming team Halloween party—one I was enthusiastically invited to as they planned out the details—and it felt like everyone had some sort of honing radar on the game whenever someone was about to make a goal or whenever the goalie made an amazing save and everyone would cheer.

In the end, the game was 3-3 and went into overtime, securing them a point. Though thirty seconds in, the Los Angeles forward scored on our goal. Our first loss of the season, and I knew that would be a rough start to the road trip.

By the time I got back to the apartment from Sophia's, I was dead on my feet. It was late, and I had to wake up early for class in the morning. I hadn't realized how quiet the apartment was without Owen until he was gone.

Was it weird that I missed him? In just a few weeks, I'd gotten so used to living together, to having him home every night when I got back from teaching. Though, I'd been missing him for the last five years, so this wasn't any different, not really. At least now we were friends. I could text him while he was gone. And it was only a few more days.

The ice skates still sat in the same spot they'd been since we'd returned from the rink last weekend, and I still couldn't believe he'd bought them. That he'd remembered what I said that first night in the bar.

I could still feel his kiss on my lips days later. And as hard as it had been, we'd needed to have that conversation. He was right, not that I wanted to admit it. I needed to come clean once he got back from his road trip. Maybe then we could finally move forward. After changing into my pajamas, I went into the kitchen to grab a glass of ice water and noticed Owen's door was open—just a crack.

I couldn't help but sneak in. God, I shouldn't be in here. I knew it was wrong—especially when we kept insisting we were just friends. Just two friends who were roommates, who *definitely* had never seen each other naked before or kissed like the world was ending. It would have been easier if I could pretend I'd never felt him inside of me.

The last time I'd been in here had been when I'd caught him in the shower, and I hadn't really taken the time to appreciate his space before. How *him* it was. Trudging over to his bed—his sheets and comforter were blue. No surprise—I pushed his pillow up against my face, inhaling deeply. It smelled like him—like ice and trees and that spicy masculine scent I loved. If I could bottle up his scent like cologne, I would.

I missed him so much.

Sitting on the edge of the king-sized bed, I almost moaned at how soft it was. This bed was *heaven*. Sure, his guest bed was comfortable, but nothing like this.

And then, even though there was a small thought in the back of my mind that knew it was wrong, I curled up under his sheet, hugging his pillow to my chest as I promptly fell asleep.

Cousins Coffee Club

TEXTS

ZACHARY

Bummer on the game last night, O.

QUINLAN

You looked great out there, though!

ELLIE

At least they got a point. And it's still the beginning of the season.

PENELOPE

Our resident hockey expert is here to school us all.

BEAU

Is anyone watching *my* game tonight?

ABIGAIL

Sorry, Beau. I'll be on a flight.

QUINLAN

To be fair, you didn't watch Owen's game either.

ABIGAIL

What can I say? I'm an equal opportunity
sports hater. I'll cheer for you if you make the
Super Bowl though, little brother.

BEAU

I'm less than three years younger than you,
you know.

ABIGAIL

So? Doesn't mean I can't give you shit.

BEAU

Love you too. 😌

ELLIE

Where are you headed, Abs? I haven't heard
about the latest trip.

ABIGAIL

A quick trip to Paris to meet with a boutique
that's interested in stocking my designs. I
doubt it'll pan out, but if they do, that would
be amazing.

Plus, you know. It's an excuse to get authentic
French food.

ELLIE

I'm jealous. I'd love to go abroad sometime.
I've still never been out of the country.

OWEN

Thanks, fam. I appreciate the support.

Even if it comes with a reminder that we lost
in OT.

Just got back to the room after post game
press and everything.

ZACHARY

Anything for you, my man. We miss you down
in Portland.

WESLEY

You still owe us drinks after bailing in May.

OWEN

Yeah, yeah. I'll be home during the holidays
and we can all go out then.

LUCY

Just rub it in that everyone else is legal except
for me, why don't you.

ABIGAIL

One day, cuz. I promise it's not as exciting as
it seems.

OWEN

Speaking of drinks, Beau, while I'm down in
your neck of the woods, we should grab one.
We have tonight off, so maybe I could swing
by the game with a few of the guys.

BEAU

Just let me know, and I'll get you tickets.

I'd love to see you, man.

OWEN

Bet. Let me talk to them and I'll let you know.

ZACHARY

What are we, chopped liver?

WESLEY

Apparently this is what we get for not being
professional athletes, Z.

BEAU

You know you two could fly down and visit
sometime. I have a guest room. It's always
open.

QUINLAN

They just like to complain.

ABIGAIL

And don't we know it.

LUCY

Sometimes I feel like I'm surrounded by
children.

ABIGAIL

You say that like I'm not ten years older than
you??

ZACHARY

She's an old soul.

WESLEY

Whatever that means.

ZACHARY

We're used to it by now.

LUCY

I'm rolling my eyes at all of you.

ELLIE

It's a good thing I keep my phone on do not
disturb during class, otherwise my students
would think someone was dying.

ZACHARY

Yeah, yeah. I gotta get back to the library
anyway.

WESLEY

Can't let your rival beat you, huh?

ZACHARY

No. She's infuriating.

ABIGAIL

You can just admit that you like her, Zach. It's
okay. Those are called feelings, and all
humans have them.

OWEN

While this is amusing, I have to go. Team meeting.

Miss you all. Talk soon.

TWENTY-FOUR

Owen
—————

NOW

*B*eing in California was really putting things in perspective for me. Especially when I watched my teammates call their wives and girlfriends, turning in early from the bar each night.

Last night, I'd met up with Beau. Brooks, Mav and Reid had all jumped on the opportunity to go to the California Cougars game with me, and I was always happy to see him play for once. Our seasons overlapped, and it was unfortunate that I couldn't make it down to see him on the field more. He'd always been one of my best friends, and I was still grateful that hadn't changed after his sister and I had broken up.

But would it change everything if we started seeing each other again? And what would happen if it ended badly this time? Our families were so close. Our moms were best friends, for fuck's sake. It would tear our families apart if something happened between us. I'd already been on the outside for the last five years, barely wanting to go home. Avoiding seeing the guys or spending time with the group because I knew she'd be there.

And now I was all alone in my hotel room, staring up at the ceiling. It was quiet. It didn't smell like Ellie's shampoo. She wasn't sitting on my couch, leafing through papers or reading a book. I was alone. And I hated it even more than usual tonight. Disappointment flooded through my veins. This wasn't enough. Not anymore.

Maybe that was why I picked up my phone, typing in a text. I was making more of an effort to be present in the cousins group chat, but I wanted to talk to her, too.

OWEN

Hi.

ELLIE

How's it going?

Good.

I caught the game tonight. Nice shot on goal. Bummer that it didn't go in.

Yeah. I'm trying not to beat myself up about it. There's always next time.

At least we'd won, though. That was better than our first road trip game. Sure, losing in overtime was better than in regulation, but it still sucked.

Also, I forgot to tell you this the other night, but thanks for giving Sophia my number. We hung out, and I had a lot of fun.

No problem. Coach asked, and it was the least I could do.

Sophia and I were friendly, but I wouldn't have called us friends. Not when Coach Donovan made it exceptionally clear to every guy on the team to stay away from his daughter. Not that I was looking.

I'd only ever had eyes for one girl.

Ellie's words flashed through my mind. *This life, Owen… This life was meant for you. You're so smart, but you're so good at hockey, too. And you love it.*

I loved you, I'd wanted to tell her.

But I'd meant what I told her, too. Because as much as I wanted her—I always wanted her—I couldn't start something if she couldn't tell me the truth. It was bad enough that she was in my space, overriding all of my thoughts. Smelling so fucking good all the time and looking so pretty. Plus, there were those tiny little sleep shorts and the way her nipples poked through her thin tank tops.

I groaned at the thought, resisting the urge to palm my cock until my aching erection subsided. *Fuck me.* I was a damn fool. All I wanted was to kiss her again. And again. And again.

No matter what she said, no matter how much her words rang true, I couldn't keep lying to myself that I didn't want her anymore.

You were always destined for this. I couldn't hold you back.

> When you get home… I think I'm ready to talk.

> I miss you.

> > I miss you too, Skater Girl.

> > Get some sleep. I'll talk to you in the morning.

> Night, Hockey Boy.

> > Sweet dreams.

I already knew I'd be dreaming of her.
I always did.

"SO, two weeks with your new *roommate*, huh?" Brooks asked me in the locker room, leaning against his stick. "How's that going?"

We were all suited up and ready to play against Anaheim. It was our last game of the road trip, and I was ready to get home for *multiple* reasons.

One of which, *yes*, was Ellie. It had been so hard to walk away from her the other night, especially when it had been so obvious that we wanted each other. But no matter how much I wanted her, I couldn't be the one to put my heart on the line. Not again.

I rubbed my hand over my jaw, which was rough with stubble. "It's… nice, honestly." I'd forgotten how nice it was to come home to someone else. To have someone to eat dinner with and talk about my day.

Maybe that was the problem. I liked it too much.

"And?"

I frowned. "And what?"

"And? Have you told her how you feel?" Brooks asked, nudging me in the side as I grabbed my helmet.

"He's asking if you two have fucked yet," Mav interjected, giving me a shit-eating grin.

I punched him in the arm. "No."

Brooks rolled his eyes at his brother. "You're ridiculous. You know that?"

He shrugged. "We're all thinking it. You saw his texts. What did you say, Harps? *I want more?*"

Fuck. Why did I have to confess everything to these guys? Looking across the room, I knew the answer. Besides my family, they were my best friends. And over the last few years, I'd spent so much time with them that this team had become my family. Blowing out a breath, I fitted my helmet on my head, antsy to get out onto the ice and start warm-ups. I was eager to burn off some of my excess energy.

"It's complicated," I said. I'd wanted to insist it wasn't like that, but… it was. The problem had never been me wanting her. It had always been her wanting me.

But there was this spark between us that no amount of time could erase. I could still feel the press of her lips against mine. How soft they'd been as I'd coaxed her mouth open. But falling into bed together wouldn't solve our problems, no matter how badly I wanted it. Craved it.

I shut my eyes, trying not to think about the look of hurt on Ellie's face when I stopped us from going further that night. Pumping the brakes had been the right call. I knew it in the deepest recesses of my brain, as much as my body disagreed.

Reid made a noise in the back of his throat from behind me as we funneled out of the away locker room and headed towards the tunnel that would take us out onto the ice. "Complicated my arse," he muttered.

"Mac, you ready to shut this place down?" One of our rookies, Andrei, shouted at Reid from the back of the line. He'd had our last game off, with our alternate goalie—Matthias Farkas—starting in the net against LA.

Goalies were some of the most intense people I'd ever met. They spent the entire game out on the ice, staying completely focused and in the zone. If a puck got past them, it wasn't just on them. It was also on us as defense for not getting it out of the zone and protecting them better.

Hockey wasn't just about one guy on the ice—it was about all of us as a team. Win together, lose together. When someone was off or someone went out because of an injury, all of us felt it. Which was why we all felt last night's loss. But that was the nature of the game. We just had to be at the top of our game. We couldn't afford to be making sloppy mistakes or letting the opposing team get a bunch of scoring chances.

Reid grinned as he pulled his goalie mask on over his face. "Damn right I am, boys. Let's go play some hockey."

"Hear, hear!" Brooks shouted.

Stefan gave his nod of approval, his eyes bright as he surveyed the team. Rhodes was at his side, that permanent frown on his face even with the A on his chest. Grumpy fucker, but he was a damn outstanding hockey player. It was an honor to play on the team with both guys.

Our fifteen minute warm-up period went by fast, per usual. Maverick was first, knocking the pyramid of pucks that sat on the boards onto the ice, and Reid was behind me. We circled the net, each taking turns shooting a puck towards the net, Reid doing his best to block all our shots. I did a few passes before skating over to the bench and bouncing a puck on my stick. At home, I'd normally throw it back into the stands. There were still some Seattle fans here tonight, but it was nothing like being on home ice.

And it was nothing compared to having my girl in the stands, knowing she was there. I wanted her to come to another game, but she hadn't asked, and I didn't want to force her. She seemed to have a good time with the other wives and girlfriends, and Sophia *had* gotten her number to invite her to hang out, but still. We were roommates and just friends. Except that kiss…

I shook the thought from my mind. Thinking about Ellie was a distraction, and I couldn't afford that. Not when I wanted that cup so badly I could taste it.

The timer ticked down on our warm-up period, and I skated off the ice, heading back towards the locker room. Brooks knocked his shoulder into mine as he caught up with me, not saying anything. It was just our quiet show of support with each other.

We weren't on the starting line tonight, which meant that when we came back from warmups, both of us slid onto the bench next to each other. We'd be ready to hop into play fairly quickly as soon as the first shift on the ice finished.

I bounced my leg as we sat, watching the puck drop.

Rhodes won the face-off, and the guys took off down the ice, passing the puck around Anaheim's players, but it was stolen before they could make a shot on goal.

"You're extra jittery tonight," he muttered. "Need to expel some excess energy, Harps? Maybe Mav is right, you do need to get laid."

"Hey," I groaned. "Not you, too, Hendy." I adjusted my sleeves, pushing them up to allow the cool air from the ice to hit my wrists and lower forearms. "It's not like that."

"You don't want to sleep with her?"

"*Fuck*." I was so fucking glad we weren't mic'd up regularly for games. If we were, we definitely wouldn't be having this conversation on the bench. "Of course, I do. But there's more to it than that. And this isn't the place to talk about it."

"Breathe, man." He patted my shoulder. "It's all going to work out."

I nodded, hoping he was right. Once we were on the ice, my mind would clear. The game always helped me achieve clarity, to get that crystal clear focus I needed to get through each shift.

A few moments later, Coach called out the line change and Brooks and I both hopped over the boards, skating out onto the ice and quickly throwing ourselves into the play.

I blocked a pass made by the other team and sent it sailing back down towards our ice. *Icing*. Damn. The whistle blew, and we reset, taking our spots at the face-off circle.

By the end of the first period, we were still 0-0. Anaheim's defense was solid, and I was pretty sure I'd pulled something in my shoulder during a shot I'd blocked. I tried to massage it during the intermission, but it wasn't bad enough to keep me out of play. At least we had tomorrow off, and I'd be able to rest. I shut my eyes as I sat back against the wall in the locker room, willing myself to focus on the game ahead and not the girl I'd left behind.

THE APARTMENT WAS dark as I trudged inside, tired down to my bones from the last week of travel and sleeping in a hotel—not to mention playing three games. I rubbed at my shoulder, which was still aching despite seeing the team chiropractor after the game and being checked out. That last body-check against the boards had really done a number on me.

God, I couldn't wait to crawl into my bed and fall asleep.

I didn't bother turning the lights on in the apartment—it was late, and I was sure Ellie was already asleep, especially since she woke up before six most days to get ready for school.

We'd both always been early risers, though these days, I got up early just to spend time with my roommate.

Two weeks had passed since she'd moved in, and it felt so *right* coming home to her.

Opening the door to my bedroom, I dropped my duffel bag on the floor, the clothes from my body quickly following behind. I'd clean them up tomorrow. Right now, I just wanted to sleep.

I froze as I heard a light moan and the rustling of sheets. Looking up, the light from outside illuminated my bed, and there was an unmistakable lump under the covers.

The moonlight caught on honey blonde strands of hair. *Ellie*. In my room. Sleeping in my bed.

What was she doing in here? I marveled at the sight for a minute, because it felt so right. Had she missed me like I'd missed her?

Slowly, I pulled the covers back, sliding in beside her. I was grateful that she'd always been a deep sleeper and didn't wake up, even as I wrapped my arms around her.

Pulling her tight against my body, I buried my nose in her hair, reveling in her scent. In the feel of her soft, lithe body pressed against mine.

I wasn't ready to give her my heart again, but damn if I wasn't halfway there already.

Exhaustion took me, and I fell right to sleep, holding the love of my life in my arms.

TWENTY-FIVE

Owen

THEN

Sophomore Year

ELLIE

Come outside.

I stared at the text on my phone for a minute, wondering if I was dreaming. If this was real. It was November, and I'd been back at college for a few months. The hockey season was in full swing, and I did my best to keep on top of classes, practices, and games.

Never mind trying to keep up with a long distance relationship. I felt guilty I couldn't talk to her more.

But she was here?

I rushed down the stairs, throwing the door open and finding Ellie standing in front of me.

"Hi." Her cheeks were flushed as I stared at her.

"Hey, El." I couldn't believe she was standing in front of me. God, it felt like an *eternity* since I'd left for school, even though it had only been a few months. Hockey season was keeping me busy, and there were more than a few nights lately that I'd passed out before I could call her or talk to her. "What are you doing here?"

She wrapped her arms around my middle, practically burying her head between my pecs. "I missed you."

I chuckled, leaning down to inhale her scent as I hugged her back. "I missed you too, El."

More than she could ever imagine. I'd never imagined it would be so hard to be away from her. Maybe I'd just taken it for granted, living next door to her for my entire life, but damn, I couldn't wait for her to be up here in Seattle, too. In Portland, everything had been so easy. Now that we were a state apart, it had gotten harder to find time for us. Even just hanging out wasn't as simple as it used to be.

Curling my hand around her chin, I tilted her face up till her eyes met mine. "I'll be home in a few weeks for Thanksgiving, you know."

"I know." Ellie's blue-gray eyes held mine, and she bit her lip. "I just wanted to see you," she admitted. "And now that I have my license, I convinced my parents to let me come up for the weekend."

Bending down, I rubbed my nose against hers. "I'm glad you're here." I grabbed the duffel bag off her shoulder and draped it over mine instead. Weaving our fingers together, I tugged her into the house. "C'mon. Come see my room."

She blushed, but nodded shyly. While Penny and my parents had helped me move in this summer, Ellie hadn't been up here for that. So she hadn't seen my room yet.

It also reminded me we were completely alone in a way we'd never been before. Sure, we'd had plenty of moments, just the two of us. I found excuses to spend time with her however I could. But besides when I took us out on an adventure, there was always family around. And while we certainly made out in my truck more than once, that was it.

"My room's on the second floor," I murmured to her,

guiding her towards the staircase. I enjoyed living in the hockey house. Loved my teammates and campus. Though some guys forwent college and playing in NCAA entirely to start their careers sooner, I liked the idea of having a degree for once I was finished with my career. My parents were both incredibly smart, and I knew after I was done being a professional hockey player, I'd be able to put my brain to work. Maybe I'd end up as a sports analyst or something like that.

Opening my door, I led Ellie into my room. There was a queen bed—because we were all big guys, and none of us wanted to remain sleeping on twin beds. Last year in the dorms had been enough.

Dropping her bag on the bed, I spun around, watching as she looked around the room. Mom had helped me pick out most of it, including my blue comforter and the little touches from home.

She ran her fingers over the framed photos of us that sat on my dresser. One of them was from prom my senior year, the two of us smiling with my arms wrapped around her from behind. There was a selfie of us from one of our hikes to Multnomah Falls. One from her seventeenth birthday party this summer.

Ellie turned to me, her face soft and full of emotion. "You have photos of us in your room."

"Course I do. Gotta make sure everyone knows about my girl."

She walked over, wrapping her arms around my middle before burying her head in my chest.

"Hey," I whispered, hooking a finger under her chin and tilting her head up towards me. "What's going on in that pretty head of yours?"

She bit her lip. "It's stupid. I just—I couldn't help but worry."

"Worry what, El?"

"That there were other girls." She shrugged. "That you'd

decide you didn't want to be with me anymore because you found someone else and—"

"There's only you, Skater Girl." I tucked a lock of hair behind her ear. "You're the only one I want. Damn, but I can't wait to have you here next year."

"Me too." She nuzzled her face against my chest again.

I ran my hand over the back of her head and her hair, inhaling her scent as I held her tight against my body. Not being able to wait was an understatement. All I wanted was for us to be in the same place again. I missed how simple things had been when we were both in high school. When a date was as easy as picking her up and taking her somewhere in the old truck.

But she was here, and I wanted to take full advantage of that.

"Do you want to meet the guys? The rest of my team-mates will start getting back from class soon. I don't have a game tonight, so normally we hang out at the house. We have one tomorrow night, though."

"I didn't even think about your game schedule," she said. "I hope me being here isn't imposing. I just—"

"It's fine," I promised. "Better than fine, actually. I'm so damn happy you're here. I get you for the whole weekend?"

She nodded. "I have to drive back down Sunday after-noon, but my parents gave me the okay for the weekend."

God, they trusted us so much. Maybe a little too much.

I dipped down my head, brushing my lips over hers. "I know of a few ways we can spend our time." I grinned at her. A weekend with my girl, *and* she'd get to watch my game? I couldn't think of anything better. Except maybe taking her on the ice and skating with her.

She surged upwards, claiming my mouth, kissing me with a fervor that I matched, stroke for stroke. The world melted away, and it was just us. I was *home*. It was a feeling only matched out on the ice. One where I knew exactly where I was meant to be. Who I was meant to be with. *Hers.*

God, I loved her. I loved her so damn much. More than might have been normal, considering how young we were. But we'd both grown up with parents who loved each other—loudly and visibly. They were as close as it came to soulmates on this planet, I was pretty sure.

And Ellie was mine. We were made for each other. I knew that, down to the depths of my soul. Who cared that we were only nineteen and seventeen? I knew I wanted to be with her for the rest of my life.

"Ellie," I murmured, pulling back after another deep kiss.

"Owen…" Her voice was hardly above a whisper as she ran her hand up my chest. "Let's have sex."

"Are you sure?" My eyes widened. I'd wanted to wait until we were ready. Until *she* was ready.

She nodded. "I want you. I want to…" She blushed. "I'm ready."

"Only if you're sure," I said. Because fuck, I wanted it too. Losing my virginity to the only girl I'd ever loved? There was no way I would turn that down.

"Yes. Yes, I'm sure." She dipped her head.

I gave her a soft kiss on her lips before grabbing one of my UW Hockey crewnecks and handing it to her. She was dressed in a cute top and tight jeans, looking adorably innocent, but also hot as fuck.

"What's this for?" She wrinkled her nose, but then brought the fabric up to her nose, sniffing it. "I tell you I want to have sex, and then you give me *more* clothes? I think you're supposed to take them off of me, Owen."

I smirked. "I want to feed you first. Show you around campus and introduce you to the guys." I dragged a finger down her spine. "We have all weekend, after all."

She sucked in a breath, and then nodded, slipping my sweatshirt on. It was chilly outside, and I wanted her to be warm. Plus, I liked that it had my name on the back and everyone would know she was my girlfriend.

The crewneck engulfed her frame, reminding me how much smaller than me she was. At five-seven, Ellie wasn't short, but she was built like her mom—a thin dancer's frame with long, elegant legs. And I was built like my dad—broad shoulders, plus the defined muscles thanks to all the hockey and working out. I needed to be careful with her. Take my time, so she wasn't in pain.

Though it would be both of our first times, I'd listened to the guys in the locker room talk about their conquests. I didn't judge them for hooking up—we were in college, after all—but that just wasn't me. Still, I'd noted some things they'd said. Especially what to do with my fingers and tongue.

"I should get condoms while we're out, too," I said, curling a hand around her waist and squeezing.

She giggled, and I raised an eyebrow. "Sorry, I was just imagining you asking one of your teammates, or that there was some communal box." Her cheeks were pink again.

Damn, I loved it.

"I'm not taking any chances. Not with you."

Something flashed in her eyes, and Ellie nodded. "That's probably smart."

Definitely smart. Neither one of us was ready for the complications or risks of going without. Especially not at the current place in our lives.

Slipping my shoes on, I tightened the laces before pulling a hoodie on over my t-shirt and jeans.

"Ready?" I asked her, grabbing my lanyard with my student ID. Luckily, our house had a digital lock, so I didn't need to carry around a key.

"Yeah." Ellie gave me a small smile.

AFTER INTRODUCING her to all of my housemates—as my girlfriend, so those horny fuckers wouldn't get any ideas—I took Ellie to the dining hall to grab dinner. We sat in one of the two person booths in the back.

It was so easy to imagine us like this next year. Spending time with each other on campus. Sneaking a few kisses in between classes. Seeing her all the time. Damn, but I couldn't wait. I wanted it to be like this between us for the rest of our lives.

"Tonight was fun." She rested her head on my upper arm as we walked back to my off-campus house. The box of condoms I'd bought was in my back pocket, and my dick swelled in anticipation.

I leaned in close, brushing my lips over her ear. "It's not over yet, baby." I squeezed her hand.

She looked around, like she was making sure no one was listening to our conversation. "You're *too* smooth, you know that?"

I grinned. "Learned from the best."

My mom being a romance author had perks, after all. It was bound to rub off. I knew exactly how to treat a woman after growing up listening to her and her best friends talk about all of their book boyfriends. They were basically instruction manuals.

Ellie rolled her eyes. "I like you just the way you are, you know. You don't have to try to impress me." She scrunches up her nose again. "I'm already your girlfriend."

"Damn right." I puffed up my chest, glancing down at HARPER written across her back. "And I won't let you forget it."

"Hey, Harps!" a voice shouted behind us, and when I turned I saw my teammate Jackson Turner—though we called him Turnip for some weird reason—jogging to catch up with us. He wasn't home earlier when I'd introduced Ellie to everyone.

"Hey, man." I fist-bumped him.

He looked at Ellie. "This your girl?"

She was the one who answered. "Yeah. I'm Eleanor." Ellie stuck out her hand. I chuckled the way she introduced herself with her full name. No one ever called her Eleanor. Maybe her parents, but she'd always just been Ellie or El.

"Hey, sweetheart." He winked at her, and I held back a growl. "I'm Jackson."

"Turner," I warned.

He held his hands up. "Relax, man. Not going to steal her."

"Better not," I muttered, tightening my grip around Ellie's hand. She squeezed mine, like she was reassuring me, and I felt a little better.

Luckily, Turner waved goodbye, heading off towards the other end of campus.

God, next year was going to be torture, wasn't it? How many guys were going to be flirting with her? I needed to get a grip. Something was seriously wrong with me feeling this possessive about her, when she'd never given a single indication that she'd even looked at another guy. And she thought I'd been with other women without telling her. That I'd *cheat* on her? There was no way. Not when she was the one I wanted.

My favorite nights were the ones where I fell asleep listening to the sound of her voice on the phone. When she told me all about her skating routine. How excited she was to continue her training at the college level next year. About her dreams of the future.

"Sorry, I know I'm being crazy," I mumbled in her ear. "I just can't help it. I don't get enough time with you, and seeing all these guys around you..." I clenched my free hand into a fist. "I feel so crazy territorial and possessive."

She batted her eyelashes a few times, leaning in close to me to whisper, "Would it help if I let you pee on me?" I burst out laughing. "You know, like a dog, mark your territory?"

"Ellie." There were tears in my eyes. I couldn't hold back my laughter, nor could I stop it. "Baby. I already did that."

"What?" She frowned.

I tugged on the sweatshirt. "You're wearing my clothes."

She always wore my jersey back in high school, too. I loved seeing it on her. It felt right. Like a reminder that some day, she'd have my last name too.

"Is that why athletes like when their girlfriends wear their jersey?" Ellie scrunched up her nose again.

I chuckled. "Yes. Drives me fucking crazy. Always has. You look so cute in my clothes, it makes me want to kiss you all the damn time."

"I want that too," she murmured.

I tugged on our interlocked hands. "Come on, my Daisy. Let's get you back so I can kiss you senseless." Among other things, because I had plans. One of them was to kiss her *everywhere.*

Her eyes heated. "Yes, please."

When we got back to my room, she was in my arms before I could blink, and I shut my door with my foot. Ellie's lips descended on mine, and we were a flurry of movement.

I tossed the box of condoms on my nightstand with one hand and sat her on the bed, kneeling in front of her. Fuck, she was pretty.

"Relax," I whispered, kissing her softly. "It's just you and I. Owen and Ellie."

Her blue-gray eyes searched mine. I wondered what she saw there. My undying love and devotion? How much I craved her very being? That I was hanging on by a thread and desperate for her?

"I love you," she murmured, wrapping her arms around my neck. "Make me yours." Ellie rested my forehead against hers. "Please."

"*Fuck.* I love you so much."
I love you.
Fuck, but those whispered words weren't enough.
They were everything.
This was everything.
She was my everything.

TWENTY-SIX

Ellie

NOW

There was a warm body wrapped around mine, and I snuggled backwards, those muscular arms tightening around me. A face nuzzled against my neck, and I felt something hard press up against my ass. My eyes flew open when I realized exactly whose body was covering mine.

"Good morning," a voice rasped against my ear. *Owen.* Because he was home. And I'd fallen asleep in his bed last night.

I rolled over to find him staring at me, his eyes full of amusement. "Hi," I whispered.

"Imagine my surprise, coming home last night and finding you in my bed."

Humming, I shut my eyes, basking in his warmth for another few moments. In a minute, I'd have to get up, and the spell would be broken. Thankfully, I had nowhere to go today and nothing to do.

"Did you miss me, Daisy?" Owen's fingers brushed under my chin.

My voice was all breath when I responded, "Maybe." I'd told him as much when twe'd texted the other night, but this felt different. More real. Watching his games on TV hadn't been enough, apparently, since I'd been sleeping in his room every night since he'd been gone. "I wanted to feel close to you," I admitted. "And your door was open and I just…" *made myself at home.*

"Mmm." He pressed his forehead against mine. "Well, I like you here. In my house and in my bed."

I thought about my text to him. *When you get home… I think I'm ready to talk.* And I was. There were things I should have confessed to him a long time ago.

"I like being here," I admitted. "I already don't want to move out when my apartment is fixed."

He brushed the hair off my forehead. "So don't. Stay with me."

"Owen…" I murmured. This was already a bad idea. So was sleeping in his bed.

But I couldn't help myself.

He kissed my nose before sitting up, climbing out of bed in only his boxer briefs. Owen was sporting an impressive erection, and my eyes zeroed in on it. He'd just had all of that pressed up against me, and my mouth watered.

"Ellie," he scolded me, an amused expression on his face as he pulled on a t-shirt.

I sat up, the covers falling off of me, revealing my choice of sleep attire. Owen's eyes filled with heat, and I did my best to look sheepish.

"You're wearing my shirt?" He let out a low groan. "Do you know what you do to me?"

I bit my lip, eyes darting down to the tent in his boxers. "I think I have some idea."

He smoothed his hand over his face. "We should, uh… Do you want some breakfast?"

Blinking, I shook my head. "No." I wasn't hungry for food.

Climbing onto my knees, I dragged his shirt up and off my body, freeing my breasts. The only thing I was wearing under his shirt—one that smelled like him—was a tiny pair of soft, lacy underwear in his favorite color. Light blue. I hadn't worn them on purpose—certainly hadn't expected this—but now, naked in front of him, I couldn't help be thankful for it.

He stepped closer, and I cupped my tits, rubbing over my nipples. The air made them pebble, and Owen's blatant perusal of my body made them tighten even more.

"What do you want, Ellie?" He stopped in front of me, hand reaching out and cupping the back of my neck, pulling our bodies together.

I moistened my lips with my tongue as he rested his forehead on mine.

"I want you," I admitted.

"Me too," he murmured, brushing back the front pieces of my hair. "So bad. You have no fucking clue, Ellie. It's been so hard trying to keep my hands off of you."

"So don't," I begged. "I can't stop wanting you. I tried, but—"

He brushed his lips over my throat, and I let out a small moan as he kissed up my neck, but not bringing our mouths together. Not yet.

No, he was apparently going to torture me.

He stepped back, pulling his shirt off before dropping it to the floor. Five months ago, I didn't have a chance to appreciate his body. God, he was beautiful. He always had been, but now he was all man. I couldn't stop myself from running my fingers down his muscular torso, chiseled and well-defined after years of playing professional hockey. I traced his abs with my finger tip lightly, and Owen shuddered, revealing his forearm with the movement.

Finally, I got a look at the tattoo I'd glimpsed last week when he'd been in the shower.

It was a daisy.

He had a daisy tattooed on his upper arm.

Somehow I knew, without asking what it meant, that he had it for *me*. He'd always called me Daisy. Of all the people in my life, he was the only one to make my middle name sound like a nickname of endearment. *My Daisy.* That nickname always made my heart melt.

"When did you get this?" I asked, running my fingers over it in awe. The lifework was thin, but detailed—exactly the style of tattoo I'd always loved. We'd talked about getting matching ones when we were younger, but obviously nothing had ever come of it.

When we'd slept together after our graduation party, we'd been in a hurry, and by the time we'd stripped each other of our clothes, it had been dark. There hadn't been a time to see his tattoo. But maybe that was by design, too. Back then, we'd both been holding back. Keeping things from each other.

Now, it was time to confess those truths. To move on —together.

He swallowed roughly. "I got it once I signed my NHL contract."

I shut my eyes, processing that news. *After* we'd broken up. "Why?"

His warm hand cupped my cheek, rubbing tenderly over my cheekbone. "You know why, Ellie."

Shaking my head, I looked down at the comforter, picking at a loose thread in the dark blue fabric. "After everything I did… I never imagined you'd still want me, Owen." Maybe I'd hoped for it, had moved back up here chasing after it, but I hadn't dreamed that he'd still want me like this.

"What did you imagine?" He brushed a piece of hair behind my ear. "That I'd be able to move on from you? Never."

Each touch was so gentle. Tender. He ran his thumb over my face, like he was memorizing it solely based on feel. Owen brushed over my lower lip, and I shuddered.

"One night wasn't enough," I admitted.

"No," he agreed. "It'll never be enough for the two of us, El."

Fluttering my eyelashes, I sat back on my heels as he climbed onto the bed on top of me, his much larger frame caging me in. "Why's that?" The murmur was hardly audible, but I knew he'd heard me.

"Fuck." He grabbed my waist, hoisting me backwards towards the headboard. His breath caught as his fingers ran down my side. "Ellie."

"Mhm?" I hummed, even though I knew exactly what he'd find on my skin.

His voice was a rasp against my skin when he asked, "Why do you have my number tattooed on you?"

"You know why, Owen," I said, repeating the sentiment.

"Tell me anyway," he begged.

I shut my eyes, picturing the moment I'd gotten it. My little secret number eight, hidden under my bra line on my side. "So you'd always be with me." I wrapped my arms around his neck, tilting my head up and brushing my lips against his.

Because I'd always been his, even with the years apart. Even though there was so much distance between us, I'd always worn his number.

Owen's mouth met mine, soft at first, but it merged into something desperate. *Needy.* I let the kiss say everything I hadn't.

Rocking my hips, I was all too aware that the only thing separating us was our thin underwear. Mine was damp already, and I desperately wanted—needed—more.

"I need to touch you," he said with one more nip of my lips. "Can I please touch you, Ellie baby?"

"Yes," I whispered. I needed it just as badly. Every part of me ached for his touch, his embrace, his warmth. He was the only man for me. He'd always been the only man for me.

"Lie back and let me take care of you," he murmured.

Gently laying me down so my head rested against the pillows, he transferred that tender touch down my body, his fingers brushing over my collarbones and then my nipples before replacing them with his mouth. He ran his tongue over the hardened peaks. Owen nipped and sucked, driving me wild with his tongue and his teeth.

"Didn't get to taste you before," he murmured as he pulled away. "To memorize your body. I'm not making that mistake again." He kissed down my stomach before reaching my thighs. I was so hopelessly turned on, and I knew it would be obvious as soon as he touched me. But I wanted this so badly.

I moaned in agreement as he pulled my legs apart, pressing his thumb over my drenched panties.

"Were these for me?" He asked, looking reverently at the fabric as he ran his knuckle over my entrance.

"They're pretty," I said, lamely, at a loss for words as he kissed my inner thigh.

"They are," he mused. "Though you've always looked beautiful in blue."

Owen pressed down, letting the fabric gather my wetness as he rubbed against my clit. His heated gaze was almost… reverent as he pulled my panties to the side and ran his finger through my slit. "Fuck, you're so wet," he rasped.

I let out a small moan, and then he hooked his fingers into the lacy waistband of the underwear before dragging them down. "Up," he commanded, tapping on my hips. I lifted them to help him pull them off my body.

He sat back, his eyes trailing down in a blatant perusal of my naked body, like he was drinking me in. "You've always been the most beautiful thing I've ever seen."

Owen settled himself in between my thighs, his mouth replacing where his fingers had just been. He used one hand to keep my legs spread apart, holding me open.

"Please," I begged. I didn't know what I was asking for, I just knew I wanted it.

He gave me a smug look as he bent down, nipping at my

inner thigh. "Patience, baby. I'm going to take my time this time. Give us what we both want."

"Oh," I squeaked as he ran his tongue up my entrance, circling my clit once, twice. "*Yes*," I cried.

He groaned as he dipped his tongue inside of my slit, lapping up all of my juices. "So sweet," he muttered.

Fuck, but that shouldn't have been so *hot*. I reached down, thrusting my hands into his hair, pushing him further against my aching pussy. He was eating me out like a man starved, but it wasn't enough. I needed more. "Owen." I tugged at his hair, trying to get his attention as he licked and sucked.

"Hmm?" He hummed against my clit, the sensation sending a wave of pleasure through me.

"I need more," I whined, bucking my hips against his mouth.

In response, he pressed his thumb against my clit, rubbing back and forth as he continued lapping at me with his tongue.

Shutting my eyes, I focused on the sensation. At how close I was to an orgasm. It had been so long, and my vibrator didn't compare to Owen's attention. Not one bit.

He squeezed my thigh, making me look down at him. At his eyes, focused on me as he licked one more time before pulling back. "Eyes open, Daisy. I want you to watch as I make you come."

I wanted that too. He slid one finger inside of me, groaning as he felt how wet I was, and then another.

And then his lips were back on my clit, sucking and giving me the most delicious pressure as he crooked his fingers inside of me, making me come faster than I ever had before. I let out a low moan as I toppled over the edge, squeezing around Owen's fingers as I practically saw stars.

After a moment, he pulled his fingers out and brought them up to his lips to suck them clean. I decided right then and there that there was nothing sexier than Owen licking my release off his hand.

Except for the sight of him reaching down, palming his cock, his erection straining through the thin fabric of his boxers. He squeezed lightly as I watched him through lidded eyes, still feeling like I was floating after my orgasm.

"Come here," I whispered, stretching my arms out towards him.

He didn't hesitate, crawling over on top of me and pressing his lips to mine, letting me taste myself on his tongue.

I wrapped my arms around his back as we kissed, feeling like somehow we still weren't close enough. Like I needed *more*. Raking my nails down his back, I slid them down to his ass, cupping that hockey butt I was quickly growing obsessed with. Any time he wore those slutty running shorts around the apartment or after a workout, I had a hard time taking my eyes off of it. Though I'd never been able to take my eyes off of him.

"Ellie," he groaned, resting his head in the crook of my neck. "Fuck, baby. I'm trying so hard to hold back. To make this last."

In response, I slid my hand into his boxers, wrapping my hand around his shaft. "You don't have to hold back."

I pumped him slowly, enjoying the look of desperation unravel on his face.

"Tell me what you want, and I'll do it."

"I want this inside of me," I whispered, running my thumb over the crown. "Please. Don't make me beg." I fluttered my eyelashes, letting go of him so he could push his boxers off, kicking them off towards the door.

His cock was oozing pre-cum, and I dipped my head down to lick the bead off of his tip.

Owen let out a groan. "Fuck."

Dragging my tongue down his shaft, I frowned when his hand cupped my chin, tilting my face so our eyes would meet.

"Why do you look like the world is about to end?"

"I don't… have any condoms." He sighed.

I sat up, blinking. "You don't?" It was crazy to me to think that in an apartment of a single professional hockey player, there wasn't a single box of condoms for the girls I was sure he hooked up with. Then again, he had promised me that there wouldn't be anyone else while I was living here. I just thought that was out of respect for me, though. "Like, they're all expired, or…"

He ran his fingers through his hair, looking towards the window. "I've never brought a woman back here, Ellie," he confessed.

"Never?" My eyes grew wide. "But…"

"I…" Owen's voice was rough. "I haven't been with anyone else."

"Since May, when we… hooked up?" He shook his head no. "But…" I froze. "Owen. It's been…"

"Five years." He nodded. "I know."

My eyes widened. "And you haven't… You *never*?"

He leaned forward, cupping the side of my face with his hand. That shaggy dirty blonde hair of his that I loved brushed over his forehead with the movement, and the look on his face was so endearing, I wanted to pull him into my arms and never let go. "I never wanted to. Didn't want anyone else… Not if they weren't you."

"Oh." My eyes filled with tears. I didn't expect that from him. Not from a hotshot hockey player, or from an NHL player. Especially not when we were broken up, and I'd broken his heart.

"I thought…" I blinked, the emotion overwhelming me. What did I think? That without me in his life, as a professional hockey player, he'd have his pick of any girl he wanted? *Yes.* That was what I'd thought. That he'd have puck bunnies warming his bed. That he would be sleeping with any girl he wanted.

It had driven me crazy for the last few years, and I didn't want to think that way anymore.

But here he was, telling me he hadn't. That he'd never wanted anyone else. That he'd always wanted me.

"I haven't either," I said, voice low. A sacred promise, somehow. It felt like *more*.

Owen rested his forehead against mine. "I need to feel you," he murmured. "Need to know you're mine. At least for now. For however long I have you." I knew what he was asking—and I wanted it more than anything. We'd only gotten to do this twice, but the first time barely counted. After all, it had been years, and I wasn't the same girl now that I'd been back then, terrified of ruining his entire life by being a clingy girlfriend.

I nodded. "I'm on birth control. And I'm okay with it, if you are." Going bare. Feeling him inside of me, claiming in a way no one else had.

There had never been another man. It had always been him. My first and only.

"I'm all clear. I get physicals with the team every year," he said, holding himself still.

"*Yes,*" I agreed. Because I'd give him anything he wanted if he asked for it. "Make me yours, Owen. Only yours."

"Mine," he agreed, cupping my face in his hands.

He kissed me tenderly before positioning himself in between my thighs and notching his tip at my entrance.

Those brown eyes I'd known my whole life looked up at me, like he was making sure I was okay.

I nodded. "Let me feel you inside me, Owen. Give it to me."

Owen pushed in slowly, giving me time to adjust to his size. He'd always been big, and no amount of time could change that.

This time, I was going to savor it. Because I knew, down to the depths of my soul, that this wasn't a one-time thing for us. It never would be. Not after this. Not after baring our souls to each other.

I wanted this too badly to hold back anymore.

234

TWENTY-SEVEN

Owen

NOW

I wasn't lying when I'd told her how much I liked her here. In my apartment, in my bed. In my arms.

Waking up with Ellie nestled into me, scooting back until her ass pressed into my morning wood, wasn't something I'd ever thought would happen for us. Not after everything. But I couldn't complain when this was how it had ended up.

Make me yours, Owen. Only yours.

She was slowly slipping back into my heart, and that terrified me. Because I knew how easy it had been for her to leave before.

Damn, it would be easier if the chemistry between us wasn't so strong. If I didn't want to spend every day just like this. Buried inside of her. Seeing my number tattooed on her. Nothing would compare. I knew that now.

Thrusting inside of her, I savored the feel of her wrapped around me. Of being bare, nestled in her warmth.

"Ellie." I kissed her neck as I slid to the hilt, her gasp filling the room. "*Fuuuck*, I missed you." I closed my eyes, trying to savor the feeling. She felt so good. So perfect. So mine.

How could I ever let her go? *I couldn't.* I'd been lying to myself all these years. It was why I'd stayed away.

But she was here now. She'd moved here for *me*. I knew she had. What I couldn't figure out was *why*.

"Owen," she groaned, wiggling her hips beneath me. "I need you to move."

"I know, baby." I interlaced our fingers, resting my forehead against hers. "I know." Pressing my lips against hers, I stroked my tongue into her mouth before pulling back, thrusting inside her with earnest.

She gasped as I bottomed out, fucking her harder with each stroke. Her nails dug into my back and I relished the feeling. Every sensation was heightened.

"Oh *god,*" she cried, tightening around me.

"Yes, that's it," I encouraged her, rocking my hips. "Don't hold back. Let me hear you." She whined as I pulled out before slamming back in, her hips rising in time to meet each thrust of mine. Each snap of my hips was met with a cry, and fuck me. I was going to come way too fast. There was no way I was lasting. "You feel so damn good, baby. Look how good you take all of me."

Ellie squeezed her insides around my cock, and I let out a low groan. "Fuck. El." I dropped my head against her chest as I held myself still. "That's too good. You feel too good. I'm barely hanging on here."

She ran her fingers through my hair, raking them over my scalp. "So let go, Owen. Give it to me." Her pussy clamped down around my cock again. "I'm so close," she moaned against my ear. "I can feel you so *deep.*" Her eyes shut, head thrown back in pleasure, and fuck me.

Ellie had already come on my fingers, but I wanted to feel her come on my cock, too. I was pretty sure nothing else would compare to the feeling of being inside of her bare, especially with the way her cunt gripped me tight. Each time I pulled out and surged back in, fucking her in a steady rhythm, her body clung to me like she didn't want to let me go.

My fingers dug into her hips, holding her steady as I rutted into her like a beast. The room was filled with the sounds of skin against skin, of groans and labored breaths as we lost ourselves in each other. Her tight, wet heat was a paradise I'd never thought I would experience again, but fuck, if it wasn't better each time.

"Touch your pretty little clit, baby. I need you to come one more time. Need to feel you clenching around my cock. Please." A gasp left her lips as I dipped my head down, running my tongue over her hardened nipples. I nipped and sucked at her breasts, lavishing both with equal attention. "Give me one more. I want you to soak me in your juices. Make me a mess."

Never mind that I wanted to make her a mess. That I wanted to see her painted in my cum, to be marked with my release in a way I could never take back.

Her cries deepened as she reached down, running her index finger over her clit and down to where we were connected. She gathered some of that wetness before rubbing a steady circle on that bundle of nerves.

"There you go," I praised her. "Such a good girl for me."

Ellie's head fell back as her fingers rubbed over her clit, her eyes fluttering shut as her breathing deepened. "*Yes*," she keened. "I'm so close. Don't stop."

"Never," I promised.

I could feel the moment her orgasm hit her, wave after wave of pleasure wracking her frame as her pussy convulsed on my shaft. Slowing the snap of my hips to shallow, pointed strokes, I followed closely behind her, pulling out at the last possible second and spilling onto her thighs, painting her skin with my seed. Neither of us moved for a moment as we both caught our breath.

Ellie hummed as I swiped my fingers through it, rubbing it

into her skin. Our eyes caught, and she giggled. "Well, we definitely made a mess."

"That we did." I heaved her up into my arms before climbing off the bed and heading towards my shower.

"Owen!" she protested, squirming in my hold. "Put me down." Her lips formed an adorable pout, and I wanted to kiss it off of her.

"What?" I asked, innocently. "I got you all dirty. Now, I'm going to clean you up." I winked, setting her down on the edge of the tub as I stepped in my walk-in shower to turn the hot water on.

Once I decided it was hot enough, I grabbed her hand, tugging her in behind me and guiding her under the warm spray. Letting the water fall down her body, admiring the look of her naked and wet. She was the most beautiful woman I'd ever seen. That had never changed.

She sunk her teeth into her lower lip as I stepped closer, running my fingers through my wet hair.

"Hi," I whispered.

"Hey." Ellie gave me a soft smile.

"I always wanted to do this with you," I admitted.

Her eyes shut, and she leaned her forehead against my chest. "There were a lot of things we didn't get to do, huh?" There were. And I intended to make up for our lost time. All five years of it. We might have missed out on college together, but there were still so many things ahead in our future.

But would she want to be by my side for all of it?

There was so much on the line. This was a distraction I knew I couldn't afford, but I wanted it anyway. Wanted her. If she wanted to be here, by my side.

I ran my hands down her side before squeezing her hips.

"Owen," she murmured, her gaze finding and holding mine.

Dipping my head down, I pressed a soft kiss to her lips before grabbing a bottle of my body wash and pouring a small amount into my palm. Kneeling in front of her, I rubbed up her legs, washing her thighs with care.

"I can do it myself," she insisted.

"Let me," I murmured, treating each inch of her reverently. She was so soft, and I wanted her to feel taken care of. We'd never gotten a moment like this before, and I sure as hell wasn't passing up on the opportunity now. Even if I had to ignore my rapidly hardening cock. I couldn't help it—just touching her like this made me want her.

Running my fingers over her slit, I cleaned her delicately. While I hated that she was no longer covered in my scent, I wanted her to know how precious she was. Because maybe, just maybe, if she saw how good this would be, she would stay.

AFTER OUR SHOWER, I wrapped Ellie in a warm, fluffy towel and dried her off, feeling satisfied at taking care of her. Once I'd finished washing her hair, she'd dropped to her knees and surprised me by wrapping her lips around the head of my cock. I'd come embarrassingly fast, but it was impossible to hold back with her mouth on me and the sight of her naked in my shower.

She stretched out her arms on my bed, looking cozy but well-sated. The towel was wrapped around her breasts, giving me just the slightest peek at the swells as she laid back. "Well, I definitely didn't expect that when I fell asleep last night."

I chuckled, rummaging through my drawers. My duffel bag was still on the floor from where I left it last night, and I needed to unpack and do a load of laundry, but that would have to wait for later. "I didn't expect to find you in my bed." My voice was rough, and I cleared it, turning back to her to find her watching me.

She did her best to look bashful. "I don't regret it."

"Neither do I," I admitted. I could never regret her. Even if it ruined everything.

"Good." Ellie hummed softly. "I missed you," she said, her voice a low whisper.

Running my fingers through my still damp hair, I pulled out a t-shirt and a pair of boxers. "I wasn't even gone a week."

"No." Ellie shook her head, like she knew I'd misunderstood her. "For the last few years, I missed *you*."

Missing her was an understatement. Dropping my towel, I pulled on the boxers before padding over to where she still lay, dark blonde strands still wet as she rolled onto her side in bed to watch me. "Well, you're here now." I kissed her cheek. "What do you think? Should we eat some breakfast?"

She hummed, stretching out like a cat, the towel slipping off her body, freeing those tits I'd had my mouth all over earlier. "Probably would be good. I should put some clothes on. Let me go grab something from my room—"

"Here. Just wear mine." I handed her the old Seals t-shirt I grabbed, watching as she wiggled it on over her frame. "Come on." I stood up, holding out a hand to her. "Let's get some food in you."

"Owen." She blushed. "You don't have to—"

Take care of her? "I do," I insisted. Some part of me— whatever feral, caveman part it was—needed to feed her. To make sure she was taken care of. It was the same part of me that got hard just from seeing her wearing my t-shirt and knowing she'd slept in my bed. "We never got to do this before. Waking up together. Bathing in the afterglow. Let's just enjoy this." I pressed a kiss to her forehead.

Yeah, I was an idiot. The guys would certainly think so. But I couldn't deny the part of me that had wanted her here always. That had jumped at the opportunity to have Ellie under the same roof as me. Knowing she was in the city was bad enough, but in my apartment? In my bed?

Maybe all along, I'd known this would happen. I hadn't wanted to stop it. We were inevitable. *This* was inevitable.

Ellie nodded. "But we need to talk."

"We do." I sighed, dropping a kiss to her cheek. "Later."

I didn't want to ruin it. There were so many things we needed to clear up. But we'd been open and honest with each other about this, hadn't we? Maybe we could keep it like that. Because part of me knew that once she told me whatever she'd been holding back, everything would change. And from the worry in her eyes, maybe it wouldn't be for the better.

Could we survive one more thing that would break us?

I interlaced our fingers together as I tugged her towards the kitchen. Lifting her up so she could sit on the counter, I pulled out the ingredients to make eggs and bacon. Normally I tried to stick to a pretty healthy diet during the season, carefully monitoring my intake of food to make sure I followed the nutrition plan the team nutritionist gave us, which was the main reason I wasn't making pancakes right now.

"Mmm." Ellie swung her legs as she watched me. "I never thought I'd see you cooking shirtless in the kitchen."

"Well, get used to it," I said, leaning over to press a kiss to her forehead. "Because I can't think of a better way to start my Sunday morning than with you."

With my girl.

Words I held back, because I needed to figure out where her head was at.

If she would stay.

TWENTY-EIGHT

Ellie

NOW

Breakfast was amazing. But then, hadn't Owen proved that everything he did was incredible?

I sat on a barstool, watching him putter around the kitchen, cleaning up after finishing the dishes. I'd tried to help him, but he'd insisted.

Not that I could complain. I liked this version of him. It reminded me of the way my dad always doted on my mom, making sure she was happy and treating her like a queen. He'd always called her *Darling*.

I rested my head on my hands as I watched him, enjoying the sight of his ass in those tight boxer briefs and the muscled abdomen I'd gotten my hands all over last night. Now that I'd seen his tattoo, I couldn't believe I'd never noticed it before. I couldn't believe that he'd gotten it, either.

It was something so small, but it proved that neither one of us had stopped thinking about the other.

I didn't know what to do with that. Five years. It had been five years since that weekend in his dorm. A weekend that had started out perfectly, or pretty close to it. We'd shared our first times with each other. He'd been so gentle and patient, trying to make sure he didn't hurt me. And then…

Then I'd ruined everything.

"Ellie."

"Hm?" I asked, my cup of coffee perched at my mouth.

He smirked. "Stop staring at my ass."

"I wasn't," I lied.

"You've had that mug in the air for five minutes, Daisy. I can practically see the drool on your face."

My cheeks warmed, and I set it down.

"It's okay," he said nonchalantly. "You can admit that you just want me for my body." Owen flexed his muscles. "I won't be too offended."

"Owen." My mouth dropped open. "I don't—"

He laughed, and his entire face lit up as he dropped the towel on the sink, clearly satisfied with his cleaning job, before walking over to me. His hands cupped my face. "I know." He kissed me softly. "Now, how should we spend the rest of my day off? We could spend it on the couch, or we could try to go down to the rink and skate. Get you back on the ice."

"Mmm…" I pretended to think about it, but I knew what my answer was immediately. A chance to snuggle on the couch? Sold.

He was right. I couldn't think of a better way to spend a Sunday.

"BYE MS. BRADFORD!" One of my favorite students called out as she rushed out the door. Halloween was this week, and the kids were so excited about their costumes and telling each other what they were dressing up as, and it was absolutely adorable. I was so excited to hear them babble about their favorite superheroes and princesses.

Sophia had texted me again to confirm that I was still coming to the team Halloween Party this week, and I reassured her I would come. Not that I'd had time to even think about a costume yet. I had no idea what I was going to wear. Especially since Owen and I weren't dating, and suggesting a couple's costume might be weird.

One day, I couldn't wait to do Halloween with my own kids. It had always been one of my favorite memories with my family. Every year, we had a big Halloween party at the Harper house with all the cousins and family friends. Everyone dressed up, and a lot of the times, each of our families had come in matching costumes. All our parents invited their friends. It was always so fun.

This year, I'd be missing that, and the thought made me a little homesick. I talked to my mom almost every day—even if it was just a text—and did my best to call her and my dad at least once a week. They liked my weekly updates, even if I hadn't told them about everything going on with Owen and I. My siblings were a different story. Abigail was busy living her insane life, jet-setting around the world with her fashion line. Beau was busy with football, which I understood even more now that I was living with Owen.

It was crazy to think this Friday marked three weeks since I'd moved with him. It was everything I'd ever wanted. I hadn't been able to wipe a smile off my face all day. Spending yesterday together had been amazing. The best sex of my *life*. Not that I had much to compare it to—I'd only ever been with him. But he was sweet and caring, and he always made sure it was good for me. I wasn't sure what else you could want in a partner. And I knew I didn't want anyone else but him.

Not that we'd had that conversation yet. He kept brushing it off. I wasn't sure if I should be worried.

But this was why I'd moved here, so I couldn't bring myself to regret it.

My phone buzzed, and I opened it to find a text from Owen.

OWEN

I have a surprise for you when you get home.

ELLIE

I'm just finishing up and then I'll head back.

See you soon, Daisy.

I hoped my surprise was him. Preferably naked.

"You look happy," Maggie said, leaning on my doorframe.

I looked up, realizing I was smiling just thinking about Owen. About the way he'd held me last night, and I'd fallen asleep in his bed again. "It was a good weekend," I responded.

"Mmm. Hockey boy is home, I take it?"

My cheeks were pink. "Maybe."

I was terrible at hiding things from my friends. Abi always said I was like an open book, showing all of my emotions on my face. For once, I wished I could keep this a secret to myself for a little longer.

The only reason all of my cousins didn't know yet that Owen and I were sleeping together—because we weren't back together, not really—was because I was two hundred miles away. Even though our group chat was always blowing up, it was much easier to keep them in the dark without them here.

"I love this for you. You're so..." She waved her hand around me. "*Sunshiney*. It looks good on you."

"Thank you." I fiddled with the hem of my thick cardigan. "It's still new, but..."

She patted me on the shoulder. "Go home and see your man." Maggie headed out, giving me a little wave.

I dipped my head, grabbing my bag and keys so I could lock up my classroom. Owen didn't have a game until tomorrow, so I was in more of a hurry to get home, knowing he'd be there when I got back. Maybe if I was lucky, we could have a repeat of yesterday morning. I wasn't opposed to the shower again. Or his exceptionally large bathtub...

There was no wiping the smile off my face as I headed out to my car and drove back to Owen's apartment.

It might have been raining outside, but my world felt brighter than ever. I just hoped it would stay this good.

OPENING the door to our apartment, I expected to find Owen in the kitchen or the living room, but they were both empty. Except… not exactly empty.

"Owen." I froze, staring at the little bundle of golden fur as a tail wagged at me. "Owen?" My voice was louder, shouting through the apartment.

"Hey, Skater Girl." He grinned as he rounded the corner, shoving his hands into his pockets.

"Owen. Why is there a dog in our apartment?"

"She's ours."

"*Ours?*" I repeated, raising an eyebrow. We weren't even together. Not really. We hadn't had the conversation about what we were yet. Maybe we were both avoiding it.

He nodded. "Uh-huh. That way, when I'm gone for away games, I don't have to worry about you being alone. Especially during some of the long stretches."

The puppy padded over to me before plopping down on the floor, pushing her nose into my legs. "*Ohmygod.*" She was so cute. "Does she have a name?"

Owen crouched down next to me, scratching the top of her head. "Not yet." His eyes met mine as he continued petting the puppy. "Figured we could name her together."

"This is insane. You know that, right?"

He hummed. "I've lived alone for the last few years and always wanted a dog, but it seemed selfish when I was leaving so much. But when I was gone last week, I couldn't stop thinking about how you were all alone here. So." Owen made a gesture like, *here we are.*

"So you got me a dog." I deadpanned.

"I got *us* a dog, baby." He reached out, brushing a hand over my face. I closed my eyes, enjoying the casual intimacy of his touch. Truthfully, I liked the sound of *us* a little too much.

Sitting criss-cross on the floor, the golden retriever puppy climbed into my lap, before putting both paws on my chest and licking my face. "Hi, little girl," I cooed. "I guess we need to name you, huh?" My parents' dog growing up had been named Brownie, and I knew Owen had grown up with one named Marshmallow, but I wasn't sure I wanted to follow the food naming trend. It felt a little… boring. I tried to think about the things that were meaningful to Owen and I, but my mind was suddenly blank.

For starters, I couldn't get over the gesture. He didn't want me to feel lonely when he was gone. Why was that so sweet? There was a pang in my heart. He had a home game tomorrow, and one more on Thursday, and then next week he had another road trip.

I laughed. "How do I have literally no idea on what to call her?" I turned to look at Owen, only to find he was watching me, eyes bright.

God, I wanted to kiss him.

But I resisted.

He reached over, petting the puppy, who was now snuggled up in my lap, satisfied from licking my face a few times. "We could name her Daisy."

I scrunched up my nose. "After *me*? No."

Playing with her soft, floppy ears, I studied her golden coat. "Sunshine."

Owen burst out laughing. "That's awful, Ellie baby."

Sticking my tongue out at him, I shrugged. "It's better than Cookie."

He chuckled. "Okay. I've got one. And hear me out before

you say no." I arched an eyebrow, and he continued on. "We both grew up on the ice, right? You know, Hockey Boy and Skater Girl?"

"If you're about to suggest we name our baby girl something stupid like Puck or Skate—"

"Zamboni." Owen smirked, and the puppy stirred and yipped at him, like she was agreeing. "See? She likes it." He reached out his hand, scratching her head, and she had her mouth open like she was smiling as he petted her.

"We can't call a puppy *Zamboni*, babe." The endearment slipped out, and I hoped he didn't notice.

"Why not? I think it's cute."

"What's her nickname going to be? Zambi?" I rolled my eyes. Even though it was kind of adorable, I had to give it to him.

He just grinned. "Yeah. Why not."

"Okay." I leaned my head against his shoulder, trying not to disturb the puppy, who seemed content where she was.

"Really?" He perked up, looking like a dog who was wagging his tail himself. It should have been a crime, how adorable he was.

I reached up, running my hair through his soft, blond strands. "Really. Zamboni is kinda growing on me." I scrunched my nose. "What does this mean for us?"

"What do you mean?" He wrapped an arm around my back, tugging me closer to him.

Furrowing my brow, I turned to look at him. "I mean, there is an *us*, right?"

He grinned. "I thought that was already decided when you told me you were mine yesterday."

My cheeks were warm, and I turned to bury my face against his shirt. "I thought that was just something we were saying, you know. In the heat of the moment."

Owen's thumb ran under my chin before he tilted my head up to his, his lips pressing tenderly against mine. "No. I meant it, El. I've always been yours." His brown eyes were so warm, full of emotions I couldn't even describe. "And you've always been mine. From the first moment, Ellie. It's always been you."

Eyes flooding with tears, I just shook my head. What could I say?

"But the five years we were broken up..." I'd broken his heart.

He sighed, but there was no frustration in it. He gave me a hesitant smile as he tucked a piece of hair behind my ear. "Didn't we already clear this up, baby? I'm not mad at you for ending things. I don't really understand *why* you did, but everything worked out in the end. You're here now. That's all that matters."

"We lost so much time," I said, shaking my head. "We can't get that back."

"We have so much ahead of us," he promised.

"Maybe." I bit my lip. But what if everything came crashing down again? Sure, we were together now, but that didn't mean we had the rest of our lives together.

His lips brushed over my forehead. "You'll see. Everything that's meant to be always works out in the end."

I hoped he was right.

Cousins Coffee Club

TEXTS

Hey everyone. Meet Zamboni.

photo attached of golden retriever puppy

QUINLAN

OMG. El, you got a puppy?

LUCY

She's so cute!! I'm obsessed!

ELLIE

Technically, Owen got her. But yeah.

PENELOPE

Dog parents!! I love this. I can't wait to snuggle with her when I come up next month.

OWEN

You guys are still coming up for Thanksgiving, yeah?

PENELOPE

Yes, that's the plan! Are we still good to stay with you? Mom and Dad wanted to know if we should book a hotel instead.

ELLIE

Why would you need a hotel?

PENELOPE

Well, I just figured that if you were still in the
guest room…

ELLIE

Oh. Right…

I can clear out of the guest room so you can
stay with Owen. It's okay.

PENELOPE

But where will you sleep?

OWEN

For the sake of the rest of the group chat, we
are not going to answer that.

QUINLAN

Are you two shacking up??

OWEN

No comment.

ELLIE

…

ZACHARY

Geez, Quin. Don't ask about their sex life. The
rest of us don't want to know.

BEAU

That's my sister you're talking about, Z.

PENELOPE

Thanks for that, Zach. You always know just
want to say to ruin the mood.

ELLIE

Anyway…

Abs, how's Paris?

ABIGAIL

It's amazing. I extended my trip another week.

I actually met someone. It's new but... I'm
having a lot of fun.

ELLIE

Oh!! Spill! I want all the details.

BEAU

Maybe not all of them...

ABIGAIL

Not yet. I want to see how things go first.

QUINLAN

Excited for you, Abs. You deserve this!

PENELOPE

I think it's safe to say all of our moms would
agree. Hopeless romantics that they are.

WESLEY

Look who's talking, Penny.

ZACHARY

It's probably all of those romance books they
read.

OWEN

Hey, you could probably learn a thing or two
from those.

Besides, I've read some, and they're good.

ZACHARY

You read romance novels? How did I not
know this about you?

WESLEY

Because he's been gone for years and we
barely see him anymore?

OWEN

Yeah, yeah. I'll make up for that, I promise.

ZACHARY

You better.

QUINLAN

We'll see you both for Christmas, right?

ELLIE

That's the plan.

Plus Zamboni. We can't exactly leave our little girl alone.

ABIGAIL

All the cousins back in one place again… Not sure our parents will survive it.

BEAU

Sounds just like old times. You are all just lucky I don't have a game on Christmas Day this year.

OWEN

I'm glad the NHL gives us a few days off, at least. It sucks that the NFL doesn't.

BEAU

You're telling me, O. But at least I'll get to see everyone.

OWEN

Avery and Amelia are coming for Christmas too. So it really will be like old times.

BEAU

Really? Man, it's been forever since your cousins have celebrated with us.

PENNY

I can't wait!!!

TWENTY-NINE

Ellie

Senior Year

I clutched the sheets to my chest as I sat up, the voices outside of the door stirring me awake as the flood of memories from last night invaded my mind. And then there was the soreness between my thighs that confirmed I hadn't imagined it. A smile lit my face. I'd lost my virginity. And it had been pretty close to perfect. Owen *was* perfect. He was so gentle and caring.

And he… wasn't here. I suspected he'd had hockey practice, and I couldn't fault him for sticking to his schedule when I hadn't even warned him I was coming up. I'd wanted to surprise him. And I had. His face when he'd come outside of the house, seeing me standing there… It had been worth it.

I sat up, finding a glass of water on the nightstand along with a sticky note.

Headed to morning skate. Will bring breakfast when I come back. Love you. -O

Smiling, I snuggled back into his sheets, closing my eyes again. I was surrounded by his scent all around me—clean and crisp, like the mountains and ice, and something uniquely him—and I breathed in deep.

I knew how badly he wanted me to be here next year. And I wanted that too. Wanted to not have the miles between us, the space that made my heart ache. But I also hated the idea of being so far away from my family. Maybe it was because I was the baby of the family, and the youngest of all the cousins until Lucy had come along, but I couldn't imagine not seeing them all the time.

Was it the right call? I didn't know.

I fell back asleep, my thoughts full of Owen and the future.

Sometime later, I woke up to the sound of voices outside Owen's door. He wasn't home yet, but clearly some of his teammates were. I tried my best not to eavesdrop, but the walls weren't very thick. Either that, or the door was just exceptionally thin.

"You ready for practice later, man?"

A second voice chimed in, "Totally. We gotta stay in top shape so we can get into the playoffs this year. I'd love to win the Frozen Four before we graduate."

"We've still got another year after this. And I think we have a shot with Harper, huh?"

"He's good, I'll give him that. They wouldn't have drafted him if he wasn't."

The first guy said something I couldn't hear, and I strained my neck, knowing they were talking about Owen.

"I heard they want him to start early." I held my breath on the other side of the door. Really? The Seals wanted him to sign a contract before graduation? That was the first I'd heard of it. But maybe Owen just hadn't mentioned it. "Lucky bastard. I'd give anything for that chance."

"We'll get there. We just gotta prove ourselves." A sigh.

"What's he doing with her, anyway?" The second voice said, loud enough that I could hear him perfectly. I furrowed my brow.

The other boy snorted. "I know. Like, why date a high schooler when there's so many puck bunnies who would want to ride his—" I stopped listening, disgusted by their conversation as the realization shocked me to my core.

Me. They were talking about… *me*. They couldn't believe he was with me.

"He's been distracted lately," one of them grumbled. "We need him at the top of his game."

"Hard to do when his pretty little girlfriend shows up for the weekend."

Then the voices moved farther away, and I couldn't hear the rest of their conversation. My eyes filled with tears. The way they were talking about me—like I was some clingy girl who wouldn't let him go—made me want to curl up in a ball and never come out.

His teammates didn't even know me. They had no idea about our plans for the future. That we'd grown up together and had been friends forever. In elementary school, when a bully had pushed me to the ground and I'd skinned my knees, Owen had been the one to pick me up. He'd wiped the tears off my face and held my hand as we walked together to the nurse's office so I could get bandaids for my skin.

He'd always been there for me.

But was I holding him back? Distracting him? If there was a chance I was putting his career in jeopardy, I couldn't live with that. He needed to put himself first. Not me. Maybe coming here had been a mistake.

I'd wanted something just for us. And now that I had it… What? What was left?

"Ugh." I groaned out loud. "Am I an idiot?" I flopped back onto the bed. Was I trying too hard to hold on to something that I should just let go? I only had eight months left until graduation. That wasn't very long, so why was I *panicking*? Why did my world suddenly feel so small?

I was supposed to come here for college. We were going to be together. But if he was this distracted just from our long-distance relationship, how bad would it be when we spent every day together? When every weekend was like this one? Or worse, if I was here—alone—and he didn't have time for me because he was too busy with class and practice.

But I knew Owen would put me first. He always had. And that was the problem. He was too good to me. Too noble. He'd come running whenever I asked him to. If I asked him to jump, he would ask me how high. And I couldn't keep doing that to him.

Pulling my knees to my chest, I buried my head in my lap and held myself tight in a ball. But I couldn't stop the tears from falling. This was too much. Everything was too much.

But I couldn't bear to be the one to ruin it. To drag him down. Because I *was* a distraction. I knew it, but I hadn't wanted to acknowledge it. I was always going to be a distraction, and he needed to be at the top of his game if he was going to make the NHL his career. And I knew how much he wanted this. How badly he desired a career on skates, spending his time on the ice.

My eyes filled with tears. I couldn't breathe. I just kept thinking about their words.

What is he doing with her?

Why date a high schooler?

He's been distracted lately.

And I couldn't. I just couldn't.

THIRTY

Owen

____

THEN

Sophomore Year

My bed was empty. It was a sight I should have been used to. I'd never come back here to find a woman in my bed before. But today, waking up next to her, finding her snuggled beside me had been everything I'd ever wanted. I'd pressed a kiss to her head before dragging my body out of bed for morning skate. I hadn't wanted to, but I'd done it.

The t-shirt she had been wearing was folded neatly in the middle of my bed, the sheets pulled back like no one had ever slept in it. And there was a note on top.

My heart sank. I could almost delude myself into thinking she was in the shower, but her stuff was gone, too. The bag of breakfast I'd gotten us sat on my desk, forgotten. I'd set it there the moment I came back to my room and finding it empty.

Ellie had left. What had I done? Had I hurt her? Last night had been something I'd waited for. I'd waited for her. And it had been special, because it was her. Us.

I'd never even looked at another girl. Didn't even want to,

because I had her. Because I knew that smiling, sunshine girl was waiting for me back home. The only one I'd ever wanted. I thought she'd felt the same way.

Hands trembling, I picked up the note on my bed.

Owen,

I can't do this anymore. I'm sorry.
Ellie

What did she mean, she couldn't do this anymore? Last night, we'd shared *everything*. And now she was just… *gone?*

I didn't even bother putting shoes on, rushing out of my house to the spot where she'd parked her car. But it was gone. Ellie was… gone. It was like it had all been a dream. A dream I'd never wanted to wake up from.

"Are you okay, Harper?" One of my teammates asked me. I was only vaguely aware of it, still looking at the empty spot of pavement.

I turned to him, blinking. "I… Uh… Did you happen to see my girlfriend this morning?"

He frowned. "I think she was leaving as I came back from the rink."

"Oh. Okay." I ran a hand through my hair. "Thanks."

Heading back to my room—at a normal pace this time—I grabbed my phone and sat down at the edge of the bed.

She hadn't called. Hadn't texted. No, she'd let me take her virginity, let me give her *my* virginity, and then fled as soon as I'd gone to morning skate.

I clicked her name from my contacts list, calling her.

"Pick up, pick up, pick up," I chanted to myself.

But she didn't answer the phone.

"Fuck!" I exclaimed, throwing my phone across the room.

OWEN

Ellie. Come back, please. Can we talk?

No response.

I'm begging you, Daisy. I can't live without you. I don't want to.

What happened? Did I hurt you? Fuck, if I hurt you, I just...

I pinched the spot between my eyebrows. All of my messages were still unread. Which, if she was driving, would make sense. What could I do?

Flopping back on my bed, I threw my arm over my eyes, blocking out the light.

"Mom," I said, my voice hoarse.

"Hi, honey," she said, tone full of concern. "What's wrong? Are you okay?"

I shook my head, even though she couldn't see me. No, I wasn't okay, not in the slightest.

"She's gone. She's gone, and she broke up with me, and I don't even know what happened, but she *left*."

I didn't know when I'd started crying, only that I'd never felt heartbreak like this before. Almost twenty years and I'd never felt a level of devastation like this. My entire future vanished in front of my eyes.

"Slow down, Owen." They were words meant to soothe. "Start over from the beginning. What happened?"

Suddenly, all I wanted was my mom. For one of her hugs that always seemed to make everything better. For the scent of baked goods & roses that always permeated our house. Instead, I was here—alone.

"Ellie came up this weekend to see me," I started. "I thought everything was great. But I left for morning skate, and grabbed breakfast for us on the way back and when I got back to my room, she'd left."

"And she didn't say anything?"

I rubbed a hand over my face. "No. Just a note. I tried to call her, but she didn't answer. She told me she loved me, Mom. How could she do this?"

"I'm so sorry, Owen. I wish there was something I could do to make it better." But what could she say? My mom wasn't there last night. She didn't know what we had shared. And then to lose her after that—after the most precious, special moment that I thought meant something to both of us—was gutting.

And I still had to go play a hockey game later today. After having my heart pulled out of my chest and stomped on. It was even worse, because I knew the Seals were looking at me. Debating on calling me up early.

"I don't know if I want to come home for Thanksgiving this year," I said, looking at the giant calendar on my wall. I'd circled the date I got to go back home, but in the end, every moment there would be one spent around her. My life was too entwined with Ellie's.

And how could I face her after she *left* me?

I couldn't.

"Maybe we'll make the trip up there," Mom offered. "It might be fun for the four of us. Seattle's a great city. Who knows, it might give me inspiration for my next book?"

I let out a small groan at her last comment—we loved to tease her for writing romance novels, but really, I was damn proud of my mom. And the way she'd raised us, we'd grown up with books all over the house. Reading was practically second nature to me. Some guys on my team struggled with assignments because they didn't enjoy it, but I would happily devour a fantasy novel whenever I had free time. Even the ones that my teammates joked could be used as a brick.

"I'd really like that," I admitted. "It would be nice to have you up here. And then you could come to my game that weekend."

It would have been a quick trip, anyway. Unlike most students on campus, I didn't have the luxury of a long weekend.

"Done. I'll talk to your dad tonight when he gets back from the University and we'll book hotels. I love you, Owen. You're so strong. You'll make it through this, I promise."

"But why?" I blinked rapidly, trying to clear the tears. "Why do I have to? It was supposed to be her and I. We were supposed to be together."

"I can't pretend to know the way the world works, hon. All I know is it's what you do after that matters. You've got so much life ahead of you. We talked to your coach, and I know he sees the promise in you. The NHL drafted you."

I nodded, reminding myself that was what was important. Hockey. My career. I loved it. I could love it enough even without her here. "Yeah. You're right. Thanks, Mom."

"See you in a few weeks. If you need me—or your Dad—we're always right here."

I wished I could hug her. "I love you."

"Love you too, O-Bear," she said, calling me my childhood nickname. "Good luck on your game tonight."

We said our goodbyes before I hung up the phone, staring up at the ceiling.

I still didn't understand.

Still wanted to cry and scream or break something.

But my mom was right. I had to be strong. Had to not let this affect me.

I'd wall off my heart with a sheet of ice, so it could never get broken again. Keep giving everyone the grinning, cheerful guy that everyone loved.

Even when I was dying on the inside.

THIRTY-ONE

Owen

NOW

Scooping Ellie up, I carried her back to my room. *Our* room, if I had anything to say about that.

Ellie thought we couldn't get back the time we'd lost, and maybe she was right. But I meant what I said, too. *Everything that's meant to be always works out in the end.* And we *were* meant to be. I knew that in my heart.

Zamboni followed behind me, already attached at the hip despite me only picking her up this afternoon after practice. I'd already shown her the new dog bed I'd gotten her in our room, and put a snuggly blanket in her crate along with toys so hopefully she'd feel safe inside.

My girl bit her bottom lip as I settled her onto the bed. "Are you sure about this? About… us?"

God, didn't she know how obsessed with her I was? How it was hard to keep my hands off of her? "Yes." The word was practically a growl as I ran my hands up her legs, pushing her dress up and exposing her pretty lacy underwear to me. My girl loved her matching sets, and I loved how delicate and feminine they all were.

I ran my nose down the seam of her panties, shutting my eyes as I breathed in her scent.

"I was so mad at you for so long," I admitted. Ellie's eyes were watery when I looked up, but I continued on, hooking my fingers into her waistband and dragging them down her legs. "For leaving me. For denying us this. For only giving me once." A groan escaped me as I pried open her thighs, catching sight of her pretty pink pussy. "Fuck, baby. It was so hard." I ran my tongue through her slit, and Ellie let out a soft moan.

Her voice was a hardly more than a whisper. "I know. I shouldn't have…"

Circling her clit, I felt her body relax under my touch as I lapped at her, blowing lightly on her clit as I kneeled in front of her. Her body jerked slightly, but my fingers held her in place.

I kissed her thigh. "I would have fought for you. For us."

"I know," she said, her entire face downcast. Like this decision had haunted her the same way it had me.

"Then *why*, Ellie? Why did you have to end it? Why did you have to leave *me*?"

She shook her head. "Why didn't you come home? Five years, and…"

"You know why, Ellie baby." I rubbed at the daisy tattooed on my arm. I'd worn a t-shirt today.

Maybe before, I'd felt the need to hide it from her. Because it had been an omission I hadn't been ready for. But now, everything was different. "If I went home, I wouldn't have been able to respect your decision. I wouldn't have been able to stay away from you." Resting my elbows on her legs, I stared up at her. The girl I'd loved. The girl who had broken my heart. The girl who I'd always wanted.

"Do you know how amazing you are?" Ellie blurted out.

I blinked. "You broke up with me because… I'm amazing?"

"No." She bit her lip, like she was deciding how much she should confess. "Do you know I've watched every single one of your games since you joined the NHL? Even before I moved up here." I wasn't sure I was breathing. *Every game?* She'd been watching all this time? My heart ached with everything we'd lost. All the time we could have had. "I could recite your stats sheet like the back of my hand." Ellie paused, taking a deep breath. "Since before you started Junior Hockey, I knew you were going to go places, Owen. And then you got drafted, and I was *so* proud of you. You went to college, and—"

"And you were supposed to come with me," I interrupted her. We were supposed to have two years together before this.

"*And,*" she repeated. "I visited you. I watched you on campus. Saw how you interacted with your teammates. How happy you were. And I heard what your teammates were saying about you. That the Seals wanted you to start early instead of waiting for you to graduate. And I knew you wouldn't go. Not if I was there." Ellie combed her fingers through my hair.

I swallowed roughly. "But we could have done it together. *Been* together."

Ellie just gave me a sad smile. "You would have been more focused on me than hockey. And I couldn't cost you your dream, Owen. I couldn't be the one to hold you back. Your teammates were right. Look at you now. Look at how much you've accomplished."

"What did they say?" I furrowed my brow.

"I don't remember. It was a long time ago and—"

"What. Did. They. Say." I growled the words.

Her shoulders dropped. "It doesn't matter now."

"My Daisy girl." I cupped her chin, forcing her eyes to meet mine. "It matters to me."

She bit her lip. "I don't want to relive that day. I was young and stupid. I just want *now.*" Her hands slid up in between my t-shirt and my jeans, running over my abs.

I placed a hand on either side of the bed and kissed her deeply.

"I'm proud of you," Ellie murmured when we pulled apart. "You made it to the NHL. You got your dream."

"No." I shook my head, her dress bunched in my hands. "My dream wasn't complete without you with me. I was so damn lonely, Ellie. I missed you so fucking much."

"So show me. Let's make up for lost time." She spread her legs, and I stepped into the space between her thighs, pressing our bodies together as she worked my shirt up and over my torso. "You don't have to be lonely anymore, Owen."

"Thank fuck." I let my shirt drop to the floor and pulled her cute little dress over her head, exposing her matching teal lace bra. There was a little bow between her breasts, and I dipped down, pressing a kiss to each swell before tugging on the bow with my teeth. I could see her hardened nipples through the fabric, and I sucked one into my mouth through the lace, enjoying the way it made Ellie's head fall back with a moan.

With one hand, I flicked the clasp open, the other buried in her hair, keeping her still.

Without warning, she unzipped my pants, her hand eagerly finding my cock—hard and ready for her. God, I wanted this beautiful woman. In my bed. In my heart.

I wanted to give it back to her so badly.

Ellie whimpered as I bent down, giving her my full weight as I captured her lips, nipping on them slightly. She gasped, and I swept my tongue in, our saliva mixing as we shared a messy kiss. My dick was practically weeping with the need to bury myself inside her tight, wet heat, and I couldn't think of anything else.

"Lie back," I murmured, pulling the bra straps off her arms tenderly, looking at her stripped naked in front of me. I pushed my jeans and boxer briefs down in one quick motion, and then I lined myself up with her entrance, burying myself to the hilt in one thrust. We both groaned as I settled inside of her, the sensations too good. It was raw and real, and there was no hiding. Not when it felt like this.

"So big," she moaned. "I'm so full."

"You're so wet for me," I said, squeezing my eyes shut as I adjusted to being inside her perfect body. "Such a good girl. So perfect."

She cried out as I pulled out halfway before thrusting in again, fucking her with shallow strokes. "Right there," she panted. "Keep going."

"I'm never letting you go again," I whispered in her ear as I dug my fingers into her hips. "Never," I promised her.

There was no going back. Not for us. Not after this.

LEANING AGAINST THE DOORFRAME, I watched as Ellie curled her hair in my bathroom, getting ready for the team's Halloween party a few days later. I was glad Sophia had invited her, even though I wanted to be the one to invite her to team stuff. Which was stupid, because I hadn't even invited her back to another game yet, too worried that she'd say no. And how could I have thought that, when this beautiful woman confessed that she'd watched *all* of my games? Thinking about her back in Portland, turning on the TV just to watch me, made my heart skip a beat.

I thought about the bag I had stashed in the closet. Something I'd had made for her after she'd shown up at my first game, even though it had been impulsive. Now it didn't feel impulsive at all. It just felt right.

"I have a question," I asked before I could lose my nerve. What about this girl made me so nervous? We'd already said we were together. She'd slept in my bed every night this week.

I'd adopted a dog for us, for fuck's sake. I could ask her to come to my games.

"Hmmm?" she hummed, turning towards me.

"You can say no if you don't want to." Hesitating, I went into the closet and grabbed the bag, and then stuck it on the counter in front of her. "But I got this for you, and, well…" I shook my head. "Just open it."

Ellie put down the curling iron after she finished her current curl, giving me a weird look. "Okay…"

Zamboni was curled up on her bed, watching Ellie get ready. She was a snuggle bug, and whenever either of us was on the couch, she was immediately in one of our laps. We'd gotten her a sparkly blue tag with her name for her collar. Of course, it was rimmed in rhinestones, because Ellie had seen that design and fallen in love instantly. I'd already bought our girl a Seals collar and toys from the gift shop—because how could I not—and she looked so darn cute when she padded around the house, wearing her collar with pride.

Yep, I was definitely going to be one of those dog owners.

My girl reached into the bag, pulling out the brand new blue sweater.

"What's this?" she asked, holding up the jersey.

I cleared my throat. "It's for you." *Obviously*. God, I was an idiot. And terrible at this. "To wear. At my games. If you want to come to them."

"Oh, Owen." Her eyes were glassy.

Stepping closer to her, I ran my finger under her eye. "Please don't cry. You'll ruin your pretty makeup."

She laughed. "*Of course*, I want to come to your games. And of course, I'll wear it. I'd be honored." She turned it around, looking at the name and number on the back. Mine. Because damn, I wanted to see her in my jersey. With my name on her back. Just like old times. The way it was always supposed to be. "I love it," she whispered, stepping up on her tiptoes to kiss me softly. "Thank you." She looked hesitantly at the floor. "I wasn't sure if you wanted me to be there. You hadn't asked me again, and I didn't want to assume, so…"

"I always want you there, Ellie baby. But I know you have to be at school early in the mornings, so I didn't want to burden you with coming on weeknights if it was too much. Whenever you want to come, you'll always have a seat."

She wrapped her arms around my waist, pulling me into a hug. I rubbed mine over her back, enjoying the feel of her body pressed up against mine. "Thank you."

"Always," I promised her.

Ellie pushed at my chest. "Now, go away. I have to finish getting ready, and we'll never make it out of here if you're being this sweet to me."

I quirked an eyebrow. "Why, because it makes you want to—"

"Owen!" She slapped a hand over my mouth, laughing. "Out. Go get your costume on."

"Fine." I gave her a quick kiss before padding into the bedroom, crouching in front of Zamboni's bed. "Your mommy kicked me out, huh?"

"I can still hear you!" She shouted from the bathroom.

I laughed as I went to put on my costume, trying to figure out how I'd gotten so lucky.

My dream girl was back in my life, and we were together, and everything else would fall into place. At least, I hoped it would.

I INTERLACED my fingers with Ellie's as we walked into the Captain's house. Though that word wasn't quite right, considering how large the place was. Stefan and Lauren had bought it after they'd gotten married, no doubt thanks to his large salary. Now, she was expecting their first child.

Would this be Ellie and I's life someday? If she chose to stay in Seattle—stay with me? I hoped so. I wanted to see her with my ring on her finger, glowing with happiness as she carried our baby. Not yet—we still had so much time to make up for. But someday. I'd always known I wanted a family. With such a large, loving family like ours, how could I not? I'd never doubted my parent's love for me. They'd supported me through everything.

I knew how I felt—how I'd always felt—but it was so hard to let myself feel it fully again, because I knew what would happen if she left me again. It would devastate me. How would I survive it?

Ellie squeezed my hand as we looked up at the door.

"I can't believe you're here with me," I admitted. "All of this feels like a dream. Ever since you showed up at the arena and I saw you on the other side of the boards."

"It's not," she said, cupping my cheek with her palm. I closed my eyes, leaning into her touch. "It's not a dream, Owen. I'm here."

"Good." I leaned down to kiss her, but then the front door opened, and I was greeted by the sight of Brooks, who was grinning as he leaned against the door.

Ellie's cheeks were pink, like we'd just been caught doing something we shouldn't have been. "Oh, hi."

"Hey, you two. Want to come inside?" He was dressed like Marty McFly from Back to the Future, and I gave him a nod in greeting. "I told Cap I'd man the door so he and Lauren can be good hosts, but really, I'm just trying to keep her off her feet."

We walked into the entryway, taking in all the decorations around the house. Brooks wandered off, probably to get another drink, and I had a moment alone with my girl.

"Should we have brought Zamboni?" Ellie whispered to me. "I feel bad about leaving her alone."

"She'll be okay, El," I promised. "She has to get used to

her crate, anyway." We were crate training her for when Ellie was at work and I was at the arena, and neither one of us was home with her. "It's just a few hours, and then we can go home." I ran my fingers through her hair.

We were dressed as Barbie and Ken, which should have felt a little emasculating, but I didn't really care. We'd picked out the costumes at the last minute, and I was just glad we'd found something that fit me. Plus, I was really digging Ellie in those boots. It was hot as fuck.

She bit her lip, and her eyes flared with heat. Yeah, I wanted to get her alone tonight. To peel that pink outfit off her body and—

"Behave," Ellie whispered.

"Can't help it," I murmured, cupping her ass and then squeezing it. "You look so hot right now, Ellie baby."

She stood on her tiptoes to kiss my cheek, and then said low against my ear, "You can show me just how hot you find me later, Hockey Boy."

I smirked. Damn right I would. "Let's go, baby." Threading our fingers together, I headed towards the living room. "Time to meet the rest of the team."

She'd met some of my teammates that night at the bar, and a lot of their wives and girlfriends, but it was a big team. And everyone was here for our Halloween party—even Coach Donovan and his daughter, Sophia. Victoria Monroe, our assistant coach, was chatting with Lauren Kovac in the living room. I was pretty sure it was the first time I'd seen her with her hair down, since she normally wore it in a braid or bun for practices and games.

Everyone was in a costume, and I grinned. Rhodes was dressed as a grumpy lumberjack, though the grumpy part was one hundred percent *him*, while the Captain and his wife were dressed as skeletons, complete with a little skeleton baby over Lauren's bump. We also had a doctor and a nurse duo, some zombies, a sexy firefighter, and more.

This was one of my favorite events of the year with everyone, because it was an opportunity we all had to relax and unwind during the season, and we could just be ourselves. No press, no hockey, no PR—just the guys, our girls, and a giant spread of themed snacks and drinks.

I took her around, pointing the rest of the guys out to her by name and introducing her to everyone as my girl. My boys Brooks and Maverick were both wearing identical, shit-eating grins as they saw me with Ellie. Rolling my eyes, I tried not to focus on how different the party felt this year. Of course, this was the first year I was bringing anyone with me to team events.

I'd never had a girlfriend to bring before. No one to sit in the wives' room waiting for me, or to cheer me on in the stands. Maybe because I knew that anyone else would pale compared to Ellie.

Ellie, practically beaming at my side, was dressed in hot pink and looking as stunning as ever. It wasn't a color she wore often—maybe because it was her older sister, Abi's favorite— but I liked the glow she had. It was kicking my heart into overdrive, and I hoped she couldn't hear how rapidly it was beating in my chest as I looked at her. Obsessed was an understatement.

Maybe that was why I was ignoring the fact that there was fringe on my matching costume.

"I'm gonna go say hi to Sophia," she whispered to me, seeing the coach's daughter in the other room.

I kissed the top of her head. "Okay. Have fun."

She smiled, heading off towards her friend, and I grabbed a beer from the kitchen.

"I'm happy for ya," Reid said, patting me on the shoulder as he joined me. He was dressed in a traditional Scottish kilt. I almost teased him for using his heritage as his costume, but damn, the guy pulled it off well. We all liked to poke fun at each other on the team. After so many years playing together, most of the guys were used to giving each other shit.

Taking a long pull of my beer, I couldn't help but grin. "Thanks, man." I'd been worried that she would be a distraction, but so far, everything was amazing.

We'd won our home game this week, and we had another one tomorrow. One that Ellie would be in the stands at, hopefully wearing the jersey I'd just given her.

"I can't believe you got a puppy," he said, running his fingers over his red beard.

After Ellie had come home, I'd texted my group chat with the guys and sent them a photo. "I've wanted one for a long time," I admitted. "Couldn't imagine leaving one behind during road trips, though."

"So what changed?"

My eyes drifted over to Ellie, who was smiling and laughing with Sophia. I chuckled. "She did." I couldn't imagine her being alone in my big empty apartment, either. I'd been lonely, but I didn't want her to be. Taking another sip of my drink, I turned back to my teammate.

"Big sap, that's what you are," Brooks said, sliding in next to us.

"Where's Mav?" I looked around the room, but didn't see his brother. Rhodes was sitting on the couch, though I couldn't help but notice the way his eyes drifted over to Coach's daughter every so often.

"Think he's flirting with Monroe again," Brooks said, rolling his eyes.

His brother had been flirting with our Assistant Coach ever since she'd taken over the role, though she kept turning him down. It was amusing for the rest of us, to say the least. The administration would never allow it, but I had to give it to him. He was bound and determined.

I laughed. "That sounds like your brother." He was a giant

flirt. Had been as long as I'd known him. "One day some girl is going to make him fall on his ass, mark my words."

"Probably." Reid cracked open his own beer, though I knew he preferred something stronger. "All the mighty succumb, eventually."

"What about you, Mack? Anyone special in your life?"

"Nope. No time for the lasses." He tapped his head. "Gotta keep everything fresh up here. Stay sharp. How else can I be the top goalie in the league?"

Brooks chuckled, adjusting his sleeves and then pulling on his puffy vest. "It's okay. Leaves more for the rest of us."

I scrunched up my nose. "Speak for yourself." I'd never been interested in bunnies or any of the girls that were hanging around on the off chance they could sleep with a pro-hockey player. Not that I'd ever been attracted to them, anyway. The only girl who seemed to get my dick hard was currently across the room in a bright pink barbie outfit, and damn if that wasn't just the way I liked it.

"Don't worry. I know you're off the market." My partner nudged me in the arm with his elbow. "I knew from the moment you introduced us to her that you weren't ever going to look at anyone else."

He was right. Even though I hated that I was so easy to read. "She's the only one for me, man." I admitted.

Brooks made a little whipped motion with his hand and a sound. "Harps, it's been nice knowing you."

I rolled my eyes. "Nothing's going to change, you jerk." I shoved at his shoulder. "Also, does anyone think Rhodes looks extra grumpy tonight? I swear, he's been scowling ever since he got here."

"Oh, yeah." Reid agreed. "Plus, he can't take his eyes off of Soph. I think Coach would kill him if he went there."

Grimacing, I tried not to imagine the look on Coach's face if someone actually dared to lay a finger on his daughter. It was one of his biggest rules, especially since Sophia was always hanging around the team lately. "No one's dumb enough for that."

I couldn't imagine what I'd do if I hadn't been allowed to be with Ellie. I'd asked her parents' permission before we ever started dating, and he'd made sure my intentions were good. And they were. I'd cared about Ellie in a way that went beyond words.

She was my sunshine, and I was happy to have my world orbit around her.

As if summoned by my thoughts, my beautiful barbie sauntered up to me, tilting her cowgirl hat back.

"Hi," she murmured, winding an arm around my waist.

"Hey, Skater Girl." I pressed a kiss to her forehead. "Having fun?" Ellie nodded, her eyes bright. "Good." I squeezed her hip.

"I'm gonna grab a drink," she said, pulling back. "Don't have too much fun, boys."

I watched her sashay away, watching the way her hips swayed with the motion, and when I turned back to the guys, I knew they'd all just seen me staring at her ass. I just shrugged.

Stefan joined us, his face paint a little smudged around his lips. I grinned. I suspected that his wife's makeup was equally messed up. "Hey, Cap. Having a good time?"

He ran his fingers through his dark hair. "I told Lo the face paint was a bad idea. Can't even kiss my damn wife without everyone teasing me about it."

"Hey, at least you aren't wearing fringe, like this cowboy here," Maverick said, throwing an arm around me.

"Look who finally decided to join us," Reid snorted. "Did you strike out?"

Mav crossed his arms over his chest. "No."

"Sure." Brooks rolled his eyes.

Our captain turned to me. "Harps. I've known you a long time, man, but I gotta say, I don't think I've ever seen you so happy. I think she's good for you."

I was pretty sure my ears were red—the Scandinavian and Irish heritage from both of my parents certainly hadn't given me a complexion that could hide my embarrassment. I also burned like a lobster in the sun, so hockey was definitely the best sport I could have chosen.

"Thanks." I didn't voice my concerns. That I'd get distracted. Most of the guys knew I'd had a serious girlfriend in high school and college before signing my contract and joining the team, but they didn't know what had happened.

How I'd almost lost everything after I'd lost her. I couldn't repeat that again.

THIRTY-TWO

Ellie

Owen kept glancing across the room at me, his eyes filled with heat. A bunch of the guys were in the kitchen with him, including the Hendrix brothers, Lauren's husband Stefan, and Reid. Was it weird to be in the same room and still miss him? We'd been here for an hour, maybe, but had spent most of the time in our little groups.

My cheeks flushed when he grinned at me. He looked so ridiculous in his Ken getup, and I couldn't believe he'd agreed to wear it. But it was perfect for us, and damn, he could pull off a black cowboy get-up. And you know what they say about cowboys… I bit my lip, thinking about all the horses I could save. Given his possessive grip when he'd squeezed my hip earlier, I was pretty sure he was thinking the same.

Damn, I couldn't get enough of him. Maybe it was because this was so new, because we'd never had a chance before, but I was ready to pounce on him already. I took a long drink of my lemonade.

"So it's serious?" Sophia asked after the third time he glanced over.

"Huh?" I looked back at my friend and then realized what she'd asked me.

I hoped it was. It felt serious. How could rekindling things with your ex be anything but? "He asked me to come to the rest of his games this season, so…" My cheeks were pink. I wasn't exactly going to tell her about his *you're mine* proclamation, even though it still made me hot just thinking about it. "And he gave me his jersey to wear."

"Oh, honey." Sophia patted my arm.

I frowned. "What, is that a bad thing?"

Lauren laughed from the couch. "No, Ellie. The opposite. If he wants you to come wearing his jersey, I'd say it's definitely serious. And the way he looks at you…" She fanned her face. Her skeleton face makeup still looked almost close to perfect, even with her husband's inability to keep his hands off of her. The Captain was pretty damn obsessed with his wife, that was clear.

"But most of you don't wear your guys jerseys to the games, right?"

Bailey just shook her head. All of them looked like I was missing something. "That's because we go to a lot of games every year, not because they don't like seeing us in them. In fact, they *really* enjoy seeing us in them." She raised her eyebrows suggestively.

"I wore Owen's sweater all the time when we were younger," I said. "Whenever I went to his junior's games." I still had it somewhere, though it was probably back home in Portland. I hadn't brought all of my stuff with me when I'd moved—I was glad I hadn't, since I'd barely lived in that apartment before moving out. It would have been so much worse if I'd had all of my belongings since childhood there.

Part of me knew I should check on my apartment. Owen said he wanted me to stay with him, that he wanted me there, and I also knew I didn't want to go back to that place, but I also felt terrible about living with him rent-free. Though now that we had Zamboni, I couldn't imagine moving out, either.

"But did you ever *just* wear his jersey?" Harlow asked, leaning over conspiratorially. "That really drives Jonah crazy."

I blushed. "Um. No." We'd been too young back then. Not that I wanted to blurt out in front of all these women that we hadn't been having sex as teenagers. Or that I could still count the amount of times I'd *had* sex on one hand.

"Try it sometime," Lauren suggested, giving me a little wink, rubbing her belly. "Pretty sure that's how we made this one."

"Oh." My face was on fire. "I mean, I don't think we're quite ready for that yet—" I was only twenty-two. We'd barely gotten back together. It had been the blink of an eye, really.

Sophia burst out laughing. "*Lauren,*" she scolded, but there was a playfulness to her tone. It was almost amusing, because normally she was the one saying the most off-the-wall, out-of-pocket things. She seriously had no filter. "You're going to scare off our poor, innocent Ellie."

Maybe I wasn't as innocent as she thought, though, because I liked the idea of it. Of Owen getting home, finding me wearing nothing else. Knowing how much he'd liked finding me wearing his shirt and asleep in his bed, I could only imagine how much he'd like that.

I'd just make sure I stayed up to date on my birth control, because we definitely didn't need any accidents. Maybe we should start using condoms. It was probably irresponsible to let him keep coming inside of me, even though it felt so good for both of us. Damn.

Owen raised his eyebrow at me, and I was sure he could read the confusion spelled out over my face. I looked towards the back door. They had a large backyard, and their covered patio had a porch swing and a space heater. Harlow and Bailey's guys came over to join us, settling onto the couches next to them, and I took that as a sign.

Okay, maybe I just wanted an excuse, but who could blame me when he was looking at me like *that?* Like he couldn't wait to get me home, strip me down, and ravish me. *Ravish?* I mentally scolded myself, because what was this, a bodice ripper?

I headed outside, letting the cool air cool my face off as I breathed in the fresh air. That was something I loved about the Pacific Northwest, and one reason I'd never been able to imagine leaving. I loved the smell of the pine trees. Of the rain in the air.

The smell reminded me of Owen.

A pair of arms slid around my shoulders, and the man in question's head rested on top of mine. I liked our height difference. How I was just short enough to fit tucked inside his body. How he was tall enough that I had to stand on tiptoes to reach his lips.

"Hi, Daisy," he said against my ear, swaying us back and forth.

"Hi." I let out a breath of relief. Just being in his arms had my body relaxing.

"What got you so flustered in there?"

I shook my head. Now was *so* not the time. "Nothing," I lied.

"Mmm." His rumble in my ear shouldn't have been so sexy. It certainly shouldn't have made my panties damp. But there was just something about *him*, about the sexual appeal that practically dripped off of him these days.

Maybe it was all the time we'd spent apart. That in that time, he'd gone from a boy to a *man*. A man with a perfectly sculpted body, like he was chiseled to perfection. Either way, it was hopeless to resist him. It always had been. That was probably why me insisting we not sleep together was a stupid proclamation. We were uniquely made for each other, and everything else was just inevitable.

"I like this," I murmured. "Being here with you." Being his girl.

Owen pressed a kiss to my neck. "Good. Because I like you being here, too."

Humming, I snuggled my back against his chest, savoring the moment.

We stayed like that for a while, enjoying the damp fall weather outside, though I wasn't cold thanks to the heater on the patio. It was just… nice. Peaceful.

After everything we'd gone through, peace was something we needed.

I wasn't taking a single moment for granted. Not with us.

WE GOT HOME AFTER MIDNIGHT, and even though I had school in the morning—and Owen had a game—I was wide awake. I'd had a few drinks over the course of the evening, but I wasn't drunk. I had a magical, happy buzz. That perfect level of tipsy when everything felt right in the world. I set my hat on the counter, running my fingers through my blonde strands of hair.

Twirling through the house on my tiptoes, I headed to the crate, freeing Zamboni from her tiny prison.

"Hi, baby," I said, showering her little golden face with kisses. "Did you miss us? Because I missed you so much." I held her head between my hands and she licked my nose. "Such a good girl, Zambi. Should we take you out for a walk?" I grabbed her leash, and when I turned around, I found Owen looking at me with an amused expression.

"What?" I furrowed my eyebrows.

His eyes dragged down my body with a heated expression. "You're going out like that?"

I was still in my hot pink Barbie cowgirl outfit. Owen had taken his hat and shirt off after we'd gotten home—which was a shame, because I loved the cowboy look on him—and was just wearing his undershirt and black jeans.

"Uh-huh." I nodded. "What's wrong with my outfit? I wore it to the party. Besides, we gotta take her out before bed, right?" I scrunched up my nose.

He chuckled, padding towards me, grabbing a sweatshirt off the chair and pulling it on over his head. "I'll take her out. It's cold outside. You can go change."

"Oh." He was right. It *was* chilly outside. And my costume didn't exactly have sleeves. "Alright."

Owen took our puppy from my arms, kissing me softly before clipping on her harness before heading out the door. I watched his ass as he walked, giggling to myself. God, it was a nice ass. I wanted to dig my fingers into it and *squeeze*.

Heading back to Owen's room, I pulled my boots off and collapsed on the bed, smiling at the ceiling. Running my fingers over my lips, I thought about how natural it was to kiss him again. How right it felt to be in his arms.

Maybe it was the alcohol in my system, the pleasant hum in my veins, but I *definitely* wasn't ready for bed yet. No. I had *plans*. We'd been making up for lost time this week, and I wanted to be on top this time. To show him just how much he meant to me. To make him feel good, like he always made me.

The front door opened and closed, and I heard Owen talking to Zambi out in the living room, telling her what a good girl she was.

Didn't he know *I* was his good girl? I pulled my bandana off from around my neck, dropping it onto the bed. Standing up, I pulled my hair over one shoulder, unbuttoning the front of the vest and letting it drop down my shoulders.

I could practically *feel* Owen's presence at the doorframe as I continued to strip, dragging the zipper down the pants and shimmying them off, exposing my panties and bra to him. Hot pink, just like my outfit.

"Ellie," he groaned. "You're going to kill me."

Running my tongue over my lips to moisten them, I undid the clasp of my bra, letting it fall to the floor before dragging my panties down my legs.

"You're so goddamn beautiful, Eleanor."

No one really called me my full name. And they certainly didn't say it the way he did, filled with so much longing and desire that I wanted to *melt*.

Heat pooled in my core and I ran my hands down my naked body, flicking over my nipples and letting out a soft moan. I was already so turned on, and Owen standing there, fully clothed while I was bared to him, made it even hotter. I ran my hands down my side, letting my fingertips trail over his number on my side. It hurt like a bitch, but it was worth it. *So* worth it, just to see the man I'd always loved barely holding back.

I smiled at his restraint, but the outline of his erection pressed against his pants made it obvious that he wanted this as badly as I did.

"Do you like what you see?" I cupped my tits, fluttering my eyelashes at him as he watched me.

"Yes," he groaned. "Fuck." Owen reached down, squeezing his cock. "Come here, baby. Let me touch you."

I shook my head as I rolled my nipples between my fingers. "Not yet."

He whimpered. "Ellie." The sound was pained. "I need you. Please."

Sauntering towards him, I dropped to my knees in front of him, sliding my hands over his waist before unbuttoning his pants. Owen grunted as I dragged his zipper down, pulling his cock out and running my tongue over his crown.

"You're always taking care of me," I said, dragging my tongue flat over his tip. "Now, let me take care of you." The other night in the shower had been the first time I'd done this, and I liked how powerful it made me feel—like even though I was the one on my knees, he was at my mercy. God, it was hot.

Owen's fingers tangled in my hair as I took him into my mouth and sucked. I wound my arms around his body, hands finding his ass and squeezing his delicious hockey butt.

"Baby," he groaned, holding me still. "Your mouth feels too good, but I don't want to come down your pretty throat."

I popped off of him, standing up to wrap my arms around his neck, his cock pressed between us against my stomach.

He dipped his head, pressing a kiss to each side of my lips before finally kissing me. "You're fucking incredible. I am constantly in awe of you."

"I'm not the amazing one," I muttered. "You are." I was just a girl who had run away from my problems for the last five years.

I'd run away from Owen because… Because *what?* I bit my lip. Because I was scared. I was scared that he wouldn't have time for me, and our relationship would crumble under the pressure. Instead, I'd broken it. Broken us. And a few months later, when I'd gotten hurt skating, I could have gotten back out there after my knee surgery, but I hadn't. I'd hidden away, convincing myself that it was safer that way.

But it wasn't. Everything I'd done to protect myself, and all it had gotten me was years of time wasted. Things I'd missed out on. *This.* We'd missed out on this.

"Take me to bed," I whispered.

He picked me up, and I wrapped my legs around his waist, kissing him as he walked us to the bed. My tongue found his, and I moaned into his mouth as he stroked inside. I rocked my hips, rubbing against his hard length, and every brush against my clit sent ripples of pleasure through my system.

Owen set me down on the bed, laying me down with my hair sprawled out behind me, but I sat up. "I want to be on top this time," I said, putting one hand on his chest and pushing him down.

His responding grin was as bright as the sun. "Okay."

"Yeah?"

"Yeah. You want to ride me, Ellie girl? I'm not a cowboy, but I'm happy to save a horse." He smirked as he shed his pants and underwear. Owen laid back on the bed, and I straddled his hips, pinning his cock between us as I moved back and forth over it, giving my clit the friction it needed.

"Put me inside of you," he commanded, running his hands up my thighs till they settled on my hips. Oh, *God*. That had no business being so hot.

I raised my hips, guiding his tip to my entrance, and then I sank down on his cock, sliding down inch by inch. My hands were flat against his chest and I dug my nails in as I worked my way onto his thick length, moaning as he filled me. Would I ever get used to the feeling of him inside of me, stretching me wide? I don't think so.

"Feels so good," I moaned, shutting my eyes as I took every last inch. When he was buried to the hilt, I started rocking back and forth, grinding my clit down over his shaft. Owen's hands trailed over my skin before he cupped my breasts, rubbing my nipples in the same way I'd been teasing him before.

"Look at you. So goddamn beautiful, the way you're riding my cock." He let out a guttural sound as I clenched down around him. "Fuck, baby."

"I can feel you everywhere," I said, sprawling my hand over my abdomen, like I could feel where he was buried inside me from the outside. The fullness and the angle like this were incredible. It was everything I needed. Everything we'd been depriving ourselves of for years. "Why haven't we been doing this since I moved in?"

He thrust into me from below, matching the movements of my hips with his own, like he couldn't hold back. "You're the one—" *Thrust.* "—who said—" Another thrust. "—that we shouldn't sleep together, Ellie baby."

Suddenly, I couldn't remember why. Not when us, *together*, was everything.

I huffed in agreement, rising on my knees before slamming back down on his cock. "That was dumb."

"Fuck being friends, Ellie. There's no way I could ever be just friends with you." One of his hands moved down between my legs, rubbing a circle over my clit, while his gaze focused on where he disappeared inside of me.

"Feel us," he said, guiding my fingers so they were spread around his cock—the same way my pussy was. "Feel the way you're spread open around me."

A whimper escaped my lips. "It's too good. I'm going to come."

"That's my girl," he praised. "Come on my cock. Make a mess of me."

Oh my god. It only took a bit of pressure on my clit before I was toppling over the edge. "*Owen*," I cried out as I came, before collapsing against his chest. My orgasm wracked its way through me, every nerve in my body coming to life with pleasure.

I could feel my pussy fluttering and contracting around Owen's length as he continued to rock into me from below at a steady rhythm, and I knew he was close as I felt him grow even harder. His hands cupped my ass, squeezing roughly, and then he let out a grunt before spilling inside of me, filling me with his cum.

"Holy shit, El." His arms wrapped around my back, keeping him pressed firmly inside of me as I stayed seated on his cock. "That was—"

"I know." I let out a contended sigh. "It just keeps getting better."

He hummed, nuzzling his face into my neck. "I don't want to leave you in a few days." The words were murmured against my hair, and I knew what he meant.

"I'm not going anywhere," I promised, my words a sacred

vow. I meant it, too. There was no way I could give this up. Give him up.

A few moments later, I sat up, our combined releases trickling out of me, some of them ending up on Owen's abs.

His eyes sparked with amusement as I blushed. "We should probably start using condoms," I blurted out. "I know I'm on birth control, but we don't want any accidents."

Owen gave me a heated look, his hand sliding over my flat stomach. "It wouldn't be an accident. Not for us, baby. Fuck, the idea of you swollen with our child..." He reached down, wrapping a hand around my neck and pulling me up to his lips. He devoured me in a passionate, all-consuming kiss, and when we broke apart, he nipped at my lower lip. "Just the idea makes me want to keep you here, full of my cum, till I know it takes." He shook his head. "But I know that's just the caveman talking. So if you want to use condoms, I'll go out and buy some tomorrow."

I bit my lip. Did I *want* to? I didn't know how to answer that. Especially when Owen's dirty talk had my pussy clenching, just imagining the thought of him fucking me until I was pregnant with his baby. Okay, yeah, that was hot. And him coming inside of me was *hot*. Maybe the risk made it even hotter. Apparently, I had a breeding kink, but I was pretty sure Owen did too.

"Stay here." He pressed a kiss to the top of my head, heading to the bathroom. When he came back out a few minutes later, he had a washcloth in his hand. He cleaned me up with the warm, wet cloth, and then pulled me back into his arms, spooning me from behind. "Sleep," he whispered in my ear. "We have another long day tomorrow."

"Mmm." I closed my eyes, sated and warm, with his body wrapped around mine, and I'd never fallen asleep so quickly. It was a feeling of peace, and I wanted to hold on to it forever.

Owen

Tonight was our Halloween themed game, so there were tons of fans in costumes, and even our mascot, Slippers, was dressed up for the occasion. Ellie stood against the glass, a bright smile on her face. She was wearing the new jersey I'd given her, and I couldn't help but admire the way she looked wearing it. *Stunning.* The bright blue color made her eyes even brighter, and she'd pulled her hair back into two half pigtails, curling the blond strands just like she had last night in her Barbie costume.

I blew my girl a kiss as I skated around the net, hitting a few pucks in and warming up my muscles.

Sophia was at her side, both of them watching warm-ups from the rink level, practically pressed against the glass. I was glad she'd made friends with Coach's daughter, because at least I knew she had someone, so she wouldn't be alone at the games. They were like two peas in a pod, leaning over and giggling with each other as they watched us skate. Ellie had also talked about inviting Maggie, her teacher friend from school, to a game.

Damn, she was perfect. She had flourished into this sexy, beautiful woman right before my eyes. When she'd told me last night that she wanted to ride me, I'd almost lost it right then and there. I'd never been harder than I was when she dropped to her knees in front of me, denying me from touching her and wrapping her lips around my cock.

Shit. I didn't need to get hard right now. And I definitely didn't need the distraction of thinking about Ellie when we were about to play sixty minutes of hockey against one of our division rivals. Sure, the season was still getting underway, but every point mattered with making the playoffs for the Stanley Cup, and I knew we all wanted to win it for the team. Our defense needed to be tight tonight, especially any potential penalty kills, to help us stay on top.

Skating over to the bench—aware of my girl watching me with every breath—I did a few stretches and centered myself, trying to get my head in the game. *No distractions.* It wasn't easy, though.

There was something about knowing Ellie was out there—knowing she was watching me—that made me want to play even harder. It made me want to get the W for her. To score goals for *her*. Because she was here for me and wasn't that just the miracle of it all? That she was in Seattle. That she was in my apartment. In my heart.

Maybe it was fate that her apartment had flooded. That I'd shown up to sweep her off her feet and bring her back to my place.

She was proving to be the sweetest distraction I'd ever had, but I still couldn't get enough of her. Couldn't get enough of the way it felt to have her here, flooding my veins with the strangest sense of satisfaction.

"Dude." Brooks punched me in the shoulder as we headed off the ice and back to the locker room as warm-ups came to a close. Rhodes followed behind us, and soon the entirety of our top line was in a huddle in the hallway. "What's up with you? You're all starry-eyed and can't stop staring into the stands."

"My girl is here," I admitted. It was better than saying *I had the best sex of my life last night. That* was what was up. The best sex of my life followed by hours of just holding her in my arms, feeling her tucked against my body.

Rhodes let out a grunt. "I saw she was here with Donovan's daughter." I noticed he didn't call her Sophia like the rest of us did. She hated only being known as his daughter and not her own person. But she was still here, at almost every game, supporting her dad. I knew she was a damn good physical trainer, one the Seals would have been lucky to have. Still, she stubbornly refused the job offer, not wanting it to look like she only got the position because of him.

"Yeah. They've gotten pretty close. I have to admit… It's nice, seeing her with everyone else's girls. Like she belongs here."

Because she does. She fit in so well, and how could she not? She was the brightest ray of fucking sunshine, this beautiful girl who was always smiling bright as a daisy, and every bit as beautiful.

Getting up this morning had been torture, and not just because Ellie had been up at six, getting ready for work. But she was still here. She hadn't left. And the sigh of relief when she showed up at the apartment right before I had to leave for the game almost rode every fear of mine that she'd leave again. *You did that to her, too,* I reminded myself. This summer, I'd left her with a goodbye note and snuck away without a word. Was it just as painful for her? Probably.

I'd let her go, but she'd… *followed me to Seattle.* My knees almost buckled at the thought. I'd stayed away, but she had come after me. She hadn't said the words to me, but when I'd asked her why she'd moved to Seattle before, she'd hesitated.

Because *she'd moved here for me.* Fuck. How had I not been on my knees for her this entire time?

"He's smitten," Maverick said, smirking at me as swung

my gaze back to the guys. "That's how you know he's a goner."

"Shut up," I grumbled.

Rhodes crossed his arms over his chest. "This is why I've sworn off love. Makes you all gooey-eyed and sloppy."

I shook my head. "*Love?* Who said anything about love?" The words felt sour in my mouth, though, and I knew it was a lie the moment it left my lips.

"Can you picture yourself without her? Her with some other man, someone else's ring on her finger?" My Captain asked, quirking his eyebrow.

"No." The word was almost a growl.

"You do, then." Stefan nodded. "You love her."

Of course, I loved her. I always had. I pulled my helmet off to drag my hand over my face and up through my hair. "Yeah, I... I don't think I ever stopped." I closed my eyes. "I just can't fuck this up, you guys. I can't lose her again. The last time I did..."

"We know." Brooks patted my shoulder. "So *don't.*"

"You make it sound so simple." I frowned. It didn't feel simple. It felt like this huge, monumental thing. The last time we were together, we'd been kids. We'd given each other our virginities and then she'd left the next morning like I meant nothing to her.

But now...

"Course it is, Harps." Stefan sounded so sure. Of the five of us, he was the one with a wife and baby on the way. "You just have to tell her how you feel."

"But what if I do, and she leaves again?" I was that same broken nineteen-year-old on my dorm bed again, crying on the phone with my mom. Fear pierced my heart. "Fuck, you guys. I'm a mess. I should tell Coach to take me off the line-up for the night. I can't..."

"Owen." Brooks grabbed me by the shoulders. "He's not wrong, Harps. And you have to decide if she's worth it."

"Of course she is." That had never been a doubt in my mind.

Stefan slapped his hand against my helmet. "Then get your damn head in the game and let's go play some fucking hockey."

"Aye, aye, Capt."

Everyone laughed, but it was the reminder I needed. After years of playing, I knew how to get into the zone. How to get out of my head. For so many years, I'd built a wall of ice around my heart. The only thing that mattered to me was Ellie. But she'd been melting it with her warmth and her beaming smile. Every time I saw her, it chipped away a little further.

But that place was as familiar to me as breathing. It was why I was such a good d-man on the ice. I knew how to block. Wasn't afraid of a few body-checks to protect my team, either.

And tonight, I had to give it my all. Because she was watching, and I wanted her to see that everything we'd given up was worth it.

That those five years apart had given me this, and I wasn't wasting that opportunity. I missed her like fucking hell all that time, but I'd become exactly what I wanted to be. A professional hockey player. At the top of my game.

By the time we came back onto the ice for puck drop, I felt sharp. *Focused.* The first shift went by in the blink of an eye, and then we were on the bench, watching a new play we'd been working on. Our second line, Campbell, Meyer, and Evans, battled for puck possession when the opposing team got it, knocking it down the ice and getting an icing call. After a few more stops in play, followed by Reid catching the puck in his glove and getting a whistle, we got the signal to swap back in.

"Hendy, Harps, you're up!" Coach called out, and we hopped over the boards, joining the forwards on the ice. Another defenseman pair, Sorensen and Tremblay, settled onto the bench we'd just vacated, finishing both of their first shifts.

Since Reid had stopped the puck, we settled in our zone for the face-off. Our primary goal was to get it away from the net and not let them take another shot on goal. This early in the period, they hadn't started out-shooting us yet, but I wasn't about to let them, either. We were back on the ice with Rhodes, Maverick, and Stefan, and *damn* did I love playing with this line.

Rhodes won the face-off, and quickly passed it to Maverick, who was on a breakaway towards the other side of the ice. He was legendary for his speed and being able to get it in deep, which was probably why he was one of our highest scoring players on the team every season. He slapped it in towards the net, but it was knocked away by their goalie, and Rhodes tried to get it on the rebound, but it didn't go in. It felt like the entire arena groaned alongside us, but then we were in motion again, chasing the puck back and forth down the ice.

By the time we were halfway through the first period, we were all desperate for that first goal. Something about tonight had us all craving it, and we wanted to take an early lead over Ottawa.

Brooks nodded at me as we started our next shift. It was a silent reminder that yeah, *we got this*. The two of us had played together for so long that I could read his body language with ease. The second line was still on the ice as we swapped out with Sorensen and Tremblay, giving us a shift on the ice with them.

After a few blocked shots—one that bounced off my skate —we had a two on one coming up the ice, and I kept possession past their blue line, my gaze focused on the goal. It was open. The perfect play set up. Ottawa's defense was behind us —a failed turnover they definitely wouldn't be happy about.

This. This right here was one of my favorite parts about

hockey. The ice under my skates, the puck between my stick, and the net in front of me.

"I'm open!" Mav shouted. He was in front of me, at the perfect angle to get a beautiful tip-in goal. I passed it to him and he sunk the puck into the net.

Their goalie didn't even have time to respond, thanks to our speed, and looked stumped as it crossed the goalpost line. The buzzer went off, and Maverick pumped his fist into the air. "YES!" The arena burst out into screams of applause. Our home crowds were always amazing, and tonight was no different.

"Fuck yeah!" I cheered, throwing my arms around him.

"Let's fucking *goooo!*" Stefan said, joining our group huddle. All five of us were grinning as we all celebrated the first goal of the game—even Rhodes, the grumpy bastard, cracked a smile. Skating over to the bench, our teammates fist-bumped us down the line.

Coach gave a nod of approval.

We needed that.

Damn, but we'd needed it.

They announced the goal, giving me the assist, and the crowd went wild.

I looked up, and my gaze collided with Ellie, who looked so proud.

Right at this moment, no matter how everything else played out, I felt like I was on top of the world.

DRIVING HOME with Ellie in my car was something I'd never imagined after a game, but fuck, I'd liked it. I loved going into the wives' room, finding her chatting with the other women as she waited for me. We'd never had this before.

A few of the guys had invited me out to the Penalty Box

after the game, going to grab some drinks, but tonight, I just wanted to be with my girl. I'd promised them we'd come together soon, which had satisfied my teammates, so at least there was that. It felt like ages had passed since Ellie had met me there at the beginning of the season, and here we were.

I had my hand on her thigh the entire drive, trying to ignore how good she smelled. God, she was beautiful. Beautiful and *mine*.

Her wearing my name all night had riled me up. It did something to me. I wanted it there—always. Wanted her to have my name, my ring on her finger. *Everything*.

When I pulled into the parking garage under the apartment, I squeezed her thigh. "Thank you for being there tonight."

"Of course, babe." Her expression was soft. Serene. "I'd go anywhere you asked. Follow you anywhere."

I dipped my head down, kissing her softly, wishing we were already upstairs in the apartment and not still in my car. Winning had me all amped up, the adrenaline in my system giving me a high. There was no way I was sleeping anytime soon, despite the late hour.

She brushed her hand up my leg, and my dick twitched. "Is it weird I miss your old truck?"

Laughing, I shook my head. "I was just thinking the same thing. It had a lot more room for… extracurriculars." I winked at her.

She bit her lip. "And to think, we didn't take advantage back then." Her eyes were full of heat. Desire. *Need*.

"*Fuck me*, Ellie. Get that sweet ass of yours upstairs." I held in a groan. "We're making up for lost time right now."

Her lips tilted up in a tiny smile, and then she was out of the car, heading up towards the elevators. I followed right behind her, crowding her inside the empty elevator car. My lips were a mere brush away from hers, and I wondered if she had any idea how badly I wanted to take her right here. I'd never been into exhibitionism before, but I was pretty sure I'd be into anything with her.

The lift stopped on our floor, and I swatted her ass as she walked out of the elevator in front of me, letting me see the back of her jersey. Damn, I wanted to fuck her in it. Wanted to take her behind, so I could see it as I thrust inside of her, as I made her scream my name over and over till she came.

Goddamn. I adjusted my cock in my suit pants. I couldn't wait to get my girl into bed.

When we got inside, I went over to the crate to let Zamboni out—luckily, she was proving to be alright when we left her for a few hours like this, but she definitely needed to go out. "I'm gonna take Zambs outside, El." We'd fed her dinner, and I'd taken her on a walk right before we left for the game, but I didn't want her having any accidents. There were puppy pads still—though she was mostly going outside. I was a proud dog dad. After we came back, I'd give her a bone to chew on, so she hopefully gave us some alone time.

"Okay!" She disappeared into my room—though it really felt more like *our* room now.

I hooked on our puppy's harness and leash, heading back down the elevator and outside into the chilly November weather.

God, I couldn't believe it was already November. That meant my family would be here in a few weekends—staying in my house. I didn't really know what Ellie and I were—neither one of us had used a label yet, even though she was *mine*—but once they were here, everyone would know. We wouldn't have our calm little bubble of peace anymore.

Though I suspected most of our cousins already had a pretty good idea.

"I'm an idiot, aren't I, Zamboni?"

She turned around, yipping at me to walk faster, and I chuckled to myself, complying as we walked towards the dog park, using the time to cool down. I wanted to take my time and not rush things.

Last night had been amazing, and I wanted tonight to be just as good for both of us.

By the time I got back upstairs, most of the lights were out in the apartment, only the under-counter lighting on in the kitchen. I unhooked Zamboni's harness and hung it up on the hook, getting her a bone and letting her take it over to her crate to chew on it.

My girl came out a few seconds later, and for a moment, I forgot how to speak. All words simply ceased to exist in my vocabulary.

"Ellie." My voice was low. A warning.

She acted like she had no idea what had me all riled up. "Hm?"

"What are you wearing?" It was hardly more than a grumble.

Her long, slender legs were bare, and that blonde hair tumbled down in sexy waves down her shoulders. She was still wearing my jersey.

Only my jersey.

"Oh, this?" She batted her eyelashes, fiddling with the hem of the sweater. "Do you like it?" She stopped in front of me, sliding a hand up my chest.

"Fuck, yes." I shut my eyes, trying to ignore my rapidly hardening cock in my pants.

She pushed the suit jacket off my shoulders, and I shrugged it off, draping it over the chair next to me.

Her eyes were lidded, like she was as turned on from this as I was. "Watching you tonight was so hot," she admitted. "I couldn't keep my eyes off of you." She bit her lip, slowly working her way down the buttons on my shirt.

"Damn, Ellie. Were you wet, seeing me on the ice?" My girl nodded. "Are you going to spread those legs for me and let me check?" Another nod, and Ellie's thighs slowly parted as she grabbed the hem of the jersey, pulling it up to give me the perfect view of her pretty pink cunt.

No panties. Fuck me. I was halfway to insisting she never wore them around the house. Especially with all the dresses she wore all the time.

"That's my girl," I praised her as I dipped a finger against her entrance, running it through her wetness. She was *soaked.* Swirling my finger over her clit, Ellie gasped as I pushed a finger inside. "I'm obsessed with this sweet little pussy."

I groaned as I kneeled in front of her. Nuzzling my nose against her entrance, I inhaled deeply. I needed to get my mouth on her. Needed just a taste of her. She let out a little gasp as I drove my tongue inside of her.

"Oh my god, Owen." She whimpered as I flicked my tongue against her clit, rolling it in circles before lapping at her entrance. I alternated between the two, taking my time eating her out. Ellie dug her fingers into my hair, holding me tight against her pussy. With my head buried between her thighs, I brought her right up to the edge, feeling how close she was, and then backed off, giving her gentle licks and slow strokes.

I didn't stop until she was crying my name, begging to come, so keyed up I knew she'd explode with the slightest amount of pressure. My thumb found her clit, and she cried out, squeezing around my tongue as she came all over my face. I licked up her release before pulling away, running my tongue over my lips. "Fuck, baby. I'll never get over the way you taste."

Ellie wrapped her arms around my neck, tilting her lips up, and I didn't hold back, giving her my mouth, kissing her hard. We stepped backwards as our mouths stayed locked together until she was pushed against the wall. Her cheeks were pink from the orgasm I'd just given her, her chest heaving, and she'd never looked more beautiful. "Owen." She curled her fingers through the back of my hair. "That was…"

"Yeah. Goddamn." I gritted my teeth. My cock was painfully hard in my pants, pressed against the zipper. "I need to be inside of you."

"I need to take care of my big, strong hockey player, huh?" Her voice was breathy, and she unbuckled my belt before sliding the zipper down slowly. Pushing my boxers down, she let my erection spring free. Her soft as sin palm ran up and down my shaft, pumping me a few times before I couldn't take it anymore, rocking my hips into her grasp.

Digging my fingers into her thighs, I picked her up, and she wrapped her legs around my waist, grinding my cock against her bare pussy. "*Oh.* Yes. Right there." Ellie dropped her head back against the wall. "That feels amazing."

"It's going to feel even better when I fuck you." I rubbed the head against her again, providing direct stimulation against her clit.

"Please," she begged. "I want you."

"I'm not going to be soft." I nipped at her neck. "Or gentle. It's going to be hard and fast."

Ellie nodded. "Yes. Just get inside of me, Hockey Boy. Fuck me."

I groaned, keeping her pinned against the wall as I guided my tip to her entrance, slamming inside without warning.

"Yes, yes, yes," she moaned, her eyes closing as I did just what I promised, fucking her against the wall. Her jersey slid up and down with each thrust, and

I gave her a light smack on her ass. "Eyes on me, baby. Watch me make you come."

They fluttered open, those blue-gray eyes I'd known my whole life. We'd grown up together. Experienced our firsts together. And this was, too. Us coming together. Losing ourselves in each other.

"Give me everything," I begged, thrusting harder. I wanted her. Her heart. Her future.

Ellie moaned as I rocked my hips into her over and over,

my fingers holding her tight enough that I was sure I was leaving marks. But I couldn't stop. Couldn't hold back.

I drove us both higher and higher, feeling the telltale signs of my orgasm building as Ellie's breaths deepened, her cunt pulsing around me in a vice grip like she didn't want to let me go.

"I'm gonna come, Ellie baby. Are you close? Need you to get there."

She nodded, dropping her head against my shoulder. "Right there, just—*yes!*" Her nails dug into my shoulder when her orgasm hit her, and I kept pumping into her, knowing I wasn't far behind. I brought her mouth back to mine, our tongues tangling in a messy kiss. Ellie bit my lip, and I grunted. Everything tightened, and then I stopped holding back, spilling everything I had inside of her.

"Fuck," she panted as she pulled back, brushing my sweaty hair off my forehead. "That was hot." She chuckled, one hand on my neck as the other combed through my hair.

"What?" I couldn't stop staring at her. Mesmerized by every aspect of her being.

"The girls were right." Her lips titled up in a devious smile.

I frowned, squeezing her thigh. "About what?"

"That wearing your jersey would drive you wild."

"You're right." I nipped at the tip of her nose, adjusted our position to wrap my arms around her ass, keeping my cock buried inside of her as I headed towards our bedroom. "It did. And I'm not done with you yet, baby."

Not by a long shot.

And I was pretty sure I never would be.

THIRTY-FOUR

Ellie

"So the jersey thing worked?" Sophia said, looking over at me from across the table. It had been a week since the last home game, and we'd decided to grab drinks to celebrate the end of the work week.

I laughed. "Yes. Maybe a bit *too* well." I scrunched up my nose, thinking about how sore I'd been the next day. Though I mostly attributed that to us fucking against the wall and then him taking me again on the bed from behind. He'd been rough, but I'd liked it. Loved it, even. Especially when he'd been so caring, tenderly cleaning me up afterwards. The next morning, he'd brought me breakfast in bed before kissing my forehead and heading to catch a plane for their first away game.

Luckily, Zamboni had cuddled up to me and kept me company while he'd been gone. I tried not to notice his absence too much, since I was supposed to be used to it by now. It helped that he called me every night, and every time his smile filled my phone screen, I felt better.

"On a scale of one to ten, how many orgasms did he give you?" She asked me, picking at her plate of teriyaki noodles. She'd brought me to her favorite Japanese place, and the food was amazing. I definitely wanted to come back here with Owen sometime.

"Sophia!" My cheeks were bright red.

"What?" She shrugged. "It's for science."

I raised an eyebrow. "What, are you thinking of sleeping with one of your dad's players?"

It was her turn to blush. "No. He'd *kill* me." She tapped her fingers on the table. "It's just…" Sophia sighed. "Never mind. It's stupid."

Laying my hand over hers, I squeezed it. "Whatever it is, I can assure you it's definitely *not* stupid. And…" I lowered my voice. "The answer is four."

"*Four?* Oh my god." She fanned her face. "I'm twenty-four, and I've never even had one." My friend gave me a little pout.

"Really?" I frowned. "Have you not…"

She shook her head, like she could guess where I was going with that. "I can, uh… have them by myself, you know. And I've had a few boyfriends. None of them could ever make me finish, though." She bit her lip. "I had to fake it. Eventually, they all kind of… fizzled out."

I could see why.

"Plus, I was never really sure if they were dating me for *me*, or because my dad was the Coach of a professional hockey team. When they started asking to come to games all the time or to meet the players, it just felt like they were… I don't know… *using me*."

Damn. "Sophia. That sucks. I'm so sorry."

She shook her head. "It is what it is. I just think I'm overdue for some good, hot sex, you know?"

"With a hockey player?"

Sophia hummed. "I mean. They have great stamina, right?"

I couldn't deny that. "*Really* good stamina. I mean, if Owen's any indication. He's the only person I've ever been with, so I don't have anything else to compare it to, but…" I held my face in my hands. "He's amazing. And he's so considerate and gentle with me, but then he's also a little wild in bed, and it's nothing like it was when we were younger."

"But?"

"Why do you think there's a but?" I frowned. "There doesn't have to be a but."

"I don't know. You seem like you're holding back. I've never even heard you call him your boyfriend."

It was weird, because calling him my boyfriend almost felt like an *understatement* of what we were to each other. He was my everything. But… "We haven't exactly put a label on it yet. I don't know. I only moved in with him because my apartment flooded, and then we agreed to be friends and…" One thing led to another, and here we were.

"He asked you to stay, though, right?"

"What do you mean?"

She blinked. "Like, stay with him. Even after they fix your apartment."

I hadn't thought about it in weeks, mostly because I hadn't even called my landlord for an update. He had told me to stay with him, but that was when I'd said I'd find a different place and not to impose on him. Had he said anything long term? "I…" Suddenly I felt sick to my stomach. "I don't know."

"I'm sure he will," Sophia said. "He's probably so focused on hockey that he didn't even think about it."

"Yeah." I forced a smile on my face. "I'm sure you're right." Besides, we had a dog together. He had to be thinking long term, right?

My teaching contract was technically only for a year, though, and it wasn't like I'd reassured him I would stay in Seattle, either.

God, I couldn't wait for him to get home. This definitely wasn't a conversation I wanted to have over the phone.

Not when the *l word* had been on the tip of my tongue for

the last week every time we hung up. But I couldn't bring myself to say it.

Maybe I was just scared that the perfect bubble we were living in was going to pop.

BEING TREATED as a WAG was a completely different experience than coming to games before. Was I Owen's girlfriend? I still didn't have an answer to that. But his expression when he'd gotten home three days ago, dropping his bag onto the floor and pulling me into his arms made me feel like I was.

Like he'd needed the comfort. Like he'd needed *me*. Zamboni had eagerly jumped on him a few minutes later, and then he was carrying me into the bedroom, showing me exactly how much he'd missed me.

Fuck, I was in too deep.

Especially when we were driving together to his games, and he kissed me before he left for the locker room and left me with Soph and the other wives and girlfriends. Tonight was no different. I hadn't worn his jersey to the game tonight—since I realized quickly why most of the girls didn't wear them to every game—but I could tell how much he loved having me there to watch him play.

"I take back what I said," she whispered into my ear after he'd walked away.

I turned to her, the expression clear on my face. "Huh?"

"There's no way he's ever letting you go, Ellie."

My cheeks flushed, but I tried to force my expression into a neutral one. "Maybe."

"Definitely," she insisted. "Now let's go get food. I'm *starving*."

"Great. I need a drink." Laughing, I let her pull me along,

chatting with the other girls and hanging out with the people that had become my friends over the last few weeks.

We went down to rink side for warm-ups, before Soph and I finally headed to our seats for the night.

Lauren was almost ready to pop, so she insisted on staying in the wives' room, saying she could watch the game on the TV. I was pretty sure her husband was fretting over her more than usual, because she was so close to her due date, but she seemed content being here, rubbing her belly as she watched the screen.

Being close to the action on the ice was my favorite, so I couldn't complain about the tickets, even if I had no desire to know how much Owen spent on them. He rarely threw his money around—or reminded me he was making millions every year—but I could tell this mattered to him.

And his coach seemed happy to have his daughter at his games. They seemed close, just from watching how they'd interact, and it made me miss my own parents. Owen's were coming up soon, and I couldn't wait to see my Aunt Noelle and Uncle Matthew—even if they weren't blood related, I'd grown up at their house. And the last few months felt like eternity when I was used to seeing them every weekend.

"I love having you here," Sophia confessed from my side as I licked ice cream off my cone. I'd wanted a sweet treat during the second intermission, and even though it was cold in the arena, I couldn't deny myself a swirl soft serve cone. "It's nice to have someone to hang out with."

"Ditto, Soph." I leaned my head on her shoulder. She was two years older than me, and in some ways, our relationship felt so much like Abigail and I's. We texted constantly—often sending each other hockey clips we'd found on social media or funny posts—and I appreciated having a friend here in Seattle. "I'm so glad we became friends."

Talking to her was just *easy*, and we hadn't stopped the entire game, unless the guys had gotten a goal so we could cheer, or when Sophia had stood up to yell at the refs for their bad calls. I told her all about my class and how school was going, and she talked to me about her job as a personal trainer and how much she loved it.

I also noticed every time Rhodes Larsen ended up on the ice, her eyes didn't seem to leave it, tracking him. She let out a little gasp when someone from the Florida team slammed him against the boards. *Interesting.*

It seemed like Sophia Donovan had a little crush on her dad's star forward. I was rooting for her—at the very least, my girl deserved some good sex to make up for her shitty ex boyfriends. Plus, the man was tall and handsome, though he wasn't my type, I could appreciate his physique.

The guys came back onto the ice as the third period started. Florida was being extra aggressive, trying to get the lead back since our guys currently were up by one with twenty minutes of regulation time left.

"Oh my god." My hand flew up to my mouth as a member of the opposing team slammed Owen against the boards in what *surely* had to have been an illegal move. He went down hard, hitting the ice. His helmet smacked the surface, and I winced, knowing that couldn't have been good for his neck.

Get back up, I willed him, unable to take my eyes off of him.

Finally, he did, heading to the bench and straight back to the locker room. He touched his eyebrow and then winced and—*was that blood?* The blood drained from my face.

"I—" I looked around wildly. "I have to go." My chest grew tight, and I wasn't sure I was breathing. "Fuck, Sophia, I —" I needed to see him. Needed to make sure he was okay. I let out a sound that was akin to a whimper.

Sophia grabbed my hand, squeezing. "Come with me. I can get you in there."

"You can? Is that okay?" I bit my lip. "I don't want to get Owen in trouble."

She nodded. "I'm the Coach's daughter. *No one* says no to me. I've got the credentials." She winked, and then tugged me towards the back area. It took a few minutes of winding through the tunnels until we stopped in front of the locker room door.

"This feels wrong," I whispered.

My friend shook her head. "It'll be okay. I promise. Don't worry."

I hoped she was right.

She softened her voice. "Hey. He'll be okay," she promised. "These hockey players—they're made of tough stuff. I've seen them go down from worse and still walk it off and play the rest of the season. They're probably just making sure he doesn't have a concussion."

I nodded. I knew that. It wasn't like I hadn't been around when he played hockey when we were kids. I'd seen his teammates get hurt and go out with injuries. But she didn't know the reason I'd stopped skating. That I'd let an injury keep me off the ice for years. That I was panicking for myself as much as I was for him.

Because seeing him go down had reminded me of my accident, and my fear had overtaken me. The logical part of me knew it hadn't been too bad, because he'd walked off the ice himself, but the other part couldn't help but be scared. I couldn't lose him. Not like this.

She knocked on the door before opening it, peeking inside, like she was making sure everyone was decent. Sophia said something to someone inside, and then was ushering me into the locker room. My eyes widened at the space. I'd seen the locker room in interviews, but never in person. It was a large, circular room with the Seals logo lit up on the ceiling, the whole thing practically in shades of blue and gray from the logo and jerseys.

I barely noticed any of it, though, zeroing in on the lone man sitting in the stall, a pack of ice pressed to his cheek as the team doctor checked him out. He'd already stripped out of his pads, just wearing a long-sleeved black t-shirt and a pair of athletic shorts. There was a bandage over his eyebrow where he'd been bleeding, and he definitely looked worse for the wear.

"Oh my god," I whispered, slapping a hand over my mouth as I moved towards him without thinking. He looked like he was in pain, and I hated it. I'd seen him take a lot of hits, but I was always grateful that he had never gotten seriously injured. Still, every game he'd ever left early from in his career was one where I'd been unable to breathe until I found out that he was okay.

Owen looked over at me, and his eyes instantly softened. The woman who had been checking on him gave him a nod, saying something else before she stepped out of the room.

"Come here, baby." He opened up his arms, and I stepped between his legs. He rested his forehead against my middle, and I ran my fingers through his hair.

"Are you okay?"

"Better now." He murmured, his legs closing in to trap me in place. "I'll be okay. Just needed you." Owen rubbed my back, holding me tight against him.

"Are you sure it's alright that I'm back here?" I'd never been inside a locker room before, especially not while a game was still being played. I turned to say something else to Sophia, but she had slipped out without me noticing, leaving the two of us alone. That felt like an impossibility. Being alone with him here with no one else around?

He shrugged. "It'll be fine. I'll explain to Coach later if he asks. If he benches me a game for it, well…"

His eyes closed as I continued massaging his head. "That scared the fuck out of me, Owen," I admitted. "Watching you go down. Not knowing if you were seriously hurt."

When he tilted his head up to look at me, his face was filled with so much emotion, I almost couldn't breathe. I had to look away to steady myself against from those beautiful, deep brown eyes that knew me better than I knew myself. Always had. Always would.

"I'm sorry, baby." He nuzzled his face against my stomach once again. "It's just part of the job. You know that."

I did. I just never thought about what it would be like to see it in person. When he was younger, he hadn't played at this level of physicality. The games hadn't been so fast-paced and... *brutal.*

"Can we go home?" I asked, instead of responding to him. "I'm guessing you're not going back on the ice for the rest of the night?"

He nodded. "In a bit." He looked down at his clothes. "I need to shower first. I'm so sweaty."

"Yeah." I wrinkled my nose. "No offense, but you stink."

Owen was hurt, a fact that I was trying to remind myself of, because he looked so hot, all sweaty and *dirty.*

He smirked. "What are you thinking, baby?"

I shook my head. "Nothing. Go shower."

Standing up off the bench, he towered over me. "Come with me."

"Owen." I looked around, my cheeks no doubt a shade of bright pink. "We can't. Someone could walk in."

"They won't," he promised. "There's still most of the period left. And the doctor already checked on me. I'm on concussion watch for the next twenty-four to forty-eight hours since I hit my head pretty hard, but I told them I had a roommate."

A roommate. Was that all I was?

His finger dipped under my chin, forcing my eyes to his. "I told them I have you, Ellie baby. That you'd take me home and take care of me."

I blinked, my eyes filling with tears. Wrapping my arms around him instead of looking at him, I buried my head in his chest. "I felt like I couldn't breathe," I admitted, my breaths heaving in my chest. "Like it was my accident all over again." My therapist had helped me after it, but I wasn't completely cured from the panic attacks.

"*Baby*." The word was soft.

He picked me up, wrapping my legs around his chest as he walked us towards the shower.

"After my accident, I couldn't get back on the ice. I kept having panic attacks any time I tried. And tonight, I just… I went back to that place." If Sophia hadn't been with me tonight, I wasn't sure what would have happened.

"I'm sorry," he whispered, kissing the crown of my head. "I should have been there."

We were outside the showers, and he stripped me out of my top—a Seals sweatshirt I'd stolen out of Owen's closet—and then my heeled booties, followed by my jeans, until I was in just my underwear in front of him. They were a matching yellow set, delicate lace with little daisies on them.

"Fuck, this color," he groaned. "It's my favorite."

I laughed. "I thought your favorite was blue?"

He looked me straight in the eyes. "It hasn't been. Not in a long time." His teeth brushed over the lace, pressing a kiss to the spot between my breasts. "Yellow always reminded me of you. When you left, I looked for it everywhere. It was like, even though you weren't with me, you were."

Owen pulled his shirt off, revealing that damn six pack that shouldn't have been so damn hot, and the deep v that continued under his shorts. He kicked them off too, and then with every piece of clothing between us shed, he led us into the large shower room and flipped on the shower.

"My favorite color is light blue," I admitted. "Because of you."

We let the warm water run over us, just staring at each other for a few beats. He still looked beautiful. A little banged up and definitely bruised, and he was still the only man I'd ever wanted.

His fingers ran over the eight tattooed onto my side, and I angled my head down to kiss the daisy he had etched on his forearm. I looped my arms around his neck and stood on my tiptoes, pressing my lips to his in a soft kiss. But he didn't let it stay that way for long, coaxing my mouth open, each stroke against my mouth spurring us on even further. Owen's hard cock pressed against my stomach, and I pulled back. Showering with him here was one thing, but sex? I blushed as he brushed his fingertips over my hardened nipples. "Owen, we really shouldn't—"

"You're perfect," he murmured, grabbing the bottle of body wash off the ledge. Before he could squirt it into his palm, I took it from him, pouring a generous amount out onto my palms and rubbing them together to make a lather.

Then I stepped close to him and ran my hands all over his muscular body. The one that allowed him to dominate on the ice and in the bedroom. The one that was always taking care of me. Making me feel special.

Loved.

He deserved that, too.

After washing his chest and arms, I turned my attention to my body, lathering up my tits and stomach before stepping in close to him, wrapping my palm around his shaft and stroking slowly.

"Fuck." He braced one hand on the shower wall as I continued washing his cock, running my fingertip around the crown. "I'm going to need to take care of this."

"I'll take care of you," I said, ready to sink to my knees in front of him.

But Owen had a different idea, grabbing my arms and holding me against the shower wall. His lips were only a breath from mine, his cock pressed against me. If I raised my legs, it would barely take anything for him to push inside of me. "Are you sure?"

I nodded. "Let me make you feel good, baby." I forgot

everything else around us—including that we were in the locker room shower and the chances of someone coming in and finding us were high—as I ran my hands through his damp, dark blond strands.

He dropped his head to my shoulder. "I don't deserve you."

"Hey." I whispered. "You do. You're the best man I've ever met, Owen Harper. So don't you dare tell me you don't deserve me, when it's the other way around."

Owen grabbed my leg, bending it and holding it up, giving him the perfect angle to slide inside of me. I gasped at the sudden entry, letting out a low moan.

"Shhh, baby," he said, his other hand coming around my waist and holding my back. "We have to be quiet, so no one comes looking for us."

I nodded, biting down on my lip to keep from gasping out from each stroke of his cock into my pussy. The angle was insane, and even though he'd fucked me against the wall in our apartment the other night, this was completely different.

Maybe it was that anyone could catch us, or the way my nipples rubbed against his bare, soapy chest with every thrust, but it didn't take long at all for me to climax, coming so hard I had to bite down on his shoulder to keep from crying out.

"Fuuuuck, baby," he groaned. "I'm gonna come now. Take it all inside that sweet cunt, okay? I want to leave here knowing it's dripping out of you." His hand wrapped around my abdomen, pressing over the spot where his cock pressed against my cervix, and the added stimulation was almost too much.

"Oh my god, Owen," I whimpered as he released inside of me, spilling his warm cum inside my body.

He kissed me softly before pulling out, finishing cleaning us up the rest of the way before we toweled off and I pulled back on my clothes. Maybe we were lucky, or maybe Sophia had just stayed outside to guard the locker room, but no one came inside the entire time. We were both fully dressed, but my hair was now damp, and anyone who had seen me before the game would definitely know we'd been up to something.

I blushed, and he pulled me in close, his lips pressing against my forehead. "Come on, Skater Girl. Let's go home."

"Wherever you go, Hockey Boy, that's where I want to be." The words slipped from my lips before I could think about what they meant, but I wasn't sure it even mattered anymore.

Because that was my truth.

I'd follow him anywhere.

THIRTY-FIVE

Owen

---

*E*llie was *radiant*. I leaned against the doorframe of her classroom, watching her with amusement as she sat at her desk, totally focused on whatever she was working on. It was her lunch break, so I knew she had a few minutes to spare before her students came back in. I'd called her school this morning to make sure it was okay that I stopped by, and her principal seemed shocked to hear from me.

I'd left practice this morning and even though I could have gone home, I'd gotten in my car and drove here instead. Instead of my usual t-shirt and team sweatshirt, I'd pulled on a nice pair of jeans and a button-up before heading over to see my girl. It was strange to think I hadn't seen her classroom before. Normally, with her schedule, she left the house before me to get to class. I couldn't deny the part of me that wanted to drive her to work, though. I was just attributing it to those same caveman instincts that made me want to take care of her.

"What's got you so focused?" I said, announcing my presence as I padded over behind her. I caught a glimpse of her computer screen, but she closed the lid before I could see what she was staring at.

"Owen. What are you doing here?" She looked shocked to see me here—which was exactly how I wanted it.

"Hey." I leaned down, pressing a kiss against her cheek. "Thought I'd surprise you." After the way she'd taken care of me the other day at the game, I practically owed it to her. Luckily, I hadn't had a concussion, and though I'd missed the next game, I was back in the lineup.

She blushed as I handed her the bouquet of daisies and a bag with a dessert in it. "Well, thank you. I'm definitely surprised."

Leaning against her desk, I stared down at her. She was wearing a mint green dress with a pair of leggings on underneath, and had twisted her hair up with some sort of clip, leaving just her shorter pieces out in the front. Beautiful.

I dipped my head down, wanting a kiss, but before our lips met, the bell rang.

A few moments later, a bunch of kids rushed into the room, eyes widening as they saw me still propped against the desk.

"Ms. Bradford?" One of her students raised her hand. "Is this your friend?" She was soft-spoken and seemed shy, looking at me hesitantly.

My Ellie looked up at me, a soft expression on her face. "Yeah. This is my friend, Owen Harper." *Friend.* Fuck, but I hated that word coming from her lips. Boyfriend, maybe. Her future husband and the love of her life, definitely. But friend no longer belonged in our vocabulary. And if she didn't see that, I needed to make sure she knew it. "Everyone say hi, Mr. Harper."

"Hi Mr. Harper," the class called out, a few dozen kids smiling back at me.

Another kid—one wearing a Seals t-shirt—had his jaw dropped open. "Miss Bradford, you're friends with a *hockey player?*"

She looked over at me, and I raised an eyebrow. Like *this is all you, babe.* Ellie gave him a soft smile. "Yes, Tommy. We've known each other for a very long time. We actually grew up together."

"Wow." He looked mesmerized. "That's *so cool.* I want to be an NHL player when I'm older."

"You do?" I stood up, walking over to his desk. "You play hockey?"

"Uh-huh." Tommy nodded. "Would you want to come to my game sometime?"

I crouched in front of his desk, grinning at him. "Absolutely, bud. Maybe you can have Ms. Bradford talk to your parents to get the details, and I'll see what I can do, huh?"

The little boy absolutely *beamed.* "Yes, please! Oh my gosh, this is so cool! Branden and Riven are going to absolutely *freak* if you show up."

A few of the other kids asked me questions about hockey and my job, which I was happy to answer. Ellie looked pleasantly surprised at the occasion, so I played along, loving her attention on me.

Mentally, I was already making plans. The team loved PR opportunities like this, but I just loved the chance to hang out with kids who loved hockey. I could probably drag the Hendrix brothers along at the very least, if not Reid as well. None of them were seeing anyone this season, besides a few hook-ups here and there, so it wasn't like they had anything better to do.

"Alright, everyone. We have to say bye to Mr. Harper now so we can start our lesson. Can everyone say thank you, Mr. Harper?

"Thank you, Mr. Harper!"

I nodded. "Bye, kids. Don't have too much fun with Ms. Bradford here." I leaned in close enough so I could whisper in her ear. "See you at home, baby. Zambi and I will be waiting for you."

I LOVED these days where I didn't have games, when I could spend the entire night with her. After I'd cooked us both dinner—making one of my dad's recipes he always fed us as kids—we watched a few episodes of some show Ellie loved on television, curled up together with Zambi's head resting in Ellie's lap. She stroked our dog's ears slowly, and I let myself just live in the moment. It was everything I'd ever wanted.

And I had it now. I had it all.

"You didn't have to do that today, you know," Ellie said, spitting out her toothpaste into the sink as we got ready for bed later. She was wearing a little blue nightgown with a bow between her breasts, and she looked absolutely *edible.*

Looking up from my book, I took off my reading glasses to quirk an eyebrow at her. "Didn't have to do what?"

Ellie gave me a look like *you know what I meant.* "Tell little Tommy Andersen that you'd come to his skating practice."

Shrugging, I put my bookmark in to hold my page and set my book aside. "It's no hardship to go support the community, El. Plus, you saw the way he was idolizing me, right? I couldn't say no to that."

She snorted. "He's loud and has way too much energy, and is a pain in my ass most of the time, but overall, he's a good kid. Still, you have a lot going on."

"It'll be fun," I promised. "I liked seeing you in action today, *Miss Bradford.*"

"Oh?" She popped her hip, leaning against the doorframe. Her nipples poked out of the silky blue nightie, and I ran my tongue over my lip.

"Yeah, baby. You were hot. I liked your little teacher outfit."

Ellie climbed onto the bed, pressing her lips against mine in a soft kiss before climbing under the sheets. "Well, I liked seeing you." She rolled onto her side, looking at me. "This is nice. I like this."

"Me too." I pinched her side. "Did you mean what you said earlier?"

"Huh?" It was her turn to give me a blank expression.

"You called me your friend at school today." I furrowed my eyebrows. "I hated that."

She frowned. "You did?"

"Yeah." I pulled her into my arms, inhaling her sweet scent. "I don't want to be just your friend. Never have."

She bit her lip. "You know, at the last game, the girls all asked if I'm your girlfriend."

"What did you tell them?" I asked, tracing circles on her bare shoulder and down her skin. She was soft everywhere, and I loved it.

"That we hadn't put a label on it yet." Her eyes fluttered as she looked up at me. "I know you said I'm yours, but…"

That was true. But it wasn't because I didn't want to. "Are you asking if you're my girlfriend again, Ellie baby?" I tucked a strand of hair behind her ear.

"Maybe."

I leaned forward, pressing my lips against her forehead. "I never should have let you doubt you were anything but. That's on me."

She smiled up at me. "It's been a long time since I called you my boyfriend. It almost doesn't feel like enough to describe… *this.*" I had to agree with that. I already had other words in mind. She was the other half of my heart. My soulmate. But maybe it was too soon for everything else I wanted. Her eyes shut as I continued to run my hands over her smooth skin. I pressed my fingers over her tattoo, tracing the loop of the eight over and over. "Do we tell our families?"

"Yes." I kissed her shoulder. "I can't keep this from them any longer."

Her lips curled up in the biggest smile. "I know. Hiding it from everyone has felt *impossible*."

"They probably already know." We weren't exactly the most subtle. And while I hadn't been posting on social media, I wanted to. There was an entire album of photos on my phone I'd taken of her over the last few months, and I wanted the world to see that she was mine, and I was hers.

Ellie's lips turned into the most adorable pout. "What do you mean?"

"El. We got a dog together." I quirked an eyebrow. "How many friends do you know that co-parent a dog?"

"Well, technically, *you* got a dog, and I just happened to be your roommate."

"You're not just my fucking roommate." I flicked her nose. "And don't say that too loud. Zambi will hear you and think her mommy doesn't want her."

My girl burst out laughing. "You're ridiculous."

"Mmm." *But you love me.* I kept the words inside. It wasn't the right time for love confessions. "Ellie." The word was hardly more than a murmur.

She hummed, not opening her eyes. "Hm?"

"Why'd you move to Seattle?" I'd asked her the same question once before, but she hadn't really answered me. Not then.

Her blue-gray eyes popped open, cheeks turned an adorable shade of pink as she stared at me. "Didn't I already tell you why?"

"No. Not really." I raised a shoulder. It was important to me to know. To hear it from her lips. "Please. I'm dying here."

"Well, I didn't have a job in Portland, and my mom had a friend who—"

I clicked my tongue against the roof of my mouth. "I know that's what you're telling yourself, baby, but I don't believe it. So what's the real, non-bullshit reason?" Staring directly into her pretty eyes, I waited for her to brush me off again.

But she held my gaze. "For you." She reached up, cupping my cheek. I rolled onto my back and pulled her onto my lap, letting her straddle my thighs. "I moved here to chase you. Because I couldn't let you go. I would follow you anywhere, Hockey Boy."

"Thank fuck," I said, and then I kissed her. "I was a fool not to chase after you five years ago, and I was a fool to leave you after your graduation. All I wanted to do was wake up next to you, but I was terrified, Ellie. I'm still terrified."

My lips found hers again, more demanding this time. I gripped her hips, holding her to me as I devoured her, the minty taste of her toothpaste invading my senses.

"You don't have to be scared anymore," she promised, resting her forehead against mine. "I'm not going to leave you again."

I didn't say anything else, just kissing her again. But it was a promise that I was going to hold on to, if nothing else could abate the fear in my heart.

"HOW'S EVERYTHING going with you and your girl?" Brooks asked from the equipment next to mine. We were both in the gym, getting in a good workout. It had been a week since I'd visited her classroom. A week since we'd officially decided we were boyfriend and girlfriend again.

Best damn week of my life.

Next week, my family would be here for Thanksgiving. We didn't have a game on the day itself, but we did on Wednesday, so they'd all be in the stands, watching me. I'd bought the tickets at the start of the season, but thankfully, I'd been able to get Ellie a seat with them, and my whole family would be together.

"Fucking amazing," I admitted. "It's better than I ever imagined. Away games suck, leaving her behind, but it's been better knowing that she has Zamboni, and that she's made friends here." It wasn't like I could ask her to quit her job and come on the road with me.

"Her and Soph do stuff together, yeah?" That was Maverick.

I nodded, doing another rep. "Yeah. They're two peas in a pod. I'm glad she has someone." Sophia had been around the team for the last few years—ever since graduating college—and she'd always been such a compassionate person. I'd also been around her long enough to know that she had absolutely no filter, and said anything that popped into her mind. Whoever was lucky enough to love her would definitely never be bored.

"You tell her you love her yet?"

My cheeks flushed. "Not in so many words." But I had in other ways. Every action. Asking her to stay. "My family's actually coming up next week for Thanksgiving. We're going to tell them we're back together then, and then we're going back home together for Christmas. Going to hit the road once we get back from our last game." It would be the first time I was seeing all of my family since May.

"That'll be nice. Mav and I already booked our flights home to see our mom for the few days of break. It's going to be nice to see her." They were from a small town in Manitoba, and I knew it was hard for her to get out here for games too often.

At least I was lucky, only living three hours from my family.

"I'm planning on looking at rings," I blurted out. "I want to ask her dad for permission when we're down there." Of course, there were other things I needed to tell her first.

Like how I'd never told her that the reason I'd picked the number eight for my jersey was for her. Because it had been her favorite number when she was little and both her birth-date and birth year ended in an eight. I'd always carried her with me.

"Oh, wow." Brooks sat up, running his hands through his brown strands. "That's serious. Do you think she's ready for that?"

"I sure as fuck hope so. I don't want to wait another moment without my ring on her finger. I just…" I shook my head. "I've been in love with her since I was sixteen years old, you know? She's it for me. Always has been. And this time apart… I know now more than ever that I want to be her husband. That I want her to be my wife." I shut my eyes, letting the fantasy play out. Our future together was so close, I could almost taste it. "I'm hers, as much as she is mine."

Maverick patted me on the shoulder. "You got this, man. Honestly, you've always been such an easy-going, happy guy, and I thought nothing could phase you. But after she came back into your life, you've been even more-so. You never stop smiling. And I'm pretty sure she's the reason, so if she makes you happy, Harps, I support you one hundred percent. And you know Brooks and I will be happy to have your back at your wedding one day."

"Thanks. Honestly, I don't know what I'd do without you both." They were my best friends, and I didn't think Seattle would be the same without them. If any of us got traded, I'd be devastated.

"Come to the bar after the next home game?" Brooks asked. "And bring your girl."

I nodded. "Yeah. It's a plan." Because I wanted her to be as close to these guys as I was. To feel like they were her extended family, too.

Because I realized that these days, what mattered to me more than anything else was her.

I could get through anything, as long as I had Ellie by my side.

Cousins Coffee Club

TEXTS

PENELOPE

Guess who's counting down the days till she's in Seattle??

ELLIE

I can't wait to see you, Penny! We have so much to catch up on.

QUINLAN

And then you need to spill to the rest of us!

ELLIE

There's nothing to spill, guys.

ABIGAIL

Yes. Because we believe that.

ZACHARY

Apparently, they think they're super sly.

WESLEY

Like we don't all know that they're K-I-S-S-I-N-G...

ELLIE

How old are we, Wes?

WESLEY

I refuse to answer that question, little
Bradford.

ELLIE

Oh my god. I'm muting the chat. Bye.

PENELOPE

She's in denial. They're obviously in looooove.

QUINLAN

Clearly. We all knew this would happen when
Ellie moved to Seattle, right?

BEAU

Someone catch me up. I feel like I'm out of
the loop??

Is this how Owen felt the last few years up in
Seattle? Damn. It sucks. Miss you all.

OWEN

Sorry, can't talk. Out at drinks with El and the
guys. See you soon, Pen.

THIRTY-SIX

Ellie

"What are you doing?" The counter was covered in sequins—and I was very aware of my current state, hunched over my Seals jersey, a tube of glue in one hand and a pair of tweezers in the other. My phone was propped up on the counter, on a video call with Owen while he was on his road trip.

"Um." I looked between my craft project and him. "Bedazzling?"

"Ellie." His voice was rough. "Is that my jersey?"

I batted my eyelashes a few times. "Maybe?" Well, it wasn't *his* exactly, but one I'd gotten with his name on it. "I picked up an extra one at the last game I went to during intermission." He opened his mouth to say something, and I interrupted him. "And before you say anything, I was with Soph. She made sure they gave me the friends and family discount."

Luckily, Owen's jersey was one of the few they carried in the store, so I didn't have to get one custom made. It helped to have a boyfriend who was also one of the top players on the team. Besides, I wanted to have both a home and an away jersey, instead of just the one.

"I would have gotten you another one if you'd asked."

I stuck my tongue out in concentration as I placed another rhinestone in the glue. "Yeah, but this was more fun."

He chuckled through the phone. "Is this a thing?"

"Oh yeah," I nodded. "It's all the rage on social media. Everyone's doing it." I was low-key obsessed with all the rhinestoned jerseys, and I loved how they sparkled. Sophia supported me in the endeavor, and I offered to do one for her next, assuming mine turned out good.

I wondered whose jersey she would wear. Her dad's old number? Or maybe she'd just pick her favorite players? She'd been talking to me a lot more about the guys on the team, and there was just this vibe I kept picking up on.

"I miss you." Owen was quiet, and I wished he was here right now so I could wrap my arms around him and tell him everything was going to be okay. Unfortunately, he was on the other side of the continent right now.

"I know." I sighed. "Me too. It's too quiet around here."

"How's our girl?"

I picked up my phone, changing the camera angle to show him our puppy, currently sleeping at my feet. "She's good. We went down to the park earlier and I let her run around for a while to tire herself out."

"That sounds fun." Owen looked exhausted, and I knew how much his travel schedule wore on him during some of these trips. It seemed exhausting, especially when the team had a back-to-back.

I bit my lip. "At least you'll be home soon, and then your family will be here? I can't wait to see Penny."

That brought a smile to his face. "Yeah. Me too. I've really been looking forward to it. My parents have been going on and on about meeting Zambi. I think they miss having a dog."

We talked for a bit longer before I finally let him go, knowing it was late and he needed his sleep. I was just glad he had time to call me during his trips or after games. As much as

I missed him, I loved watching him play, even if it was on my TV while he was across the country.

I might have had to share him with the world, but when he was home, he was still mine, and that was all that really mattered in the end, right?

THERE WAS a crisp quality to the air as I walked Zamboni down to the park. It wasn't currently raining—for once—and we were enjoying our last moments of quiet. Owen was getting back from an away game in the morning, and then his family would arrive in the afternoon.

At least I didn't have school tomorrow, since I was off for the rest of the week.

It was crazy that I'd blinked, and it was almost December. We'd be going back home in less than a month to see our cousins. I missed them all, but especially my family. I'd never spent this long away from Portland before. And while I knew my parents would have driven up here in the blink of an eye if I'd told them I missed them, I'd wanted to do things myself.

And I had. Owen and I were back together, and everything felt brighter. Easier. My job was great, I had friends here —*good* friends—and we'd even gotten a dog. I laughed to myself, thinking about telling seventeen-year-old me about my life now.

There was no way I'd believe it.

I tilted up my head as Zambi sniffed around the grass, letting the sun's rays warm my face as a smile touched my lips. Since we were inside the fenced dog park, I'd let Zamboni off her leash, letting her run around. She had already grown so much in the last month, and I missed how small she'd been.

My phone vibrated in my back pocket, startling me out of

the serene moment, and I furrowed my brow as I pulled it out, not recognizing the caller ID. "Hello?"

"Miss Bradford?"

"Yes?" I asked. "Who is this?"

"Sorry, sorry. This is Mr. Wright. Your landlord?"

I frowned. "Oh. Sorry, I wasn't expecting to hear from you." It had been three months since my apartment had flooded, and not a peep on how repairs were going.

He made a sound with his throat. "Right. Well, I wanted to let you know that we're finished renovations on the apartment and you're free to move back in about two weeks."

"I am?" My mouth went dry. "I just figured—" I squeezed my eyes shut. Maybe I'd forgotten that this arrangement was only supposed to be temporary. Because Owen had never brought it up again. He'd asked me to stay. At least… I was pretty sure he had. I'd confessed to him I didn't want to move out when my apartment was fixed, right? *Don't. Stay with me.* "Okay. Thanks for letting me know. If I won't be moving back in, is there a date I need to tell you by?"

"Ah. Well. I guess as soon as possible. That way, I can find someone else to rent it. You'll need to pay the fee to break the lease, however."

Even if I moved back in, I wanted to see it first before I agreed to it. But having to pay to break it when the place had filled with water didn't sit right with me.

"Alright. Well, let me talk to my boyfriend and I'll let you know."

"Is that the young man who helped you move out? The hockey player?"

I nodded, like he could see me. "Um, yes. That's the one." I blushed. Back then, we'd been struggling to navigate our friendship. But all along, that attraction had been there, simmering. It was a miracle we'd kept our hands off of each other for as long as we had.

After letting me know some other information about the

apartment and saying our goodbyes, I hung up, finding my way over to a bench. I needed a minute to process everything.

God, it fucking sucked that I couldn't talk to Owen. He had a game tonight, though, and I knew how important his routine was before games. If I brought it up, would it ruin his game? There was no way I could do that to him. Being a distraction was what I'd been scared of years ago, and here I was.

I loved him so much that I couldn't do that to him.

He'd be home tomorrow. I'd bring it up then.

Zamboni put her paws onto my knees and pushed her nose into my lap. I scratched at her head. "You're such a good girl, Zambi. Mommy loves you very much." Kissing her snout, I thought about what it would be like if I moved out.

Not seeing my puppy every day? Not seeing Owen the second I got home from work, or when he got back from an away game? I hated that idea.

I'd call my landlord back and tell him I wasn't going to be moving back in and break the lease as soon as I talked to Owen about it.

As soon as I made sure that he wanted me to stay.

"ELLIE!" Penny's voice shouted, and then I was engulfed in a hug from my ginger-haired best friend, who was wearing a yellow sweater dress that hugged all of her curves.

"God, I missed you so much," I said, tightening my arms around her back.

"Never leave me for that long again," she groaned.

I laughed. "I'll try not to. You can come up too, you know." Penelope and I had spent the last twenty-something years of our lives hardly spending any time without the other. We were only nine months apart, and since we'd started school together and gone to college together, moving away from her had been weird.

"I know, I know. It's just a lot back home, and I've been working at the coffee shop a lot, and—"

A few moments later, the door opened, and everything else faded away as Owen came into view. My grin was so wide, there was no hiding it. He'd gotten in this morning when I'd still been sleeping, and slid into the covers, pulling me against his hard, warm body. Neither one of us had gone back to sleep, instead indulging ourselves in each other's bodies—twice—before we finally got up and showered. And now the Harpers were here.

He'd carried in two suitcases, and I was pretty sure one of them was his sister's. Owen had always been good like that, making sure his younger sister didn't have to do any heavy lifting. Though he was the same with me, too. It was a wonder I'd only realized in high school he liked me when I thought about all the things he'd done for me growing up.

Matthew and Noelle entered behind their son, their faces lighting up as they saw me. My eyes watered, seeing two of the people I'd grown up with, that I considered my family because they *were*.

"Hi." I sniffled. "It's so good to see you."

"Oh, Ellie." My Aunt Noelle wrapped me up in a hug. "We've missed you."

"Me too," I whispered. "I'm glad you could make the trip."

She nodded. "We always try to come visit Owen for Thanksgiving. We just had to wait until Matthew finished his last class before we could head up."

"And who's this?" Uncle Matthew said, crouching down in front of Zamboni, who had been running between everyone, licking and trying to find someone to pet her. Our cute little golden girl was a bit of an attention whore. She was the same way whenever Owen's teammates came over, wiggling her way across whoever was sitting on the couch, determined to lick everyone's faces.

"That's Zamboni," Owen said, pulling me in closer to him and kissing my forehead. He looked proud, like the golden retriever at our feet was our kid. "She's ours."

Of course, he knew that. I knew Owen talked to his parents regularly, and we'd sent it in the group chat, so I knew he was aware we'd gotten a dog.

Well, that Owen got a dog. Technically, she wasn't mine. But every time we laid together on the couch, watching Owen's away games on the TV, she certainly felt like she was.

His dad chuckled, pretending to shake Zambi's paw. "It's very nice to meet you, Zamboni." He stood back up, wrapping his arms around his wife. Even all these years later, it was clear how very much in love the two of them were.

I hoped that was us some day, too. Still in love even after two kids and a whole life together.

"Well, we were thinking maybe we could go out to dinner tonight?" I looked over at Owen, who nodded his agreement. Tomorrow night, we had his game, which I was looking forward to. It was the first time since high school that all four of us would be in the stands for him. And then Thanksgiving day, we'd be cooking here.

"That sounds great," Noelle offered. "Gives us time to catch up, too."

"The guest room's already for you two," I said to Matthew and Noelle. "And we made up a bed for you, too, Penny."

"We didn't kick you out of your room, did we?" Noelle asked me, looking between Owen and I.

"Ah..." I looked up at him. "No."

Owen wrapped his hand around my hip and squeezed. "Ellie's in my bed. We're together again."

I blushed. "Surprise?"

Penny laughed. "Told you!" She smirked at her parents. "I knew you moving in here would lead to this."

"Yeah, well…" I looked over at my boyfriend and found him smiling.

I couldn't complain about that. Even if the call from yesterday was still weighing on me. I hadn't told Owen yet. I knew I should have this morning, but when he'd wrapped his body around mine, I'd forgotten about everything else. My damn horny brain was to blame, but who could blame me when Owen gave me orgasms like candy on Halloween?

"We're happy," he said, interlacing our fingers. "And that's all that matters, right?"

"Of course, Owen." His mom reached up, patting his cheek. "We're just glad you two kids figured it out. Charlotte and I hated watching you two be heartbroken and avoid each other all those years."

Owen looked away, a guilty, haunted expression on his face. "We both were young," I said, squeezing his hand. "I think maybe we needed those years apart to grow and find our way back together."

"Yeah." He kissed the top of my hand. "And we did."

We found our way back together. And here we were. He was everything I'd ever wanted. When I was with him, I felt complete. Like he was the missing piece of a puzzle I hadn't even known I was missing.

I loved him more than ever, and I wished his family weren't here so I could show him just how much. Even if I hadn't told him yet.

"I CAN'T BELIEVE you're actually dating my brother again," Penelope said, resting her head on my shoulder as we watched the guys warm-up from our seats.

"It's great, right?" I smiled, my eyes tracking my man with his every movement.

This was my favorite part—I loved watching Owen stretch and hit pucks into the net, and I especially loved it when he bounced a puck on his stick. As a bonus, I got a healthy amount of forearm porn, because he wore his jersey pushed up onto his pads, and I was pretty sure I was the only person who appreciated his slutty little wrists.

But damn. He was *hot*. And all mine.

We were all decked out in Seals merch, since apparently Owen made sure all of his family had jerseys with his name on them, too. Even Uncle Matthew, who played basketball in college, fit right in wearing his bright blue jersey.

Penny sighed happily, weaving a finger around one of her red curls. "Every time I come to one of his games, I totally get why women love hockey romances."

Noelle laughed from her other side. "The numbers don't lie, sweetie. Athletes are the perfect romance hero." She looked over at her husband, wiggling her eyebrows. "Right, babe?"

"Sunshine." His voice was low. "You're going to be the death of me."

She pressed her lips to his cheek, and he just shook his head. I didn't miss the hint of a smile on his face as he looked at his wife.

"I'd love him no matter what he did," I said, the words rushing out of me. "Even if he didn't play another game of hockey in his life. He's just... He's my Owen."

"Oh, El. I know." Noelle looked up at Uncle Matthew and then back at me. "We've always known that what you two had was special." She reached over Penny to squeeze my knee. "You're his girl. Plain and simple. Nothing could ever change that."

I hoped she was right.

"And just think," Penelope interjected, grinning. "One day, I'll get to call you my sister."

"We'll see," I said with a small smile. Was he thinking that far into the future? About what our lives would look like together in one, five, ten years? If he got traded, would he want me to go with him?

Owen looked over at that moment, pulling his helmet off and dragging his hands through his hair as he drank deeply from his water bottle. And he waved, giving me a gorgeous grin.

My heart fluttered as I blew him a kiss back.

We were Ellie & Owen. Hockey Boy & Skater Girl. We could get through anything.

We would, right?

THIRTY-SEVEN

Owen

December came in the blink of an eye, and every day brought us closer to the holidays. Unfortunately, that also meant my family's quick trip was over.

"It's always great to have you guys here," I said, wrapping my arms around my mom for a hug. I loved when they came up to visit.

There were so many things I missed about Portland. But the NHL didn't have a team there, and I was just glad to be in Seattle. What would happen if the team tried to transfer me somewhere like Florida, on the opposite side of the country from my family? I wasn't sure I could accept that, because I couldn't imagine leaving here. But hockey wasn't forever.

One day, I liked to think we'd end up back in Portland, raising a family there.

My dad hugged me next. "Don't be a stranger, son."

I looked over at Ellie, who was animatedly talking to my sister, her eyes bright and cheeks pink. So fucking happy, and she lit up the whole damn room when she smiled. I cleared my throat, looking away. "I'll be home in a few weeks," I promised. "We're bringing Zambi down for Christmas." For the first time in a long time, I was really looking forward to going home, because this time, Ellie was going to be at my side.

"Let us know if you want us to make up your old room," Mom added. "Or if you and Ellie want to stay somewhere else—"

"I will, Mom," I said, cutting her off. The back of my neck was probably red, but I definitely didn't need to discuss my girlfriend and I's sleeping habits with my mother. Nor did I need her talking about it with Ellie's mom.

We hadn't discussed it yet, but I didn't really care whose house we slept at, as long as I could sleep with her in my arms. It was the thing I missed the most every time we were on the road. With Ellie nestled against my body, and Zamboni sleeping at our feet, I had my entire world right next to me. God, I fucking loved it.

Mom lowered her voice. "Take care of her, Owen. I know how much she means to you. Don't let her go."

"I don't intend to."

Another promise I didn't plan on breaking. I'd started ring shopping, and I was going to ask her dad when we got into town. Just like I'd asked him all those years ago for permission to date his daughter.

It was crazy to think that almost ten years had passed since then. Since I'd taken her to prom, and she'd been the most beautiful girl in the room. I'd been a goner long before that, but damn.

Ellie was it for me. Always had been.

"Love you guys."

Penny and Ellie hugged, and then she came to stand at my side, wrapping her arm around mine and leaning on my shoulder as we stood at the curb.

"Hi, baby," I said, pressing a kiss to the crown of her head. "You good?"

"Yeah." Her voice was soft. "I just didn't realize how much I missed them until they came up to visit."

We watched my family load up in the car and drive away, and I hugged her tight. "We'll be home in a few weeks," I said to her.

"I know." She snuggled into me. "And while I'm looking forward to it, I'm also glad to have you back to myself for a bit."

"I couldn't agree more." Cupping her cheeks, I looked down at her. "I wish I didn't have to leave you again so soon." Just when we were alone, I had another away series.

"I hate that you have to go," Ellie said, giving me a little pout.

Running my hand down her hair, I cupped the back of her head. "I know." This was our longest road trip of the season —with six away games in a row—and I already hated the idea of being gone for so long. But at least at the end, we'd be that much closer to leaving for Portland.

Ellie sighed as she rested her head against my chest. "Hockey is important, Owen. I know that. I don't expect you to sacrifice anything for me."

Little did she know I would sacrifice the world for her. Gladly. If I had to, I'd give up my career tomorrow to be with her. I could go back to school and finish my degree, plus I'd already made more money than I knew what to do with for my entire life. If I invested wisely, there was no reason I'd have to worry. "You're worth it," I said against her lips. "Don't ever doubt that, Ellie baby."

She smiled, tugging at my hand. "Come on. Let's go upstairs and snuggle with our puppy. I think she's feeling a little neglected."

"Spoiled princess," I said, snorting as I followed her to the elevator. Our dog had figured out how to manipulate everyone to get the maximum amount of pets this week.

Ellie pressed the button for our floor and then leaned back against the wall. "Yeah. But she's kind of the cutest thing ever, isn't she?"

I stepped in close, arching my back to lean over her, my mouth only a breath away from hers. "That's you, Daisy."

"Owen," she murmured.

"It was so hard to stay away from you the last few days," I said, settling my hands on her hips. "But there was no way we were going to be able to stay quiet with my parents in the apartment, huh?"

She shook her head, brushing her lips over mine with the motion. "No." Her voice was breathy, and I helped guide her legs so they wrapped around mine, pressing my cock against her pussy. Layers of fabric kept us apart, but we both groaned at the sensation. "*Fuck*, Owen." Ellie dropped her head against my shoulder.

"I know, baby." Nipping at her shoulder, I dropped my lips against her ear. "I'd fuck you right here in the elevator if I could." She squirmed, whimpering. "Does that turn you on, my dirty girl? So needy."

Thank fuck, the doors opened. I didn't waste another second, throwing the apartment door open and heading directly for the bedroom, ready to show my girl exactly how much I'd miss her.

IT WAS a chilly morning as I took Zamboni out for a walk, already dreading having to leave later today. We had practice this morning, and then we'd hop on a plane to start our long east coast road trip.

She was still a puppy, one who loved to nip at our fingers with her sharp little teeth and who tried to eat her leash when

I took her out. I was working on leash training her, enjoying our time together and these little moments each morning. There was no way I was asking Ellie to get out of bed any earlier than she already had to, especially since I was the one who had brought home a dog.

It was selfish, but coming home and seeing my girls cuddled up on the couch reinforced that I'd made the right decision. Because seeing how much Ellie loved Zambi, and how attached our puppy was to her mommy? Yeah. I was smitten. With both of them.

My feelings were bubbling up inside of me, but I hadn't told her how I felt. I'd confessed to her I was scared, and yet I still couldn't say the words.

Maybe because last time we'd said I love you, everything had fallen apart.

What if she didn't feel the same way? I thought she did, but she hadn't said it either. Or what if she left again, and I fell apart?

In college, I'd been a mess for weeks afterwards. I'd missed blocking shots that cost us goals against. I'd missed passes that would have helped us score. It was only when my coach had told me to get my head out of my ass or I'd lose my opportunity to work in the NHL that I'd finally shaped up. I'd given my all to hockey, and the next year, when I'd gotten called up to the NHL for my rookie year, I hadn't looked back.

Now... I didn't know. Of course, I still loved her. I'd always loved her. And I wanted to ask her to marry me. Wanted her to be my wife.

"Fuck me," I groaned.

Why was I being this stupid? I needed to tell her how I felt. Preferably, before I got on a plane and left for a few days.

I headed back upstairs, Zamboni happily trotting through the apartment and finding one of her bones once I took her off her harness. Heading into our bedroom, I saw Ellie's phone was sitting open on the nightstand and I heard the shower running. I didn't mean to look at it, but I noticed she had a notification from an unknown number, and I frowned.

UNKNOWN

Did you decide what you wanted to do with the apartment yet?

If you're going to move back in, I just need to know in the next week.

Move back in? *What?* I frowned. Ellie hadn't mentioned her apartment in months. Honestly, I'd forgotten about it entirely. That place was a shithole. She wanted to go back there?

Did she not want to live with me anymore? I thought everything was going great. How could she want to leave? I sat on the bed, trying to process the idea. I was out shopping for wedding rings, and she was planning on moving out?

"Owen?" Ellie's voice called out. I looked up, finding her wrapped in a towel, her damp blonde hair hanging down around her creamy skin. "Are you okay?"

"I—" I blinked at her. Was I okay? *No.* "You're moving out?"

She paled. "What?"

Fuck. "So it's true? You're moving back to that shitty apartment?"

"Owen. Wait. Let me explain."

I shook my head. "You don't have to. I just… Fuck, El." This was the worst possible timing. "I have to go. I need to get to practice and then I have to catch a flight." If I was late to practice, I risked not getting to play the next game at all.

Her eyes filled with tears. "Please don't leave right now. I was going to tell you when I got the call that they were done repairing it, but you had a game that night, and I didn't want to be a distraction."

"Dammit, Ellie!" I smoothed a hand over my face. "And what is this? How long have you known?"

She bit her lip. "A week?"

"A *week*?" She'd known about her apartment for a week and hadn't told me? "I can't do this right now."

"Please, Owen." Ellie grabbed my wrist. "Don't leave. Don't walk out on me."

"Like you did?"

She crossed her arms over her chest. "That's not fair."

Fuck. I knew it wasn't fair. But I couldn't help it.

I grabbed my duffel bag off the floor, followed by the suitcase I'd packed last night. "We'll talk later. I just…" I leaned in, pressing a kiss to her forehead. "I don't want to fight."

Tears streamed down her face, and I knew this was the worst possible thing I could do to us. But what else could I say?

I love you.

I want you to stay.

I want you.

But I didn't. Instead, I left.

This time, in the middle of the day. No note need.

Maybe in the end, this would be the thing that destroyed us.

And it felt like my world was falling apart.

BOARDING THE TEAM PLANE, I popped my earphones in, not wanting to talk to my teammates. Even Brooks and Maverick had questioned why I was in such a bad mood earlier, but I didn't know what to say.

How do you explain to your friends that your girlfriend—the one you wanted to marry, that you'd been looking at rings for—had been keeping a secret from you like that? That she had been considering leaving me?

I wasn't enough for her.

Maybe I'd never been.

My job made it so I was gone for half the season, and I was sure it couldn't be easy. But didn't she love me? Didn't she love Zamboni?

Why weren't we enough?

Why wasn't *I* enough?

THIRTY-EIGHT

Ellie

I couldn't stop crying, and Zamboni was licking my face. She whined, and I knew she was trying to make me feel better, but what could she do? She couldn't fix this. She couldn't bring Owen back.

It was my fault that I'd pushed him away.

I should have told him sooner. I'd been waiting for his family to leave, and then I'd just been so happy in our little bubble that it had completely slipped my mind. I didn't even think about my landlord texting me to ask for an update.

SOPHIA

Are you okay?

I heard that Owen's been in a bad mood ever since they left.

ELLIE

Honestly, babe, I don't even know.

I'm just… numb.

We've never fought like that before.

I'm here if you need me. Just say the word.

Even if it's just to bring over a bottle of wine to commiserate. I've had my fair share of shitty breakups.

Not that this is a break-up. Just... I'm in your corner.

Thank you. You're such a good friend. I'm lucky to have you.

Right back at ya, Ellie.

"YOU LOOK LIKE SHIT," Maggie said, leaning against the door of my classroom a few hours later. Both of us had the same period as our planning period, though I wasn't exactly getting any planning done. At least I was here, trying to put on my best face for my students.

I blew out a breath. My eyes were red and puffy from crying. "Yeah, well, I feel like it, too."

"What happened? Did you and your hockey boy break up?"

"Not exactly. We just got in a fight, I guess?" Now I just felt like I was being dramatic.

No, we hadn't broken up. He'd had to go, and yes, he'd *left*, but he looked just as devastated as I had. The pain in his eyes had broken my heart. Because I'd done that to him. I was the one who was ruining everything. *Again.*

I couldn't let us go another five years apart. I wanted him forever. Wanted to be by his side every day for the rest of my life. Wanted the future I'd been dreaming of. He was the only one who held the key to my heart.

She came over to me, rubbing my back. "Then why are you crying, babe?"

"Because he left. And it just brought up all these old feelings and I feel like my life is imploding. I want to be with him. But I just…" I dropped my head against my desk. "What am I going to do, Mags?"

"Go after him." She quirked an eyebrow like it was obvious. "Tell him how you feel. You love him, right?"

Shaking my head, I frowned. "You say that like it's that simple. I can't just *go*. He's gone on a long away series, and I have a job. I have to teach."

She nodded. "Well, I guess that's fair. When does he get home?"

"Like, a week and a half," I said, biting my thumbnail, pretending I didn't have the Seals game schedule basically memorized at this point.

Maggie hummed, looking deep in thought. "Is there a game this weekend?"

"Yes. Why?"

She shrugged. "Just a thought."

Could I really book a flight and just *go?* Show up at his game and tell him how I felt? That I'd never planned on moving out. That I'd told my landlord I was happy where I was. That I loved him.

My god, I loved him so much.

My friend headed out of my classroom, turning to look at me as she got to the doorway. "Go get your man, Ellie. Don't wait to tell him."

I nodded, hearing the truth in her words. Honestly, I couldn't deny there was some logic to her point. This wasn't a conversation I wanted to have on the phone—if he'd even pick up—and I didn't want to wait almost two weeks to see him in person.

But there was something I needed to do first.

Something that was just for me.

I LOOKED AT THE RINK, and then back to my ice skates Owen had bought me. They were still in my hands. *I could do this.*

We'd come to the iceplex a few times over the last few months, ever since he'd brought me here the first time. Still, I'd never gotten back on the ice without him. The anxiety was still there, even after all this time. My chest felt tight, and I wanted to shut down.

My thoughts were filled with Owen.

How soft and tender he was with me.

The way he made love to me.

His face when he'd brought Zamboni home.

The way he'd looked at me when I'd worn *his* jersey for the first time.

Every time he'd gotten up early and made breakfast just so we could have time together in the mornings.

The way he believed in me, wholly and completely.

I didn't deserve him. Not by a long shot. He was everything good and right in the world, and I was hopelessly, desperately in love with him. He was my other half. The Hockey Boy to my Skater Girl.

I thought about how proud of me he'd be if he was here, watching me skate all on my own.

But I wasn't here for him. I was here for myself. So I sat down on the bench, pulling my boots off and letting them drop to the floor. Lacing up my skates, I took the time to appreciate the smooth white leather. I'd broken them in well enough, but they were still like new. *Beautiful.*

I walked over to the wall, popping in my earphones and putting on one of my favorite playlists. Putting one foot in front of the other, I stepped onto the ice, employing the breathing methods my therapist had taught me years ago.

Owen's words rang out in my head. *Put one foot in front of the other. Remind yourself that the world isn't over. Pick yourself up and dust yourself off. Try again.*

I would. For him, for me, and for our future, I would try again a million times.

Then, I *skated*. Gliding across the ice, I let my muscle memory take over. While running through one of my old routines that I'd always loved, I remembered everything I loved about figure skating. Maybe I couldn't do a triple axel anymore, and I definitely wouldn't be attempting any jumps, but the rest of it came back to me like an old friend.

What I missed the most? *This*. Not the competitions or the insane regimen my coach had me on. The moment I'd walked away from that life, none of it had mattered anymore.

I just missed loving the ice. Feeling the wind whip around me and the ice under my blades. The smell of the rink. It was a smell that would always remind me of Owen.

I remembered what it was like to fall in love with him, slowly, then all at once. Being that five-year-old girl, mesmerized and begging her mom for skates. I remembered being the teenager who couldn't help but stare at her best friend's brother. The girl who had him—and lost him.

I stayed out on the ice until my muscles cried, screaming at me to take a break.

The rink had always been where I'd done my best thinking.

It was also where I'd fallen in love with Owen Harper.

And it was time to do just what Maggie said.

I picked up the phone, clicking on the only person in my contacts that I knew could help me.

"Hey, Sophia? I need a favor."

THIRTY-NINE

Owen

___

We lost the game. Maybe it was because I'd been distracted, but I was *pissed* at myself. I'd missed an important pass in the third, one that would have gotten us the game winning goal. Instead, I'd fumbled the puck, and they'd scored on us instead.

I felt defeated. And knowing we were only half done with our road trip made everything feel even more exhausting. All I wanted was to go home and curl up with my dog and my girl, but I was in a hotel tonight, alone in a strange city.

And I didn't even know if Ellie would be there when I came back.

"Owen." It was Rhodes, of all people, following behind me as we headed to our hotel rooms for the night. "You're playing like shit, bud."

"Fuck." I thrust my hands in my hair, pulling at the strands. "I know."

He crossed his arms over his chest, quirking an eyebrow. "If you know, why do you keep doing it? You're sloppy on the ice. We can't afford sloppy, Harps."

"Tell Coach to scrap me at the next game." I shook my head. "I'm not any good to the team right now."

"No." He gave me that look. And while Rhodes Larsen might have been a grump, he was also a damn talented hockey player. He'd been with the Seals his entire career, and I had no doubt he'd finish it out here, too. "You're going to go back to the hotel, fix your shit, and then at the next game, we're going to kick some ass."

I shook my head. "What if I can't fix it? What if it's too fucked up?"

"This is why I told you that love is too much work." He sighed, and then patted me on the shoulder. "But if anyone can make it work, I know it's you, Owen. You love that girl too much to let whatever's going on break you apart. Alright?"

"Thanks, Rhodes. That was surprisingly… nice?"

He frowned. "Don't get used to it. I have a reputation to uphold." And then he walked away, leaving me trying to figure out what had just happened.

But he was right. I loved Ellie more than anything else in the world. Fighting with her before I left had fucked me up. All I wanted was for her to be here, to talk to her, to hold her.

Only… she was thousands of miles away.

And I still had to make it through the rest of this away series.

WE WERE PLAYING A BACK-TO-BACK, and even though I'd told Coach Donovan to leave me off the line-up for tonight, worried that I'd fuck up and let more shots in, he'd refused. *Win together, lose together,* he'd told me.

It wasn't your fault, Owen. Words I hadn't realized how much I'd needed to hear. Because maybe last night's loss hadn't been my fault, but my overreaction with Ellie had been.

I'd thought about texting her, but what would that do? Would she even respond? I'd been an ass. Something I needed to remedy as soon as I got home. A home that I hoped she'd still be in when I returned, that is.

"Hey, Harps. Isn't that your girl over there?" Brooks asked as we settled onto the bench after our first shift of the game.

My neck snapped up, looking to where he was pointing behind the penalty box. And sure as fuck, two heads of blonde hair were right behind it. My girl. Standing next to Sophia.

"Ellie?" I blinked. "What is she doing here?"

She wore that jersey she'd been gluing rhinestones on the other week, and it was impossible to miss her because it caught the light every time she moved. She fucking *sparkled*, and I loved it.

My girl smiled at me, and I was pretty sure I was hallucinating.

"She's really here?" I asked him. "I'm not seeing things?"

"Nope."

I noticed someone else had stopped on the ice, staring at the same place I was. Rhodes.

Ellie unrolled a piece of paper, holding up a sign.

#8, I love you.

Fuck. "I was supposed to be the one to do the big grand gesture thing," I said to Brooks.

He smirked. "Well, looks like she beat you to it."

Which was torture, actually. Because for the next twenty minutes of gameplay, I couldn't go to her. Couldn't talk to her or touch or tell her *anything*.

She loved me. She was here, and she *loved me*.

I didn't know what I'd done to get so fucking lucky in this life, but I was damn grateful.

A fight broke out during the next shift, and while it was broken up quickly, a player from both teams ending up in the penalty box.

"Penalty to Seattle number eleven for roughing, and DC number eighty-six gets a double minor for boarding and unsportsmanlike conduct." Maverick and the player on the opposing team were already inside, and it meant we had a power play. We had one of the top power plays in the league, but the other team had one of the top penalty kills, so we still needed to be at the top of our fucking game to score.

And here I was, jealous as fuck that Mav was sitting in the penalty box and not *me*. Because he was only a few feet away from my girl.

The girl that I wanted to spill my heart to.

But until then, I jumped over the boards, heading onto the ice as Coach called the line change, ready to play my fucking heart out.

MY HEART STOPPED when I headed back to the locker room at the end of the first period. There she was, standing in the middle of the hallway. I dropped my helmet and gloves on the ground without even thinking.

"You're here." I wasn't sure I was breathing.

She nodded, taking a hesitant step forward. "I'm here."

"Thank fuck." I opened my arms. "Come here, Ellie baby. I need to hold you."

She stepped into my arms, and I pressed my nose against her scalp, inhaling her scent. "I can't believe you're here."

I pulled away, the question finally popping into my mind. "How *are* you here? And who's watching Zamboni?"

Ellie reached up, brushing a damp blond curl off my forehead. "I couldn't let you go one more minute, thinking I didn't want to be with you." She chucked. "And Mikhail's fiancée, Bailey, is watching her."

Sorensen's girl had always been sweet, and I appreciated her helping mine. "I'm glad you're here." I dropped my head, resting our foreheads together. It was kind of our thing.

"El… you're my best friend. You've *always* been my best

friend. And I've missed you so much." I'd missed her for the last week. I'd missed her for the last five years.

I loved hockey, but I loved her more. Always had. Always would.

She was everything good in the world. Her smiles were like the sun rising over my dark sky. Like somehow, Ellie Bradford's sheer existence could brighten up any day.

I didn't want to lose her. Couldn't bear to lose her again. To go back to being that heartbroken shell of a man I'd been for the last five years. I'd survived, sure—but I hadn't lived. The other half of my soul hadn't been complete without her.

"I missed you too," Ellie admitted. "Even when I knew I shouldn't. Even when I cursed myself for leaving. For walking away from this, from us." I knew she wasn't talking about the last week anymore.

I smiled. "What are you saying, baby?"

"I never want you to worry about leaving and not coming home to me, Owen Harper. Because you're *mine. You're* my home."

And there was no way I could go one second longer without kissing her. Ignoring the fact that I was still in my pads and all my gear, I cupped her neck, bringing her mouth to mine. It was everything I'd needed. Everything I wanted.

When I pulled back, our chests heaving, I cupped both of her cheeks. "My favorite place in the world, without question, is right next to you." I kissed her again, softer this time. "I gave up on us once, Skater Girl. Believe me when I say I'm never going to again."

"Good." She nodded. "Because I don't want to move out. I never did. I told my landlord that when he called the first time. There was no way I could ever want to leave you and Zambi." Her eyes were glassy. "Not *ever*."

"Ellie." I reached out, brushing a strand of hair back and tucking it behind her ear. "God, I love you. I always have. I never stopped, not for one fucking moment. I carried you with me in here," I said, tapping over my heart, and then pressed a kiss to my tattoo. "And I never forgot about you. Not for one single second. How could I? It's always been you. You're it for me, Eleanor Daisy Bradford. Always have been. Always will be."

Her beautiful blue-gray eyes filled with tears, and I brushed them away with my thumb.

"Say something," I murmured. "Please."

"Owen." She shook her head. "I don't deserve you. I—I broke your heart."

Her breath shuddered as I stepped closer. Like even she couldn't deny how affected she was by the physical contact. "But do you still love me?" I knew the answer. I just wanted to hear it.

"*Yes*," she whispered, looking more beautiful than ever. Standing in my jersey, adorned with hundreds of sparkling fucking rhinestones, with her blonde hair tumbling down her shoulders and her eyes bright.

"Are you going to leave me again?"

She shook her head. "No."

I curled my hands around her hips. "Say it." I pressed our bodies closer together.

Her eyelashes fluttered, a small whimper slipping from her lips. "Say what?"

"Say you love me. Tell me you'll stay with me forever. Tell me you're mine. That I never have to wake up without you ever again. That I'm yours."

"You are," she agreed, nodding mindlessly. "You're mine." I captured her lips with another punishing kiss, and then she wrapped her arms around my neck. Dug her fingers into the back of my blond hair, even as she pulled apart to look into my eyes. "I love you, Owen Ryan Harper. More than anything in this world, I want to be yours. Always have. Always will."

"Fuck," I muttered, wishing I didn't still have two periods of hockey to play and I could take her back to my room already. "I love you so much. I hate that you ever had any doubts about that."

Ellie sighed. "I hate that you ever thought I wanted to move out."

"I'm sorry," I said—something I should have said from the beginning. "You tried to explain, and I didn't hear you out. That's on me. I was hurt and scared, and that wasn't fair to you."

She leaned up and kissed my cheek. "We both messed up. Let's just promise not to do it again, okay?"

That I could agree to. "Okay."

I bent my head down again, ready to steal another kiss, when—"Oi!" That was Reid's voice. "Harper! Stop kissing your girl or else you're going to miss the start of the second!" When I turned, I saw him with his arms crossed, fully decked out in his goalie attire.

"Fuck." I gave her another soft kiss. "I love you. I'll see you after the game?"

She nodded. "Before I go, I—I don't exactly have somewhere to stay tonight. Do you think I could stay with you?" My girl fluttered her eyelashes.

I chuckled. "Like I'd let you stay anywhere else."

Ellie smiled. "I was hoping you'd say that."

After one last kiss, she pulled away. "Now go out there and win the game for me, baby. I'm rooting for you."

"You're the best damn thing that ever happened to me, baby. Every point I score—they're all for you."

FORTY

Ellie

___

Leaning my forehead against his chest, I inhaled deeply. He'd always smelled like mountains and clean air—like the *ice*, and like man. The scent comforted me, steadying me.

The Seals won their game against D.C. tonight, and I was pressed against Owen in the back of the hotel bar, because the guys had decided they needed to celebrate their win. I wasn't complaining, but I was desperate to be alone with him.

Sophia was across the booth from us, stuck in between Maverick and Rhodes, the latter of who hadn't stopped looking at my friend. Her dad had been surprised when she'd called, but apparently, Owen had been in such a shitty mood over the last few games that he had immediately agreed to let us fly out. Apparently, team morale depended on it. Considering they'd won tonight, I was trying not to question that.

"Are you having fun, baby?" Owen murmured in my ear. He'd ordered me a whiskey sour when we got here, the same thing I'd ordered whenever we went to the Penalty Box, because he never forgot anything when it came to me.

"Yeah," I agreed, though I'd stopped paying attention to the surrounding conversation over twenty minutes ago. His hand was wrapped around my middle, resting on my stomach, and I'd been doing my best not to squirm for the last few minutes. Truthfully, every brush of his skin against mine was setting me off.

Owen pressed a kiss to my neck. "Whenever you're ready, we can go back to the hotel."

I practically sprang out of my seat. *Yes.* I was definitely ready to go. Owen chuckled as he slid out behind me. "We're heading out. Y'all have fun."

Sophia winked at me.

"You good here, Soph?"

She looked at the guys—though I noticed her eyes lingered on Rhodes' for a beat longer—and then nodded. "Yeah. I'm fine. Have a good night."

"Thanks. I couldn't have done it without you." Truly, without her, none of this would have been possible. Sure, I could have gotten on a plane, but this went way beyond tickets. "I owe you one."

Owen slipped his hand into mine, interlacing our fingers and guiding me towards the elevator. Once we got inside, he picked me up, lifting me onto the rail.

I wrapped my legs around his waist and slid my hands up his chest, resting them on his shoulders. "Hi," I whispered.

"Hi." He traced a finger over my cheek. "I missed you."

"You said that before," I said, unable to hold back my smile.

He huffed. "Doesn't mean it's not true."

"I missed you too. All of you." I let my eyes flick down lower, showing him just what I meant by *that.*

Owen's eyes darkened, and he pressed his cock against my crotch, giving me just the smallest hint of friction that I desperately needed.

"That's *mean,*" I said, letting out a ragged breath, trying not to moan. "You know what you do to me."

"You started it," he groaned against my skin.

Luckily, the elevator opened, and he carried me the rest of the way to the room, letting me stay wrapped around his front. I nuzzled my face into the crook of his neck, enjoying his freshly showered scent. There was something about watching him on the ice tonight. He'd been *unstoppable*.

My man wasn't a top goal scorer—he was a solid defenseman and did it well—but he'd been like a beast out there. Not even halfway through regulation time, and my panties had been *soaked*.

And he'd scored a shorthanded goal for me in the third period.

I knew it was for me, because he'd kissed his tattoo after it crossed the line and then looked directly at me. God. I'd been ready to straddle him right there and then.

He was *mine*.

"*Owen*," I whimpered, rubbing my nose in his neck. He had the lightest amount of stubble, and I loved the feeling of it against my skin. "I need you."

"I know, my Daisy girl. I'm right here. I'm going to take care of you." He rubbed his hand down my back, opening the door and not setting me down until we were in front of the bed.

It was a pretty standard hotel room—one king bed, with Owen's suitcase in a corner. I wandered to the window, looking out at the lights in the city.

When I turned back, he was staring at me with an expression of awe. Like he couldn't believe I was here.

"I wanted to do something big. Order you a room full of daisies. Tell you how much I loved you and that I couldn't live without you. Ask you to move in with me permanently, not just as my roommate, but as my girlfriend. As the love of my life. If soulmates exist, I know you're mine."

I smiled. "Yeah?"

He nodded. "But you beat me to it."

"I didn't want you to think I didn't value you, Owen. Or our relationship. Like I told you before, I don't want you to worry about me leaving. I never should have in the first place. If I could get us those five years back, I would."

He shook his head. "I wouldn't."

"No?"

"Come here," Owen murmured, holding out his hand.

I took it, stepping in close to him.

He held me in his arms, swaying us slightly, even though there was no music. "I'm grateful for every moment with you. It might not be perfect, but this is our story, and I'll always love it because of that."

"Owen…" I choked up. God, did he have any idea how perfect he was?

His hand threaded through his hair, and then his mouth met mine, tongue tangling as we gave each other everything. His lips moved against mine like it was the single most important thing in the world to kiss me. And I felt the same. There was nowhere I'd rather be than right here, right now, being kissed by him.

When Owen spun me around, I knew he was looking at his name on the back of my jersey. His fingers traced down my spine until he was tugging up the hem, slipping his hands underneath and up my bare stomach. He cupped my breasts, squeezing lightly. I let out a low moan, unable to hold back when he pulled the cups down, flicking his thumbs across my nipples.

"Thank fuck I don't have a roommate," he said as I whined again, pushing my hips back against him. "Now be a good girl and sit on the bed, El."

The bossy tone in his voice made the heat rise in my body, and I quickly complied, sitting on the edge and looking up at him expectantly.

He kneeled down in front of me, unzipping my heeled

boots before pulling them off my foot, tossing them across the room before repeating with the other one. My socks followed, and then he was tugging my skinny jeans down my legs, my blue polka dot panties following until I was bare in front of him.

Owen pushed my legs apart, dragging his tongue up my entrance without preamble. Like he would die if he didn't taste me. Like he was starving, and I was his last meal. He sucked and licked at my clit and my pussy, until I was begging him to let me come, his tender strokes with his tongue driving me wild. I dug my hands in his thick blond strands, pulling him tighter against me.

"Please," I cried. "*Owen.*"

He finally pulled back, his mouth wet, coated with my juices, and I practically orgasmed on the spot just from the sight.

I sat up, pulling off the jersey and my bra, and then wiggled backwards on the bed until my head hit the pillows. Owen quickly divested himself of his own clothes before joining me on the bed, draping his body over mine.

"I love you," he murmured, tracing his lips down my skin, taking his time like he was memorizing every inch of my skin. His tongue circled over one nipple, and then the other, before kissing down my stomach, sitting up and staring down at me. His hair was messed up from my fingers, and his eyes were dark as his gaze roved over me. "You're so beautiful, Ellie. Like every dream of mine made into a reality." He shook his head. "I'm so fucking lucky that you came back into my life. If you hadn't come chasing after me, I'd never have gotten this opportunity. I'd never be this wonderfully happy."

Sitting up, I practically launched myself into his lap, hugging him tight. "I love you so much. I've loved you as long as I can remember, honestly. From the very beginning, you always took care of me. Looked out after me. I remember when I was learning to ride my bike, and I fell and scraped my knee. I was crying, and do you know who came out with a bandaid and stuff to clean me up?"

He did his best to look bashful. "Me?"

I nodded. "You were always like that. I remember watching you when you started skating, too. I think I told you once that was why I asked to learn. Because I watched you out there, playing peewee hockey, and I was entranced. God, it was mesmerizing. And then we got older. Every day, I fell in love with it a little more. With *you*, a little more. And then I blinked, and there you were. This older guy who I had this massive crush on. My best friend's older brother, who was the hottest guy in High School, and then you know what he did?"

Owen popped a little smile. "What?"

"He asked *me* out on a date. He asked *me* to go to prom with him. And god, I was enamored. Like, me? He liked me?"

"Ellie." He laughed. "I was the one who couldn't believe you wanted to go out with me."

"Luckiest girl in the whole damn school, that's what I was. Everyone was jealous of me when I wore your jersey at your games. I used to get death glares when we walked out to the parking lot together."

"No way."

I nodded. "Yes way. But I didn't care. Because you were mine, and we were Ellie and Owen, and I knew we were gonna make it."

"Making out with you in my truck probably helped, too."

"Oh yeah." I smirked, poking him in the arm. "I think we're gonna need some repeats of that."

"You might have mentioned that before." He smoothed a piece of hair over my ear. "I'll get another one."

Closing my eyes, I let a feeling of calmness wash over me. "I love you and I don't want to lose you. I never should have tried to keep things from you. You were scared, and I knew it.

You'd told me that. And I still kept such a big secret." He opened his mouth to say something, but I shook my head and kept going. "I promise, from now on, that I will always be honest with you. I'll be open about how I'm feeling and where my head is at. That way, we don't have to get into another stupid fight ever again."

"We're going to fight." Owen's finger brushed under my chin. "But I never want to go to bed mad at each other. I never want to leave the house upset ever again. Leaving you behind made me feel like *shit*, baby. You were so far away, and I couldn't come home. It wasn't a conversation I wanted to have on the phone, and I was just miserable."

"I know. That's why I came to you."

A smile touched his lips. "You're fucking amazing."

Owen scooted us farther on the bed, letting his back rest against the headboard and stretching his legs out underneath us. I stayed happily on his lap, my arms wrapped around his shoulders.

"I still can't believe you're here. That you did this." He kissed me, and it quickly grew passionate, until I was rubbing against him, every rock of my hips making my clit brush over his hardened cock.

I moaned, and he dropped his head, his mouth claiming my nipple. Lifting my hips, I wiggled until the tip of his cock pressed against my entrance, and then I sank down, taking all of him inside me.

It felt right. Like he was home.

Because I was home with him.

"Ellie," he whispered, running his fingers over my cheeks. That was when I realized I was crying. They weren't sad tears at all. Owen rubbed his hands down my back. "Baby."

I shook my head. "I love you."

He pressed his lips to mine, holding me tightly to his body until neither of us could hold back, moving in tandem. It wasn't fast or hard, but slow and tender.

We made love to each other as he held me tight, and I knew it was what we both needed right now. The reminder that we were here.

Together.

And I'd never let him go again.

Ellie

CHRISTMAS

"Merry Christmas!" My sister's arms flung around me, pulling me into a hug.

"Hi, Abs," I said, hugging her back just as tight. "I missed you."

She squeezed tighter. "Me too. I know why you left, but damn, it's weird having you so far away."

I rolled my eyes. "Says the professional jet setter who stayed an extra two weeks in France because she was having such a good time."

My older sister's cheeks pinked. She'd inherited our dad's coloring—thanks to the Italian American on his side—and tanned beautifully, plus having dark, thick hair. But just like me, all of her emotions showed on her face. "About that..."

"What?" I raised an eyebrow. "You're not going to tell me the two of you eloped, right?"

"No. God. Of course not. It was just a fling." She waved me off. "He was good in bed, but I don't foresee it going any further."

Oh. "I'm sorry, sis." I wanted her to find her person. Especially now that everything with Owen and I was so good. I wanted her to have someone to love.

"But I wanted to tell you I—"

"Girls!" My mom's voice interrupted us, and she practically squealed.

I turned to her, and I couldn't hold back the tears even if I wanted to. "Mom." I'd missed her so much.

"Oh, my love." She pulled me into her arms. "I'm so glad you're home." She rubbed my back in that comforting way she had ever since we were kids. "When did you get in? I thought you wouldn't be here till later?"

"Well, we left Seattle earlier than we originally planned. Owen couldn't wait to be home." I looked over to the living room, where he was sitting with my dad, and I had to bite my lip to stop from smiling. "Honestly, neither could I. I can't believe how long it's been." We'd brought our bags in earlier, and he'd carried them up to my childhood bedroom. Never in all my teenage fantasies had I ever imagined us sharing a bed in my parents' house, but apparently it was happening tonight.

"I'm so happy you two worked things out, sweetie." My mom cupped my cheeks, squishing them together slightly like I was still her toddler and not a grown woman. "It was hard seeing you two mopey all those years."

Crossing my arms over my chest, I frowned. "I wasn't *mopey*." Maybe I hadn't really been living as fully as I was now, but I'd still made it out the other side.

"Don't give her a hard time, Mom," Abigail said. "Ellie figured things out in the end, didn't she?"

My mom nodded thoughtfully. "She did. Now it's your turn." She poked my older sister in the arm. "Someone's going to give me grandkids eventually, right?"

Abigail winced, but quickly recovered. "Just don't hold your breath that I'm going to blink and find the love of my life just standing in front of me." She rolled her eyes. "I'm perfectly capable of doing life without a husband." Abs bit her lip, like she wanted to say something else, but decided against it.

I wondered what she was going to tell me before mom interrupted us. Hopefully, I'd find out later.

"You can do anything you put your mind to, sweetheart. But you never know," my mom added with a shrug. "Your father and I were best friends for almost a decade before we realized we were in love with each other."

I was glad it hadn't taken Owen and me that long to figure it out. Sure, we were still young—he turned twenty-five next month—but we hadn't needed a marriage pact to decide to be together. A part of me would always love my parent's story, though. Just like I loved mine.

Owen was my first and only, and I was his.

I slung an arm around my mom and my sister. "Come on. Let's go put our pjs on and watch some cartoons. It's Christmas, after all. I want to spend every second of these next four days celebrating."

If it was all the time we had, I wanted to make it count.

I HAD ALWAYS LOVED this time of year. There was something about the magic of Christmas, of the chill in the air and the way it brought everyone together that couldn't be beat. This year, it was even more special.

Because everyone I loved was under one roof. I sat on Owen's lap as we watched Christmas cartoons until the late hours of the night, drinking cider. The house was warm and full of laughter, and it was perfect.

Everything that I'd ever wished for.

I smiled, snuggling deeper into the covers and enjoying the warmth of my bed.

Something hard pressed into my ass, and I rubbed against it, letting out a small moan from my throat.

"Ellie?" There was a rasp against my ear. Blinking my eyes

open, I opened my eyes to find a smiling, handsome face looking down at me.

"Morning," I yawned, stretching out my arms. "What time is it?"

"Time for presents," Owen grinned.

It was almost strange having him here, sleeping in the bed of my childhood bedroom. When we were younger, we'd never had sleepovers. Our parents might have trusted us, but that had always been the rule. We could have stayed over at his house last night instead, but everyone was coming to my parent's house for Christmas breakfast this morning.

He kissed the tip of my nose. "Come on. I already let Zambi out."

I sat up, the sheets falling off of me, exposing my little red nightgown. "She likes the yard, huh?"

"*Loves* it." It was the perfect yard for a dog. I felt bad that our girl was cooped up in an apartment and didn't have one, but with how much time he spent taking her for walks at home, she probably barely even noticed a difference.

"Mmm. Guess we'll need to get our own one day."

He smirked, grabbing a shirt and pulling it on, covering up those glorious muscles. I pouted a little, and he laughed. "You don't like my apartment?"

I shook my head. "I *love* your apartment. Are you kidding? It's beautiful." That was an understatement. And I had no desire to know how much it cost every month. "But I don't want to live in the city forever."

He leaned down, pressing a soft kiss to my lips. "Me either. Now get that sweet ass out of bed and put something on so we can go open presents with your family, baby."

I crossed my arms over my chest. "This isn't acceptable?" I circled a finger over my cleavage, lifting the little bow between my breasts. "You don't think my family will like it?" I batted my eyelashes innocently.

Owen's responding growl made me glad I wasn't wearing

any panties, because they would be soaked. I giggled, getting up and finding an old pair of Christmas pajamas that still fit, pulling them on and tossing my nightgown back on the bed.

He quirked an eyebrow as I turned to him, pulling my hair up into a high ponytail. "What?"

"You're seriously not putting any panties on?"

"Nope." I popped the p, and blew him a kiss. "Now come on, Hockey Boy. Let's go open presents with our family. And then you can open yours later." I winked.

His only response was a resounding groan.

THE ENTIRE LIVING room was full of us kids, and our parents had escaped to the kitchen. We'd already had Christmas dinner, and now we were enjoying the night, trading presents with each other and hanging out for the first time since May.

My brother had flown in last night, and I was so happy to have my whole family back together. Owen was sitting at my side, his hand resting on my hip possessively. I let him keep it there, because I loved how he needed to touch me all the time, like that reminder of my physical presence was enough to calm him.

Plus, after we'd opened presents and I'd tortured him all morning, we'd fucked in the shower and even though it had been a tight fit, *my god.* Teasing him was the hottest thing ever. I was considering asking him to wake me up with his tongue tomorrow, because I couldn't get enough.

"What are you thinking about?" Owen murmured in my ear, brushed a piece of hair back. I'd curled it and left it down with my champagne covered glitzy dress and a pair of heels.

"How glad I am that we could be home this week," I answered, saving my dirty thoughts for later. I was so glad the

NHL gave their players a few days off for the holidays, because it meant we'd be able to come back. "I've missed everyone."

"Me too." He nuzzled his face against mine.

Penelope was sitting on the couch across from us, deep in conversation with her cousin, Avery, who looked like a model. To be fair, she actually *was* one. She'd grown up going between Hollywood and Portland, since her mom—Owen's Aunt—was a famous actress. Her younger sister, Amelia, was sitting in the corner with my youngest cousin Lucy, since the two of them were the closest in age.

It was too loud to eavesdrop, but I was warm, tipsy, and content in my boyfriend's arms, so I didn't even mind that I had no idea what everyone else was talking about.

All of our parent's friends were here too. Owen's dad's best friend from college had brought their kids—Theo and Jenna—who were older than the rest of us by a few years. Theo had turned twenty-eight this spring, and Jenna was the same age as Abigail. My sister and her were chatting off to the side, probably about Ab's clothing brand.

Zach, Wes and Beau were all in a little huddle. If Beau wasn't my brother, I swear, I would think those three were triplets. Aunt Angelina always liked to joke that the Bradford genes were strong, and damn if it wasn't true. My Aunt Angelina and Uncle Benjamin's boss, Nicolas, had brought his family too. His wife, Zofia, had been his assistant when they'd fallen in love, and they had Alexander around the same time mom had Abigail. The two had grown up together, and I knew at one point my sister had a giant crush on him, but nothing had ever come of it. His younger sister, Bianca, was best friends with Wes, and she was sitting with Quin, who was showing her photos of the new baby animals that had been born at the zoo over the last few months. Bianca was a singer, and though she hadn't made it big yet, her voice was beautiful.

God, there were a lot of us. But this was my family. And I

loved them. I loved our little coffee shop dates. Our silly quips and the way we all teased each other. We were close, and in a world when so many people lost touch with their families or had a falling out with their siblings, I knew how important it was that we all loved each other.

Owen leaned over, pressing a kiss to my forehead. "I love you."

"I want this," I blurted out. My voice was low enough with everyone talking around us that no one else paid attention to me, but my boyfriend's lips curled up in a soft smile.

"Yeah?" He gave me a soft smile.

I nodded. "I love our families. I want this. All of us being together every year, catching up and celebrating."

Kids. A family of our own. Lauren and Stefan had their baby a few weeks ago, and my ovaries had cried the moment they'd placed that tiny, sleeping baby in my arms. She was precious. Not that I was ready for that. Not yet. Some day, though.

He pressed his lips to my head. "Me too. One day, after I've retired, I'd love to move back home."

I rested my head against his chest, humming my agreement.

"Merry Christmas, baby," he whispered in my ear.

"Merry Christmas, Owen." I snuggled against him, letting my eyes drift shut, feeling more love than I ever thought possible. "Love you."

OUR TIME in Portland passed quickly, and on our last full day, I couldn't help but feel a little blue. Life would go back to normal soon. I wouldn't be surrounded by my parents or my cousins, and though I loved the life I'd found in Seattle and the friends I'd made, it was still bittersweet. But Owen only had four days off of hockey, with a game on the twenty-eighth, so we couldn't stay longer.

I didn't want to drive home by myself just to stay a few extra days. Besides, he was my person. I loved being with him.

Abigail and I had gone on a shopping trip yesterday, and I'd bought the most adorable new sweater. This morning, when I'd been getting dressed, I hadn't been able to resist wearing it.

Zamboni jumped on my bed, and I rubbed her snout. "God, you've gotten so big, Zambi girl, huh?"

When I looked up, there was Owen, leaning against the doorframe. He was wearing a pair of jeans and his favorite hoodie—a Seals one, no surprise there—and yet, he'd never looked more handsome.

"Hi, Hockey Boy."

"Hey, Skater Girl." He pushed off the door, coming to stand in front of me. He wrapped his hands around my waist. "Did you bring your skates?"

I nodded. "Of course. They're in my bag in the car." I'd thrown them in the car at the last minute, just in case. Since I'd been going to the rink more by myself these days, I hadn't even second guessed the decision. It felt… right. I narrowed my eyes. "Why?"

He flashed me a grin. "It's a surprise. Come on."

I looked down at my outfit. My new sweater was yellow and adorned in daisies, and I'd paired it with a white skirt, tights, a pair of matching yellow leg warmers and a pair of boots. "Am I dressed okay?"

Owen laughed. "Yes, Ellie." He leaned down, pressing his lips against my forehead. "You look beautiful, baby."

"Thank you," I said, kissing his cheek. "But that's not what I asked."

His expression gave nothing away. "It's perfect, Daisy girl." He tightened his grip on my waist, holding me close. I shut my eyes, relishing this feeling.

After softly kissing my forehead, he interlaced our fingers, leading me downstairs and into the car. He was uncharacteristically quiet as we drove, and I wondered what was going through his mind.

"Owen." My voice caught in my throat.

We pulled up to an outdoor ice rink, one that was normally crowded at this time of year but looked completely empty. Of course, it was later in the evening, but I still figured someone would be here. There were string lights hung around the edges of the rink, and it reminded me of all the times when I was younger that we'd come out here.

While we were constantly at the practice rink, Owen had brought me here for dates, too. It was one of the few times we really skated for fun, with no expectations or requirements. We weren't practicing. It was just us, enjoying each other's company as we circled the ice.

"Come on. I rented it out, so it's all ours for the night."

"You... you rented it out?"

Owen chuckled. "Ellie baby. You gotta stop being surprised when I do things like this. NHL superstar, remember? I have more money than I know what to do with." I punched him in the arm as we got out of the car.

He interlaced our fingers after grabbing our bags from the trunk, and led me towards the gate.

A few minutes later, after he'd laced up my skates and then his own, we both stepped onto the ice.

"This is truly the perfect way to finish our time in Portland," I said, doing a little spin before taking his hand again. "Thank you." We started a slow lap around the rink, never dropping our combined hands. It was peaceful. Just what I needed.

"You don't have to thank me for making you happy, Eleanor. I just want to." He pinched my cheek.

"I know I don't have to. It's one reason I fell in love with you." I pressed a kiss to his hand. "You're my best friend and the love of my life."

We stopped in the middle of the ice after another loop, and Owen cupped my cheeks, kissing me softly. *Tenderly.* Like this, right here, was the only thing that mattered in the world.

When we pulled apart, I shut my eyes for a moment, letting my smile creep over my face.

"Look," he murmured, tracing a line across my face.

"What?" I opened my eyes, looking in to his deep brown ones. Full of love and emotion. Pride.

His smile filled my heart. "It's snowing."

It was the beautiful ending to a perfect holiday.

The first of many to come.

FORTY-TWO

Owen

NEW YEAR'S EVE

I wrapped my arms around my girl, looking out over the skyline of Seattle. It was New Year's Eve, and the entire team was out at a party. We'd rented out a restaurant with views of the city, and it even had a covered rooftop bar, though most of my teammates—and the girls—had stayed inside.

Coach and the entire team's staff were here as well—likely to ensure we didn't go crazy, considering we had a game in two days. We still had half the season to play—and even though we liked where we were in the standings, anything could happen.

"This is nice," I said, resting my head on top of hers. She fit so perfectly into my arms. In the last few days since we'd been back home in Seattle, we'd settled into our rhythm again. Ellie was still off from school for a few more days, and I loved every second of her break. We'd spent a lot of time on the couch, binge watching old TV shows and cuddling with Zamboni, who was in heaven having us both home.

We talked about our pasts. Every detail I could think of from the years we were apart. She told me about everything I'd missed with all our cousins and friends.

We'd talked about what we wanted for the future, our dreams and hopes. A big house with a yard. Kids—one day, once we were a little older and more settled. And of course, we wanted to be married first.

I just wanted her to have my last name. *Ellie Harper*. Just the way it was always supposed to be. I'd been crazy about it ever since she'd worn my jersey again.

She still had no idea that I'd talked to her dad, and I was glad to keep it that way. He hadn't been surprised at all when I told him I was planning on proposing and already had a ring. I'd bought it the moment I got back from my long away game trip last month, not wanting to wait another second. Now, I was just waiting for the right moment to ask her to marry me. To be with me forever.

Ellie hummed, taking another sip of her champagne. "You guys really go all out for these, don't you?"

"If you can't party in style, what's the point?" I winked at her. Of course, it was so much more than just a celebration of a new year. It was one way we thanked our team, giving back to the people who supported us all year. Plus, the open bar didn't hurt.

Sophia was at the bar, though I noticed she hadn't touched a drop of alcohol all night. *Huh.* That was strange. She normally had a glass of wine in hand at these kinds of events, being her normal, bubbly self.

I looked around, trying to find the rest of my teammates. Stefan was in the corner talking to Coach, his wife wrapped around him. It was the first time they were somewhere without their newborn, and I was pretty sure they'd dip early.

Jonah, Carter, Finn and Mikhail were all dancing with their girls, while I spotted Brooks leaning against one of the high-top tables next to Rhodes. Maverick was still trying to flirt with Coach Monroe, who still wasn't giving him the time of day.

They were my boys. Being on a team with twenty plus

players who all had super competitive personalities, you would think we would clash more, but I was grateful that we all got along like a family. I couldn't imagine leaving here. If they tried to trade me, I'd be hard pressed to find a reason to go. This was my home, and these guys were my family.

And no matter what else… the girl at my side came first.

"Want to sneak outside?" I whispered in Ellie's ear.

She nodded. "Yes, please."

They were about to set off fireworks to celebrate the new year, but I didn't care about that. Mostly, I just cared about the woman in front of me, and I wanted a bit of time for us.

"It's beautiful out here," she said, looking around the empty patio and pulling her wrap tighter against her shoulders as she leaned on the railing. "Yeah," I agreed, not taking my eyes off of her. "It is."

There were lights strung up out here, illuminating the patio, and a little bar tucked into the corner, that I was sure were in use during the warmer months. Right now, though, it was just us outside, and that was exactly how I wanted it.

How it had been from the beginning. Just her and I.

Hockey Boy & Skater Girl.

Ellie and Owen.

She looked beautiful tonight in a dark blue velvet dress that hugged her body in all the best ways. Her blonde hair was curled, half pinned up, and she'd put some shimmery eyeshadow on her eyelids that made her blue eyes pop. Ellie was stunning. So stunning, I'd almost dropped to my knees before we left the apartment and asked her to marry me right there. But I had a plan.

I reached into my back pocket, pulling out the box I'd stashed away when my girl had been in the bathroom getting ready. It had been in my sock drawer for the last few weeks, just waiting. The moment I'd seen it, I knew it was meant for her.

"Should we go back inside for the countdown?" She pulled back from the railing, turning her head to look at me.

I shook my head, wrapping my arms around her. "Just wait."

She frowned, but turned her head back towards the skyline.

The moment the first firework went off, I dropped to one knee, holding out the box in my hand. When she turned around, she saw me kneeling, and her eyes widened as I took her hand.

"Owen…" she murmured, her other hand resting over her heart.

"Ellie," I said, grinning as I stared up at her. "Maybe this feels fast, but to me, it doesn't. I've been waiting my whole life to love you. From the very first moment to the very last, I've been yours. I'll always be yours. Just like you'll always be mine." I took a breath. "My beautiful Daisy, my Skater Girl. I don't want to go another minute without knowing you'll be mine for the rest of our lives. Tell me you'll be my home, no matter what happens or where we go. That every day—unless I'm on a road trip and out of town—I can wake up next to you." Her eyes filled with tears, and I opened the box, revealing the white gold princess cut engagement ring. The stone was three carats, and the band was adorned with smaller diamonds.

"Eleanor Daisy Bradford, will you do me the honor of being my wife? Will you marry me?"

She nodded. "Yes. Yes. Oh my gosh." I stood up, sliding the ring onto her finger, and then cupped both of her cheeks, kissing her softly.

"She said yes!" I shouted, holding up Ellie's hand, and the patio exploded with our friends and my teammates. I'd told the guys that I planned to propose tonight and asked to have a few extra minutes alone on the patio for this reason.

The guys slapped me on the back, everyone coming over

to congratulate us, and Ellie was beaming the whole time. Sophia's cheeks were flushed when she came over, inspecting the ring and hugging my girl tight. I was so glad they were friends, and that Ellie already felt like a part of the group. She fit right in with the rest of the girls, and that made everything so much sweeter.

When everyone finally left us alone, grabbing glasses of champagne and all chatting amongst themselves on the deck again, I pulled her back into my arms.

Ellie rested her left hand on my chest, staring down at the ring I'd put on her finger. "Owen, this is just... It's so gorgeous. I can't believe you did this."

I pressed my lips to the crown of her head. "Turns out, I couldn't wait any longer before making you mine." Grinning, I wrapped an arm around her waist. "I asked your dad when we were down in Portland last week."

"You did?"

I nodded. "Got his blessing. Turns out your parents are really fucking happy we're back together, baby."

My girl—my fiancée, now—laughed. "Yeah. Tell me about it. They went on and on to me when we were there." She stood on her tiptoes, wrapping her arms around my neck. "Can you believe we're the first ones out of everyone to get engaged?"

"Honestly? No." I laughed. "But I know deep down that even if we hadn't lost those five years, we'd still be in this same spot tonight. No matter what had happened, I would have asked you to be my wife tonight."

"Owen." Her eyes were wet, expression soft.

"I love you, my Skater Girl."

"I love you too, Hockey Boy."

I kissed her again, and the fireworks went off around us, signaling the countdown for the new year. Everyone around us started counting. *Ten, Nine, Eight, Seven, Six, Five, Four, Three, Two...*

But I was just looking at her.

One.

"Happy New Year, Ellie."

"Happy New Year, Owen."

And somehow, I just knew it was going to be our best year yet.

Cousins Coffee Club

TEXTS

I think?

ABIGAIL

When's the wedding? Have you guys started planning yet?

ELLIE

We were thinking about summer of next year. We're still young, so a long engagement doesn't sound so bad.

And if it's in the off-season, it should be easier for everyone to be there.

PENELOPE

I'm so excited!! I can't wait for you to become my sister—officially.

BEAU

Hey, this means I finally get the brother I always asked for.

ABIGAIL

Thank god our parents stopped at three. I can't imagine the menace you would have been if there had been two of you.

ZACHARY

Hey.

ABIGAIL

Case in point.

OWEN

I'm excited for you to be my brother too, Man.

QUINLAN

You know this means our family trees are all officially linked? Which means we're like, actually all related. Mostly. In a roundabout way.

PENELOPE

Cousins at heart. That's what matters.

ELLIE

Once the hockey season and school is over, I'm going to need about a dozen coffee shop dates when we're back in Portland.

ABIGAIL

You're coming home for the summer?

OWEN

Yeah. Maybe not for the whole time, but for a few weeks. We miss all of you. And I still owe the guys drinks.

ZACHARY

Hell yeah, you do.

BEAU

Sounds like I have another reason to come home this summer too.

WESLEY

What was the other one?

BEAU

...

No comment.

QUINLAN

Oooo, B, do you have a crush? Tell us, tell us.

BEAU

No.

ABIGAIL

The plot thickens...

QUINLAN

Speaking of, apparently we're getting a new head vet this summer at the zoo. Should be interesting.

ABIGAIL

Did you hear anything about them?

QUINLAN

Not really. Apparently he's coming from a zoo in Texas.

PENELOPE

Oooo. Keep us updated, Q!

QUINLAN

About what??

PENELOPE

Your hot new boss, obviously.

QUINLAN

We don't even know that he's hot. And besides, he could be like, 50.

ABIGAIL

But is he?

QUINLAN

Guess we'll find out when he gets here, won't we.

ELLIE

Rooting for you, Q!

You, too, Abs.

ABIGAIL

I'm perfectly happy just the way I am, thank you. I certainly don't need a man to complete my life.

ELLIE

Come on. Can't someone else please be in a relationship? I want to go on double dates.

OWEN

What about Soph?

ELLIE

She's not dating anyone.

OWEN

Come on. You've seen the way her and
Rhodes look at each other, right?

ELLIE

Her dad would KILL him. No way.

OWEN

Just calling it like I see it, Ellie baby.

ABIGAIL

Ok, new rule. No sickeningly sweet nicknames
in the chat. I think I might throw up.

ELLIE

Love you too, Abs.

We're gonna go celebrate, but miss you all!
Can't wait to see you in a few months!

Epilogue

ELLIE

Two and a half years later...

O wen?" I called out, dropping my bag onto the kitchen counter and pacing through the apartment I'd been calling home in Seattle for the last few years. One we wouldn't call home much longer, since we'd just bought a house in the suburbs. It was still close enough to the rink for him, but not too far from the school I was now teaching at.

Sometimes I still missed skating, the feel of the ice under my blades and the rush of flying around the rink, but I *loved* teaching. It fulfilled me in a way I couldn't explain. The *best* way.

But then again, so did Owen.

A sparkling ring rested on the second finger of my left hand. The one he'd given me two years ago, when he'd gotten down on one knee and proposed to me.

Maybe we were still young, but I was blissfully happy. Our second chance had given me everything I'd ever wanted. I had a career, a fulfilled life full of friends I loved, and family that was close enough to see multiple times a year, but far enough away that they weren't over every evening. And a dog, who normally was wagging her tail and waiting for me when I got home from work.

I frowned. "Zambi? Babe?" Heading into the bedroom, I found a little note on the bedside table. Two years later, and he still left me notes all the time. It was just our thing.

Took Zamboni out for one last run in the park. Be home soon. Love you. -O

One last run, since tomorrow the movers were coming. Sitting on the bed, I looked around our bedroom. It was bittersweet to leave. We'd had so many wonderful memories here. Moving in back when we were trying to convince ourselves we could be friends, like we weren't inevitable. Like I hadn't loved him all my life.

I would have followed him anywhere, and I knew that was true now more than ever. Even if one day he got traded to a different team, I'd be right behind him, cheering him on.

For now, though, we both loved Seattle, and we loved our friends. Sophia had been one of my bridesmaids at our wedding last year, along with my sister, Penelope, Quinlan, and Avery. She was Owen's cousin, but we were friends, and now I got to call her my cousin, too.

Owen and I had tied the knot last summer, since it was a *lot* easier to host a wedding during the off-season, with their hockey schedules being what they were. And now he was *mine*.

My husband. I sat on the bed, fidgeting with my ring.

"Ellie baby," he called out as the front door opened, and I heard the sound of Zambi's nails clicking against the hard-wood floor. "We're home!"

His footsteps padded into our room, and there was that gorgeous smile I loved.

He ran his hands through his blond hair, our fully grown

golden retriever trotting behind him. She jumped onto the bed and laid her head in my lap, and I scratched her head. "Hi, sweetie pie. Did you have a good walk with Daddy?" I made some kissy noises at her, and she barked excitedly at me.

She was my girl, one who loved cuddling with me, always sleeping next to me in bed when my husband was gone on a road trip. And though I'd never expected him to get us a puppy when he did, I'd never regretted it. Not once.

When I looked up, Owen's eyes were full of heat. It was intoxicating, even after all this time, to see how much he wanted me. To know how much he loved me, every single day.

He kneeled in front of me, his arms resting on my knees. He laid his head on them, looking up at me. "What are you thinking, El?"

"That everything is about to change," I admitted. "That I'm going to miss this place. It's where we'd brought Zamboni home. Where we…" I bit my lip. "You know."

He smirked, leaning in to press his lips to mine, and his hand slid over my still flat stomach. "Oh, I know."

It was still *really* early, but I'd found out last month that I was pregnant with our first baby, and we were over the moon. Owen's mom was even more excited to have her first grandchild, though I wasn't the first of my siblings to have a baby. Though that wasn't my story to tell.

Owen kissed me again, his hand still resting over my still-flat stomach.

"I love you so much," I murmured, cupping both of his cheeks in my hand. "Thank you for loving me. For our second chance."

"Oh, El." He nuzzled his nose against mine. "I'm the one who should thank you for chasing after me. For showing me just how much I'd been missing for all those years. What a fool I was to not fight for you sooner." His lips brushed my mouth, just a tender touch. "I love you and our little Daisy. I can't wait to meet her."

My eyes watered. "You think it's a girl?" We wouldn't find out for a while, but I liked the idea.

He nodded. "I can't think of anything better than having a little you running around our house."

God, my ovaries were crying. If he hadn't already knocked me up, that would have had me melting for him. I placed my hand over his. "I know it's too early to know, but I feel like it's a girl, too. As long as they're healthy, that's all that matters." Girl or boy, they would be cherished.

"Our little skater." He looked at my stomach in wonder.

"What if they don't want to skate?" I asked, raising an eyebrow.

He just gave me a look. I reached up, combing my fingers through his long blond hair. "Honestly, Ellie baby. With a NHL Superstar and a Figure Skater as parents? Our kids are going to grow up on the ice."

"Don't get ahead of yourself," I laughed. "One at a time."

He kissed me softly. "However many you want to give me, I'm all in."

I hummed. "I can't believe we're moving tomorrow."

This apartment was large, but the house had more space. A yard for Zamboni. Room for a nursery. Bedrooms for our future kids. *Kids,* because we both wanted more than one. I'd grown up the youngest of three, and Owen had always been close with Penelope. I wanted that for this baby, too. Our families would always be big—overwhelming, considering the sheer amount of aunts and uncles they were going to have— but there was so much love.

Owen shifted his position, sitting on the bed and wrapping his arms around me to press me into his front. "I'm so happy that we're going to have a place that's *ours.*"

Shutting my eyes, I leaned my head back against his chest. "Me too."

As much as this apartment was home, it had always been his. He'd lived here before me. This new place would be one that we always shared. We'd picked it out together, and everything in it was *ours*.

"You know, my mom sent me up a package," I said, resting my hands on his arms.

"Mhm?"

I tilted back my head so I could look at his face. "Yeah. She found one of my boxes from high school."

He raised an eyebrow, the question obvious on his face. "And what did she find?"

Turning around, I straddled his lap, lowering my lips to his ear. "Your old hockey sweater from high school. The one I always used to wear to your games."

"Fuck." He shuddered. "Don't tell me that right before I was going to take you for a surprise."

"I could put it on for you," I said, fluttering my eyelashes. "We could live out whatever fantasies you had in high school."

"Don't need to," he grinned, dragging his lips down my neck. "They all already came true."

I tilted my head back, luxuriating in the sensations of his mouth on my skin. "You're the best thing that ever happened to me, Owen Harper."

"Ellie Harper, my wife, the love of my life, my everything… I think it's safe to say, without a doubt, that you're the best thing that ever happened to me."

How could I argue with that? Still, I laughed. "You could have just said *ditto.*"

"Where's the fun in that?" He kissed my neck. "I love you."

"Love you too," I murmured, relaxing into his hold. He kept both hands over my middle, over where our baby was growing, and I shut my eyes, the warmth of his touch lulling me to sleep. It didn't take much these days. Between the all day sickness—whoever called it morning sickness was a liar— and everything else that came with growing a baby, I was constantly exhausted.

When I woke up a few hours later, feeling well rested after my nap, Owen was no longer wrapped around me. He'd draped a blanket over me and tucked an extra pillow under my head.

That was my husband. No matter what, he always took care of me.

Yawning, I stood up, walking into the living room. Everything was pretty much packed, so we'd been going out to dinner the last few nights and just getting takeout instead. I was about to ask him what we wanted to order, but… I blinked a few times. The entire room was full of candles, and there was a vase of daisies sitting on the counter.

When had he had time to do all of this?

There was also a spread of breakfast food—because he knew that was my favorite—sitting on the counter. I let out a moan. It smelled amazing. "Okay, I'm *starving.*"

"Now, don't go making that sound yet," Owen said, padding up behind me and wrapping his arms around me. "I have to feed you first."

A girlish giggle slipped free from my throat. "I can't believe you did all of this."

"Of course I did. It's our last night in our first apartment together. The apartment that brought us back together. Even if it was because yours flooded." He kissed the crown of my head, leading me over to the barstool. "We got our second chance here, and that means more to me than you'll ever know. So I wanted to celebrate this place. Us. Even if we're about to embark on a new chapter, I don't want to forget this one, either."

I leaned my head against his shoulder as he sat down next to me, moving his barstool close enough to mine that our thighs would touch. "Thank you." My emotions were all over the place, and I was definitely blaming that on the tears that sprung from my eyes as he plated me pancakes, eggs, and perfectly cooked bacon.

Owen wiped the tears away from my face, and I just laughed. "Sorry you have to deal with all of this. I know I'm a lot right now."

"You're *not* a lot." He shook his head. "You're pregnant, and carrying my baby, that's the biggest miracle ever. So I don't care if you want to cry while you eat your eggs, as long as you're eating."

Laughing, I took a bite of the pancake, moaning at the flavor as it hit my tongue. My husband watched me eat with heated eyes, and I licked every tong of the fork as I pulled it out of my mouth, knowing it was driving him crazy.

By the time I finished eating, he threw me over his shoulder, carrying me back to our bedroom, and for the last time in our apartment, made me come so hard that I saw stars.

I fell asleep in his arms, dreaming of our little ice skater who was growing inside of me and all the wonderful memories I knew we'd make in our new home… together.

Extended Epilogue

OWEN

Two and a half years later...

My wife stood in front of the glass, hefting up her little mini-me in her arms. She wore a Seals jersey—both of them did—with my last name on the back.

Our last name.

My girls. A smile brightened my entire face. Everything Ellie and I went through—every obstacle we faced to get here—was worth it. Of course it was. She'd always been the most important thing in my life. Even more than hockey. I skated over to them, pressing my gloved hand against the glass.

I love you, I mouthed.

Her blonde hair was pulled back with a light blue bow, and even though seeing her in my jersey—and nothing else— was still the sexiest thing I'd ever seen, nothing compared to *this*.

Ellie was glowing, holding our two-year-old daughter in her arms, the gentle swell of her belly showing through all of her layers. Satisfaction and a rush of possessiveness run through me, like it always did when I saw her like this.

She grinned at me, bouncing our daughter, making her little blonde curls move with the effort.

Mine. And I couldn't be happier about that. Soon, we'd be welcoming another little girl into the world, and I couldn't fucking wait.

I was convinced I was born to be a girl dad, and I was perfectly happy with only having girls, even if my teammates teased me and asked me if we were going to try again for a boy. I was happy to have however many kids my wife gave me. If she wanted three, we'd have another. I knew she'd loved growing up with her older sister and brother. But if she only wanted the two, I knew our lives would be complete with them.

The team had gone through changes over the last few years. Rhodes and Stefan had retired, and I was the one with the A on my jersey now. I still couldn't believe I was an alternate captain now. Or that I'd been playing on the team for almost a decade. It didn't feel like it had been that long.

I loved my girls being here to watch me warm up on the ice. Sometimes Ellie would leave Skyler in the wives' room, since they had childcare for them during the games, but lately, she'd gone back after the first period and waited for me to be done with the game.

Not that I minded. Just having her nearby was like my lucky charm, and I always thought I played better when she was watching.

Every goal I got was for my girls. I'd tattooed a second flower next to the daisy on my arm—a lily, for Sky's middle name. And I planned to add another one in a few months, too. I'd have a little bouquet representing the loves of my life, and then they'd be with me everywhere I went.

Every home game, every away game, I carried them with me.

"YOU WERE AMAZING, BABY." Ellie's eyes were bright as I wrapped an arm around her, tugging her tight against my body. I'd taken a quick shower after the game, finished the press, and headed straight for her. God, there was nothing quite like this. Skyler was scribbling on a coloring book on the floor, happily babbling away to herself.

"Thanks." I kissed the top of her forehead. "How are you feeling? How's the baby?"

She ran her hand over her bump. "Good. She was moving around like crazy when I was watching you on the ice."

"That's because she knew her dad was out there scoring goals for her." I leaned down, pressing a kiss to her bump.

We were over halfway through this pregnancy, and Ellie's morning sickness had been awful for the entire first trimester. She'd barely been able to keep anything down. Luckily, it had been in the off-season, so I could stay at home and help take care of her. I would have felt like shit if I'd had to leave her for a long road trip while she felt like that *and* was taking care of our toddler.

"Daddy," my daughter said, tugging at my leg. "Up."

Bending down, I picked Sky up in my arms. "And how's daddy's perfect little girl?" I nuzzled my nose against hers, and she tucked herself against my neck, cuddling into me. God, I fucking melted anytime she let me hold her like this. Ever since she was a baby, she'd been like this.

"Go car?" Skyler asked me, blinking up at me with her big blue doe eyes.

"Yes, little skater." I kept holding her with one arm as I grabbed Ellie's bag off the floor and took my wife's hand in my other. "We're going to go home now."

Our little girl didn't even make it to the car before she was out like a light. I buckled her into her car seat, helping Ellie into the front seat before buckling myself in and heading out of the arena lot.

"I can't believe how much I've popped already," Ellie murmured, resting her hand on her belly. "We still have so many months to go."

After I pulled on the interstate towards our home, I kept one hand on the wheel and let the other drape over her lap. "You're beautiful, baby."

She groaned. "You're just saying that. I feel *huge*, and I'm only going to get bigger. I wasn't this big with Sky until way further along."

I chuckled, because *fuck me*, my wife was adorable. "Do you forget how sexy I think you are when you're pregnant? Or how much you begged me to breed you again, Daisy?"

Her cheeks were pink.

Yeah, my girl had a breeding kink. Turns out all the times we'd skipped condoms while she'd been on birth control had made us feral animals, and I was totally a caveman about getting her pregnant. It was hot as fuck when she begged for my baby.

"Owen..." She looked backwards at our daughter in the mirror, but Skyler was still fast asleep.

"Don't worry." I squeezed her thigh. "I'll remind you how much I love your body when we get home." I winked.

Never underestimate a hockey player with an insane amount of stamina. I was happy to eat her pussy until she came all over my face, soaking my beard with her release. I'd let it grow out over the last few years, since Ellie always seemed to like when I had a bit of scruff on my face, though I kept it well-groomed and trimmed to my face.

I ran my tongue over my bottom lip. Even all these years later, and she was still my favorite dessert. How had I gotten so lucky?

Almost five years ago, I'd thought I'd lost her forever. That the love of my life was gone. And then, by some miraculous change of fate, we'd reunited.

Spent the hottest night of our lives together.

One last night to get it out of our systems.

I'd tried to move on, but I think a part of me knew she was always going to be it for me. She was the love of my life. The other half of my soul. She held my heart in her hands. I'd never stood a chance.

And when I put that ring on her finger, asking her to be my wife, I got everything I'd ever wanted.

Now we had it all. A house. A beautiful daughter, and another on the way. The most spoiled dog in existence. Friends who were like family. Our actual families, big and loud and messy, but the best people we could have asked for.

And we had each other.

Because after all of that, here we were.

Ellie & Owen.

Skater Girl & Hockey Boy.

Husband & Wife.

As long as we had each other, we'd always be home.

The End.

Want to read more Ellie & Owen? Click here to sign up for my newsletter and read about their first family skate, or follow the link below! https://dl.bookfunnel.com/ztopr1h0lz

The Cousins Coffee Club will continue with Quinlan's workplace romance, dislike to love story, *Wildly in Love,* coming in 2026.

Acknowledgments

To Hannah: thank you for letting me rope you into my hockey obsession and watching so many Bolts games with me. Without you, this book would never have come together the way it did. Thank you for being my sounding board and for letting me scream about Ellie and Owen from the beginning. I appreciate you and everything you do for me!

To Maren: you mean so much to me, and I am so grateful for our friendship. Thank you for always encouraging me to keep going and for being there for me through every step of my author career. I don't know what I'd do without you!

To my ARC Team, thank you so much for constantly hyping me up and for all the excitement over this book. I hope it lived up to your expectations! I always appreciate all the posts, edits, and videos you all make. You're the best!

To the Tampa Bay Lightning, thank you for making me completely fall in love with hockey. #GoBolts!

To Mom: thank you for always being my assistant at signing events, for taking my packages to the post office whenever I need it, and for always helping me when I need it.

Also by Jennifer Chipman

Contemporary Romance

Best Friends Book Club

Academically Yours - Noelle & Matthew

Disrespectfully Yours - Angelina & Benjamin

Fearlessly Yours - Gabrielle & Hunter

Gracefully Yours - Charlotte & Daniel

Cousins Coffee Club

(Best Friends Book Club Generation 2)

Uniquely in Love - Ellie & Owen

Wildly in Love - Quinlan & Sawyer (coming soon)

Castleton University

A Not-So Prince Charming - Ella & Cameron

Once Upon A Fake Date - Audrey & Parker

The Bookworm and the Beast - Izzy & Adam (coming summer 2025)

A North Pole Christmas

Elfemies to Lovers - Ivy & Teddy

Paranormal Romance

Witches of Pleasant Grove

Spookily Yours - Willow & Damien

Wickedly Yours - Luna & Zain

Bewitchingly Hers - Eryne & Barrett (coming fall 2025)

Science Fiction Romance

S.S. Paradise

A Love Beyond the Stars - Aurelia & Sylas

A Passion Beyond the Galaxy - Kayle & Leo (coming soon)

About the Author

Originally from the Portland area, Jennifer now lives in Orlando with her dog, Walter and cat, Max. In her free time, you can find her with her nose in a book or going to the Disney Parks. She loves writing romance heroes who fall first and hard for their women. Jennifer writes Contemporary Romance, Paranormal Romance, and Sci-Fi Romance.

Website: www.jennchipman.com

amazon.com/author/jenniferchipman

goodreads.com/jennchipman

instagram.com/jennchipmanauthor

facebook.com/jennchipmanauthor

x.com/jennchipman

tiktok.com/@jennchipman

pinterest.com/jennchipmanauthor

www.ingramcontent.com/pod-product-compliance
Lightning Source LLC
Chambersburg PA
CBHW070308310726
48976CB00005B/1623